Praise for [obscured]

"A distinct[ively] modern tale that [...] past masters H. P. Lovecraft and A[...]. A finale that veers [unexpec]tedly [...] [disp]lay of supernatural [...] works [...] [disar]ming [...] only underscores [...] [...] behind this [...] tale of awe-inspire[...] [...] —*[Publishe]rs Weekly*

"*Threshold* [...] [pro]claiming [...] Kiernan's elevated position in the [...] [...] literature. It [...] [ex]ceptional novel you m[...] [...] bluntly [...] —*Cemetery Dance*

"[Caitlín R. Kiernan [...] [...] voice [...] the genre since Neil Gaiman po[...] [...] [S]tephen King made movies live inside books [...] Beginning with [the] instant-classic *Silk* [...] [con]tinuing through her short fiction to this extraordinary [new] novel, Kiernan h[asn't] [...] yet [...] If you haven't samp[led her work yet, you haven't really been rea]ding the *future* of ho[rror and dark fantasy, only its past]."
—[Lisa DuMond, SF]site, M[...]ews.com

"Kiernan's p[rose is] [...] [to]ugh and [char]acterized by nightmarish description. Her brand of horror is subtle, the kind that is hidden in the earth's ancient strata and never stays where it can be clearly seen." —*Booklist*

"*Threshold* confirms Kiernan's reputation as one of dark fiction's premier stylists. Her poetic descriptions ring true and evoke a sense [...]

Praise for *Silk*

"A debut novel of a level of accomplishment most young horror/dark fantasy writers could not begin to approach. [Caitlín R. Kiernan's] tightly focused, unsparing, entranced gaze finds significance and beauty in the landscape it surveys." —Peter Straub

"A remarkable novel. [Caitlín R. Kiernan] tells a powerful and disturbing story with creepy intensity and a gift for language that borders on the scary. Deeply, wonderfully, magnificently nasty."
—Neil Gaiman

"A daring vision and an extraordinary achievement."
—Clive Barker

"Caitlín R. Kiernan writes like a Gothic cathedral on fire. If the title alone doesn't make you want to read *Silk*, the first page will do the trick. Kiernan's work is populated with the physically freaky, mentally unstable, sexually marginalized characters who have caused so much consternation in conventional circles—but Caitlín Kiernan is headed in an entirely different direction. Her unfolding of strange events evokes not horror, but a far larger sense of awe." —Poppy Z. Brite

"[Kiernan] has what it takes to excite me as a reader . . . think of Poppy Z. Brite with slightly more accessible prose and characters who aren't quite so outré. . . . I just loved this book and can't wait to see what she writes next." —Charles de Lint

CAITLÍN R. KIERNAN

LOW RED MOON

A ROC BOOK

ROC
Published by New American Library, a division of
Penguin Group (USA) Inc., 375 Hudson Street,
New York, New York 10014, U.S.A.
Penguin Books Ltd, 80 Strand,
London WC2R 0RL, England
Penguin Books Australia Ltd, 250 Camberwell Road,
Camberwell, Victoria 3124, Australia
Penguin Books Canada Ltd, 10 Alcorn Avenue,
Toronto, Ontario, Canada M4V 3B2
Penguin Books (N.Z.) Ltd, Cnr Rosedale and Airborne Roads,
Albany, 1310, New Zealand

Penguin Books Ltd, Registered Offices:
80 Strand, London WC2R 0RL, England

First published by Roc, an imprint of New American Library,
a division of Penguin Group (USA) Inc.

First Printing, November 2003
10   9   8   7   6   5   4   3   2   1

Roc REGISTERED TRADEMARK—MARCA REGISTRADA

LIBRARY OF CONGRESS CATALOGING-IN-PUBLICATION DATA:

Kiernan, Caitlín R.
    Low red moon / Caitlín R. Kiernan.
        p. cm.
    "A Roc book."
    ISBN 0-451-45948-2
    1. Hallucinations and illusions—Fiction. 2. Women—Alabama—Fiction.
3. Serial murders—Fiction. 4. Married women—Fiction. 5. Psychics—Fiction.
6. Alabama—Fiction. I. Title.

PS3561.I358L69 2003
813'.54—dc21   2003048782

Set in Sabon

Printed in the United States of America

For Spooky

In memory of Elizabeth Tillman Aldridge
(1970–1995)

AUTHOR'S NOTE

Though I've shown great care with the phases of the moon for the month of October 2001, any readers familiar with the marshlands east of Ipswich, Massachusetts, will immediately realize that I have taken considerable liberties with the area. My decision to have the Castle Neck River double for Lovecraft's fictional (or fictionalized) Manuxet River is based on my own reckoning, drawing largely from comparisons of "The Shadow Over Innsmouth" with various topographic and geological sources. I realize this conclusion is at odds with the work of some Lovecraft scholars, though it agrees favorably with the conclusions of still others (see, for example, a footnote in Jack Morgan's *The Biology of Horror*). I should also note that *Low Red Moon* owes much to the poetry and prose of William Blake, especially *Songs of Innocence and of Experience*, *The Pickering Manuscript*, *The Book of Thel*, *America: A Prophecy*, and *The Book of Los*. Once more, I am indebted to Martin Gardner's invaluable notations to Lewis Carroll's work (and, of course, to Carroll himself), as well as to the works of Charles Fort (particularly *The Book of the Damned* and *Lo!*), H. P. Lovecraft, Tennyson, W. B. Yeats, Angela Carter, Joseph Campbell, and Carl G. Jung. This novel's title, and some of its matter, was inspired by Belly's 1993 album, *Star*, and I would also like to acknowledge the influence of Poe's 2001 album, *Haunted*.

Finally, grateful thanks to my agents, Merrilee Heifetz and Julian Thuan, to my editors, Laura Anne Gilman and William

Schafer, and to Jennifer (both of them), Kathryn ("Minister of Continuity"), Jada, Jim, Byron, Dr. David R. Schwimmer for bringing dinosaurs to Atlanta, and to Rogue (for coming to the rescue). This novel was written on a Macintosh iBook.

Moon you made me cry when I was young
& I was young

        —Belly, "Low Red Moon" (1993)

Swimming out with tears in my eyes
looking for the shore . . .
        —The Crüxshadows, "Tears" (2002)

PROLOGUE

Providence

The motel room smells like blood and shit and air freshener, the aerosol can sitting empty on top of the television set and the air in the room *still* smells like blood. Spring Heather, the purple can promises, and Narcissa Snow has never smelled spring heather but she's pretty sure it doesn't smell like an abattoir. She watches the telephone from her place by the window, the hard, uncomfortable chair the color of spicy brown mustard and her ass keeps going numb. The drapes, which almost match the upholstery on the chair, are drawn against the rainy night outside and the prying eyes of anyone who might walk by and see her naked and crying. She's left the plastic DO NOT DISTURB sign hanging from the doorknob and her gun lying on the table within easy reach, the safety off, just in case.

A watched pot never boils, someone whispers, one of the corner voices or the hooker's head wrapped in newspaper and tied up snug in a Hefty bag, either or both or neither. Maybe she whispered it herself and just didn't notice. A watched pot never boils and the phone is never going to ring.

Narcissa Snow's stomach rumbles and rolls like the thunder in the black Rhode Island sky and she thinks about going to the bathroom to throw up again. She imagines standing under the shower and letting scalding water wash away the blood drying on her face her lips, the blood caked beneath her nails and in her tangled blonde hair. Blood and soap and the sour smell of vomit, she thinks, and goes back to watching the telephone.

"You simply should have known better, dear," Madam Terpsichore said, scowling Madam Terpsichore three long, long hours ago in the cellar of the old house on Benefit Street. "It's not as if we're a club. You don't apply for membership." And that made all the other ghouls laugh, of course, set them to chuckling their ugly dog-bark laughter until Madam Terpsichore turned her head and scowled at them instead.

"But I'm not telling you anything you didn't know already," she said. "You're a very bright young girl, Narcissa, and you know. I don't have to tell you."

And then she went back to work, the body on the slab laid open like a holy book, a flick of claws and rusted scalpel blades, an eye lifted from its socket, a severed tendon, and none of them had said another word to her. Not another word, just the busy, secret whispers passed between them like scraps of flesh and gristle, nothing meant for her ears, and she watched them for a little while longer from the rickety stairs that led back up to Miss Josephine's old house filled with antiques and vampires. All their red-yellow eyes and the wary prick of their ghoul ears at the smallest sound from the tunnels or the floor overhead, slender hands and surgeon fingers, everything that Narcissa was not and would never be no matter how many prostitutes and transients she murdered, no matter what exotic victuals she brought them pickled in balsamic vinegar and rosemary. Lucky they were letting her leave with her life, Madam Terpsichore had said, with her skin still on her bones instead of stretched tight and nailed up to dry. Lucky, lucky girl.

"Is *that* what I am?" Narcissa Snow mutters, asking the walls, the blood-soaked sheets and carpeting, the bits and pieces of the dead woman she hasn't bothered to gather up yet. "Am I a lucky, lucky girl?" The corners whisper and snicker the contemptuous way that only corners can whisper, and *Damn straight,* they reply. *You're the luckiest goddamn girl alive.*

"Fuck you," she spits back. "I wasn't asking you. I wasn't really asking anyone at all."

And how many hours left until dawn, how many days now since the last time she slept? No answers from the whisperers in her head and she closes her eyes, wishing the room didn't smell so bad, that she didn't *think* it smelled bad, because that's one of the reasons they didn't take her. Like her smooth, pale skin and pretty face and she can't even keep down a bellyful of fresh meat and kidneys.

"Your great-grandfather was a fine man," Madam Terpsichore

said and licked her thick black lips. "Now *there* was a man who knew his way around a stew pot. Yes, indeed. I can *still* taste his sweetbreads with cloves and cinnamon."

They cut out the dead man's tongue and set it aside in a blue porcelain bowl; Narcissa reached into her leather jacket, laid her right hand on the butt of the pistol, the full clip of .45-caliber cartridges and *I could kill them all,* she thought. *I could kill them all right now, this minute, and slice them up with their own knives. I could dump their bodies in the Seekonk River for the fish and seagulls. I could strew them across the land like fallen leaves.*

The one named Barnaby glanced at her nervously, his eyes shining in the candlelight, and maybe he knew exactly what she was thinking. Maybe they *all* knew and were only waiting, biding their time until she was stupid enough to try something. She winked at him and smiled, and the ghoul snarled silently and went back to work.

"Ring," she whispers urgently to the telephone beside the bed, but it doesn't and the corners all laugh at once. The hooker's head in the garbage bag has started crying again, begging to be let out, begging for its body, its intestines draped about the motel room like Christmas garland.

"Shut up," Narcissa Snow growls. "*All* of you just shut the hell up right *now,*" but they ignore her, every one of them, and she picks up the gun, slides the barrel across her lips, her teeth, slips an index finger through the trigger guard. The sudden, sharp flavors of gunpowder and steel, metal cold against her tongue, the sight blade tickling the roof of her mouth, and she gags.

Do us all a favor, the corner voices whisper.

And the telephone does not ring.

"Will we ever be seeing you again?" Miss Josephine asked too cheerfully, taking Narcissa by the hand and showing her to the tall front doors. She shrugged, tried to smile, but the woman's hand like ice and marble, her eyes like cut and polished sapphires burning in her skull. "I hope so," Narcissa said and gave her the sealed manila envelope with the videotape inside, the tape and the motel's phone number and maps of the necropoleis beneath Swan Point cemetery and Boston and Stonington, Connecticut.

"Give this to Madam Terpsichore, please," she said. "I almost forgot. She's expecting it."

"Yes, of course, and do come again."

Coward, the corners whisper. *Pull the goddamn trigger and get it over with.*

And that's all it would take, one sizzling, bright instant, more pain than even she can imagine, and then oblivion or hell, whichever she has coming.

"I don't usually do this sort of thing," the hooker said.

"What? What don't you usually do?" Narcissa asked and rolled the Mustang's window down a crack to get some fresh air, despite the cold rain beating against the glass. The woman smelled like cigarettes and sweat, cheap perfume and stale, careless sex.

"Chicks," the hooker said. "I'm not into that. I don't usually sleep with chicks. I'm not a dyke."

"I'm paying you enough," Narcissa said very quietly, holding everything in because she wouldn't have to hold it in much longer, and yes, the woman nodded, yes, and she looked down at the three one-hundred-dollar bills wadded together in her hand.

"How many men you gotta blow to make that much cash?"

"I just wanted you to know."

"Baby, I don't really give a shit one way or the other," Narcissa said and then they were at the motel on Oak Street, pulling into the parking lot and at least the hooker stopped talking for a little while.

Go on and do it. We're getting tired of waiting.

And the last thing the girl said, before Narcissa opened the Italian stiletto and cut her throat from ear to ear, the very last thing she said before she died, "I still go to church, sometimes."

Hurry up, girl. Pull the fucking trigger. That phone's never going to ring.

Narcissa closes her eyes and grips the barrel of the gun with her teeth.

You're not a monster. You're just a crazy girl. Just a pathetic freak who hears voices and one day, Narcissa, they'll catch you and lock you up forever.

She starts counting backwards from ten, and all the corners and the head stuffed in the Hefty bag get quiet and listen.

And when she reaches three, the telephone on the table beside the bed begins to ring.

PART I

The Children of the Cuckoo

There are no longer any gods whom we can invoke to help us. The great religions of the world suffer from increasing anemia, because the helpful numina have fled from the woods, rivers, and mountains, and from animals, and the god-men have disappeared underground into the unconscious. There we fool ourselves that they lead an ignominious existence among the relics of our past. Our present lives are dominated by the goddess Reason, who is our greatest and most tragic illusion.

—CARL JUNG (1961)

CHAPTER ONE

Deacon

"You feelin' any better, Mr. Silvey?"

Deacon doesn't answer the cop, stares instead out the front of the coffee shop at the autumn-bleached sky above Third Avenue. Palest pale blue, almost white that shade of blue, and hung so very high, so completely out of reach.

"Is your coffee okay?"

"Yeah. My coffee's fine," Deacon says, but keeps his eyes on the plate-glass window. There's an airplane up there, the chalk streak of a jet's contrail, and he imagines himself sitting on that plane, thirty thousand feet above the city, far away above the world, him and Chance going anywhere else but Birmingham.

"How's your head?"

"Just getting started."

"I think I have a bottle of Excedrin out in the car. Want me to go get it?"

"You've never had a migraine, have you, Detective Downs?"

The cop doesn't answer right away, like maybe he's not so sure exactly what Deacon's asking him, and outside the coffee shop a city bus glides ponderously by in a charcoal cloud of diesel smoke.

"No," he replies, after the bus noise has faded.

"Lucky son of a bitch," Deacon whispers and stares back at himself from the plate glass, imperfect, see-through reflection peering out between the Halloween decorations Scotch-taped to the window; *Jesus Christ*, he thinks, *I look like death on a cracker*. The stubble on his hollow cheeks because he hasn't shaved in days and the circles beneath his eyes gone dark as bruises, and he thinks he probably looks a lot more like the hard end of fifty than thirty-nine.

"We didn't know you knew the victim," the cop says. "I swear to god, man, we didn't have any idea."

"I never said you did."

"Yeah, I know. I just didn't want you thinking otherwise."

Silence then and Deacon sips a little more of the coffee, so sour it might have been brewed last week, bitter and getting cold but it gives him something to do besides stare at the sky or his ragged face in the window. Once upon a time, back in the day, he thought all coffee tasted like this and he wishes he had a big cup of the Jamaican Blue Mountain stuff that Chance likes so much.

"I don't believe in all this psychic mumbo jumbo, you know," Detective Downs says and he pours another packet of sugar into his coffee, like that's going to help. "Some sort of fuckin' voodoo con job, if you want to know the god's honest truth what I think. I'm only doing this because I got orders. Nothing personal, but—"

"You just didn't want me thinking otherwise."

"Look, I got enough problems right now without you busting my balls, all right? I'm just doing what they tell me."

"You think *they* believe in this psychic mumbo jumbo?"

"What *they* do or don't believe, that ain't none of my business, Mr. Silvey. Someone in Atlanta says you helped solve a few murders and someone down here thought maybe we should talk to you. That's all I know and all I really want to know."

"Well, hell, I can see how you made detective," Deacon says, smiles even though it makes his head hurt worse, and the cop pushes away from the table, the legs of his chair squeaking loud across the linoleum floor. Sudden anger on his clean-shaven, twenty-something face, anger and disgust, so maybe now he'll give up and go away and Deacon can have his headache in peace.

"Nothing personal," Deacon says and takes another drink of coffee.

The cop shakes his head and runs his fingers through his thinning hair, glares across the table at Deacon. "I thought this guy Soda was a friend of yours?"

"I didn't say he was my friend. I just said I knew him. I'm not sure Soda had any friends, exactly."

"So . . . now you want me to fuck off and leave you alone."

"Something like that."

"And you're not even gonna try to help?"

The brass bell hanging above the coffee shop door jingles and an old black woman in a Coca-Cola sweatshirt and nappy leopard-print house shoes glances suspiciously at Deacon and the detective on her way to the counter.

"You asked me to look. So I fucking looked."

"And you didn't *see* anything or *feel* anything or whatever the hell it is you're supposed to do?"

"No," Deacon says, wishing it weren't a lie, wishing that he'd never gotten out of bed and answered the phone, never agreed to take the ride across town to the squalid little apartment where they found Soda's body. But mostly wishing he had a drink, a bottle of beer, a shot of whiskey, anything at all but the sour coffee and the dry place in his soul.

The detective looks at the old woman and the skinny kid taking her order, then looks back at Deacon and licks at his chapped lips.

"This is the *third* one we've found like this in three weeks," he says quietly. "So far, we've managed to keep the details out of the news. That shit you saw painted on the wall, the things that were done to the body, three times so far. And it doesn't take a rocket scientist to know it's gonna be four real soon if we don't get a break. I want you to think about that, Mr. Silvey."

"Why would I lie to you?"

"That's precisely what I'm askin' myself," and the detective takes a white card from his coat pocket and lays it on the table in front of Deacon. "If you change your mind, you call me."

"Right," Deacon says, staring out the window again at the blue October sky. The plane is gone and already its white contrail is fading. The brass bell jingles as the door swings open and shut and he watches as the cop crosses the street to his car parked on the other side.

"I tried to tell him to put a dead bolt on his fucking door," Deacon said and Detective Downs stopped picking at a Band-Aid on the back of his left hand and stared at him.

"What?"

"You gotta be fucking nuts, living in a dump like this with nothing but a chain on the front door."

"You knew this guy?"

"Half the crack whores and dust heads on Southside crash in this shithole. Fucking junky's paradise."

"Mr. Silvey, are you saying that you *knew* the victim?"

"Yeah, I knew him."

"Oh god, man, I'm sorry. I swear, we didn't have any idea—"

"His name was Soda," Deacon said and took another step into the bedroom of the tiny basement apartment. Colder than October down there, colder than January, cold like black ice water lapping greedily against his skin, and the smell of blood and mildew so thick he was beginning to think he might be sick before he even touched the corpse.

"Charles Ellis," the detective said. "At least, that's what his driver's license and social security card both say."

"He was just Soda. I never heard anyone call him Charles."

"So that was a nickname, then? Soda?"

"I never heard anyone call him anything else," and Deacon swallowed once, swallowing nothing but spit and the stinking, frigid air, and walked quickly from the doorway across the sticky, damp carpet to stand at the edge of the bed. The body was still lying there, of course, because they wanted him to see it all, every little gory detail.

"Where the fuck's his head?" he asked and the detective coughed twice before answering.

"In the bathroom, tied up in a pillowcase, just the way we found it. Did your friend here use drugs?"

"What do you think?" Deacon replied and stared at the dark and empty cavity of the torso laid open for the whole world to see; it made him think of cantaloupes at the grocery store, split in half and scooped clean. Both Soda's arms dangled over the sides of the narrow bed, and his right hand, clenched into a fist, curled up like a dead spider, was lying under a card table a few feet away.

"Are those bite marks on the body? Did the killer bite him?"

The cop chuckled softly and "Not unless the sonofabitch has teeth like a fucking rottweiler dog," he said.

"So he might have had an animal with him?"

"That's my guess," the detective answered and added, "We haven't accounted for all the internal organs yet, or the eyes, either."

"Or the eyes," Deacon whispered, as though what the detective had said might make more sense if he heard it coming out of his own mouth. Words he understood perfectly well, three simple syllables, but no sense left in them anywhere. He swallowed again and looked past the body and the bed at the wall above the headboard.

"Maybe you can tell us what that means," the detective said and pointed.

An almost perfect circle drawn in Soda's blood, crusty maroon ring maybe three feet across to stain the dingy drywall. And written all around the outer rim were characters that Deacon thought might be Arabic. Below the circle, a line had been drawn in what looked like charcoal, a straight black line drawn parallel to the floor.

"What the hell makes you think I'd know that?"

"Well, I figured it's part of some sort of pagan ritual, you know, witchcraft or—"

"And some asshole in Atlanta told you I'm an expert in that sort of shit, right?"

The detective started picking anxiously at the Band-Aid again and nodded his head once.

"Well, they lied to you, man. I've got just the one trick up my sleeve and everything I know about witches I learned from watching *Dark Shadows* on TV."

"Oh," the detective said and "I'm sorry," sounding more disappointed than apologetic, and Deacon looked from the thing on the wall back to the thing lying spread out on the bed beneath it.

"The lettering could be Arabic," Deacon said and squeezed his eyes shut tight, wanting to be back out on the street, wanting to be home, wishing he'd told the cops to go to hell.

"Arabic, as in Saudi Arabia? As in *A*-rabs?"

"Yeah, but I'm guessing. It might just be something the killer invented. It might not be anything at all."

"Okay, so what next? Is there anything special you need before, you know . . ." and Deacon shook his head, took a deep breath, filling his lungs with the stench of the place, with its freezing, slaughterhouse air. Without opening his eyes, he reached out and laid his right hand on the footboard of the bed.

"Do you *have* to touch the bed? I mean, that's gonna play hell with forensics. We haven't even dusted—"

"What do you think the press is going to say," Deacon asked, "when they find out the Birmingham police are using a psychic to do their work for them?"

"They ain't gonna say jack shit, Mr. Silvey, because no one's ever going to tell them this happened. I thought we were clear on that point."

"Clear as mud," Deacon said and the detective was still talking, veiled threats for anyone who ever breathed a single, solitary word of this to *anyone*. But the cop's voice was growing faint, as though he'd stepped back out into the hallway, as if maybe he were only shouting at Deacon from the sidewalk somewhere outside the old apartment building.

And nothing at first, and he hoped that meant there would be nothing at all. It happened sometimes, when he was very lucky, the trail grown too cold or his head firing blanks; the process still a mystery to him, which was fine. The less he had to think about it the better, and *Please,* he thought, *please dear fucking god let this one be a dud,* and then he could tell Detective Downs to fuck off, thank you very much, and catch the bus back across town, try to pretend this whole thing had never happened. But Deacon Silvey had always had an uncomfortable relationship with luck, at best, and slowly the mold and gore smells were replaced by the sweet and sickly blend of citrus and fish that always accompanied his visions.

"You gettin' anything?" the detective asked impatiently and Deacon shrugged. "Well, we ain't got all day, Mr. Silvey," Detective Downs grumbled.

"Chill out, copper," Deacon whispered, trying not to start laughing, riding the storm-front edge of whatever was coming at him from the bed, from however many hours ago Soda had died, licking at his emotions like lightning bolts and thunder.

"*What'd* you just say?"

"It's coming," Deacon said, and it did, then; he gripped the bed so hard his knuckles popped, and hung on as though his life depended on it. His life or only his sanity, and for a moment there was nothing in the world but the pulp of ripe tangerines and the clean, white flesh of freshly gutted fish.

"Sorry the place is such a pigsty," Soda said, that stupid, silly grin he got whenever he was drunk or stoned, and keen, silver light glinted off the blade of a knife. "Someday, man, someday I'm just gonna call the fire department and have 'em hose the place out."

Wind through tall grass and the not-so-distant sound of waves.

"Maybe that'll kill the fucking roaches, too," and Soda sat down on the bed, bottle of something in his hand, and the old thirst stinging at Deacon's throat even through these sights and sounds locked up inside his skull.

"Wish I had a goddamn twenty-dollar bill for every cock-roach in this place," Soda said and set the bottle on the floor beside the bed. "Man, I'd be a millionaire. I'd be Bill fucking Gates by now."

The knife dividing the air like pure and holy fire, the burning sword of Heaven to cleave the sky from horizon to horizon, sky above the sea, sky above all Creation, to slice skin and muscle and bone. Red hands busy at their work, hands as sure as a surgeon's and as careless as a butcher's. Deacon grits his teeth and opens his eyes, but it's all still there. Red hands and the sea, grinning Soda swigging from a half-empty bottle of Thunderbird, and the storm turning wild about them all, rolling like a hurricane, a Ferris wheel, the indifferent wheel of fate and fortune.

"Has any mortal name, Fit appellation for this dazzling frame?"

Soda's brown eyes so wide, so wide and drunk and scared, and the blood flowed from his lips, spilled thick and dark down his chin. The silver blade falling across his face again and again and again and soon it was not even his face anymore, only raw meat, only a tattered mask for a dead man to wear.

The red hands traced a perfect circle on the wall above the bed and the body.

"I have no friends," the Lamia said, *"no, not one."*

And Deacon slipped off the spinning wheel, sank to his knees on the sticky carpet before the detective could catch him.

There's a mirror on the other side of the room and the naked thing squatting above Soda's body turns its shaggy head and stares at Deacon with eyes like scalding amber stars.

"Shut, shut those juggling eyes. . . ."

"Christ, man, what's happening to you? Snap out of it," Detective Downs said, sounding very frightened, breaking the spell, the eggshell moment, and suddenly the storm folded itself closed again, collapsing to leave Deacon Silvey alone at the still, blind center of its soulless soul.

"What the sam hell was that?" the cop asked, and his words,

his breath, were so loud, so hard, a hammer to pound the first migraine spike deep between Deacon's eyes. "What'd you see?"

Deacon looked at the footboard, his hand still wrapped tight about the wood, his fingers numb, white knuckled, and "Nothing," he lied. "I didn't see anything at all."

Deacon leaves the coffee shop five or ten minutes after the detective and stands on the sidewalk outside for a while, smoking a cigarette and gazing vacantly at the marquee of the Alabama Theater directly across the street. Grand old movie palace saved from the wrecking ball, and THE PHANTOM OF THE OPERA in ruby-red plastic letters, LON CHANEY OCTOBER 27; he exhales a gray cloud of smoke and the breeze along Third Avenue picks it apart. Only five blocks home, but what then, Chance away in Atlanta today on business and their big, empty loft waiting there for him, full of nothing at all but television and his aching head, time alone he doesn't need and the desert in his throat. He reaches into his coat pocket and there's the cop's white calling card, and another card, too, the one with the phone number printed on the back, the number he never goes anywhere without, the number to call if the thirst ever gets the upper hand again. *Today it just might do that,* he thinks and allows himself the hazardous indulgence of imagining endless liquor store aisles, pint bottles filled with gin and rum and Jack Daniel's whiskey, alcohol fire to soothe the pain behind his eyes, to burn away the memories of Soda's mutilated body and the thing he saw looking back at him from the mirror.

That hundred would buy a good, long drunk, wouldn't it, Deke?

The shaggy thing he hadn't told Detective Downs about, and *Not yet,* he tells himself again. Maybe later on, maybe, and maybe not. Some questions you never answer, no matter who's doing the asking, no matter how many badges he has or how much money he's offering.

"Just start your ass walking," he says out loud, no one around to hear him so no one to give two shits if he talks to himself. Better than the booze, talking to himself, walking in the cold, and so he turns left, following the sidewalk east to the corner of Twentieth Street. There's an old man, old bum standing there in a brown corduroy jacket and filthy jeans, work boots a size or two too big for his feet, and he glares at Deacon with his cloudy blue eyes.

"Gotta dollar fifty?" he asks. "Only need a dollar fifty to get my medicines. Help a feller out, mister."

The bum smells like soured wine and body odor, and Deacon reaches into his back pocket for his wallet. "Yeah, I got a dollar fifty," he says. "You better start thinking about finding a warm place to sleep tonight. You know they won't let you in Jimmy Hale if you're drunk."

"I don't go to that damned old mission no more," the bum replies. "I go over to the Firehouse. The preacher over there, he ain't such an ass."

"Well, they still won't let you in if they know you're drunk."

"I ain't gonna be drunk tonight. Just gotta get me my medicines, that's all. Doctor says it's my goddamn liver. Says I prob'ly ain't even gonna live till Thanksgivin'. Now, ain't *that* some fine shit, mister? Somebody sayin' you ain't even living till Thanksgivin'?"

"I'm sorry," Deacon says and there's nothing in his wallet but the hundred-dollar bill the detective slipped him, the bribe so he'd get in the car and take the ride across town to Soda's apartment.

"Maybe he was wrong," Deacon says and the old man blinks and looks confused.

"Who?"

"Your doctor. Maybe he was wrong."

"Oh, no. I don't think so."

Deacon looks at the hundred a moment, remembering when that would have been a small fortune to him, not that long ago, and then he hands it to the bum.

"Don't you lose this, you hear me? Whatever you don't spend today, you put it away someplace safe."

"My god," the man mumbles, licking his chapped lips and staring at the bill in his hand. "No way, mister. No, no, no. You can't just give me a hundred-dollar bill."

"Why not? You need it more than me."

"*Why not?* Jesus. 'Cause someone's gonna think I stole it, that's why not. Or someone'll hear I got it and bash my brains out to steal it. You can't just go givin' a bum who ain't even gonna live to see Thanksgivin' a goddamn hundred dollars."

"I already did. It's yours now. I don't want it," and Deacon glances anxiously southeast, at the tall brick buildings standing between him and home.

"But somebody'll kill me, mister. I'll wind up dead or in jail. Maybe both. Ain't you got nothin' a little smaller?"

"No," Deacon says. "I don't. Just take it," and he leaves the bum staring dumbfounded at the detective's blood money; he turns north up Twentieth, walking quickly away from home.

"I only needed a buck fifty!" the bum shouts after him.

Deacon ignores him and keeps walking, past vacant storefronts and alleyways, four banks at one intersection and an Episcopal church cringing in their shadows. Keeps his eyes on the cracks in the sidewalk, the litter and pigeon shit smears; if he doesn't have to stop, he'll be at the park soon, the park and the library and he can spend what's left of the day reading. Hiding in books and magazines until Chance gets home, and he feels a little better already, the money gone and with it at least some small part of the temptation. The thirst is still there, still burning, but not so easy to quench now, and at least that's something.

He looks both ways, then crosses Seventh Avenue to Linn Park and the two bronze soldiers standing guard on their tall, granite pedestals. The one on the left a remembrance of the first World War, a doughboy frozen forever in his last, desperate dash across no-man's-land, bronze barbed wire twined about his ankles, his rifle and bayonet clutched in verdigris hands. And the soldier on the right to honor the men who died in earlier, half-forgotten conflicts—the Spanish-American War, the Boxer Rebellion, the Philippines insurrection—and he stands at attention, his rifle held across his chest, proud soldier who's never even dreamed the nightmares of trench warfare and machine guns, mustard gas and tanks. And in between these mute and immobile sentries stands a fifty-foot limestone obelisk dedicated to the Confederate dead. Deacon pauses on the steps near the base of the obelisk, last opportunity for a smoke before the library and he fishes a pack of Camels from his shirt pocket. He's smoking way too much these days, but he supposes that's like talking to himself, better than the drinking, at least as far as Chance is concerned.

"Hey there, stranger," someone says, familiar girl voice grown unfamiliar because he hasn't heard it in so many months now—a whole year, almost—and when he looks up from his lighter and the burning tip end of his cigarette, there's Sadie Jasper walking towards him from the library, Sadie's quick, determined stride, as if she always has someplace to be and she's always five minutes late. Her cultivated pallor and hair like a fire engine, black lips and her blue eyes paler than the October sky and ringed by so much mascara and eyeliner they look bruised. Seeing her again, not just Sadie but the old life she represents, Deacon feels something in his throat, his belly, an almost-pain that's part nostalgia and part dread. Sadie's carrying a bundle of books in her arms and she sets them down on the sidewalk at his feet.

"No one ever sees you around anymore," she says and frowns. "But I guess you're respectable now, right? Can't risk being seen hanging out with a bunch of freaks and barflies."

"Is that how it is?" and Deacon fidgets self-consciously with the simple white-gold band on his left hand. It glints dull in the afternoon sunlight and he takes a deep drag off his Camel. His headache is getting worse and he can't think, doesn't know what to say next.

"I don't know which is harder to believe, that Deke Silvey's sober or that he's married."

"There's a difference?"

"You tell me," and then she bums a cigarette and he lights it for her and they stand smoking beneath the obelisk.

"You hear about Soda?" Sadie asks and Deacon can feel the goose bumps on his arms and the short hairs prickling at the nape of his neck, the shiver inside that his mother always said meant a possum was walking on his grave.

"Yeah," he says. "I heard."

"He was a weasel, but damn, I never pegged him for a suicide."

"Is that what you heard, that Soda killed himself?"

"Yep," and Sadie makes a pistol of her right thumb and index finger and sets the barrel against her temple. "Sheryl's big brother's a cop and he told her that Soda blew his head completely off. Said he used a shotgun."

"Yeah, well, word sure gets around fast," Deacon mutters and shakes his head, glances down at the stack of books that Sadie's deposited on the steps, a copy of the *Mabinogion* on top and Bruno Bettelheim's *The Uses of Enchantment* underneath that. "You still working on the novel?" he asks her.

"On and off," she replies, sighs and kicks gently at the stack of books with the pointy toe of her boot. "I think it's just about de-cided it doesn't want to *be* a novel. Maybe I'll write something else instead. Maybe it wants to be short stories. But thanks for asking. I'm surprised you even remember that."

"Of course I remember. I liked that one chapter you let me read last year. I liked your style. You know, your voice."

"My *voice?*" Sadie laughs and takes a long drag off her ciga-rette. "My last rejection slip called my style 'obtuse' and 'con-trived.'"

"That's bullshit. I'd call it Faulknerian, à la *The Sound and the Fury.*"

"Oh, you mean the way I liked to run words together to make new adjectives? Well, I don't do that anymore. It just kept pissing people off."

"Yeah, well, I still liked that one chapter you let me read."

"It sucked ass."

"Hey, what the hell do I know."

"That's not what I meant, moron," and she looks up at him with those cold blue eyes and for a moment it might still be the world before, the long days and nights of boozing and the careless ease of a life filled with slackers and layabouts, dead-end hipsters, people without ambition or all their ambitions out of reach and they know it so what's the use trying. The life he walked away from for Chance, the bars and punker shows replaced with AA meetings and his monthly counseling sessions. And it would be so simple to go back, as simple as twisting the cap off a bottle of Popov or Mad Dog. As easy as following Sadie home or to the nearest watering hole.

"I gotta run," she says. "There's gonna be a thing for Soda at The Plaza tonight and I told Sheryl I'd help tend bar. You should drop by. You could bring the little wifey thing. Tell her we won't bite."

"You know I can't do that, Sadie."

"Yeah," she says. "I know. I was just thinking out loud, that's all." And she stands on tiptoes and hugs him around the neck, hugs him hard, and Sadie Jasper smells like vanilla and roses and the spicy smoke of clove cigarettes. He hugs her back with one arm, surprised and noncommittal hug, and "I miss you," she says, al-most whispering. "We all miss you, Deke."

"I miss you, too. Don't think I don't."

She releases him then, smiles her strange, sad smile and for a moment Sadie just stands there, very still, staring at Deacon until he feels the possum scamper across his grave again. Always something a little *too* spooky about this girl, like maybe the death-rocker affectations are only a mask to hide a more genuine darkness; he smiles back and drops the butt of his cigarette to the sidewalk, grinds it out with the heel of his shoe.

"I gotta run," she says again, finally taking her eyes off him, and she stoops to retrieve her library books. The *Mabinogion* slides off the top of the stack and Deacon catches it before it hits the sidewalk.

"Thanks," Sadie says. "Now, you take care of yourself, Deke. And tell that wife of yours if I ever hear she ain't doing right by you, she's gonna be in for a serious butt-whuppin'," and sure, he laughs, sure, you bet, and then she's gone, crossing the street to the bus stop. She waves once and Deacon waves back, before he turns and walks quickly past the magnolias and statues to the sanctuary of the library doors.

Deacon had been sober for almost four months when Chance sold her grandfather's big house, the tall white house overlooking the dingy gray carpet of Birmingham from the side of Red Mountain. The place where she'd lived most of her life, since her parents died when she was barely five years old and her grandparents took her in. The little attic bedroom that Chance had been unwilling to vacate even after they were married, never mind they had the whole house to themselves, her grandfather dead three years, and sometimes Deacon thinks she only married him because she couldn't stand the thought of living in that house alone with the ghosts of her grandparents.

He made the mistake of saying that once—"Sometimes I think you only married me so you wouldn't be alone," reckless words he should have always kept to himself, but that was one of the endless, thirsty days when he could think of nothing but having a drink, just *one* drink, one very *small* goddamned drink. The anger and desperation building up inside him all day long, piling up like afternoon storm clouds on a sizzling summer day. And finally Chance had done or said something to piss him off, something inconsequential, something he'd forget a long, long time before he would ever forget the way she turned and stared at him with her hard green eyes. Even his thirst shriveling at the look she gave him with those eyes, the look that said *I can leave you anytime I want, Deacon Silvey. Don't you ever think I can't.*

He apologized and spent the rest of the day alone in the basement, banging about uselessly with a crescent wrench, pretending to work on the house's leaky copper plumbing. Those ancient pipes one of the reasons that Chance finally gave him for wanting to sell the place, the pipes and the furnace that rarely worked, the termites that were eating the back porch, the roof that needed reshingling, property taxes and the grass that Deacon couldn't be bothered to mow. Her dissertation finally finished and there'd been a good job waiting for her at the university, an assistant professorship in the geology department.

"I just don't want to have to worry about the place anymore," she said one morning at breakfast and Deacon watched her silently across the kitchen table, uncertain how much of this was his decision to make, and what, if anything, he ought to say.

"I don't know how Granddad kept it together all that time. I feel like it's about to come crashing down around my ears."

"It's not that bad," Deacon said and she shook her head and stared out the window at the weedy backyard.

"It's bad enough."

Deacon sipped at his scalding black coffee, waiting for her to say something else, waiting for his cue to say anything useful.

"Alice wants me to look at some lofts down on Morris," she said without taking her eyes off the window.

"You think we could afford that, I mean—"

"I'm making decent money now, and we should get a good price for the house. It wouldn't hurt our savings account."

And Deacon waited for her to say, *You could get a job,* but she didn't, looked away from the backyard and took a bite of her toast and apple butter instead.

"I just don't want you to do something you might wind up regretting," he said. "I mean, this is your home. You've lived here all your life."

"That doesn't mean I have to live here the *rest* of my life."

Deacon shook his head, already sorry that he'd said anything at all. "No, it doesn't," he agreed.

And so Chance sold the house, the house and half the things in it, antiques and her grandfather's guns, and they moved downtown into a renovated warehouse at the eastern end of Morris Avenue. What the woman from the realty agency kept referring to as the "historic loft district," though Deacon could remember when the long cobblestone street had been something else entirely. Not so long ago, the early '90s, back when Morris was only a neglected patchwork of warehouses struggling to stay in business and abandoned buildings dating to the turn of the last century and before. A couple of gay bars and one punk hangout called Dr. Jekyll's, a coffeehouse and The Peanut Depot, which sold freshly roasted peanuts in gigantic burlap sacks. A place where homeless men slept in doorways and built fires on the unused loading docks, and sensible people avoided the poorly lit avenue after dark. But most of that time had been scrubbed away to make room for offices and art galleries, apartments and condos for yuppies who wanted to flirt with city life without leaving the reliable provincialism of Birmingham behind.

"And what do *you* do, Mr. Silvey?" the real-estate agent asked him while Chance filled in the credit history on their application.

"Mostly I try to stay sober," he replied and Chance glared at him from the other side of the room.

A nervous little laugh from the agent and then she coughed and smiled at him expectantly, suspiciously, waiting for the *real* answer, and he wanted to take Chance and drive back to the big white house on the other side of town. Wanted to tell this woman she could go straight to hell and take her "historic loft district" with her. And who cared if the pipes leaked or there was no heat in the winter, so long as they didn't have to answer questions from the likes of her.

"Deke's thinking of going back to school soon," Chance said before he could make things worse, and the woman's face seemed to brighten a little at the news.

"Is that so?" she asked him and he nodded, even though it wasn't.

"Deke was at Emory for two years," Chance said, looking back down at the application, filling in another empty space with the ballpoint pen the real-estate agent had given her.

"Emory," the woman repeated approvingly. "Were you studying medicine, Mr. Silvey, or law?"

"Philosophy," Deacon answered, which was true, a life he'd lived and lost what seemed like a hundred years ago, before the booze had become the only thing that got him from one day to the next, before he'd come to Birmingham looking for nothing in particular but a change of scenery.

"Well, that must be very interesting," the woman said, but the doubt was creeping back into her voice.

"I used to think so," Deacon said. "But I used to think a whole lot of silly things," and then he excused himself and waited downstairs behind the wheel of Chance's rusty old Impala while she finished. He smoked and listened to an '80s station on the radio, Big Country and Oingo Boingo, trying to decide whether he should just cut to the chase and take the bus home instead. When Chance came downstairs with the real-estate agent she was smiling, wearing her cheerful mask until the woman drove away in a shiny, black Beemer and then the mask slipped and he could see the anger waiting for him underneath. Chance didn't get into the car, stood at the driver's-side door and stared down Morris towards the train tracks that divided the city neatly in half.

"Go ahead," he said. "Unload on me. Tell me what an asshole I am for queering the deal."

"Deke, if you don't want to do this, why the fuck don't you just say so and then we can stop wasting our time?"

Deacon turned off the radio and leaned forward, resting his forehead against the steering wheel.

"All right. I don't want to do this."

"*Shit*," she hissed, and he shut his eyes, trying not to think about how much easier all of this would be if he were only a little bit drunk. "Why the hell didn't you say so before?"

"I didn't want to piss you off."

Chance laughed, a hard, sour sort of laugh, and kicked the car door hard enough that Deacon jumped.

"I don't want to live in that house anymore, Deke. There are way too many bad memories there. I need to start over. I need to start clean."

"I just wish you'd slow down, that's all. I feel like we're rushing into this."

"Well, after the way you behaved up there, I expect you'll be getting your wish."

And Deacon didn't say anything else, slid over to the passenger's side and neither of them said another word while Chance drove them back to the house, and, as it turned out, he *didn't* get his wish. Their application was approved three days later and Chance put the house that her great-grandfather had built up for sale. A month later the house sold, the house and its acre and a half of land, and the week after that they found out she was pregnant.

Through the library doors and past the winding marble stairs that lead up to the mezzanine, past the marble statue balanced on its marble column, headless angel, armless angel, and Deacon follows the short hallway back to the pay phones. A quarter just to get a dial tone and then he punches 411 and tells the operator he needs to place a collect call to Detective Vincent Hammond, Atlanta PD, Homicide Division, so she transfers him to an Atlanta operator. A long moment of clicks and static across the line, and Deacon waits and watches the towering, gold-framed portrait of George Washington hung on the wall opposite the hallway's entrance. Washington stares back with his ancient, oil-paint eyes that are neither kind nor cruel, the unflinching face of authority and history, and after just a few seconds of that Deacon looks down at the scuffed toes of his shoes instead.

"Is anyone there?" Deacon asks the phone and "Just one moment, please, sir," the Atlanta operator says impatiently and then a phone begins to ring at the other end.

"This is Hammond," the man who answers the phone says in a smoky, tired voice, gravel voice, and just hearing him again, Deacon can smell the menthol Kools that dangle perpetually from Vince Hammond's thin lips.

"You did this," Deacon says. "You're the one that told them where to find me."

A pause and "Deke?" the cop asks, trying to sound confused or surprised, but Deacon knows it's just an act. "Hey, bubba, is that really you? Goddamn. I haven't heard from you in a coon's age."

"Don't 'hey, bubba' me, you sonofabitch. You did it, didn't you? You fucking *knew* I didn't want any more of this crazy shit in my life and you did it anyway."

"Yeah, well, let's just say I owed someone a favor."

Deacon wipes at his face, at flop sweat and the pain piling up higher and higher behind his eyes. Really no point in any of this, the call to Hammond, the accusations and anger, because the damage is done now and there's no undoing it.

"Just calm down, bubba. You guys have a bad one over there. They needed some help."

Deacon takes a deep breath, holds it, and glances back at George Washington; serene, certain George in his justaucorps and white wig, and Deacon exhales very slowly.

"I'm married, man," he says. "I have a pregnant wife. I'm doing everything I can to stay sober. I can't have this sort of shit in my life anymore."

"I'm sorry. I didn't know that. Congratula—"

"You could have fucking asked. You could have called me first and asked."

"And you would'a told me to fuck off, right? Look, I just thought maybe you could help those boys out down there, that's all. This one's something special, Deke, something *bad*."

"Yeah, and that's *exactly* why it's not my goddamn problem."

"Good to know you're still the same philanthropic soul I remember from the old days."

"Fuck you, Hammond," Deke growls into the receiver, raising his voice and a passing librarian scowls at him.

"Just don't do it again, okay? Don't ever do it again, do you understand me?"

"You have a gift, Deke—"

"I have a *wife*," and he hangs up and stands glaring at the phone, waiting for his heart to stop racing, for the fury to drain away and leave him with nothing worse than the headache and his thirst.

CHAPTER TWO

Deep Time

Alice Sprinkle's old Toyota pickup bounces over a rut in the interstate pavement and Chance moans and opens her eyes. She's been trying to doze since they left Birmingham, catch some shut-eye while Alice drives, but it's impossible to get comfortable in the cramped cab of the truck and she's tired of trying. Tired of staring at the insides of her eyelids, the bright sunlight shining through her flesh, and, besides, she has to piss again.

"Better stop at the next exit," she says and Alice sighs and nods her head.

"Wouldn't you rather wait until the rest stop? We're almost to the state line."

"I can try," Chance grumbles, shifting in her tiny bucket seat, trying to find any position that'll make her back ache just a little bit less. "But I'm not making any promises."

"I'm thinking the rest stop would sure be a hell of a lot cleaner, that's all," and Chance glances over at Alice behind the wheel, the woman more than twenty years her senior and all the lines in her face right there to show every moment of her life. All the long days of scorching sun and freezing wind, her weathered, rugged face sculpted like the rock walls of the quarries and strip mines that she's lived half her life in. *My face someday,* Chance thinks.

"I feel like a beached whale," she says. "A goddamned pregnant beached whale with hemorrhoids."

"Only a very small whale," Alice smirks. "Maybe a manatee."

"Thanks a lot," and Chance adjusts the pillow behind her back again, but it doesn't help.

"Them's the hazards of living that damn heterosexual lifestyle, dear. You should've listened to me and found yourself a good woman. *She* wouldn't have gotten you into this sad predicament."

"I swear to god, Alice. I'm gonna pee in your floorboard if we don't stop soon."

"Not much farther, I promise," and there's the reflective blue interstate sign to back her up, WELCOME—WE'RE GLAD GEORGIA'S ON YOUR MIND, and underneath that the big peach that Chance has always thought looked more like someone's naked butt. She leans forward and braces one hand flat against the dash, wanting to un-buckle the seat belt, but she knows Alice would have a fit. It was hard enough just convincing her that she was up to the drive to At-lanta, lucky she's not sitting in her office grading freshman papers instead while Alice makes the trip alone.

"You should've stayed in town," Alice Sprinkle says, like the woman can read her mind. "You should have listened to Deacon and let me handle this."

"Christ, I think the urine must have backed up into my brain. I could have sworn you just agreed with Deke."

"Hey, even *he* can't be wrong all the time."

"Can I quote you?"

"Have you looked in the mirror lately? You're about to pop, kiddo," and Alice makes a sound with her lips like pulling the cork from a bottle of wine.

"Yeah, well, they're my fossils," Chance says glumly and she looks out the window at the green pine trees and the autumn-wide sky. "And I've been trying to put this exhibit together for six months. Now I'm gonna see it through."

"Chance, you're almost as stubborn as your grandpa was, you know that?"

"I consider that the highest of compliments."

"I'm sure you do," and Alice slows down and takes the exit for the Georgia Welcome Center, wrestling with the Toyota's tempera-mental stick shift. A loud, grinding noise from beneath the hood and "One day this old bitch is just gonna roll over and give up the ghost," she says; Chance nods, too busy trying not to wet herself for words.

"Here you go, Puddles," Alice says and pulls in between a bat-tered minivan and a yellow Corvette with California license plates.

The truck's engine sputters and dies as soon as she shifts into park. "Sit still and I'll give you a hand."

"I'm pretty sure I can still get out of a truck on my own," but Alice is already on her way around the front of the Toyota to get Chance's door. "I'm *not* a cripple," she whispers, talking to no one but herself. "I'm eight months pregnant, but I'm not a goddamn cripple."

Alice opens the passenger-side door; "Six of one," she says, "half dozen of the other."

"How did you possibly hear that?"

"We lesbian paleontologists got ears of steel, didn't you know that? Comes from not squandering all our precious bodily fluids having babies." Alice laughs and puts one arm around Chance's waist, holds her right hand, strong arms to keep her steady until she has both feet planted firmly on the parking lot asphalt.

"You think anyone would care if I squatted down and peed right here?"

"Now, we ain't in Alabama no more, Mrs. Silvey. They got laws against that sort of thing in Georgia."

"I can make it the rest of the way on my own," Chance says and Alice frowns and looks doubtful. "Hey, if I'm not back in ten minutes you can send the cavalry in after me, okay?"

"You're sure about that?"

"Yes, I'm sure. Just check on the crates while I'm gone," and before Alice can object, Chance is already halfway up the sidewalk to the door, moving as quickly as she dares. Her legs and feet, her back, hurt so badly that she might as well have *walked* all the way from Birmingham. A fat little boy sitting alone on a concrete bench stares at her like maybe she's grown an extra head, like he's never seen a pregnant woman before and babies come from cabbages. Then a bearded man in a red, white and blue Budweiser cap holds the door open and she thanks him.

Alice Sprinkle waits until Chance is safe inside, waits another minute to be sure, and then she begins inspecting each of the nylon ropes securing the wooden crates of fossils packed into the back of the pickup.

Cold water from the tap and the restroom stinks of cleansers and disinfectants, the fainter smell of human waste, and Chance splashes her face again. Her reflection in the long mirror above the row of sinks, her wet face, the whites of her green eyes bloodshot because she hasn't been sleeping so well lately. Tall and pregnant woman looking back at her, the silly maternity overalls because she's always hated dresses; water dripping from her coffee-colored hair, trickling down her face, falling back into the porcelain bowl. Her face so puffy that she hardly recognizes it sometimes, always so thin before this, and Chance reaches for a paper towel from the metal dispenser on the wall.

I should hurry, she thinks, imagining Alice waiting impatiently in the truck, long since finished checking the crates and now she's probably sitting out there behind the wheel, restlessly tapping her foot, mumbling to herself. A few more minutes and Alice will most likely come looking for her.

"Yeah," Chance says aloud. "I *should* have stayed home," and then she feels the baby kick again. That strange and gentle pain from inside, and she knows she'll never get used to it, that the kid will be born long before she could ever hope to take it for granted. The precarious life held inside her belly, the half-Deacon, half-Chance person growing in there, and it makes her dizzy, just the thought of such an extraordinary, unlikely thing. She splashes her face again, the cold to clear her head, wash away the fog, and glances once more at the mirror.

I should hurry. Alice is waiting for me.

A large drop of water as red as a ripe cherry gathers on a strand of her wet hair, swells there for a moment and then pulls free and lands in the sink with an audible *plop*. Chance stands staring at it, speechless; not water, blood, a crimson spatter of her blood in the sink and when she touches her forehead her fingertips come away smeared red.

"Oh Jesus," she whispers, her heart racing, fear and confusion and the sick-sharp punch of adrenaline. "Oh fuck," and there's no one else but her in the rest room, no one to help, though she could have sworn there was someone only a moment before. An elderly Hispanic woman with a child, only a moment before. Chance's face in the mirror, stark and pale in the rest-room light, and now the blood is running in a thin stream down the right side of her face.

And the baby kicks again, harder than before.

Chance looks from her frightened, reflected face to the blood staining her fingers, *her* blood, and she touches her scalp again. No pain there at all, no sign whatsoever of a cut or a lesion, and she leans closer, parting her hair for a better view.

But her scalp isn't bleeding.

Another drop of blood falls from her face and spatters the white sink.

"Alice," she says, never mind that Alice is outside with the truck, with the fossils, and can't possibly hear her. "Oh god, Alice, something's wrong with me."

There's a noise behind her, then, a dry and crackling sound like October leaves crunching loud underfoot, and she turns quickly around, slinging blood onto the dingy beige tiles that cover the rest-room floor. No one and nothing back there, nothing at all but sterile walls and fluorescent lights, and suddenly her legs feel so weak that Chance thinks she might fall. She's never fainted in her life, but she thinks maybe this is how it feels before you do, and she leans against the countertop. Chance looks at the rest-room door and surely it'll open any second now and Alice will come barging in, bitching about having to wait in the truck. Or someone else, a stranger, anyone she can send to get Alice.

The crackling sound again and this time it seems to be coming from directly overhead, probably nothing more than squirrels on the roof of the building, the roof covered with fallen leaves and squirrels rooting about up there for acorns or pecans or something.

She wipes the blood off her hand onto the denim bib of her overalls and takes a deep breath. She's always been so strong, always self-sufficient, and nothing worse than this helplessness; overhead, the crunching, scritching sound grows more frenzied, but now she's pretty sure it's only squirrels digging for fallen acorns. Only squirrels, squirrels or maybe birds, and she looks back at the sink.

And it's completely spotless—a few fat, lingering drops of water that haven't drained away, and nothing else. She looks at her face in the mirror and there's no blood there, either, only her wet bangs plastered flat against her forehead, only her wide, tired eyes. A fleeting moment of relief that isn't really relief because she knows what she saw.

"Shit," Chance says and stands very still, waiting for her racing pulse to return to normal again, for the strength to return to her legs, still wishing that Alice would come walking through the door. At least ten minutes since Chance left her alone in the parking lot, ten or even fifteen, she thinks, and *Where the hell are you, Alice?*

No blood in the sink. No blood on her face. No blood smeared across the front of her overalls. Just clean porcelain and busy squirrels scampering about on the roof. She takes another deep breath and shuts her eyes for a moment, opens them again and slowly exhales.

I'm tired, that's all. I'm not sleeping enough and I'm just really fucking tired. Worrying about Deacon all the time and the situation at the university, most of her work neglected for months now. Terrified of the pain, the delivery, and too proud to confess that part to anyone, and *It's a miracle it's taken this long for me to start seeing things,* she thinks.

The baby shifts slightly and kicks her again. But this time there's only comfort in the sensation, and she places a hand on her swollen belly.

Chance hears the rest-room door swing open, hears heavy footsteps, and "Hey, kiddo," Alice says. "You okay in here? I was starting to get worried."

"I'm fine," Chance tells her, turning away from the mirror. "I was just coming. I didn't mean to take so long."

Alice stares at her uncertainly for a second, and Chance forces a small smile to prove she isn't lying. "My back's killing me, that's all. I'm not looking forward to getting back into that damn truck."

"Well, I'm sorry, but we're going to be late if you don't get a move on. I told you to stay home."

"Yes," Chance says. "Yes, you did."

And then Alice takes her hand and leads her out of the rest-room and back to the truck.

When Chance was only six years old, her grandfather asked her what she wanted to be when she grew up. Not a second's hesitation before her reply, "A paleontologist," and Joe Matthews smiled and hugged her. "Well, that would be nice," he said. "But you just do what you want to do. We'll be proud of you no matter what." Joe Matthews was a geologist, and Chance's grandmother, Esther, an invertebrate paleontologist. Joe had spent his life teaching and studying the sedimentology and stratigraphy of the Late Cretaceous rocks in the west-central part of the state, the Black Belt prairies that had been covered by a shallow seaway at the end of the Age of Reptiles. Esther studied trilobites closer to home, collected her strange little bugs from the Paleozoic shales and limestones exposed across most of the northern part of the state. In her lifetime, she named two new trilobite species—*Tricrepicephalus conasaugaensis* and *Cryptolithus gigas*.

Her grandmother died when Chance was still a teenager, a suicide that no one ever really understood; no convenient, exegetic note left behind for the living, no warning signs before Esther Matthews got dressed late one stormy night and hanged herself from a tree behind the big house on Red Mountain. Her grandfather lived on for almost another ten years, his final heart attack coming shortly before Chance received her MA. Together they'd been half her life, and paleontology the other half, all she'd ever needed until Deacon Silvey came along to complicate things. The little girl who really did know what she wanted from the world when she was only six, a life like her grandparents', a life spent teasing answers from the rocks, all the mysteries of time laid out before her and she never seriously considered doing anything else.

And this trip to Atlanta to supply fossils for a temporary display at the Fernbank Museum of Natural History—"At the River's Edge: Fish with Feet." A whole exhibit built around the work that Chance had begun when she was still an undergraduate, after she'd discovered the fossilized remains of a creature that straddled the evolutionary fence between fish and amphibians. The past seven years of her life spent collecting from the strip mines and road cuts where she'd first found her "missing link," gathering bits of skull and vertebrae and eight-fingered feet that were not quite done with being fins. Her "indecisive pollywogs," as Alice Sprinkle liked to call them.

The exhibit was already scheduled before Chance learned that she was pregnant, and she was determined to see it through to completion. It was one of her *other* babies, after all, just like the fossils and her publications. Her responsibility, her obligation, and she wouldn't have Alice or anyone else tying up her loose ends, not if she could help it. Most of the day before spent packing the fossils for the two and a half hour drive from Birmingham to Atlanta, carefully wrapping each specimen in tissue paper and cotton and

Bubble Wrap before placing them between layers of foam rubber carved out to accommodate each piece. The packing and the paperwork, making sure that all the loan forms were in order; more than fifty specimens, all told, that she was entrusting to someone else's care, six months that they would be out of her protection and Alice joked that at least it was good practice for motherhood.

"I won't be that kind of a mother," Chance said, wrapping a siderite concretion containing the skull of a small coelacanth.

Alice stopped nailing the lid shut on one of the army surplus ammo crates that would contain the fossils during the drive to Atlanta and she stared at Chance, shook her head and chuckled.

"Right. I can just imagine the first day you have to leave the poor kid with a nanny, or at preschool. Hell, you'll probably pack it in excelsior and write a catalog number on its butt."

Chance's latest discovery, and the fossil that would form the centerpiece of the Fernbank exhibit, was an almost complete skeleton of a creature that would have been a veritable titan in the steamy Coal Age swamps where it had died. Something that must have looked more than a little bit like a stubby, snub-nosed alligator when it was alive and breathing, three hundred million years before she found its petrified skeleton exposed by bulldozers clearing a patch of land north of Birmingham to make room for a new Wal-Mart.

The university had managed to persuade the construction company to halt work at the site for three days, just long enough for her to oversee the specimen's recovery, and then Chance spent four long months preparing it. Slowly, painstakingly removing the hard siltstone matrix with an Air Scribe until the entire left side of the skeleton was exposed in bas-relief, jet-black bones set in stone the color of charcoal. The bulldozer's blade had destroyed the very tip end of the tail, but the rest was there, all twelve feet, eight inches of the creature's spectacular frame. In a paper published in the *Journal of Vertebrate Paleontology,* she described the fossil and named it *Megalopseudosuchus alabamaensis.*

The week the paper was released, the Geology Department had thrown a surprise party for Chance, including a huge layer cake baked into something vaguely approximating the shape of her monstrous amphibian and covered with dark green, lime-flavored icing. Deacon came, though he spent most of the party sitting alone in a corner drinking a Coke and pretending to read an old issue of *Scientific American*. Pretending all of it didn't make him uncomfortable, the noise and nerdy academic jokes, Chance's success. But she knew better. Knew that some part of him resented her and sooner or later that was something they would have to face, one way or another.

Driving home afterwards, a cold rain and the sky like folds of purple-gray velvet. "I'm really proud of you, you know," Deacon said. "Maybe I never say it like I should, but I am. I'm very proud of you. Your goddamn brain, it amazes me . . ." and he trailed off, then, turned onto Morris Avenue, the tires *bump-bump-bump*ing over the wet cobblestones.

"Thank you," she said softly and leaned over to kiss him on the cheek.

"No, I mean it. You really do amaze me."

"I know," she said and smiled and for the smallest part of a second Deacon smiled, too. The rain drummed softly on the roof of the old Impala, and in a couple minutes more they were home.

Alice drives slowly past the main entrance to the museum, squat and sensible building of brick and glass, past the visitor parking lot to a loading platform located in the rear. There are two young men waiting there to unload the heavy crates from the back of the Toyota, and the collection's manager, a middle-aged woman named Irene Mesmer, is waiting with them. Alice talks to her and Chance watches nervously and chews at a thumbnail while the men transfer her fossils from the truck to the concrete platform, a job she'd be handling herself if she were able. When one of them sets a crate down too roughly for her liking, she scowls and asks him to be more careful, please, and he apologizes and goes back to work.

"Have you ever visited Fernbank before, Dr. Silvey?" Irene Mesmer asks in a heavy Charlotte accent and Chance nods, not taking her eyes off the workmen and the crates.

"Yeah. But I was just a little kid."

"So you haven't seen the new dinosaurs?"

"No," Chance says.

"Well, then, why don't I give you both a quick tour?"

"I think that would be great," Alice says enthusiastically, glancing at Chance, who sighs and shrugs her wide shoulders.

"I don't know. Maybe I should wait here. I could catch up with you guys later on."

"You'll have to excuse her," Alice says, speaking to the collections manager. "She had to pee back at the state line and I'm afraid I might not have stopped soon enough. There may have been irreversible brain damage."

"I just want to *watch,*" Chance says, annoyed now, wishing Alice and the other woman would leave her alone, wishing she were in any shape to lift the crates herself. The last hour spent trying to forget whatever she did or didn't see back at the welcome center and now she'd just like to be left alone to oversee the unloading.

"I promise, Dr. Silvey, Bill and Andrew here know what they're doing. They've unpacked fossils before."

"They've never unpacked *my* fossils before."

One of the men, skinny, muscular man in a gray Atlanta Braves sweatshirt and a red baseball cap turned around backwards, sets down a crate marked THIS SIDE UP and MORRIS FISH; he smiles for Chance and nods his head reassuringly.

"No, ma'am. But last summer, I worked for the High Museum and helped unload a whole shipment of those fancy Fabergé eggs. And I expect they're a whole lot more fragile than your fossils here."

Chance stares at him, offended, and "No," she replies. "Not necessarily."

"They can *handle* it, Chance." Alice says, "C'mon, let's go see some dinos," and she takes Chance's arm and leads her into the building.

The museum was designed around a great central atrium capped with a vaulted dome of steel and glass, whitewashed beams to form the formerets and tiercerons, the transverse arches and diagonal buttresses. An industrial cathedral of welds and bolts instead of keystones and mortar, and the October afternoon sunlight floods into the atrium, warm and clean, illuminating the Cretaceous giants below. Chance stands with Alice on one of the balconies, staring in wonder at the skeletons, her fossils and the two workmen momentarily forgotten, even the weird shit at the rest stop forgotten for now.

"They're not the *real* skeletons, of course," Irene says apologetically. "They're only fiberglass and resin casts. The real bones are still in Argentina."

"Of course," Chance says and she takes a step closer to the edge of the balcony. Below, the skeleton of an impossibly immense titanosaurid sauropod, *Argentinosaurus,* is pursued by the skeleton of a hungry *Giganotosaurus.* The sauropod is one hundred and twenty-six feet long from its small head to the end of its whiplash tail, too enormous to have ever been real, a creature to put all other dragons to shame. Its pursuer, larger even than *Tyrannosaurus rex,* seems puny by comparison. The air around and above the dinosaurs is filled with the delicate skeletons of flying reptiles suspended on not-quite invisible wires, a whole flock of *Pterodaustro,* their peculiar flamingo-like jaws lined with bristles for filter feeding, and a couple of the much larger *Anhanguera* like something a desperate, escaping vampire might become. A moment forever lost in time, some South American floodplain or tropical forest more than ninety million years ago, and these giants striding beneath the light of a younger sun, the earth literally shaking beneath their feet.

"It's beautiful," Chance says.

Irene makes a satisfied sound deep in her throat and "Yes," she says. "We're very proud of it, Dr. Silvey."

"Please, just Chance. Only my students call me Dr. Silvey."

"That's an unusual name."

"That's what everyone keeps telling me," Chance says and she leans a little way out over the railing, letting the yellow-white sun bathe her face. "I wish I'd brought my camera."

"Too bad we don't have anything like this in Birmingham," Alice says and puts one hand on Chance's back, twining thick fingers protectively around the straps of her overalls.

"I'm fine," Chance mumbles. "I'm not going to fall," but Alice holds on anyway.

"Whatever became of the Red Mountain Museum?" Irene asks. "They had that wonderful mosasaur skeleton."

Alice frowns and shakes her head. "The city decided it would rather have a science center for the kiddies than a real museum. They closed Red Mountain down back in '94. Now that wonderful mosasaur's sitting in a crate in the attic of the kiddy place."

"Oh," the collections manager says. "Well, that's a shame."

"Yeah, it is," Chance whispers, still warming her face and staring down at the magnificent Patagonian dinosaurs. "But that's Birmingham for you. One step forward, two steps back."

A moment of silence, then, and Chance shuts her eyes and imagines the flutter of leathery pterosaur wings, the deafening bellow of the *Argentinosaurus* as the *Giganotosaurus* hisses and lunges at the sauropod's unprotected flanks.

"Would y'all like to see the hall where your fossils will be displayed? It's right downstairs."

"Yes, we would," Alice says and Chance opens her eyes, reluctantly letting go of the daydream, and the brilliant noise and violence of a Cretaceous day dissolves instantly back into fiberglass bones and the black iron support rods that hold them up.

"The diorama's almost finished. The exhibits department at the Field Museum in Chicago helped us design it, you know. We'll be keeping it on permanently."

Chance takes a 1st look at the giants, silently wishes the sauropod luck, and then the collections manager leads them along the balcony to a waiting elevator.

"Some lives are more unlikely than others," Chance once wrote in her diary, seventeen years old and already it had seemed to her that she'd enjoyed more odd luck and misfortune than most people twice her age, more than some people might experience in their entire lives. Small unlikelihoods and bigger ones, the trivial and profound weaving accidental trails about her. The death of her parents and her unlikely survival, to start with, both of them killed and her left with nothing worse than a broken arm. "A miracle," one of the doctors said, though Chance had always suspected he'd actually meant something a little more prosaic. Not a miracle, just damned unlikely.

And the fact that Chance ever met Deacon Silvey at all, much less fell in love with him, as unlikely as anything else in her unlikely life. Inhabitants of the same small city, but existing in two entirely different worlds. Deacon lost in his ruin of bars and dead-end jobs, firmly stuck on the fast track to nowhere, and Chance rarely looking up from her textbooks, the Golden Key honor student, Phi Kappa Phi, Sigma Xi, and her first scientific paper published when she was still an undergraduate. The good girl, too-smart girl all set to write her own ticket out into the real world hiding somewhere beyond the rust and slag-heap confines of Birmingham.

But she met him anyway, the summer night that she and Elise Alden got drunk on Jack Daniel's and walked from Chance's house to the homely little park at the end of Nineteenth Street, a few months before Elise moved away to Atlanta. Not really much of a park at all, though it had a few dogwood trees, a weathered, graffiti-scarred gazebo with a picnic table, and the gated entrance to the city's old water works tunnel. A place that Chance had always avoided because it had a reputation as a hangout for junkies, a reputation that had earned it the nickname Needle Park.

Following the "nature trail" down from Sixteenth Avenue into the park, limestone gravel scattered between railroad ties, a crude footpath for curious urban hikers who'd never seen kudzu and poison ivy and blackberry briers up close. Halfway down and Chance and Elise heard voices, angry voices, someone shouting and "Come on," Chance said, leaning against a tree so she wouldn't fall down. "Let's go back home."

"Wait a minute. I want to see what's happening," and Elise took another step along the trail, then stopped and peered through darkness and a thicket of briers at the dimly lit park below.

"What's happening is none of our goddamn business," Chance said, wishing she wasn't starting to feel nauseous, that the world would stop spinning just long enough for her to drag Elise's dumb ass back home where it was safe and she could at least be sick in a toilet instead of in the bushes.

"Oh, Christ. It's a couple of big guys beating up a hippie."

"Too bad," Chance said. She took a deep breath and looked up at the sky, the branches overhead, Heaven far too stained by streetlights for her to ever see the stars. A cacophony of hateful male voices and the cicadas screaming in the trees and she tried to remember why coming down here had ever seemed like a good idea.

"I think they might be skinheads," Elise whispered excitedly.

"They're not skinheads."

"Well, one of them has a big swastika on his T-shirt."

"Good. I'm going home now."

"Oh god, Chance. He has a *knife*."

"*Now,* Elise."

"Hey, fuckface!" Elise shouted at the guy with the knife. "Yeah, you. Leave him alone or I'm gonna call the cops!"

The guy growled back something that Chance couldn't quite make out, but she understood his meaning well enough, no need to speak pit bull when one of them starts barking at you. She grabbed for the collar of Elise's shirt and missed, just a humid handful of night air for her trouble, and Elise was already scrambling towards the little gazebo at the end of the steep trail.

"That asshole's gonna cut your throat!" Chance screamed and stumbled after her.

But there was someone else, waiting in the gazebo, someone they hadn't noticed before, gaunt man hidden in the shadows, and Chance almost screamed when she saw him. He was sitting alone at the picnic table, a pint liquor bottle in front of him. When he saw Elise and Chance he held one hand out like a traffic cop.

"Is that your little girlfriend, faggot?" the guy with the knife asked the hippie. "Is that your girlfriend coming to save your sorry faggot ass?"

"Don't move, either one of you," the man beneath the gazebo whispered. "Don't make a single goddamn sound," and he stood up, then, and Chance could see how tall he was. She saw something clutched tight in his right hand, too, but she didn't realize what it was until he stepped out of the shadows. A piece of board that might have been part of the picnic table once, and the guy with the knife turned towards him while the other guy, the one with the swastika on his T-shirt, kicked the hippie in the stomach. The tall man from the gazebo held the piece of board concealed behind his back as he walked quickly towards the skinhead with the knife.

"Hell no, it ain't your little girlfriend. It's your goddamn faggot *boy*friend."

"Maybe he wants a taste of this shit, too," the guy in the Nazi shirt said and kicked the hippie again. "Maybe he wants to suck our dicks."

"Is that it?" the skinhead with the knife asked. "You want to suck on my fuckstick, faggot?"

The board came out from behind the tall man's back and smashed the skinhead in the face, a black spray of blood from his nose and mouth, his shattered front teeth like broken ivory pegs, and the knife slipped from his hand to the grass. The tall man kicked the knife away and swung the board again, catching the second guy hard across the back of his shaved head. A loud crack, the sound of someone hitting a baseball, hitting a home run, and the skinhead dropped to his knees without a word, then fell face forward over on top of the hippie.

"Fuck," Elise whispered, her voice equal parts shock and admiration, and Chance, who'd finally had enough, sat down at the picnic table and puked on the ground between her shoes. And maybe she passed out for a while, because just a moment later the tall man was bending over her, wiping her face with a handkerchief, and both the skinheads and the hippie were gone. She could hear police sirens in the distance, getting closer. Chance's stomach rolled again, cramped, and she doubled over.

"Take deep breaths," he said. "Slow and easy. It'll pass."

"Dude, that was *so* fucking cool," Elise bubbled drunkenly. "I mean, *shit*, you must know kung fu or karate or something, right? You must have been in the marines or something."

"No," he said. "I'm just a drunk with a stick."

"My name is Chance," Chance said and swallowed, trying to keep from throwing up again. Her mouth tasted like bourbon and bile, and her throat burned.

"Good to meet you, Chance. I'm Deacon," the tall man said. "But I think we'd better get moving now. It'll probably be best if we aren't still here when the cops show up."

"Yeah," Chance said and heaved again.

"Better give me a hand," Deacon said to Elise and together they carried Chance back up the trail to the street.

Downstairs, Chance and Alice follow the collections manager past the Patagonian dinosaurs, between the legs of the *Argentinosaurus* and Chance cranes her neck and stares up at the rib-hollow belly of the beast, suspended fifteen feet or more above her head.

"I only study things I can hold in my palm," Alice says and waves a hand dismissively at the giants. "That's my motto."

"What is your specialty, Dr. Sprinkle?" Irene asks.

"Depends. Sometimes, it's Ordovician brachiopods. Other times, it's Oligocene bryozoans. I don't like to be pigeonholed."

And then Chance's cell phone starts ringing and "That's mine," she says quickly, fishing it out of a pocket of her overalls.

"Is that safe?" Irene says. "For the baby, I mean?"

Chance shrugs. The number displayed on the phone's tiny, oil-gray LCD screen is nothing familiar, but there's a 205 area code, so she knows it's Alabama. She presses TALK and holds up one finger to show that she'll only be a moment.

"Chance?" Deacon says, his voice faint and far away, stretched thin and flat by distance and digital electronics. "Are you okay? Are you at the museum?"

"Yeah, yeah. I'm just fine. What's up?"

"Nothing. I'll tell you about it when you get home. It's been a weird day, that's all," but Deacon's voice has that brittle edge it gets whenever he's anxious or afraid, the way he sounded the first couple of weeks he was sober. "I just wanted to hear your voice."

"Where are you calling from?"

"The downtown library. I thought I'd do some reading."

Chance glances at Alice and the collections manager. Alice is staring thoughtfully up at the underside of the sauropod skeleton, and Irene Mesmer seems to be staring at its shadow on the stone floor.

"But you're *okay*, right?" Chance asks him, turning the tables and Deacon doesn't answer.

"Deke?"

"Yeah, baby, I'm just fine. It's not that. I promise. You know I'd tell you if it was that."

"Honey, I gotta go. We're about to have a look at the exhibit."

"So, all the fossils got there in one piece?"

"As far as I know. Nothing's been unpacked yet."

"Well," he says, and she can tell he doesn't want to hang up, trying to squeeze a few more seconds out of the conversation. "I guess I should let you go. You're busy."

"You're sure nothing's wrong?"

"Yeah, I'm fine. Everything's jake."

"I wish you were here. I'll have to bring you to see these dinosaurs. They're incredible," and she looks up at the pelvis of the *Argentinosaurus,* big as a Volkswagen.

"I'm just gonna hang around the library for a while," Deacon says. "I'll head home before dark."

"You should take the DART. It's only fifty cents."

"I'd rather walk."

Alice is glaring at her impatiently now. "I really gotta go, okay," Chance says. And yeah, he says, yeah, I know, but the reluctance easy enough to hear.

"I love you, Chance," he says and she still hasn't gotten used to hearing that.

"You too, Deke. You stay busy, okay?"

He hangs up first and Chance apologizes, returns the phone to her overalls pocket.

"Is anything wrong?" Alice asks, but she sounds a lot more irritated than concerned.

"No, Deke just wanted to be sure I was okay, you know."

"Shall we?" Irene asks and motions towards the banner hung above a nearby doorway—AT THE OCEAN'S EDGE: FISH WITH FEET. Tall letters, swirling shades of blue and white and deep green on a canvas banner.

"That's not the title we agreed on," Chance says.

"Oh, yeah. We decided that 'ocean' would sound better. It has a sort of romance that 'river' doesn't."

"But it's not *right*. The earliest amphibians were almost certainly not marine. And all my Pottsville and Parkwood specimens are freshwater."

Irene smiles a strained, slightly embarrassed smile. "Yes, but 'At the River's Edge' just doesn't have quite the same ring to it."

"Yes, but this is *wrong*."

"Let's see what's inside, Chance," Alice says. "We can work this out later."

"I'm very sorry," the collections manager says. "I didn't think it would matter that much."

"Well, it does. In fact, it matters a great deal," Chance grumbles and then she walks quickly beneath the mistaken, ocean-colored sign before Alice can tell her to shut up.

Her first date with Deacon a few weeks after the night in the park. Dinner at Pizza Hut and then she drove them to Irondale to see a cheesy big-budget movie version of *Lost in Space* and Deacon snuck two cans of Budweiser into the theater tucked inside his shirt. The movie was ridiculous, silly time-travel clichés dragged out at the end to tie things up somehow, and afterwards they sat in the parking lot outside the multiplex and watched teenagers and talked. Deacon had four more cans of Bud stashed beneath the front seat of the Impala, warm, but he didn't seem to mind.

"You drink a lot," she said and he nodded and opened another can of beer.

"Yes, I do. It's sort of my chosen vocation."

A Lincoln Continental, blaring rap music and loaded down with black kids, rolled slowly past, *thump thump thump,* and there was no use trying to talk until they'd gone.

"You don't listen to that hip-hop Snoop Dogg shit, do you?" Deacon asked and Chance shook her head. "Well, that's good, 'cause I don't date girls that listen to that junk."

"I don't listen to any music very much. Not since I was a kid."

"Is that so? Damn," and he took a long drink from the can of Bud and wiped his mouth on the back of his hand.

"So what do you like?"

"You mean besides beer?"

"What kind of *music* do you like?"

Deacon belched, excused himself, and stared out the windshield at the black sky above the strip mall. "Lots of shit, just not rap. Jazz, blues, Muddy Waters, Nina Simone and Billie Holiday. Joy Division. Nick Cave. The Clash."

"I like Billie Holiday," Chance said.

"Well, anyone who digs Lady Day can't be all bad."

"I was really into The Smashing Pumpkins for a while," she said. "Back in high school, I thought Billy Corgan hung the moon."

"But you're all better now, right?" Then Deacon finished the Bud, crumpled the can, and tossed it out the window. It clattered loudly on the asphalt.

"What's that supposed to mean?"

"Oh hell, half of what I say don't mean shit, Chance. Half of it you can just ignore."

"How am I supposed to know which half I'm *not* supposed to ignore?"

Deacon turned around in his seat and stared at her instead of staring at the August sky, fixed her with his sleepy eyes the color of magnolia leaves and broken Coca-Cola bottles. "You're smart," he said. "You'll figure it out eventually."

"I need to tell you something important, Deacon, but you have to fucking *promise* me you won't freak out or laugh at me or anything."

Deacon rubbed at his chin, the dark stubble there like sandpaper, and "Darling," he said. "I might not be the sort of person you want to start spilling all your deepest, darkest secrets to. Anyway, none of it matters to me."

"Well, it matters to *me.*"

He nodded his head and then reached beneath the seat for another beer. "Well," he said. "Let's see. Either you're about to tell me you used to be a guy, or that you're a dyke, or a Mormon or one of those—"

"Will you please just shut the hell up for a second?"

"Sure," Deacon said, grinned, and opened the beer, which foamed and dripped all over his jeans and the Impala's floorboard. "I just like to imagine all the worst-case scenarios up front. Kind of takes the sting out of whatever's coming. And Mormons really do annoy the bejesus out of me."

"I swear, if you fucking laugh at me, you're gonna be walking home."

Deacon sipped his beer and didn't say a word, one way or another.

"I just wanted you to know you're the . . ." and she trailed off and slumped forward, resting her forehead against the steering wheel.

"The cat's meow? The bee's knees?"

"No," Chance said, beginning to get annoyed with him, and she took a deep breath and slowly let it out again. "You're the first guy I've ever been out with. I've never been on a real date before tonight."

And then both of them were silent for a long, uncomfortable moment. Chance with her forehead pressed against the steering wheel, Deacon sipping at his beer, another car stuffed with teenagers rolling past in a bass-heavy thundercloud of noise.

"I'm flattered," Deacon said finally. "A little surprised, but flattered."

"It just never seemed important enough," Chance said, lifting her head and looking at him. "I always thought it would be a distraction. I was always so busy with school."

"You know what they say. All work and no play—"

"You think I'm dull?"

"No, I don't think you're dull. If I thought you were dull, I wouldn't be here. I hate dull even more than I hate rap."

"Jesus," Chance whispered. "Life is so goddamn weird."

"You don't know the half of it," Deacon said and finished his beer in a single, long gulp, crushed the can and stared at the wad of red and white aluminum in his hand.

"What do you mean?"

"Nothing. I don't mean anything at all. I guess it's safe to assume you're a virgin?"

Chance reached across the seat and punched him in the arm, not hard enough to hurt, but he yelped anyway and tossed the crumpled beer can at her.

"You're not shy, are you Deacon Silvey?"

"No ma'am," he said, reaching for the last can of beer. "Shy ain't nothing but a waste of time. And life's short."

And then, quick, before she lost her nerve or he started talking again, she asked "Are you an alcoholic, Deke?"

He set the unopened beer can down on the dash and cracked the knuckles of his right hand, and already she wished she'd kept her mouth shut.

"No," he said. "Alcoholics go to meetings and twelve-step support groups and therapists. I can't afford that shit, so I'm just a drunk. Is that a problem?"

"Why? I mean, why are you a drunk?"

"Maybe someday I'll tell you," and he picked up the Bud and popped the pull tab. Loud beer hiss, but this one didn't foam over. "If you stick around long enough."

"I think I'd like to try. But it's something that we're going to have to talk about, sooner or later. It's something I don't understand."

"Nothing mysterious about drunks, Chance. We just move a little slower than sober people, that's all."

"You didn't move slow that night in the park."

"Well, I have my moments."

She smiled and changed the subject, talking about the movie instead, confessing that she'd sit through almost anything with Gary Oldman in it; Deacon admitted he didn't go to too many movies, or watch much television either. She talked about school and he complained about the teenagers and their crappy music, and in a little while she drove them back to Southside.

Chance is standing with Alice and Irene in front of the huge coal forest scene, smiling even though she's still pissed off about the banner. "It's very nice," she says. "I'm impressed."

"Well, that's a relief," Alice says and pats her gently on the back.

At least half the gallery space is occupied by the Pennsylvanian diorama, like an impossible snapshot of the tropical peat swamps that spread out north and south of Birmingham almost three hundred million years ago. Swamps along a vast delta created by an ancient river, wide as the Mississippi, as it flowed down from the newborn Appalachians across coastal lowlands to a shallow inland sea. The scene is dominated by a dense grove of bizarre vegetation as tall as tall trees: the lycopods *Lepidodendron* and *Lepidophloios,* both towering, cone-bearing plants with bark like the diamond scales of garpikes, along with the giant horsetail *Calamites* and the tree-sized gymnosperm *Cordaites* with its long, razor-strap leaves. Alien trunks expertly cast in plastic and airbrushed to life, rising up to meet the ceiling and the painted illusion of a rain-forest canopy spreading out a hundred and fifty feet overhead. An understory of ferns and pteridosperms among the gnarled roots, the most minute details of the fronds and seedpods so well sculpted that Chance can identify half a dozen familiar genera at a single glance. The forest seems to run on for miles and miles, as though the museum's wall has simply dissolved in some warping of time and space. There's a dragonfly as big as a crow, spiders and millipedes and giant cockroaches.

"I wish the soundtrack was finished," Irene Mesmer says. "Then you could get the full effect. But we're still trying to get the insect noises right."

"Still working the bugs out," Alice says and Chance laughs.

A broad streambed winds between the trees, no water in it now but the collections manager says there will be later, just pebbles and dry sand for the moment, the pretend decay of fallen lycopods. And at the edge of the stream, a wide patch of fiberglass mud and Chance immediately recognizes the creature sprawling there, staring back at her, ink-black eyes the size of Ping-Pong balls set in that wide, flat skull, her own *Megalopseudosuchus* resurrected after three hundred thousand millennia. A dying lungfish dangles from its toothy jaws.

"That's *him*," Chance says. "My god, Alice, that's really him."

"Yeah. Ugly bastard, isn't he?"

"Are you kidding? He's absolutely beautiful," and she leans awkwardly over the railing, difficult because her belly's in the way, and strokes the amphibian's bumpy snout. "Hello there," she says.

There's another, much smaller amphibian nearby, peering cautiously out at the *Megalopseudosuchus* from behind a *Calamites* stalk. The temnospondyl *Walkerpeton*, another primitive tetrapod that Chance discovered in a Walker County strip mine her junior year. Eight webbed toes on its splayed front feet, and "I see you, too," she says.

"I'm so glad that you like it," Irene says. "The artists and technicians followed your notes and instructions whenever possible."

"It's almost like going back, isn't it?" Chance asks no one in particular. "I can almost imagine the way it would smell."

"Like a stinky old swamp, I expect," Alice says.

"It's *so* real," Chance whispers, ignoring Alice, and then a dark trickle of blood leaks from the mouth of the *Megalopseudosuchus,* from the plastic lungfish trapped between its plastic jaws, and spatters on the fake mud.

Chance gasps and takes a sudden step backwards, bumping into Alice.

"Is something wrong, Dr. Silvey?" Irene asks anxiously, and Chance stares at her and then back at the diorama.

"I'm okay," Chance replies, but she hears the quaver in her voice and knows she must sound anything but okay.

"Well, you're white as a sheet," Alice says. "You look like you just saw a ghost." And then she puts a hand to Chance's forehead like someone checking for a fever.

They don't see it. They don't see anything there at all.

"Do you feel ill?" the collections manager asks. "Do you need to sit down?"

"No," Chance says, brushing Alice Sprinkle's hand away from her face. "I'm fine," but the fish is still bleeding and she turns her back on the Pennsylvanian diorama. The rest of the gallery is cluttered with other related exhibits in varying stages of incompleteness—a wall devoted to the economic importance of coal, empty display cases to hold her fish and tetrapod fossils, a *Cordaites* stump for the kids to touch. The walls have been painted the color of moss.

"Are you sure?" Alice asks.

"I'm *fine*," Chance says again. "Really. It's silly. I just got a little too excited, that's all."

They don't see it, because there's nothing there to see.

"Let me get you a glass of water," Irene says and is already hurrying out of the gallery before Chance can stop her. When she's gone Alice sighs and "Well, at least we're rid of her for a few minutes," she says quietly. "Maybe it's time we got you back home."

"Yeah, maybe so," Chance whispers and glances back over her shoulder at the coal forest, bracing herself, expecting more of the crimson splotches like the stigmata of some inexplicable Catholic effigy.

But if the blood was ever there, it's gone now.

CHAPTER THREE

Haunted

Narcissa Snow parks the black Oldsmobile at the dead end of Cullom Street and sits watching the house a moment before she gets out of the car. Only the second time that she's seen it, the first just yesterday, but the real estate agent wouldn't shut up, so she couldn't *really* see it. The fat, smiling woman chattering on and on and on about things that would never matter to Narcissa—new kitchen appliances, work on the roof, the fresh coats of white paint.

"It was a terrible mess a few years back," the woman said. "Just falling apart. A bunch of hippie kids used to live up here and they'd let it go. A shame. It's a good old house, really."

"I'm sure," Narcissa said.

"Did you live in Savannah long? I have an aunt—"

"It's exactly what I'm looking for," and Narcissa smiled and thought that the woman's expression might have changed, then, a flickering, almost imperceptible shift, there and gone again, fear or something finer, and "Very good," the woman said. "We can take care of the paperwork back at the office."

The house built more than a hundred years ago, the real estate agent said, raised at the other end of that late, bloodred century so recently deceased; war and murder, deaths and shattered minds, broken spirits, the shit and piss that men have dragged themselves through in their hunger for an end.

"I see you," Narcissa says, aloud though she knows this house could hear her perfectly well without words, without her voice, that a house like this hears everything. The house it is *because* of everything it's heard and seen and felt playing out inside its walls, beneath its ceilings. Mad house, sour place, once upon a time ago good place driven insane by happenstance, driven sick by the minds that have lived and dreamed inside its rooms. Not evil, no, Narcissa knows evil houses well enough to be sure—not evil, only mad. Left at last to rot in this lonely patch of trees and strangling kudzu vines on the side of this mountain and Narcissa imagines how much the house would have welcomed that decay. *I will die, finally,* it must have thought. *I will forget everything, forever,* but then the hateful carpenters and painters and plumbers, their busy hammers and brushes and PVC transplants, to patch it back together again and haul the house on Cullom Street back from the precious edge of oblivion.

"Maybe, when I am done," Narcissa tells the house, "maybe then I will burn you to the ground. I can be merciful." But it can see inside her and the house knows she's a liar.

Narcissa takes the slender leather satchel from the passenger seat and gets out of the Olds, the car she stole in Charleston almost a month ago. "Just a few more bad dreams, that's all," she says and the house cringes, floorboards drawing back the smallest fraction of an inch, the stiff flinch of tar-paper shingles and goose bumps down cloudy windowpanes.

"You don't have to be afraid of me," she says. "You're a far, far more terrible thing than me, after all. Think about it," but she can tell that the house has no intention of believing anything she says. The doubtful shadows crouched apprehensive on the wide front porch, a stubborn darkness clinging there despite the noonday sunshine and the blue October sky sprawled above the trees.

"Well, then. Have it your way," Narcissa whispers. "We could have been friends, though. And I don't think you've ever had many friends. We could have told each other stories." She glances back towards the rear of the Oldsmobile, thinks about her heavy suitcases in the trunk, a cardboard box with her books, another, larger satchel with her knives and scalpels, her tools, but all those things can wait until later. There will be plenty of time to unpack later, and she walks slowly across the weedy, leaf-littered front yard to the door.

All Narcissa's life like someone else's fever dreams locked up inside her head and wanting out, or something scribbled down by a crazy woman for her to have to live through, red-brown words stolen from her mother's diary; all her days chasing delirium's legacy, measuring the ever-narrowing space between nightmares and visions, and she cannot even remember a time before this was the way she saw her life. No guiltless beginning, no damning moment when childhood's hollow innocence melted into disillusionment and all the casual atrocities of her twenty-six years.

Her birth on the last freezing night at the end of a long year of horrors—earthquakes in Burma, volcanic eruptions in Hawaii, a subway wreck in London that killed forty-one people, the fiery crash of a Vietnamese cargo jet carrying two hundred and forty-three orphans. And all of these things written down in her mother's diary, all of these and a thousand more, a pregnant woman's book of splintered days, and then her mother died in childbirth, before she saw Narcissa's face, before she even heard her child draw its first breath and cry. One life lost, one life gained, tit for tat, and the only daughter of Caroline Snow was raised by her grandfather, Aldous, in his tall and crumbling house by the sea. He read to her from his strange books, reading by beeswax candles and oil lamps because the electricity had been shut off long ago, and she walked with him along the rocky Massachusetts beach below the house.

"The sea is the mother of the world," he told her. "The sea is Mother Hydra and one day soon she'll rise again and swallow her ungrateful children."

"Will she swallow me, too?" Narcissa asked and the old man nodded his bald head.

"She will, child. She'll have us all."

May 20—The demons have stopped coming to my windows. They know what has happened to me. They can smell the life growing inside me. Sometimes, when I have only the sound of the waves for company, I miss their faces pressed against the glass. Last week a woman in Maine was convicted of drowning her six-year-old son while he was bathing. She simply held him under the water. I wonder if he opened his eyes and watched her? I thought about taking a coat hanger from my closet and ending this, but I haven't got the courage. I'm not ready to die.

The ocean black and green, always-wheeling gulls, the ragged granite and salt-marsh wastes at the mouth of the Manuxet River, and Narcissa did not go to school or play with other children. Nothing for her beyond the house and its jealous secrets, the seashore and the Atlantic horizon running on forever. Everything she needed to know old Aldous taught her—how to read and write, astrology, the rhythms of the tides, history, the cruelty of this life and the ones to come, the red, wet mysteries beneath concealing skins.

When she was six years old, Narcissa killed a stray dog with a piece of driftwood, beat it slowly to death and then dragged the sandy, flea-seething carcass back up the hill to her grandfather's house. She cut it open with a kitchen knife and the old man watched, neither approving nor disapproving. A wooden mallet and cold chisel to break its sternum, her small, bare hands to pry open the bone and cartilage cradle of its rib cage. Then she spread the dog out around her, like the pictures in his books, naming organs for the old man as she cut them free and laid them on the porch. "This is the heart," she said, naming valves and ventricles, and "This is a kidney. Here's the other one." She ate an eye because it looked like the hard candy he sometimes brought her from his rare trips into Ipswich. After that, she killed gulls and wild geese, rats, a fat raccoon, whatever she found that couldn't get away.

When Narcissa was eight she discovered her mother's diary, hidden in a small hole in the wall behind the headboard of the bed where she'd been born and Caroline Snow had died, and it became her bible. She kept it secret from Aldous, though she'd never kept anything from him before; something told her *this* book, the yellowing pages in her mother's perfect cursive hand, was hers and hers alone. The book was bound in red leather, with a strip of fine gold cloth to mark the pages. It was only half-filled, the last entry made three days before Narcissa's birth. The first page dated April 29, and "I will put it all down, whatever seems important, everything I can remember," Caroline had written in ink the color of dried blood.

Narcissa kept the diary in the hole behind the headboard. It was safe there, she reasoned, because her grandfather wouldn't come into this room. Some nights he even poured a double line of salt in front of the threshold, if he didn't like the look of the moon and stars, and he'd written things that Narcissa couldn't read on the door. Charms to keep something he feared in or out, but nothing to stop her.

June 27—Lights in the skies above Tennessee yesterday. A school bus hit by a train outside Sacramento, thirteen dead. Father doesn't like me reading the newspaper but he keeps bringing it to me anyway. I'm starting to show.

When Narcissa was nine a shower of blood fell on the house for two hours straight, thick red rain against the gambrel roof like bacon frying in a skillet and her grandfather watched the storm from his seat by the parlor window.

"Is this your doing, child?" he asked Narcissa without taking his eyes off the window.

"No sir," she said and crossed the room to stand beside him.

"Are you sure?"

"Maybe it's Mother Hydra," Narcissa said and she wasn't surprised by the fear in his eyes or the small tingle of satisfaction it made her feel, deep inside. "Maybe she's coming back."

"You still remember that damn story?" he asked and his dry voice trembled.

"I remember everything you tell me, Grandfather."

"Well, that was just a tale I made up to keep you away from the sea. It's greedy and little girls who aren't afraid of it might wind up drowned."

"I think you were telling me the truth," she said.

"You believe whatever you want. I don't give a damn no more."

And he sat in his chair and she stood at his side until the blood stopped falling from the sky.

August 14—Last night a motel in Cincinnati burned. 35 people died. A man in Los Angeles shot his wife and two daughters and then hung himself. One of the daughters will live. Father is spending more time in the cellar. He doesn't think that I notice. He doesn't think I know about the tunnels.

On her tenth birthday, Narcissa's grandfather gave her one of his books, one of the antique volumes that he kept locked inside the walnut barrister cases in his study and the keys always hidden somewhere she was never able to find. He wrapped it in an old newspaper, tied it up neat with twine, and made a bow from a scrap of china-blue silk they'd found on the beach the week before.

He left the package lying outside her mother's bedroom door, where Narcissa had started sleeping months and months before, and she unwrapped the gift sitting on the edge of the dead woman's bed. The title and author were stamped in gold letters across the brittle black cover—*Cultes des Goules* by François Honore-Balfour, Comte d'Erlette. There were pictures, terrible, wondrous pictures that she stared at for hours on end, and the book became her most prized possession, even if she couldn't read the French. She thought the bow was pretty and kept it in the hole in the wall with her mother's diary.

She kept other things in the hole: coins and seashells she'd found among the dunes, a shark's tooth, a black and shriveled mermaid's purse, pretty shards of blue and green beach glass. An arrowhead. A string of purple plastic beads.

"Have you read the book yet?" her grandfather asked one day when they were walking along the beach together. She'd just found half a sand dollar and was busy wiping it clean on the hem of her dress.

"You know very well that I haven't," she replied. "You know I can't read French."

He stared at her silently for a moment, as if that had never occurred to him, and then Aldous Snow glanced longingly back towards his tall house, grown small in the distance.

"We should start back," he said and rubbed at his chin. "The tide will be coming in soon."

"Do you *want* me to read it?" Narcissa asked him.

"You're stronger than your mother ever was. I never would have given her a book like that."

"Do you want me to *read* it, Grandfather?"

"It's your book now. Read it if you want. I should have burned that goddamned thing years ago and dumped the ashes into the sea."

"Then why didn't you?"

But he didn't answer her, turned around instead and started walking back up the beach towards the house alone. Narcissa stood watching him, listening to the cold wind, the waves, and in a little while she slipped the broken sand dollar into her coat pocket and followed him home.

The shiny, new silver key the real estate agent gave Narcissa opens the front door and she eases it shut again before reaching for the light switch on the wall. The foyer's much darker than it should be, plenty of sunlight from the big living room to her left, but it seems diffused, stretched thin, drained of the simple strength to keep the shadows at bay. The electric light doesn't work much better, and Narcissa turns the new dead bolt on the door, the dead bolt and the safety chain. Not that such flimsy things would ever keep anyone out, not anyone who really wanted in, but they might buy her time. Locks have bought her time before.

The air in the old house smells sweet and sickly, fresh paint and a fainter undercurrent of mildew, a smell of age and neglect that the workmen couldn't scrub away or cover over. There's a closed door leading off the foyer and Narcissa reaches for the brass knob, cold metal in her hand, and opens the door to the bedroom where a young woman once hanged herself, where that same young woman's mother died of cancer years before. These aren't things that the real estate agent would ever have told her, things she would probably have denied had Narcissa asked, but she knows how to find what she's looking for on her own. Bruised places, houses with enough misfortune in their past that she can trust them to keep her secrets.

The bedroom is empty, just like the living room, no furniture and nothing on the stark, white walls. The newly refinished hardwood floor glints wetly in tiger stripes of sunlight getting in through the plastic slats of brand-new Levolor blinds covering the big windows. A chintzy ceiling fan, the closet door standing wide open and it's very dark in there. The faint mildew smell from the foyer is stronger in here.

Narcissa shuts the door and thinks briefly about closing the blinds, too, wiping that ugly chiaroscuro pattern from the floor. But the voices haven't found her yet and she doesn't want to encourage them; they'll track her down soon enough—they always do—and right now she needs to think, needs her head clear to consider the work and the days ahead. She sits down on the floor and undoes the straps and buckles on the leather satchel, folds it open and removes a thick sheaf of papers and spreads them out in front of her. There's also a new box of thumbtacks in the satchel and she takes that out, as well.

" 'Poor fragments of a broken world,' " she whispers and smiles vacantly, stray line from an old poem she memorized as a little girl, words meant to console herself, but they never do, never any consolation anywhere except the grim, violent work and already last night seems like something from months and months ago. The skinny, tattooed kid with the skateboard that she picked up in a park just after sundown, the one who told her his name was Soda. Narcissa closes her eyes tight, remembering his fear, the musky taste of him, the way his lips kept moving long after she'd slashed his throat. Thin, pale lips to shape a silent prayer or curse or plea for mercy.

Shit, maybe the stupid motherfucker was just pissed at me for killing him.

She opens her eyes, takes a deep breath, and slips her pistol from its shoulder holster hidden beneath her jacket, checks the clip, the safety, and then sets it down beside the satchel. There's a red Sharpie pen in her jacket and she takes that out, too.

Narcissa selects a dog-eared, photocopied map from the careless scatter of papers on the floor, Birmingham with its roads laid out neat as a game of ticktacktoe, the grid of streets running northwest and southeast, avenues running northeast and southwest, but everything getting warped and tangled when it reaches the foot of Red Mountain, ancient topography to foil the contrivances of men and their machines. She pulls the cap off the Sharpie and draws a very small red circle around the spot where she killed the boy named Soda. A circle at one apex of the nearly perfect diamond she plotted on the map the day before, sitting in a Southside diner drinking coffee and chain-smoking, waiting for the sun to set, reworking her plans again and again in her head.

"That's one," she says, because the first two Birmingham kills don't count, not really, only rehearsals, and she uses the Sharpie to carefully trace over the line leading from the circle she's drawn to another corner of the diamond. "One for sorrow," and Narcissa snaps the cap back on the pen.

"Two for mirth."

Outside, a sudden breeze rattles all the bright, dry leaves that haven't fallen to the ground yet, this slow Southern autumn so strange to her, and Narcissa turns her head and watches the restless limb and branch shadows.

Only the wind. Nothing out there but the wind.

"Three for a wedding," she says, speaking low just in case the voices have slipped in on the breeze and are listening. If walls have ears, if plaster and lath and paint could talk, and the wind subsides as suddenly as it began.

Narcissa opens the box of thumbtacks and uses one to pin the map to the closest of the white bedroom walls. Then she sits cross-legged on the floor and gazes out the windows at the trees, the red-gold-brown leaves, the shifting swatches of blue sky, and "Four for a birth," she whispers. All the long months since she left Providence, all the roads and cities and empty rooms leading her here, all those other circles she's drawn on other maps pinned to other walls. How many sides, if she were to add them up, how many dimensions necessary to accommodate that polygon? Geometry of blood and time, pain and misdirection, but *this* is where it ends, where it all begins itself over and Madam Terpsichore and her Benefit Street lapdogs will never laugh at her again.

There's a bird on the windowsill watching her intently with its beady, black eyes, a big gray mockingbird staring in though the blinds like she has no business being here. Narcissa picks up her gun and aims it at the bird, but it doesn't fly away. So many spies to take so many forms that no one could ever keep count and so it's always better to be safe than sorry.

Someone will hear, a voice mumbles from the open closet, voice like someone talking with his mouth full and it's a wonder she can understand a word he says. *Someone will hear the shot and call the police.*

"I'll say it was an accident. I was cleaning the gun and it went off."

You think they won't ask to see a permit? And what if they run the plates on the car? What if they look in the trunk?

The mockingbird cocks its head to one side and she knows damn well that birds can't fucking smile, but maybe this one's smiling at her anyway. And all she has to do is pull the trigger and there won't be anything left of it but a sticky spray of blood and bone and feathers that will never go peeping in windows at anyone again.

"It's just a lousy bird," Narcissa says, because whether she believes it or not the words feel good to say, and the mockingbird bobs its head and hops a few inches along the sill, taps once at the glass with its beak. "I'm not blowing out that windowpane over a goddamn, stupid bird."

Remember the crows in Philadelphia? a woman's voice asks her from the closet. *Remember that black dog outside Richmond? What were they, Narcissa?*

"Shut up," she says and the mockingbird taps at the window again, harder than before. In Philadelphia, crows had watched her for days, dozens of them following her through the city, perched on sagging power lines or watching her from the lawn of Logan Circle, always there when she looked for them. She'd killed the black dog and left it hanging from a highway sign.

They know your every move, Narcissa, the woman's voice says. *Every breath, every step, every time you take a shit, they're watching you. They can take you anytime they want.*

"Then why the hell haven't they?"

Soon now, the woman whispers. *Soon they will.*

The smiling mockingbird taps at the glass and Narcissa fixes it in the pistol's sights. Fuck the windowpane, fuck the noise. No one's going to hear it and even if they do, who's going to give a shit? No one ever wants to get involved and if they do, so what? It's not as though she hasn't dealt with cops before. Cops are easy. Cops are a fucking walk in the park.

The wind rattles the leaves.

"Say bye-bye, you nosy little shit," and she pulls the trigger, but there's only the sharp, metallic *thunk* of the Colt jamming. The bird taps on the glass one last time, taunting her, and then it spreads its wings and flies off in a blur of gray-white feathers.

"*Shit!*" Narcissa growls and hurls the pistol at the window. It tears through a couple of the plastic Levolor slats and disappears from view; the sound of glass breaking is very loud in the empty room.

Behind her, one of the voices from the closet begins to giggle hysterically to itself and she gets up and slams the door, then opens it just for the pleasure of slamming it again.

You're so close, Narcissa, a voice that almost sounds like her dead grandfather says. *So goddamn close now. You gonna throw it all away over a bird? That wasn't a spy. Keep your head, girl.*

"Why don't you leave me alone? Why don't all of you please just leave me the hell alone? Let me finish this."

You wanted our lives, and this voice could be the hitchhiker from Atlanta, or the waitress from Myrtle Beach, or someone that she's forgotten altogether. Narcissa knows it doesn't matter anyway, one ghost as good as the next, all of them buried deep in the soft convolutions of her brain to drive her insane before she can finish, all of them spies. *You wanted our lives and now you have them. You took us inside you, digested us, made us a part of you, and you'll never be rid of us.*

"Yeah, I know," Narcissa says and she nods her head and stares at the white closet door; all the voices have fallen quiet now, and in a few minutes she goes outside to find the gun.

From the first night that she read her mother's diary, first night that she held it in her hands, Narcissa knew there were missing pages. Ragged bits of paper left behind to show where they'd been torn out, whole days skipped, entries that ended or began in mid-sentence. All these evidences to prove the point, but easy enough to imagine that Caroline Snow had written things she'd come to regret. That she'd ripped those pages out herself and for years the only thought that Narcissa ever gave the matter was to wonder what confidences had been lost to her, what might have been said on those missing pages.

> *October 9—I'm beginning to understand it now. But I can only say these things in fragments. The whole is too terrible. Father has started bringing me the paper again, but he always slides it under my door and won't ever look me in the face or answer my questions. I think he's seen the whole, seen it all at once, and now it's driving him insane. Yesterday, in Glen Savage, Penn. three people watched a "black monster" floating above a field. In Montevideo, MN a woman named Helena Myers cut her own—*
>
> *—almost three days. I sit at the top of the stairs when he doesn't know I'm watching him. I can never see who he's talking to. I think about leaving this house all the time now. Maybe I could get away. Maybe I could save my baby. I could go to Boston, anywhere but here. I don't think he would even try to stop me. I almost think he would be relieved to see me go.*

Sometimes Narcissa made up stories to fill in the gaps. She'd peeled off strips of wallpaper and pulled up loose floorboards looking for places where her mother might have hidden the missing pages, but she never found anything but silverfish and dust and spiders.

When she was twelve, she awoke one muggy July night to find Aldous standing over her. His cloudy, yellow eyes glowed softly in the darkness. He held something clutched in his right hand that reflected the scraps of moonlight leaking through the rotting drapes.

"Grandfather," she said and he sighed then, a drawn-out, ragged sound as if he'd been holding his breath for a long time, suffocating, waiting for permission to breathe again. "Is something wrong?"

"I thought they would come for you," he said, something in his voice that could have been either disappointment or anger, a little of both, maybe. "I've kept you for them, and taught you things, because I thought they would want you. They never wanted me or your mother, but I thought they would want you."

"Who, Grandfather? Who did you think would want me?" and she spoke calmly and kept her eyes on the silvery thing glinting cold moonlight in his hand, the same knife she'd used years ago on the beach dog, the knife she'd used on so many other things since. The carving knife from her bureau drawer.

"I *gave* you the book . . . a year ago. But you still haven't read it."

"I still can't read French."

And then he slapped her so hard that Narcissa's mouth filled with blood and her ears rang. His ragged, thick nails tore a deep gash in her right cheek and she scrambled to the far edge of the bed, just barely out of reach, ready to run if that was what she was going to have to do.

"You fucking cunt," he growled, rabid dog growl from his old throat and his eyes flashed in the dark. "Don't you *ever* talk to me that way again. You hear me?"

"I hear you, Grandfather," Narcissa replied quietly, a salty-warm trickle of blood leaking from her mouth, her voice still as perfectly calm as it had been before he struck her.

"We are damned, Narcissa."

And then he leaned across the bed, moving faster than she would have ever thought he could, and held the blade of the knife against her throat. He smelled like sweat and aftershave and the faintest hint of rot on his breath.

"If I *truly* loved you, I'd kill you now and get it over with. I'd save you from the shit you're going to have to try to live through. I'd be doing us both a favor. Yes, little girl, I'd being doing everyone a favor."

"Why are we damned?" Narcissa asked. She thought briefly about the ice pick she kept hidden underneath her pillow. "What does that mean, Grandfather?"

"I'm not your damned grandfather," Aldous said and took the knife away from Narcissa's throat. Her skin stung slightly and later she'd find a shallow cut just beneath her chin. "Don't you ever call me that again, because it isn't true and I'm sick of lies."

"Why are we damned?" she asked again.

"Read the book, Narcissa. That bitch-cur, my *mother*," and he laughed then and turned to stare at the window. "We're mongrels, child, and we can never be anything else."

He stood there for a while, silently watching the sea through her drapes, watching the summer night, and she didn't ask him anything else. She slipped her hand beneath the pillow and gripped the wooden handle of the ice pick tightly, but he left a few minutes later, without saying another word, without even looking at her again, left the carving knife lying on the bureau and shut the door behind him. Aldous Snow would only enter her bedroom one more time in his life.

October 30—There are terrible noises from the cellar tonight and I'm too afraid to go see. I'm afraid all the time. I don't want to know anymore. I don't want to know any of it. This afternoon I watched my father standing at the edge of the sea, talking to the sky. I think he was arguing with the sky. I was all the way back at the old boathouse and couldn't hear what he was saying, but he did it for over an hour. And I think he's started keeping animals in the cellar. I can smell them if I stand at the cellar door. I can hear them moving around.

The day after Aldous held a knife to her throat, Narcissa walked and hitchhiked into Ipswich. She didn't tell him that she was going, not because she thought he would try to stop her, but because she didn't care whether he knew or not. She was starting to think that he *couldn't* hurt her, that if he could, he would have done it already. She crossed the dunes behind the house, then followed the Argilla Road until a man in a green pickup truck stopped for her.

"Where you bound?" and she told him Ipswich.

"But you ain't no runaway?" he asked suspiciously and Narcissa shook her head no, told him the story she'd made up that morning about her sick grandfather and how their car had broken down a week ago, how she had to pick up his heart medicine from the drugstore in Ipswich. Narcissa had never ridden in a car and the thought of gliding along so effortlessly on those black rubber tires made her a little dizzy.

"Well, I guess you better get in, then."

The man didn't say much on the drive into town, glanced at her in his rearview mirror from time to time, hesitant, nervous glances, but just before he let her out on Market Street, "You ain't by any chance any relation to Old Man Snow?" he asked.

"Yes sir," Narcissa said politely. "He's my grandfather. How'd you know that?"

"You just got that look about you," the man said and shrugged, not looking at Narcissa, pretending to watch a woman pushing a baby carriage along the sidewalk. "You got the old man's eyes."

"Thank you for the ride," she said and got out of the truck.

"Anytime," the man said. "Hope your granddad's feeling better soon," and then he drove away. Narcissa walked past the drugstore to a smaller shop that sold books and magazines and bought a paperback French-English dictionary with five dollars she'd taken from one of the snuff tins Aldous kept his money in. On the way back, no one stopped to pick her up and it was almost dark by the time she got home.

After she found the Colt where it had landed beneath a crape myrtle bush and unpacked the car—four trips from the porch to the Olds and back again, four trips across the dandelion- and pecan-cluttered yard and all her boxes and bags finally safe inside the house—Narcissa fell asleep near the broken bedroom window. No sleep for almost forty-eight hours and the sunlight, the clean, afternoon-warmed air through the broken window, almost as good as the tiny violet Halcion tablets she takes when the voices won't let her sleep. She promised herself that she was only going to close her eyes, only for a moment, a ten-minute nap at the most, and she lay down with a stolen motel pillow beneath her head and the gun within easy reach.

"Rise and shine, girl," her grandfather growls at her from some fading dream place; in an instant Narcissa is wide awake, adrenaline sharp and her heart pounding loud as thunder. The long shadows and half-light filling the white room, so she knows she's slept for hours, not minutes. The day almost gone and she closes her hand around the butt of the pistol, its comforting, undeniable weight, and listens for whatever it is that woke her—not her grandfather or his ghost, something flesh and blood, something that can hurt and die.

But there's only the brittle rustle of the wind playing with leaves, two squirrels chattering angrily at each other somewhere nearby, the distant, steady sound of traffic. Down the street a woman calls out.

"Taylor! It's getting dark! Time to come in!"

Narcissa takes a very deep breath and holds it, waiting impatiently as her heart begins to return to normal, as her body quickly burns away the adrenaline clogging her bloodstream.

"Five more minutes. It's not even dark yet."

"*Now*, young man!"

Narcissa exhales and sits up, slides across the floor until her back is pressed firmly against the wall and then she steals a glance out the window at the porch and the yard cut up into neat twilight slices by the blinds. Nothing that shouldn't be there. The sleek black car almost lost in the gloom. The untrimmed shrubbery lining the driveway. One of the noisy squirrels races itself from the trunk of one tree to another.

"It was nothing," she whispers. "It was nothing at all," and she turns to face the almost-empty room again, three closed doors, the map thumbtacked to the wall, her papers scattered on the floor.

And from somewhere in the house, the creak of a floorboard to contradict her.

"Old houses make all sorts of sounds," one of her voices whispers reassuringly from a corner. "You know that."

Narcissa raises the Colt and rests the barrel flat against her left cheek, straining her ears to see if the voice is right or wrong. She flips the safety off with her thumb and takes another deep breath.

Old houses make all sorts of sounds.

From the north side of the house, the living room or perhaps the kitchen, somewhere off to her left, there's another, louder creak and then a third immediately after that. She stands up very slowly, keeping the wall at her back, silently cursing herself for having fallen asleep.

"You can't expect to stay awake forever," the voice in the corner sighs.

"But she's getting careless," another voice whispers. "These fuckers, you screw up just once and you're history. Just once, and you're toast."

Narcissa takes one cautious step towards the door leading to the foyer and the floor squeaks softly beneath her bare feet.

"If you can hear them, you better bet they can hear you," one of the voices chuckles and Narcissa stops and aims the pistol at the corner the voice came from.

"Best ignore those voices in your head," her grandfather grumbles from behind the closet door. "They're just trying to distract you. They still think it'll save them, if you get yourself killed."

The sudden flutter of wings then, a hundred wings hammering the air somewhere above the house, ink-black feathers battering the October dusk, and she fires two shots through the bedroom ceiling.

"You should have killed that damned bird when you had the chance," her grandfather says.

Sheetrock dust like powdered sugar settles to the polished floor from the fist-sized hole in the ceiling, hangs suspended in the air, drifting lazily through the last rays of the setting sun. The birds are already far away, high above the city, crying her name to anyone who will listen. And now there's a new sound coming from the other side of the door, something animal pacing back and forth out there, its steel claws *click-click-click*ing against the wood, its breath the endless rise and fall of ocean waves against granite boulders.

"You can run," one of the corner voices sneers. "But you know they can run faster."

"I'm tired of running," she says and never mind if the thing on the other side of the door can hear her; after the birds, she can't imagine it matters much whether she's quiet or not. "I'm sick to fucking death of running. I'm going to find what I fucking came here to find and then I'll never have to run again."

"Open the door, half-breed," the thing in the foyer snarls and she can smell it now, decay and red, raw meat, ashes and gasoline.

"You're such a disappointment," Aldous Snow mumbles from his closet. "My only daughter died for you."

"Not your only daughter, you twisted old fuck," one of the corners reminds him. "Now shut up and go back to sleep."

"Make it easy on yourself," the thing behind the door says. "Save us the trouble. You might as well. This story ends exactly the same, either way."

And Narcissa looks down and sees the thick, red-black liquid leaking into the room from beneath the door, viscous soup of shit and blood and rot, bile and half-digested hair, and backs away as it spreads itself out across the bedroom floor. She raises the pistol and fires three times at the door, and the shots are as loud as the world cracking itself apart at the end of time.

"Wake up, girl," her grandfather says.

—The vision ended. I awoke
As out of sleep, and no
Voice moved—

"There's someone here to see you."

Narcissa opens her eyes, the dream spitting her back into herself, back into the sunny-bright afternoon room, sweat-soaked and gasping for air like a drowning woman. She lies still for a moment, staring up at the bedroom ceiling, waiting for her heart to stop pounding. Waiting to be absolutely sure it isn't all a trick, some magic far too subtle for her to have ever learned; but no monsters have followed her back here, no black-bird spies, and in a few more minutes she rolls over and hides her face in the stolen pillow, crying as quietly as she can so the voices won't hear.

As her twelfth summer dissolved into a bleak and drizzly twelfth autumn, Narcissa sat alone in her room in the tall house by the sea. Day after night after day, alone with *Cultes des Goules* and her French-English dictionary, impatiently struggling to tease some sense from the book's crumbling, yellow-brown pages and archaic grammar, fragments of sentences adding up to no more than fragments of meaning. Slowly transcribing the text onto stationery that she'd stolen from a drawer in her grandfather's study, writing paper that had once belonged to Mr. Iscariot Howard Q. Snow, Esq., and she was pretty sure that must have been her great-grandfather's name. The relic and her cipher and little time left over for anything else, pausing only for the bland meals Aldous left outside her door twice a day and as little sleep as she could get by on. This blind urgency something new to Narcissa, like *passé simple* and the baffling French conjugations, this small voice in her head that whispered incessantly, *Hurry, there's not much time left, hurry.*

Dépêchez-vous.

The revelations given up to her in stingy, oblique bits and pieces, murky enlightenments, and by early October she was finally finished, or at least as finished as she ever thought she would be. Several pages of the book had been written in languages other than French, and those would remain closed to her for many more years. But she'd gleaned enough to begin to understand, at last, the things her mother's diary had only hinted, her grandfather's fear and anger, her own golden eyes—that there was a world behind and beneath the world she knew, as hidden from the minds of men as the bottomless, black depths of Mother Hydra's drowning oceans. Hidden, but there *were* intersections, thin places where the one sometimes met the other, and there were the children of these meetings, the forsaken creatures Comte d'Erlette had simply called *les métis.*

"Do you see now?" her grandfather asked, watching from the safety of the bedroom doorway, his face become a skeleton mask by the light of his kerosene lantern. When she didn't answer him, he asked again, "Do you *see*, Narcissa?"

Narcissa didn't bother to look up from the stationery pages crowded with her sloppy handwriting, pages of pencil and fountain pen scrawl, pretending to read the words she'd written there.

"Leave me alone. Close the door and leave me alone," she said.

"I wouldn't have given you that book, but I still thought they would take you away. I shouldn't have—"

"Are you going deaf, Aldous?"

"It was old Iscariot. *He* started all of this. It wasn't me—"

"Do you really think that matters, who started it?"

"It isn't my fault," he mumbled ruefully, staring down at the floor, at the threshold of his lost Caroline's bedroom, his eyes grown wet and distant. "I'm the same as you, Narcissa."

"No, old man," she snarled, baring her sharp white teeth for him. "Whatever you are, you're not the same as me. You'll never be *anything* like me," and she got up and crossed the room, slammed the door in his face and then stood there listening to the sound of his slippers shuffling slowly down the long corridor towards his own bedroom door.

"Nothing like me, you lying bastard," she whispered, her lips pressed hard against the door, driving her voice through the wood like nails. "Nothing like me at all."

November 18—They all left the cellar last night and danced around a big bonfire father built in the dunes behind the house. He spent the whole day gathering enough driftwood. I sat on the porch, bundled up in my coat and gloves and read the newspaper while he walked up and down the beach talking to himself. The things I read in the paper seem less and less important. I thought they were the key, but maybe they're something else altogether. Maybe they're only a distraction. Small evils, small cataclysms. It's all a game and there's no time left for me to learn the rules. They howl all night long from the dunes and my baby kicks in my belly as if it wants to join them and run beneath the moon. Be patient, dear. Your damnation will find you soon enough.

On the morning of Narcissa's thirteenth birthday she began to bleed, crimson stains like rose petals tattooed onto her sheets, her thighs, and that afternoon two upstairs windows and a porcelain figurine in the parlor shattered. She'd always hated the figurine, two Irish setters and one of them with a dead pheasant gripped in its jaws. *I think Aldous is afraid of me now,* she wrote on one of the blank pages in her mother's diary. Lying on her bedroom floor that night as one year died and another was born, corpse of 1987 traded for 1988, and *He doesn't want me here,* she wrote. *He's never wanted me here. I'm something he wants to forget.*

Aldous swept up the pieces of the Irish setters, but ignored both the broken windows, and the fierce Atlantic gales blew snow into the house that gathered in small drifts upon the stairs.

December 3—My daughter came to me last night. She told me not to be afraid anymore, that it's almost over now. She was beautiful and wore a necklace of small blue flowers, seashells and fish bones bleached white by the sun. She kissed my cheek and I was a gull soaring high above this awful place. I could see the marshes and the Manuxet shimmering silver beneath the full moon, the glittering lights of Ipswich and the beacon at Cape Anne. I turned towards the ocean and she said, "No, mother, don't look at it." I shut my eyes and was back in my bed again. My daughter leaned close and whispered in my ear, so that father wouldn't hear. She had her father's eyes.

And three nights after the new year, Narcissa awoke with Aldous standing there beside her bed again. This time he was naked, his pale and wrinkled flesh draped loose on spindle bones, worn-out old man with tears rolling down his sunken cheeks. He had the carving knife, though she'd hidden it under a loose floorboard after his last visit.

"I *know* what you've been thinking, girl," he said. "Every dirty little thought. Every lie—"

"Go back to bed, Grandfather," she said, keeping her eyes on the carving knife. "I need to sleep."

"I told you not to call me that ever again."

"Then what would you have me call you instead?"

His head bobbed up and down and then slumped forward so his chin rested against his chest. His eyes flashed iridescent gold and red and orange in the dark.

"Go the fuck back to bed, Aldous," she said, trying to sound groggy, slipping her hand beneath her pillow.

"There's a yellow house in Providence," he said, "a house on Benefit Street full of monsters. There are entire cities built from the bones of the dead."

"You've been having bad dreams again," Narcissa said.

"My father . . . he walked streets paved with human bones. They took him to Providence and showed him the roads winding down to the very bottom of the universe. They showed him every goddamn thing he ever asked to see."

The old man stopped talking then, nodded, and stared silently for a moment at the knife clutched in his left hand as if he'd forgotten it was there.

"I saw him last night, Narcissa, watching me from the beach. I nailed the cellar door shut, but there he was on the beach."

"You saw your father?"

"He said that *I* had to finish this. He said there wasn't any other way. They aren't ever coming for you."

"Are you sure, Aldous? Are you absolutely certain this is what you want?"

"I'm so sorry, child," he said and raised the carving knife high above his head.

And Narcissa plunged the ice pick deep into his skinny chest, burying it all the way to the handle, piercing his heart, and the knife fell from his fingers and clattered loudly to the floor. Aldous stumbled backwards, crashed into her dressing table and collapsed. So much simpler than she'd ever dared to imagine, and Narcissa sat on the edge of the bed, amazed, listening as his breath grew shallow and uneven, hearing all the sounds an old man makes dying. His eyes were open, straining towards the sagging, water-stained ceiling or the night sky, the cold and treacherous stars he would never have to see again.

When it was almost over, Narcissa went to him, crouched on the floor and wiped the tears from his cheeks with the hem of her flannel nightgown.

"Thank you," he whispered, his voice wheezing raggedly out between blood-flecked dentures.

"No. Don't try to talk," she said and outside, somewhere among the dunes, something began to howl, a long, low, mournful sound, more human than animal. Aldous Snow's chest rose one last time, shuddered, and was still. Narcissa glanced over her shoulder at the bedroom window, then closed his eyes and stayed with him until the thing in the dunes stopped howling and there was only the wail of the January wind around the eaves of the house.

She dressed, then packed her clothes—everything she wasn't wearing—into a big canvas suitcase that she'd found in the very back of her mother's closet: her clothes and *Cultes des Goules,* Caroline's diary, the French-English dictionary and all the pages of her transcription. She pulled the ice pick from Aldous' chest and covered his body with the sheets and blankets from her bed, impromptu shroud because it didn't seem right to leave him lying there naked on the bedroom floor. Narcissa packed the ice pick and the carving knife in the suitcase, as well, and went downstairs, taking the steps one at a time, careful not to slip on the tiny drifts of snow that had accumulated beneath the shattered windows.

She opened both the front doors, letting in the storm, left the suitcase sitting on the snow-covered porch, and walked quickly through the silent, empty house, truly alone now for the first time in her life and only the echo of her own footsteps for company. The door to the old man's study wasn't locked, wasn't even shut, and she used a heavy brass paperweight shaped like a sleeping lion to smash the glass fronts of the walnut barrister cases. Narcissa lit the lamp from his desk, then took her time searching the spines and covers of all the books until she found the ones she was looking for, the ones that she knew would be there somewhere, rare and terrible volumes that François Honore-Balfour had mentioned or quoted. She packed them carefully into an empty cardboard box and carried it and the kerosene lamp back through the entryway to the place on the porch where she'd left her suitcase.

"Good-bye, old man," she said, wanting to sound brave but her voice seeming very small and insignificant, a child's voice lost inside the rambling, dark house looming up around her like the tomb it had always been. She hurled the lamp into the gloom and it burst against a wall, spilling fire, and the flames spread quickly to the floor and up the stairs, a roaring, burning creature devouring everything it touched.

I could stay, she thought. *I could stay and burn, too,* and she imagined her charred skeleton jumbled among the timbers and blackened masonry, her bones abandoned to the weather and time and before long there'd be nothing left of her at all. Nothing to hurt, nothing to be afraid of what was coming next, nothing to hope that the world could ever be any different than it was.

Go, Narcissa, Aldous growled angrily from the whirling redorange heart of the fire. *Go now, while there's still time,* and she turned and left the house, gathered her things and pulled the doors shut behind her. Outside, the storm wrapped her in a million shades of gray and white and black, and the freezing banshee wind hurried her stumbling towards the future.

Hours after dark and her face staring back at her from the mirror above the bathroom sink, the face of someone who has never had any trouble passing for human, and Narcissa holds the razor blade between her thumb and index finger and pretends that she has the courage to cut away the mask and find the truth secreted beneath her skin. Her yellow eyes the only outward hint, the windows of the soul, and even they're proof of nothing at all; plenty enough normal people born with yellow eyes, T. S. Eliot had yellow eyes, and they only get her stared at every now and then. Her face as pretty as every runway model's, unlikely Hollywood pretty: the fine, arched line of her unplucked eyebrows, her thick blonde hair and full lips, the delicate bridge of her nose. A monster locked helpless somewhere inside this shell, chained to this waxwork perfect husk, and sometimes, like now, staring at that face staring back at her, she wonders if half the things she remembers ever happened at all. If perhaps there never was a house beside the sea and Madam Terpsichore and Benefit Street are only a schizophrenic's delusion, shreds of truth warped inside out by a mind unwilling or incapable of facing dull reality.

No more or less a monster than any killer.

Only a lunatic lost in the labyrinth of her own dreams, in stray lines from ghost stories she might have read as a child she can't remember ever having been. Only a murderer.

Weary of myself, and sick of asking . . .

You're getting sloppy, girl, Aldous Snow mutters at her from the bathtub. *Renting a house, shitting where you eat. You're getting sloppy.*

"I'm getting close," she replies and sets a corner of the blade against her chin. "He's here, old man. I saw him yesterday. And when I carry his child back, they'll have to take me in."

If they wanted the child that bad they'd come here and take it themselves. They don't need you doing them favors.

A sting when the razor finally draws blood, and Narcissa watches as it gathers on the blade and her pale fingertips and drips into the rust-stained sink.

You don't have the nerve, do you? one of the corner voices taunts. *You fucking coward, you fucking phony, why don't you go ahead and see what's waiting under there. It's only meat, isn't that what you always say?*

"They'll *have* to take me," she says again.

Who are you talking to, Narcissa? Who do you think is listening? and she shuts her eyes and the razor makes hardly any sound at all when she lets go and it falls into the blood-spattered sink.

CHAPTER FOUR

Gyre and Gimble

Dark by the time Alice Sprinkle pulls up in front of Chance's building, shorter days as autumn spins the world farther away from summer, and from the sidewalk Chance can't see any lights burning in the windows of their third-floor apartment. She opens the door of the pickup and Alice peers doubtfully up through the windshield.

"Do you think he's home?" Alice asks. "Want me to see you to the door?" and Chance shakes her head.

"He's probably just taking a nap or something. Don't worry. I'll be fine."

"You sure?"

"Yeah, of course I'm sure."

"It's no trouble."

"I'll be *fine*," Chance says again, trying not to sound annoyed. "Thank you."

"Then I'll wait here until you get inside. Turn on a light so I know you're okay."

And Chance starts to tell her that's silly, but there's no point arguing once Alice has made up her mind, and all she really wants now is to sit down and take her shoes off.

"See you tomorrow," she says and closes the truck door.

She can feel Alice watching her as she enters her code into the security pad by the front door, types *0 and BUFO, and the door buzzes and the lock clicks open. Inside, the brightly lit lobby smells faintly of disinfectant and cigarette smoke, and she turns and waves at Alice, who smiles and waves back at her.

"Alice dear, you're going to drive me absolutely bugfuck before this is over," she mutters quietly to herself and waddles to the elevator, pushes the white plastic UP button and waits impatiently while invisible gears and cables whir and groan and creak to life. She fishes her keys from the bib pocket of her overalls and when the silver doors slide open, she inserts her elevator key and pushes another white plastic button with a black 3 on it. *Like peppermint and chocolate,* she thinks, wishing she had a York peppermint patty, wondering if there's anything in the apartment to eat.

The elevator smells more strongly of cigarettes, and there's a small puddle of dog piss in one corner. At their front door, 307 in tasteful black sans serif, she unlocks the dead bolt and the brass doorknob, and steps into the dark apartment.

"Yo, Deke," she calls out, reaching for the switch on the wall beside the door. A moment of silence as she flips the switch and one of her grandparents' antique lamps, stained-glass willow boughs beneath a gnarled, bronze trunk, illuminates the small foyer. She takes off her sweater and hangs it on the coat-tree.

"Deacon? Are you asleep?"

Two hallways branch off the foyer, a short one leading to their bedroom and the unfinished nursery, and a longer one leading towards the front of the building, to the living room and kitchen. Either way, there's only darkness beyond the warm edges of the lamplight, and Chance calls to Deacon again.

"In here," he calls back, his voice drifting to her down the long hallway leading to the living room. She leaves the light behind, following his voice like bread crumbs.

"Deke, why are you sitting here in the dark?" and she turns on another lamp, another of her grandparents' Tiffany relics, and Deacon curses and immediately covers his eyes with his left hand. He's sitting on the big sofa and there's a pint bottle of Jack Daniel's on the coffee table in front of him. She stares at Deacon and the whiskey bottle for a second or two, long enough to be sure that it hasn't been opened. There's a prescription bottle on the table too, a month's worth of powder blue Fioricet tablets inside amber plastic.

"What's that?" she asks and points at the whiskey.

"That, my dear, is a bottle of Tennessee bourbon."

"Were you going to drink it?"

Deacon curses again and slowly lowers his hands, blinks and

squints at Chance. "I was thinking about it," he says. "Will you please turn the light back off? I've got a headache."

"No, I will not turn the light back off. I want to know what the hell's going on."

Deacon shuts his eyes and leans his head against the back of the sofa, the timeworn upholstery almost the same shade of brown as his hair, and Chance picks up the bottle of Jack Daniel's.

"I had a very bad day," Deacon says.

"So you bought this fucking bottle of whiskey and you've been sitting here in the dark trying to decide whether or not you were going to get drunk?"

"I had a very, *very* bad day, Chance."

She looks at the bourbon, the tea-colored liquor inside the sealed bottle, and thinks a drink or two wouldn't be such a bad thing right now, something for the pain and the worry, something to make her forget the rest stop and the blood she thought she saw dripping from the mouth of the fiberglass *Megalopseudosuchus.*

"Why didn't you call Harold?" she asks Deacon and sets the bottle down a safe distance away, out of reach, on top of the television.

"I didn't *want* to talk to fucking Harold. I wanted a drink."

"You could have called Dr. Winman. You could have said something when you called me."

"I have a headache," Deacon said and rubbed at the furrowed spot between his eyebrows. "And I don't want to have this conversation right now."

"Well that's just too bad, Deke. Because I'm not going to let you throw away everything you've accomplished over one bad day."

Deacon opens an eye and glares at her.

"No offense, babe, but you don't have any goddamn idea what you're talking about."

"Then why don't you *enlighten* me," Chance replies, pushing down the anger, resisting the weary, exasperated part of her that wants to give the bottle right back to him and tell Deacon to go fuck himself.

"You remember a guy named Soda? Skinny little fuck with a skateboard."

"No," Chance says. "I don't. What about him?"

Down on the street a horn blows and Chance remembers Alice,

waiting dutifully in her truck. "Shit," she hisses and crosses the room to one of the tall front windows. She waves and Alice honks the horn again.

"What the hell is that all about?" Deacon asks and "It's just Alice," Chance tells him. "She wanted to make sure I got inside okay."

"Maybe you should have married her instead."

Chance ignores him and watches as the old Toyota pulls away from the curb and heads east down First Avenue.

"I'm sure Alice would've made you a fine husband."

"Deke, can we please not do this tonight?" and she rests her forehead against the windowpane, stares down at the sidewalk bathed in the glow of streetlights. "I'll talk if you want to talk, but I haven't had such a good day myself and I just don't think I'm up to fighting tonight."

"Whatever," Deacon says and when she turns around he's popping the top off the bottle of Fioricet.

"How many of those have you taken today?" she asks him.

"Not nearly enough, obviously."

Chance clumsily eases her body into an armchair near the window and watches while Deke dry-swallows two of the tablets. Maybe if she'd listened to Alice and stayed in Birmingham, or maybe if she'd had a little more time when he called, and *If wishes were horses,* she thinks, *beggars would ride.*

"What happened to Soda?" she asks.

"Soda is dead. Someone—" and then he stops and silently stares at the prescription bottle for a moment. "You really don't want to hear this."

"If it's got you this upset, I have to hear it, Deke. I can't help you if I don't even know what's going on."

Deacon takes a deep breath and shuts his eyes again. "You're half right," he says.

"Damn it, if you're not even willing to let me try—"

"Did all the fossils make it in one piece? All your little frogs and fishies?"

"I don't want to talk about the damned fossils right now. I want you to tell me what's going on."

Deacon opens his eyes and turns his head towards her; his bleary green eyes grown so much darker tonight, filled with the thirst and all his secret pains, all the things he'll never tell her no matter how many times she asks. The blind spots he keeps for himself, and most of the time that's fine by Chance, if that's the way he wants it, as long as he stays off the booze.

"Someone killed him last night," he says, the words slipping reluctantly from his lips. "Gutted him like a catfish and left his head in a pillowcase under his bathroom sink."

"Jesus, Deke."

"So the cops came to see me this morning, about an hour after you left, because that prick Vince Hammond in Atlanta told them I might be able to help."

"You might be—" Chance starts, then stops and looks down at her hands folded across her swollen belly.

"I told you that you didn't want to hear this."

"But you told them to leave you alone, right?" Chance asks him, almost whispering now. "You told them you didn't know what they were talking about."

"No," he says. "I didn't."

"You promised me, Deke. You promised me that was all in the past. You said you didn't want anything else to do with that shit ever again."

"Yeah, I know."

"Then why'd you do it? Why'd you go with them?"

"I didn't say I went anywhere with them."

"But you *did*. That's why you've got a migraine now, isn't it? That's why you bought that bottle of whiskey."

Deacon sighs and rubs at his forehead again. "I haven't held down a job in almost a year," he says. "I sit here, day after day, waiting for you to come home—"

"Your *job* is to stay sober. That's all I need you to do."

"Hell, you're not asking for much, are you?" he mumbles and the bitterness in his voice, the cold resentment, is almost more than she can handle right now, almost that one last straw. Chance bites hard at her lower lip and keeps her eyes on her belly.

Inside her, the baby moves.

"I'm sorry," Deacon says and gets up off the sofa, stands there a moment squinting at the bottle of whiskey sitting on the television set. "Sometimes I think it's eating me up inside, like a cancer."

Chance nods, because she knows he's telling her the truth, but she doesn't look at him. She's determined that she isn't going to start crying, not this time, not tonight, not with Deacon so close to the edge.

"So . . ." she says, and has to stop and swallow before she can go on, her mouth gone as dry as sun-bleached bones. "They asked you to look at Soda's body."

"I didn't know it was Soda. I didn't know it was him until we pulled up out front of his place. They said they didn't have any idea I knew him."

"You think they were telling you the truth?"

"Probably. They didn't have anything to gain by lying to me."

"Maybe they thought you wouldn't go with them, if you knew."

"Yeah, maybe," Deacon says, turning away from Chance, and he goes to the refrigerator, the small kitchen divided from the living room by nothing but empty space and imaginary boundaries. She looks up and he's standing there framed in the white icebox glare, so tall and thin. Deacon takes out a bottle of water and shuts the refrigerator door again.

"Are you hungry?" he asks her.

"I'm all right. I'll get something in a little while."

"I wouldn't have gone if I'd known it was him," Deacon says, and then he screws the cap off the bottle and takes a long drink.

"It was your decision," Chance whispers, speaking so low now she's not even sure he can hear her.

"God, I hate this stuff," he says, grimaces and wipes his mouth on the back of his hand. "If it comes from the tap, it tastes like a goddamn swimming pool. If it comes out of a bottle, it tastes like plastic."

"It's good for you," Chance says.

Deacon sets the bottle down on the kitchen counter and stares at her across the wide room. Outside, a big truck rumbles past the building and the windows rattle softly in their aluminum frames.

"I should have told them no," Deacon says when the truck has passed and it's almost quiet again, only the muffled sound of someone's stereo coming from the apartment next door. "I should have told that detective that Hammond was pulling their leg."

"Well, so what happened? What did you see?" and she watches while he takes another drink from the bottle, wishing she could come in again and start this whole scene over, wondering if there's any way it could play itself out differently. *No,* she thinks. *It would be the same, exactly the same.*

"You don't have to humor me, Chance."

"I'm not humoring you. I just asked you a question."

Deacon screws the cap back on the water bottle and returns it to the refrigerator. "There's leftover Chinese in here," he says, "if you're hungry."

"What did you see there, Deke? Did you see the person that killed him?"

He shuts the fridge and stands with his back to her, pretending to inspect the assortment of magnets and sticky notes on the freezer door.

"You don't believe I *saw* anything. It's all just part of my addictive, delusional personality, remember?"

"Maybe it doesn't matter anymore what I believe," she says, wanting to sound sincere, wanting to get past this to some place she can help him, and the pint of Jack Daniel's won't be an ax hanging over them. Deacon shakes his head and comes back to his place on the sofa, his bare feet making hardly any sound on the hardwood floor.

"Did you see what they *wanted* you to see?" Chance asks and he shrugs and props his feet on the coffee table.

"I saw something. I wouldn't have this splitting fucking headache right now if I hadn't seen something. But I'm not sure what it was. And I'm pretty sure it wasn't anything they wanted me to see."

"But you told them, whatever it was."

"Nope," Deacon says. "I lied. I told them I didn't see anything at all."

"What'd you do that for?" Chance asks, surprised, and she leans as far forward in the chair as her belly will allow, straining to close the distance between them, and the baby moves again.

"You don't tell the man what the man don't want to hear."

"But you think you saw the killer?"

"I already told you, I don't know what I saw."

Chance leans back in the armchair again. The lamplight through the whiskey bottle is casting a tea-stained reflection on the wall. She looks up at the high ceilings, the crossbeams lost in shadow, and "I'm sorry," she says. "I'm sorry I can't believe you about these things, and I'm sorry I got upset. It doesn't help either of us if I get upset."

"How'd the exhibit look?"

"It's beautiful," Chance says, too tired to tell him that they changed the name without asking her and the new name doesn't even make sense. Too tired to tell him about the dinosaurs and the Coal Age diorama. Too scared to tell him about the blood.

"I think they'll leave me alone now," Deacon says. "If they don't think I can help them, they won't be back. I called Hammond from the library and told him to leave me the hell alone."

"Do you think he will?"

"I told him I was married now and you were pregnant. I told him I was staying clean and I don't have time for this psychic shit. He doesn't try to be an asshole. It just seems to come naturally."

"Deke, honey, will you please help me get these shoes off?" and Chance kicks at the corner of the coffee table with the toe of one sneaker. "I swear, I think my feet have died and gone to hell."

"I'm sorry I bought the bottle," Deacon says. "It was stupid."

"Let's just forget about it, okay? How's your head?"

"Either it'll kill me or it'll get better in a couple of days," and Deacon slips off the sofa cushions, squats on the floor in front of Chance and begins unlacing her shoes. "I've got the Fioricet there, and I've got the Imitrex if it gets unbearable."

Chance runs both her strong hands though his short, uncombed hair; her fingertips pause at the sides of his head and, gently, she begins to massage his temples as he slips her right sneaker off.

"Your feet are swollen," he says.

"I think I'm holding enough water to float the goddamn *Titanic*."

Deacon pulls off her other shoe and rubs her ankles while she continues massaging his temples. He closes his eyes and sits down on the floor at her feet.

"I'm sober, Chance, and this time I'm going to stay sober."

"I know," she whispers, but then glances nervously back at the whiskey bottle on the TV, as if it might have moved, as if it might have slithered away when she wasn't paying attention.

"I know," she says again, and outside another truck rumbles past and the windows rattle.

*   *   *

After Chance has fallen asleep, Deacon sits at the foot of the bed and stares out the window at the street, the whitewashed brick office building on the other side of Twenty-third, the limbs of the tall and spindly trees planted between the sidewalk and the asphalt tossed by the wind and all their dry leaves rattling together in the cryptic tongue of autumn. There's a storm coming and already he can smell the rain. The drapes billow in the breeze and Deacon thinks maybe he should go ahead and shut the window now, before he dozes off and everything gets soaked. But the air pushed along before the thunderstorm feels clean and healthy, untouched and uncontaminated by the world; he doesn't want to close the window and he doesn't want to go to sleep.

His head feels like a bucket of broken glass and raw meat, and he wishes he had a cigarette. But Chance would raise hell if she caught him smoking in the apartment, especially the bedroom, and he doesn't feel like getting dressed and standing alone in the stairwell. So he ignores the craving, so much of his life these days spent ignoring cravings that there are times when he thinks he could best be defined entirely in negatives, the collection of things he doesn't do. The man who doesn't drink. Or work. Or have visions of the secret things that murderers do when there's no one around to stop them. The man so thirsty he would sell the last hour of his life for one sip of alcohol, something wet and warm to soothe the pain behind his eyes.

He glances over his shoulder at Chance, lying on her back beneath the cornflower-blue comforter, the big goose-down comforter that she bought to match the walls. Her pregnant belly is a great blue dome and her mouth is open slightly, her hands clasped together beneath her chin so she almost looks like she's praying. But Deacon doubts that Chance has ever prayed in her life, both her grandparents the sort of evangelical rationalists who subscribe to *The Skeptical Inquirer* and feel sorry for anyone still shackled by the chains of religion or any other stultifying superstition. Deacon suspects that Joe and Esther Matthews would have packed Chance off to a shrink at the first sign of an irrational thought.

He turns back to the window and the night, annoyed at himself that he feels guilty for thinking such sour thoughts about her dead grandparents. Esther died years before he met Chance and Joe was never anything but kind to him, even on the occasion or two he showed up drunk. But there are times when he wishes their influence on their granddaughter had been a little less profound.

"You're just jealous, asshole," he says, not loud enough to wake her, and the drapes flap and flutter their agreement. The clean air washes over him like a balm, like clemency, something to scrub away the sights and smells of Soda's gore-spattered hovel.

They ordered a pizza for dinner, because that's what Chance wanted, a huge pizza with extra olives, and then he watched CNN while she took a shower. Afterwards, despite his headache, he read to her from Dr. Seuss' *McElligot's Pool,* because Chance was convinced it was good for the baby to be read to, that Deacon's voice could somehow help to gift their unborn child with its parents' love of books. A hopeful, harmless Lamarckian trick to bias the roll of Darwinian dice, insurance against a stupid kid, but mostly he suspects Chance just wanted to hear the stories herself. Tonight, he only made it as far as the furry Eskimo Fish bound for warmer waters before she was asleep and snoring softly; Deacon closed the book and laid it aside, wondering if he would sleep, too, if he would make it to dawn without dipping into the Imitrex. The injections almost always work, but can leave him nauseous and vomiting, and he usually prefers taking the Fioricet tablets and riding out the migraines.

He closes his eyes and there's Soda's corpse waiting for him, lying beneath the red wheel and words painted on the wall in a dead man's blood, the hard black line drawn underneath. The naked thing gnawing at Soda's flesh is there too, the naked *woman,* but a woman from some freak-show nightmare. She stops and looks towards him, her irises flashing iridescent red, and Deacon opens his eyes.

The dry October leaves rattle in the wind, and the drapes make a sound like pterodactyl wings.

She's out there somewhere, Deacon thinks, not wanting the thought in his head. *Whoever she is, whyever she does it, she's out there somewhere.*

Deacon sits on the bed until the first heavy raindrops begin to fall, coming in and splashing themselves against the floor. He gets up and closes the window, pulls the drapes shut, and lies down next to Chance waiting for morning.

*   *   *

The next day, and Chance sits in a chair near the lectern, sipping a can of Sprite, as the last students drift indifferently into the small, windowless auditorium. Her final day at work before maternity leave begins, and then Alice will be taking over her sophomore-level Evolution and the History of Life survey course. Biology-lite for non-majors, a magnet for business and humanities students looking for required science credits without getting in over their heads, and most of them are in way too deep anyway. She glances at the clock above the blackboard, 10:30, so it's time to get things started, five minutes past time, but her back hurts too much for her to care.

Students shuffle loose-leaf paper, cough, hastily flip textbook pages, talk among themselves in loud and hurried whispers, the muffled clamor caught between the lime-sherbet walls, beneath the too-bright fluorescent glare. Chance sets down her drink and slips on her reading glasses, picks up a stubby piece of chalk and turns to the blackboard. She writes NATURAL SELECTION = MECHANISM in tall, blocky letters, and then DARWIN and WALLACE underneath that, before turning back to the lectern and her notes.

"Well," she says and licks her dry lips. "Here we go again," and a few of the students laugh, though most of them are too busy scribbling down the four words she's written on the blackboard to notice that she's said anything.

"If you read the assignment, there shouldn't be anything mysterious about any of this," and Chance waves one hand in the general direction of the blackboard. "In 1859, Charles Darwin proposed a mechanism that would account for how new species arise from pre-existing species, explaining Earth's present biodiversity and the fossil record. Or, as he so eloquently wrote, 'As buds give rise by growth to fresh buds, and these, if vigorous, branch out and over-top on all sides many a feebler branch, so by generation I believe it has been with the great Tree of Life, which fills with its dead and broken the crust of the earth, and covers the surface with its ever-branching and beautiful ramifications.' "

The sound of seventy or so pencils and ballpoint pens scritching down her every word, and Chance braces her elbows on the corners of the lectern, sighs, and gazes out at the class over the tops of her spectacles.

"You don't have to write all that down. It's in the book," she says, but most of them keep scribbling anyway. "I want you to grasp the concept here, the elegance of Darwin's argument, not memorize the precise words he used to express it. I want you to see how his observations, of artificial selection by pigeon breeders, for instance, led him to the theory of *natural* selection."

And near the very back of the room, high up, near the doors, a thick-necked boy with auburn hair cut close to his scalp raises his hand. He's leaning back in his chair, tapping arrhythmically, deliberately, on his unopened textbook with the eraser end of an unsharpened pencil. Chance takes a deep breath. So much for an easy last day, so much for hoping she could get through this one lecture without a duel. She takes another swallow of her Sprite and "Yes, Larry," she says. "Do you have a question?"

"You really think people and pigeons are the same thing, Dr. Silvey?" he asks and taps a little harder at the cover of his textbook. There's a nervous smattering of laughter and Chance smiles and nods her head.

"In that human beings and pigeons are both animals subject to the process of natural selection," she replies and stares resolutely back at the auburn-haired boy, hoping that she's said enough to shut him up and knowing that she hasn't.

"Animals don't have souls," the boy says, staring stubbornly back at her. He leans forward, letting the front legs on his chair rock back down to the floor. "My creator gave me an immortal soul. That's what separates me from animals like pigeons."

The rest of the class is waiting quietly, expectantly, for whatever Chance is going to do or say next; all eyes on her or Larry, grateful for any diversion that might possibly shorten the lecture. She glances down at her carefully typed notes, but there are no answers there and she tries to recall all the things that Alice has told her about dealing with creationist students, the value of a witty comeback to break the tension, humor to turn the tables.

Never let them see you sweat, kiddo.

"Larry, are you familiar with *Inherit the Wind*? It's a play."

"Yeah. We had to watch that movie in high school," the red-headed boy says and watches her suspiciously.

"So, do you remember when Matthew Brady's on the stand, and in response to one of Drummond's questions about the age of a fossil, he says, 'I am more interested in the Rock of Ages, than I am in the age of rocks'?"

"Yeah," Larry says and taps his pencil against the cover of his textbook. "I remember that. That was right before Brady explains how Archbishop James Usher calculated the true age of the earth by—"

"That's right. So, what do you think Brady meant when he said that, about the Rock of Ages and the age of rocks? What do you think he was getting at?"

Larry stares dubiously at Chance for a moment, then stops tapping his pencil and says, "That what mattered to him is not how old rocks are, but his faith in God."

"Right, I think that's exactly what Brady was saying. We can agree on that?"

"Sure," Larry grunts and shifts uneasily in his seat.

"Okay. Now, what I need you to understand is that in this class, which is a biology class and not a religion class, I *am* concerned about the age of rocks and *not* the Rock of Ages."

A girl near the front of the room snickers softly and Chance glares at her until she stops.

"But you want us to believe that people are just animals," Larry says. "You want us to believe—"

"I honestly don't care what you *believe,* Larry," Chance tells him, careful to hide her impatience, careful to sound reasonable. "If you'll stop trying to disrupt class and as long as you learn what I'm trying to teach you, whether you believe any of it or not is really none of my business. If you don't want to be in here, you should consider taking another course. You might try Dr. Parker's excellent introduction to astronomy, or maybe a chemistry course for non-majors."

"What's the difference?" Larry asks, finally opening his textbook and looking down at it instead of at her. "You're all atheists, all you scientists. None of you believe in God or try to show both sides of things."

"I happen to know that Dr. Parker is also an ordained Unitarian minister," Chance says and Larry snorts derisively and leafs through the pages of his copy of *Biology: Diversity and Function.*

"You're all evolutionists," he says. "And you're all afraid to give creation science equal time in your classes. You're all afraid to tell us the truth so we can decide for ourselves what's right."

Chance sighs and takes another sip of her Sprite, which is beginning to get warm and go flat. Larry stops flipping pages and frowns down at the textbook, pretending to read something printed there.

"Larry, let's just cut the crap, okay? We both know that the very last thing you want is for people to make up their own minds about anything, much less evolution. When's the last time your Sunday School teacher gave a lecture on population genetics or geological time?"

"When's the last time you went to church, Dr. Silvey?"

"That's none of your business, Larry."

"Oh, I see. It's okay for you to question our religious convictions, but it's not okay for us to question yours?"

"I *haven't* questioned your convictions—" but then Chance stops herself, hearing the anger beginning to creep into her voice, and she looks back at the blackboard, reading over what she's written while she tries to clear her head.

"Maybe it doesn't seem that way to you, Dr. Silvey," Larry says, "because you don't have any convictions. The Bible tells me that I'm not an animal, that I was *created* in the image of my God, not evolved from a bunch of monkeys."

Chance turns back to the class, and now almost everyone's watching her, like the auditorium has become a chessboard and it's her move. The first day, she passed out copies of a questionnaire to gauge their knowledge of and attitudes towards biology and paleontology, so she knows a lot of them are probably enjoying this; more than half these kids fresh out of local high schools where evolution isn't taught at all, or only presented by nervous teachers as a nonthreatening, dumbed-down "alternative" to creationism.

Chance takes a swallow of the flat Sprite, sets the green-and-silver can back down on the lectern, and gazes at Larry across the sea of curious, watchful faces. The auburn-haired boy is smiling confidently, triumphantly, still pretending to read his textbook.

"Larry, I'm not trying to undermine your faith or anyone else's," Chance says, trying to choose her words carefully. "I'm here to teach you what science has learned about the history of life, not argue religion."

Larry nods his head and glances up at her, glancing down on her from his seat on the top row of the auditorium, and now his smile has melted into something more like a sneer.

"What are you going to tell your baby about God?" he asks. "Aren't you afraid?"

"Afraid of what, Larry?"

"Aren't you afraid it's gonna go to Hell because you're going to teach it that it came from monkeys and has no soul? Doesn't that bother you, Dr. Silvey, that you're going to send your own baby to burn in Hell for all eternity?"

A surprised murmur from the class, then, perhaps everyone getting just a little more than they bargained for, and Chance grips the edges of the lectern and doesn't take her eyes off the boy.

"Larry, I'd like you to leave now, please," she says calmly, straining to hide the shaky edge in her voice, loath to give him the satisfaction of seeing that he's gotten to her. "We'll continue this conversation in my office after class, if you like."

"Don't bother," he says, standing up, gathering his things. "I'll just drop. There's nothing you have to say that I want to hear anyway."

"Well, I'm sorry about that," Chance says, though she isn't, and all she really wants right now is for him to leave the room before she says something she'll regret. "Bring me the drop slip after class and I'll sign it."

"Whatever you say," the auburn-haired boy mutters, picking up his backpack from the floor. He slings it over his left shoulder and walks halfway to the doors, then stops and looks back at her again. "But one day you're gonna have to answer to God for all the lies you're telling," he says. "One day you're going to have to pay for trying to make people doubt His word. I wouldn't want to be you when that day arrives—"

"*Good-bye,* Larry," Chance says and goes back to her notes, the straight and sensible lines of text, Charles Darwin and Alfred Russel Wallace, the Argus pheasant and Galápagos finches. In a moment she hears the auditorium doors open and swing closed, and she apologizes to the class for the disruption and begins her lecture over.

After class, Chance takes her time walking the short distance across campus from the lime-sherbet auditorium in the Education Building to her tiny office in the Earth Sciences Annex, nestled among a few dogwood and crape myrtle trees behind the Physical Sciences Building. The annex a hasty afterthought of brick and glass, built during the oil shortages of the 1970s, when geologists and micro-paleontologists were in short supply and high-paying jobs were plentiful. Those days long gone though, and the university has been making noises about cutting the program altogether, money that might be better spent elsewhere, and already the geology department, faced with indifferent or hostile administrators and state proration, has had to cancel a couple of courses and subscriptions to several journals. Something else to make Chance wonder if selling the house was such a great idea, one more thing for her to worry about.

She checks her mail—a new Ward's catalog, fliers from Columbia University and Academic Press announcing books she can't afford to buy, a dues reminder from the Society of Vertebrate Paleontology—and then ducks into her office and shuts the door behind her. Chance squeezes awkwardly around the corners of the desk that takes up most of the room and then eases herself into the chair wedged in against the back wall. There are galley pages waiting for her on the desk, a long paper on vertebrate biostratigraphy in the Carboniferous rocks of Alabama that she needs to proof quickly and get back in the mail to *Palaios,* and she sits down and stares vacantly at the photocopied pages.

Chance reaches for a red pen, is pulling the cap off, when she starts crying, a sudden, hot rush of tears, all the emotion she's been swallowing for days now bubbling suddenly to the surface, and she throws the pen at the office door. It leaves a jagged crimson streak across an old *Calvin and Hobbes* cartoon taped there, Calvin fashioning a "dinosaur" skeleton from bottles and tin cans and discarded silverware he's dug up from his backyard, while Hobbes watches on doubtfully.

"Fuck it," she growls, looking frantically about for something else to throw, when there's a knock on the door and it takes her a minute to calm down enough to ask who it is.

"Alice," the someone replies and Chance wipes at her eyes, her runny nose, quickly dries her tear-and-snot-damp hands on her jeans.

"Yeah," she calls back. "Come in," and Alice Sprinkle opens the door and stands there a moment, staring at Chance.

"I just heard about what happened with that Larry character," she says. Chance takes a deep, hitching breath and wipes at her eyes again, shrugs her shoulders. "Oh," she says. "That was fast."

"Well, from what I heard, you did the right thing."

"Did I?" Chance whispers, the tears still so close, and she covers her face with her right hand.

"Oh, hey. Come on now," Alice says. "Don't do that," and she steps into the office and shuts the door.

"I'm sorry," Chance mumbles through her fingers. She can smell and taste the salt from her own tears, and that reminds her of the exhibit banner at the Fernbank—AT THE OCEAN'S EDGE—and she starts crying again.

"That little shit's not worth it," Alice says and knocks over a stack of books trying to get around the desk to Chance.

Chance wipes at her eyes and shakes her head. "It's not him. It's not *only* him. Everything's so fucked up. I swear Alice, most of the time I don't know if I'm fucking coming or going."

"It's just your body, all those hormones," and Alice squats down to retrieve the fallen books; she picks one up and stares at the cover. "You know that."

"My body," Chance says and frowns forlornly down at her stomach. "Is *that* what this is?"

"I'm afraid so, darling," and Alice sets the book on the corner of the desk, picks up another and reads its cover.

Chance pulls open a drawer and rummages about until she finds a packet of tissues; she blows her nose loudly, then tosses the damp wad at the wastebasket and misses.

"Half the time I look in the goddamned mirror, I don't even recognize myself anymore. I feel like someone's stolen my body and now I'm stuck in this bloated . . ." and she trails off, reaches for another Kleenex and blows her nose again. "I'm absolutely disgusting," she says, staring into the Kleenex.

"You're not disgusting and it's almost over." Alice returns the last of the books to the desktop, then sits down in the floor and smiles up at Chance. "You are a beautiful, radiant paragon of femininity, a marvel of nature, Mother Gaia incarnate."

"You're full of shit, you know that?"

"Always tell the ladies what you think they want to hear," Alice says. "That's what my daddy always said."

"I don't want it to be almost over, Alice. I want it to be over now. I want my life back." Chance drops the soggy, crumpled tissue on the desk, picks up the paper-clipped galley pages and stares at them. She finds another red pen and tests it on her palm.

"I'm afraid it's a little late to be getting cold feet. The only way out is straight ahead."

"I have to get this thing proofed and back in the mail today," Chance says. "Look at that. I misspelled 'Famennian,' right there in the damned abstract. I tell you I'm losing my mind," and she taps the paper once with an index finger and then turns the pages around so Alice can see.

"Yeah. You're getting stupider just sitting there."

Chance ignores her and goes back to reading the first page of the galley silently to herself. "When this is all over," she says, "I'm spending a whole goddamn month in the field."

"Whatever you say, Momma Bear."

"I mean it. I think my legs are atrophying. Pretty soon, there won't be anything left of me but a belly and a pair of leaky tits."

"So, what're you gonna do about Mr. Larry?" Alice asks, changing the subject. Chance shrugs, marks a comma splice, and turns the page. About the only thing she wants to think about less than being pregnant is the ugly scene in the classroom, the arrogant sneer on the boy's face, the spite in his eyes, as he told her that she was damning her baby to Hell.

"He says he's bringing me a drop slip. I'll sign it and hope I never have to see his face again."

Alice bobs her head thoughtfully. "If he said what I heard he said to you, I think it qualifies as harassment. Maybe you should think about taking disciplinary action."

"No," Chance says and inserts a missing period. "I just want him out of my class. I'm not in any shape to get involved in something like that, not now."

"It's your decision. I just feel sorry for whoever gets him next time around."

"Whoever gets him next time around won't be eight months pregnant."

"This isn't the first time he's done something like this, you know," Alice says and Chance stops reading and looks at her. Alice nods and continues. "That's right. Last semester he signed up for physical anthropology with Joan Forty and dropped out three weeks into the course. She calls him Holy Larry."

"I think Scary Larry would be more accurate."

"Yeah, well, get this. He actually told her that whites were created separately in the Garden of Eden, that blacks are the children of Cain, and teaching evolution leads to miscegenation."

"I doubt he can even spell 'miscegenation.'"

Alice laughs and presses the soles of both her tennis shoes against the side of Chance's desk. "When you're one of God's chosen people, I don't think it much matters whether or not you can spell."

"Then maybe there's hope for me yet," Chance says and reaches for the paperback *Merriam-Webster's* on her cluttered desk.

"So you're going to be okay?"

"I'm fine," she says, whether it's true or not, because it's what Alice wants to hear. "I'm just tired, that's all. I just didn't need that creationist crap today."

"Good," Alice replies, getting up from the floor. "Let me know when you're finished in here and I'll give you a ride home, okay?"

"Thanks, but I have the car. As soon as I finish with these corrections and get this ready to go back in the mail, I'm out of here."

"Okay. But be careful, and don't you wait around here for Scary Larry to show up. He told Joan he was going to drop, too, but he never did. He took an F instead. I expect he'll do the same with you."

"I'll call you tonight," Chance says, "I promise," and manages a weary smile.

"You do that, Momma Bear," Alice tells her, and then she leaves Chance alone with her red pen and galley pages, her Kleenex and self-doubt. Chance leans back in her chair and stares at the office door, at the defiled *Calvin and Hobbes* strip and a postcard from her visit to the Yale Peabody Museum taped up next to it. She tries in vain to recall the world before she met Alice Sprinkle, or a world without her, and in a few minutes she gives up and goes back to work.

In the dream, and he knows that it's a dream, Deacon is standing in the doorway of Soda's apartment, watching while the blonde woman undresses. Soda's sitting in the center of the bed, sitting there cross-legged in nothing but a dirty pair of navy-blue boxers and a smile, talking his white-boy shit, the king of the goddamn world, Mr. Smooth, and if this were not only a dream, Deacon would try to warn him. If he knew, instead, that he was wide awake and these moments were not already history, he would tell Soda about the knife. If he were awake, he would tell Soda lots of things. But Soda is already dead, sliced and diced, decapitated and carted away to the city morgue, where the police pathologists have already had their turns at his corpse. Soda is already evidence of the murder that still hasn't happened in this dream, this now inside his brain, and Deacon sits down on a wobbly chair near the door and watches.

"Hey, man," Soda shouts at him. "Were you raised in a fuckin' barn or what? Shut the goddamn door!" So Deacon closes the door and the latch clicks loud, like someone cocking a gun on TV.

"Maybe I'll leave a few scraps for you, dawg," Soda says and grins at Deacon, showing off his crooked, yellow teeth.

"I'm a married man now," Deacon says. "But thanks, anyway."

"Oh, hell," Soda giggles. "You ain't that married, bro. Ain't nobody with a dick *that* married."

Deacon knows this is a dream because his migraine has stopped.

The tall woman unbuttons her blouse, and Soda's drooling like a kid waiting for the ice-cream truck; her long fingers with their long unpolished nails work the buttons one after another, bottom to top, and her belly is as flat and smooth and white as milk.

"Oh yeah," Soda says, "That's what I want to see," and Deacon reaches for the bottle of Jack on the floor beside the chair. He breaks the paper seal, twists the cap off, but when he raises it to his lips, he realizes that there's nothing inside but sand. Sand that smells like the sea and he thinks if he were to put the mouth of the bottle to his ear he would hear waves crashing against the shore, somewhere far away.

"Have you ever seen the moon bleed?" the woman asks Soda and he nods his head enthusiastically, still grinning that stupid grin.

"I'll see whatever you want me to see, baby."

"Have you ever seen it red and swollen and hanging so low above the world you could reach out and brush it with the tips of your fingers?"

Her voice like satin and rust, and "Baby, I'll say I seen Elvis and the Pope scootin' around in a goddamn flyin' saucer, if that's what you wanna hear."

Deacon sets the bottle of beach sand back down on the mangy, gray-green carpet. "Dude, peep this," Soda says, as the woman slips her blouse off her shoulders and it falls to the floor. There's a stiff mane of short, blonde hair running from the base of her neck all the way to the waistband of her jeans.

"Maybe I should go now," Deacon says and Soda laughs and shakes his head.

"Hell no," he says. "This shit's just gettin' interesting. You know you gotta stick around. You gotta see what this fine bitch is gonna do next."

If the woman knows that Deacon's watching them, she's chosen to ignore him. Her yellow eyes on Soda and nothing else, ghost of a smile on her full red lips, and Deacon tries to remember if he's ever seen anyone with yellow eyes before.

"When I was a little girl," the woman says and steps out of her jeans, "the moon came down from the sky and scraped itself raw against the sharp edges of the horizon. When I was a little girl, the moon bled for me." Now Deacon can see that the stiff mane runs all the way to the base of her spine, where it ends in a whitish tuft of hair. A single tattoo on each side of her ass, black ink and shades of gray against her pale skin, unfamiliar runes or ideograms, and Deacon tries to memorize them because they might be important later.

"Is that a fact?" Soda says, his eyes on her breasts, her hard brown nipples. "That must'a been a sight to see."

"She gets lonely, so far away," and now the woman's reaching for the knife tucked into the leather sheath strapped around her left thigh. "It's cold in Heaven. Cold and dark and the stars are farther away than God."

"Show me," Soda whispers and there's a sound from directly overhead, something heavy dragged slowly across a floor, something rolled end over end, and Deacon glances up at the ceiling. There are dozens of stains blooming on the cracked and sagging plaster, opening themselves like red-brown roses, living flowers pressed flat by the weight the woman carries in her soul. One of the stains begins to drip, and soon the others follow its example.

"You don't have the eyes to see such things," the woman says, "not yet," and opens her mouth very wide, and at first Deacon thinks that she's only yawning. Her teeth like polished ivory, white daggers in her pink gums, lion yawn, hyena yawn, and now there's so much of the red shit dripping from the ceiling of Soda's apartment that Deacon's getting wet and wishing he'd thought to dream an umbrella.

Upstairs, men and women laugh softly among themselves, the clink of glasses and there's orchestra music, and the dragging, rolling sound grows suddenly louder. The blonde woman draws her knife and it flicks open in a flash of silver fire before she slices Soda's throat. More surprise in his wide eyes than either fear or pain, and dark blood dribbles from the corners of his mouth to stain the sheets.

"Now, you're a different story, Deacon Silvey," the woman says softly, turning away from Soda gasping and strangling on the bed. "You have vision an oracle would envy. You can see all the way down to the rotten heart of creation."

"I never asked for it," Deacon says, unable to look away, the sticky rain from the ruined ceiling painting her pale flesh in streaks of crimson, her yellow eyes flashing red orange in the gloom of Soda's basement. "I never wanted it."

"Do you think that matters?" she asks. "Do you really think I give a shit?"

"No," he replies and the phone begins to ring, but it's all the way on the other side of the room. He'd have to walk past her to answer it and never mind if this is only a dream, the phone can ring all night long before he takes one goddamned step closer to the woman with her burning eyes and stiletto fingers.

"You have a lovely wife, Deacon Silvey," the woman growls with the voice of storms and hungry dogs, and he opens his eyes, then, awake in an instant, but the phone's still ringing. His clothes and hair are drenched in a clammy, cold sweat, and his heart's racing, his body bathed in the afternoon sunlight spilling warm across the bed. And his head's pounding, the invisible railroad spike driven deep into his skull, so he knows for sure that he's awake. Deacon shuts his eyes again, digs his fingers into Chance's cornflower-blue comforter, hanging on, and in a minute or two the phone gives up and stops ringing.

*   *   *

Chance slows down and turns off Twenty-second onto Morris, trading asphalt for the bumpity cobblestones, and there's Deacon walking past The Peanut Depot, Deacon in his black sunglasses, unshaved and his hair so wild and spiky he looks like a punk rocker or a crazy, homeless man. She honks the horn and he stops beside a stack of burlap sacks filled with roasted peanuts, stops and glances behind him as if maybe the sound came from somewhere back there. Chance pulls over and parks the Impala directly across the street from him.

"Deacon!" she shouts from her open window and his head snaps around again so that he's staring straight at her, but still no evidence that he's *seen* her, no hint of recognition on his stubbled face. *He looks lost,* she thinks, and then, *No, he looks drunk,* and the sudden, dizzy surge of fear and anger and adrenaline so strong her heart skips a beat, and the baby kicks sympathetically.

He takes one hesitant step in her direction, bumps into the burlap sacks and stops again. Chance curses, kills the engine and opens her door, unfastens her seat belt and wriggles out from behind the steering wheel. By the time she's standing on the pavement, Deacon's crossing the narrow street towards her.

"Where were you going?" she asks. "Why didn't you answer the phone? I tried to call before I left campus."

"I was just walking," he replies and hooks his thumbs into the front pockets of his jeans. "I needed to get out of the apartment for a while, so I was just walking."

"Have you been drinking, Deke?"

He takes a deep breath, then shakes his head very slowly and gazes past Chance at the car.

"There's no point lying to me about it."

"I'm not lying. If I want to get drunk, I'll fucking get drunk. You know that."

"Right," she says, and leans against the Impala, taking some of the weight off her feet. "I know that."

"It's my head. It's bad, and I had a nightmare."

"I tried to call you."

"Yeah, the phone woke me up. But I didn't get to it in time."

"Jesus," Chance whispers, feeling more ashamed of herself than relieved, and she looks down at Deacon's feet because she can't see her own; one of his black tennis shoes is untied. "I'm sorry. I was scared, that's all. I had a really shitty day and I shouldn't have accused you—"

"No, I understand. I've definitely been *thinking* about getting drunk. I been thinking about it long and hard. But I was only going for a walk."

For a moment neither of them says anything. A train whistle wails, far off but coming closer, and a tall black man in overalls and a white T-shirt brings out another sack of peanuts and stacks it by the curb.

"I may have to do this thing," Deacon says. "I don't think I'm going to have any choice."

Chance looks up, stares into the flat black lenses of his sunglasses. "Of course you have a choice," she says. "You always have a choice, so don't stand there and tell me that you don't."

"You weren't there. You didn't see his body."

"But you promised me, you *swore* you'd never get mixed up in this shit again."

"I know what I said."

"This isn't your responsibility, Deke. That's why we have policemen. Let them do their job."

Deacon takes off his sunglasses and squints at her with his watery, bloodshot eyes.

"We aren't going to argue about this, Chance," he says. "Not this time."

"Fine then, you do whatever the hell you want to do," and she turns back to the car, better to get away from him now before she says something she won't be able to apologize for later. She gets in and shuts the door, turns the key in the ignition and the Impala grumbles reluctantly back to life again.

"I'll be home in a little while," Deacon says. "I just need to walk," and he puts the sunglasses on again.

"I'm not stopping you, Deke," and she drives away, leaves him standing there in the middle of the street. When she reaches their building at the intersection with Twenty-third, Chance glances at the rearview mirror and he's gone.

CHAPTER FIVE

The Circle and The Line

Scarborough Pentecost and the pretty black-haired girl who usually calls herself Starling Jane climb the concrete stairway leading up and up to the long viaduct beside the old steel mill. As they go, the girl counts off the steps aloud—fifteen at the first landing, thirty-one at the second, and then she notices a nest with three robin chicks tucked into a cranny beneath the highway. She stops and leans out over the handrail to get a better view of the baby birds and, "Will you please come on," Scarborough says impatiently, wishing again that he could have left her in Atlanta, or Charleston, or anywhere, wishing that he'd never gotten stuck with her in the first place.

"But just look at them," she says and cautiously reaches out towards the birds, three gray-brown, cream-speckled chicks huddled in a nest woven from twigs and dead grass, strips of plastic and paper and bits of a foam coffee cup. The cement behind them is spattered with chalky white smears of robin shit. All three birds remain absolutely motionless as her fingertips hover in the air just above their heads and the traffic roars past overhead, three sets of wide black eyes staring silently back at her.

"If you touch them, their mother will let them starve to death," Scarborough warns her and he glances at the angry momma robin perched on a nearby power line. She squawks twice and glares at them with all the fury a robin can muster.

"That's not true," Starling Jane says, skeptical, indignant, and her fingers drift an inch or so nearer the chicks. "She wouldn't do that."

"Oh yes, she would," Scarborough says, watching the distraught mother bird.

"No. Not just because I touched them."

"If you touch them, then they'll smell like you."

"I don't stink."

"She thinks you do," and Scarborough points at the bird on the wire. "If her chicks smell like you, she won't believe they're hers and she won't take care of them anymore."

"That's the stupidest thing I've ever heard."

"I'm afraid robins aren't terribly bright creatures."

Reluctantly, the girl pulls her hand back from the nest and frowns up at Scarborough, then at the momma robin. "Just because I *touched* them?" she asks. "That's absolutely wicked. What kind of mother would do such a thing?"

"We don't have all day," Scarborough tells her and Starling Jane sighs, shakes her head, and follows him up the stairway, goes back to counting steps and there are forty-seven at the top.

"That's not a bad number," she says. "Four and seven are both lucky numbers for me, because I was born on the seventh day of the fourth month of—"

"Bullshit. You don't *know* when you were born, Starling," and Scarborough takes a very small pair of binoculars from the inside pocket of his black leather jacket. "Just like the rest of us."

"They told me I could pick a birthday," she says. "And I picked April seventh a long time ago."

"Good for you. But it doesn't mean anything."

"Meaning is in the eye of the beholder."

"That's beauty, you silly twit."

"Same thing," Starling Jane sneers back at him and then she watches the cars and trucks rushing past while Scarborough peers through his binoculars at the low, tree-covered mountain two or three miles south of the steel mill. To the west, Birmingham's stingy, uneven skyline blocks out the horizon and the setting sun; to the north and east, a gray, industrial wasteland threaded with back streets and railroads stretches away from the viaduct. There's a chilly breeze and she hugs herself, buttons her violet cardigan and wishes she'd worn something warmer.

"The damned trees are in my way," Scarborough grumbles and starts walking again, searching for a better view, leaving her behind. Starling Jane stands beside the guardrail and watches him go, willowy boy with his quick, determined stride, his narrow shoulders and straight brown hair tied up in a long ponytail. He stops and scowls back at her.

"Well, what are you waiting for?"

"I was just looking around, that's all," she says and pretends that she was examining the old steel mill instead of watching him. She glances over the guardrail at the odd little park that's been fashioned from the ruins of the mill, fifty feet down to a wide green lawn with its artful scatter of metal sculptures, rust-red skeletons like the shells of giant insects or the wrought-iron bones of dinosaurs. There's an ancient steam shovel and a toothy ring of severed steam-shovel jaws laid out like megalithic stones near weathered heaps of slag. Farther on, a long casting shed where men once poured molten iron to cool in sandy channels, and past the shed, the towering smokestacks and blast stoves, rickety catwalks and a silver water tower with SLOSS printed across it in tall black letters. Starling Jane hugs herself tighter and hurries to catch up with Scarborough.

"Who was Sloss?" she asks, pointing at the water tower.

"How the hell am I supposed to know?"

"Sorry. I thought you knew *everything*," and she smiles a sly, secretive smile and looks back down at the steam shovel.

"Maybe it was the name of the mill. I don't know."

"Maybe so," she says. "Do you think she knows we're here yet?"

"Maybe," Scarborough says. "Probably," and he peers through his binoculars again. There's a gap between the casting shed and the furnaces and from here he has an unobstructed view of the mountain. The tawny, autumn-browned heads of trees, the roofs of buildings, a cast-iron giant standing on a stone pedestal at the mountain's summit.

"That's Vulcan," he says. "The house is supposed to be somewhere just west of there."

"Will she be waiting for us?"

"She's always waiting for someone," he replies.

Starling turns towards downtown, thinking how cities all start to look the same after just a while. The same harried loneliness behind tinted skyscraper windows and stone walls and she wishes she were more like Scarborough and never got homesick.

"Vulcan was the god of the forge," she says.

"That's what the Romans said," and now he's examining a great gash through the mountainside that men have carved out for the highway, tries to imagine how the mountain must have looked before that wedge of rock was blasted loose and hauled away.

"The Greeks called him Hephaestus," Starling Jane says. "He was born deformed and his mother cast him down from Mount Olympus. Of all the gods, he was the only one who was ugly."

"Is that a fact?" Scarborough asks her, returning his binoculars to his jacket pocket. He turns his back on the steel mill and the mountain and sits down on the guardrail.

"I don't know if it's a fact or not, but it's the truth."

"Poor fucker," Scarborough laughs and he jabs a thumb over his shoulder at the distant statue. "And the best gig he could get was guarding this dried-up old cunt of a city." He takes a crumpled pack of Camels out of his jacket and offers one to Starling Jane.

"It doesn't even have a river," she says sadly, glances at the pack of cigarettes and shakes her head. "If I died here, how would my soul ever find its way down to the sea?"

"I'm sure they have sewers," Scarborough mutters around the filter of his Camel. He tries to light it with a match, but the wind immediately blows the flame out.

"That's not funny."

"Yes it is," and he strikes a second match, but the wind blows it out, as well. "You just don't have a sense of humor."

"I just don't want to die here."

"No one from Providence has a goddamn sense of humor."

"There are bad places in the world to die. I think this is one of them," she says quietly and Scarborough curses when the wind snuffs out another match. Starling Jane takes the book away from him and strikes a fourth one, cups a hand around the flame long enough for him to light his cigarette, then she blows it out and drops the smoldering match over the edge of the viaduct. Scarborough takes a long drag and then breathes out a smoky gray ghost for the wind to shred between its invisible teeth.

"You're not going to die here, bluebird," he says, trying very hard to sound certain even if he isn't, her apprehension starting to rub off on him and Scarborough wonders how much trouble he'd be in if he put her on a train straight back to New England.

"I'm sure that's exactly what the others thought, but that didn't stop her from killing them."

"Yeah, well just do me a favor and shut the fuck up about it for five minutes, okay?" and he doesn't look at her because it's easier if he doesn't have to see her eyes; he smokes his Camel and watches the cars passing them by, all the careless, oblivious faces safe behind windshields and steering wheels, and no one looks back at him. After a minute or two, Starling Jane starts whistling an old gospel song she heard on the radio the day before. Scarborough takes a last, deep drag and flicks the butt to the asphalt at their feet, zips up his leather jacket and starts walking back towards the concrete stairway.

"What now?" she calls after him and "It's time to have a talk with Mr. Silvey," he says and keeps on walking.

At first he doesn't even know that he's going to Sadie, just walking, motion for the dumb and simple sake of motion, a talisman against inertia, and Deacon leaves Morris Avenue behind him and crosses the arched beam bridge on Twenty-second Street. Leaving Chance behind, too, and maybe later he'll try to explain it to her and she won't listen because she's never been able to talk about that part of him or even acknowledge that it might be real. The old bridge carries him high above the train tracks, orderly tangle of iron rails and wooden ties below, the Rainbow Bridge according to a bronze plaque at the top, and the many crumbling balusters have been wrapped round and round with silver-gray duct tape, the city's half-assed idea of repair after chunks of falling concrete smashed through the windshields of cars in the streets and parking lots below. That was a couple of years ago and now the duct tape has begun to fray and disintegrate, as well.
"Leave it to Birmingham to try and fix a bridge with duct tape," Chance said the first time they saw what the Street and Sanitation people had done.

Deacon pauses at the crest of the bridge to watch a freight train passing underneath, rattling away towards the sunset. Rusted boxcars and tankers filled with chemicals, empty bulkhead flats and gondola cars, finally the red caboose bringing up the rear. By morning that train will be all the way to New Orleans or Memphis or Biloxi, he thinks, and some part of him wishes he were going with it. He waits until the train has grown small and far away, and then Deacon follows Twenty-second southeast, past used-car lots and gas stations, finally crosses Eighth Avenue into a tract of run-down Eisenhower Era housing projects.

"Yo, white boy," a husky, male voice shouts from a backyard and someone laughs. "You lost? You need directions?" and Deacon doesn't reply, keeps walking, keeps his eyes on the sidewalk, counting cracks and dandelions, the distance from one streetlight pool to the next, until he's safely out the other side again. The street curves gently and climbs a hill, and there's the apartment building where Sadie Jasper lives, red and chocolate-brown bricks and screened-in front porches, low rent but not quite a slum, so she could be doing worse. Next door to the building is a seedy little nightclub, The Nick, like a house trailer built from cinder blocks; one of his old haunts, a mecca for cheap beer and deafeningly loud rock music, pool tables and smoky darkness.

Deacon glances back the way he's come, towards the projects and downtown, towards home, the dusk deepening quickly to night, and then he looks back at the apartment building. There's a light burning in one of Sadie's windows and he imagines her busy at the noisy old Royal typewriter she writes her stories on, the desk she built from a door and two sawhorses. By now, Chance is probably starting to wonder where he is, when he's coming home, if maybe he's found a liquor store.

He follows the short, crunchy path of crushed brick and limestone gravel from the sidewalk to the front door of the building, finds it unlocked and steps inside. The hallway smells like Indian food and stale cigarette smoke, the fainter stink of mold, and he walks down the short hall lit by bare, irregularly placed forty-watt bulbs. Sadie's place up on the second floor and Deacon climbs the stairs two and three at a time before he can think better of it, before he talks himself out of seeing her.

Her place is right at the top of the stairs and he knocks a little harder than necessary, afraid she won't be there after all, that maybe she only left the light burning so it wouldn't be dark when she comes home. No one answers, so he starts to knock again, and then "Hold your horses," Sadie calls out from inside. "I'm coming."

Deacon takes a deep breath and lets it out slowly, wishing that his heart would quit racing. Not like he's doing anything wrong, seeing an old friend he's hardly spoken to in ages, not like he's come here looking for booze or a fuck, just someone to talk to, someone who'll listen to the things Chance won't.

The door opens and Sadie's standing there in a long black T-shirt a size or two too large, BAUHAUS and a silk-screened shot of the sleepwalker from *The Cabinet of Dr. Caligari,* fishnet tights and a pair of pink socks on her feet. At first she looks confused more than surprised to see him, Deacon Silvey the very last person she expected to see tonight, and then Sadie laughs and smiles. Her startling ice-blue eyes seem very bright in the dim light.

"As I live and breathe," she says in her worst Tennessee Williams drawl. "Will you just look at what the cat dragged in," and he smiles nervously back at her.

"Are you busy?" he asks. "I know I should have called first, but I—"

"Are you kidding me?" and she steps over the threshold and throws both her arms tight around his neck, washing him in her private aroma of cloves and tea rose, vanilla and the stuff she uses to dye her hair the color of ripe cherries. Her hands are warm and damp.

"If you're busy, I can come back some other time. I really should've called first," Deacon says again.

"Phooey. I was just doing dishes," she says. "So you practically saved my life." And then she takes him by the hand and drags him out of the hallway and into her small and cluttered apartment. The smells of Indian cooking and cigarette smoke are immediately replaced by sandalwood incense and a slightly stronger, more pervasive version of the Sadie smell, something he'd probably find cloying if it weren't so nostalgic. She points him at a threadbare sofa upholstered in corduroy the color of mustard and "Sit your fanny down," Sadie Jasper says. "I'll be right back. Want some coffee?"

"Sure, if it's not too much trouble."

"Milk, no sugar, right?"

"Yeah," Deacon says.

"Coming right up," and she disappears through a curtain of amber plastic beads.

Deacon steps past the magazine-littered coffee table, sits down on the sofa and its shot springs groan and creak loudly beneath him. He glances around the room, at the plaster walls decorated with an incongruous mix of horror movie posters and Pre-Raphaelite prints, Dario Argento and John Carpenter rubbing shoulders with Rossetti and Waterhouse. The floor is stacked with books and videotapes because there's no room left on any of the shelves. A moth-eaten, taxidermied raccoon stands sentry on top of the television set, surrounded by a circle of votive candles and a couple of bird skulls. Almost everything exactly the way it was the last time he was in Sadie's apartment, and he tries to remember how long ago that was.

"Does Mrs. Silvey know you're here?" Sadie calls from the kitchen and "No," he shouts back at her.

The curtain parts again, Sadie carrying two steaming, mismatched coffee mugs, and then the beaded strands swing and clack noisily together behind her.

"I'd just made a fresh pot," she says. "The milk's skim. Hope you don't mind."

"Er, no," Deacon says, taking the mug she holds out to him. "That's fine."

She sits down at the other end of the creaky yellow sofa and blows on her coffee. "Would it piss her off if she found out?" she asks and it takes Deacon a second or two to realize what she's asking. He shrugs and stares at his milky coffee; it smells like chicory and he hates the taste of chicory.

"These days I never know what's gonna piss Chance off," he says. "But yeah, I think it probably would."

"Does she think I'm a bad influence?"

"Something like that."

"I'm flattered," Sadie says and sips tentatively at her coffee.

"She's just afraid I'll start drinking again. I can't say that I blame her. I'm a bastard when I'm drunk."

Sadie nods her head and dips a pinkie finger into her coffee.

"Hell, I'm a bastard period, but you know what I mean."

"Yeah, I know what you mean," Sadie says and licks a drop of coffee off her fingertip. "When's the kid due?"

"Almost any minute now," he says and sets his mug down on a magazine cover.

"That's gotta be a total mind-fuck, Deke. I mean, I can't even begin to comprehend how someone copes with that sort of responsibility."

"Join the club," Deacon says, wishing he hadn't left the apartment without his cigarettes. He considers bumming one or two off Sadie, but she probably doesn't have anything but Djarum cloves, and he'd rather smoke a dirty old mop.

"Do you know if it's going to be a boy or a girl? They can tell you that now, can't they?"

"If you want to know, but Chance wants to wait until it's born and find out the old-fashioned way."

"Have you guys decided on names already?"

Deacon picks up his coffee cup again, chicory or no chicory, and takes a swallow before he answers.

"Joe, if it's a boy, after Chance's grandfather."

"And if it's a girl?"

"If it's a girl, either Emma Jean or Elizabeth. Chance hasn't made up her mind yet."

Sadie shakes her head. "If *I* ever had a daughter," she says, "I'd name her Hermione, after that girl in the Harry Potter books."

"I'm sure she'd just love you for that," Deacon replies and drinks more of the coffee, trying to ignore the peppery aftertaste.

"It's no worse than *Chance*. Why didn't her parents just name her Opportunity and get it the hell over with?"

"You might just have a point there, Miss Jasper."

Sadie laughs out loud and leans back against the sofa, pressing herself into the tattered cushions; she props her feet up on the table and Deacon can see that there are small holes worn in the toes of both her pink socks.

"I've really fucking missed this, Deke. I mean, I've really missed you. There isn't anyone else I can talk to the way we used to talk."

"Yeah," he says and sets his cup down again. "I guess that's why I'm here. There's something I need to talk about and I couldn't think of anyone else who wouldn't think I was crazy."

"What do you—?" she starts, but the phone in the kitchen rings and "Shit," Sadie hisses. "Just a minute, okay? I'll be right back, I swear. It's probably just my mother." And then she leaves Deacon alone on the mustard-colored sofa and vanishes into the kitchen again. He sighs and stares across the room at the stuffed raccoon, which seems to be watching him intently from the top of the television with its dark glass eyes.

"Yeah, well fuck you too," he mutters at the raccoon and finishes his coffee.

Deacon was drunk the night he met Sadie Jasper for the first time, back in the day, years ago now but just a few months after he'd finally left Atlanta. The boozy good old days, and he worked every other night at a Southside coin-op laundry and then at a produce warehouse in the mornings, sleeping away the afternoons and staying drunk as much as possible, as much as he could afford. A steamy August evening and she'd talked him into going to an abandoned warehouse with her to see a ghost. Nothing half as simple as that, but that's what they would say whenever it came up later—"Remember the night we saw the ghost in the Harris building?"

Sadie had heard people talking, rumors that Deacon had once worked for the police, that he could find dead people and missing bodies and even murderers just by visiting crime scenes, by touching an article of clothing or a corpse.

"So you're Deacon Silvey," she said and smiled, a triumphant, pleased-with-herself sort of smile. "The psychic criminologist," and Deacon shook his head. "Not exactly," he replied. "I'm just a drunk who sees things sometimes."

"That's not so unusual," Sadie said.

"That's what I keep telling people, but no one ever seems to listen."

But he followed her to the old Harris Transfer and Warehouse Building on Twenty-third Street, walking a few steps behind her, sipping from his quart bottle of McCall's, the cheap gin so none of it would ever matter, not now or in the morning, and what could this little goth girl have to show him, anyway? Just a game and maybe if he played along, maybe if he looked at her spooky place, oohed and aahed whenever oohs and aahs were called for, maybe he wouldn't have to sleep alone for a night or two.

"I used to know a girl," Sadie said. "Back when I still lived with my parents down in Mobile. She was a clairvoyant, too, but it finally drove her crazy. She was always in and out of psych wards."

"I'm not clairvoyant," Deacon said. "I get impressions, that's all. What I did for the cops, I helped them find lost things."

"Lost things," Sadie said thoughtfully. "Yeah, that's a good word for it."

"A good word for what?" he asked and glared up at the building, late-nineteenth-century brick, rusted iron bars over broken windows and those jagged holes either swallowing the streetlight or spitting it back out because it was blacker than midnight under a coffin in there, black like the first second before the universe was born and Deacon was beginning to wonder if he'd underestimated Sadie Jasper.

"You'll see," she said and this time when Sadie smiled it made him think of a very hungry animal or the Grinch that stole Christmas. Deacon took another long pull off the bottle of gin and wiped his mouth.

They didn't go in through the front door, of course, the locked and boarded-up front door set inside its marble arch and HARRIS chiseled deep into the pediment. Instead, she led him down the narrow alley to a spot where the iron burglar bars had been pried loose and there were three or four plastic milk crates stacked conveniently under the window. Sadie scrambled up the makeshift steps and slipped inside, slipped smooth over the shattered glass like a raw oyster over sharp teeth, like she'd done this a hundred times before and for all he knew she had. Deacon looked apprehensively up at the building again, had another swallow of McCall's, and then checked for cops before he followed her.

However dark it had seemed from the outside, it was twice that dark inside, and the broken glass under Deacon's boots made a sound like walking on cornflakes.

"Better hold up a sec," Sadie said and suddenly there was light, the weak and narrow beam from a silver flashlight in her hand; white light across the concrete floor to show glittering chips and shards of window, a few scraps of cardboard and what looked like a filthy sweater lying in one corner. Nothing else, just that wide and dust-drowned room, and then Sadie motioned towards a doorway with the beam of light.

"The stairs are right over there," she said and started walking towards the doorway. Deacon stayed close, not wanting to get too far away from the flashlight. The air in the warehouse smelled like mildew and dust, a rank, closed away from the world odor that made his nose itch and his eyes water.

"Oh, you'll want to watch out for that spot over there," Sadie said and the beam swung suddenly to her left and down and Deacon could see the gaping hole in the floor, big enough to drop a pickup truck through, that hole, big enough and black enough that maybe it was where all the dark inside the building was coming from, spilling up from the basement or subbasement, perhaps, and then her flashlight swept right again and he didn't have to look at the hole anymore. Now there was a flight of concrete stairs instead, ascending into the nothing past the reach of Sadie's flashlight.

"It's all the way at the top," she said.

"What's all the way at the top, Sadie? What's waiting for us up there?"

"It's easier if I just show you, if you see it for yourself," and then she started up the stairs, taking them two at a time and carrying the light away with her, leaving him alone next to the hole. Deacon glanced forlornly back towards the broken window and then hurried to catch her. They climbed up and up and up the spiral stairwell, like Alice tumbling backwards and nothing to mark their progress past each floor but a small landing or closed door or a place where a door should be, nothing to mark the time but the dull echo of their feet against the cement. Sadie was always three or four steps ahead of him and finally he yelled at her to slow the fuck down.

"But we're almost there," she called back and kept going.

And then there were no more stairs left to climb, a final landing and a single, small window, but at least it wasn't quite so dark at the top as it had been at the bottom. Deacon leaned against the wall, wheezing, trying to catch his breath. His sides hurt and his legs ached; he stared out through the flyblown glass at the streets and rooftops below, a couple of cars and it all seemed a thousand miles away, or only a film of the world and if he broke this window, there would be nothing on the other side at all.

"Over here," Sadie whispered and the closeness of her voice did nothing about the hard, lonely feeling settling over him. "This hallway here," and she jabbed the flashlight at the darkness like a knife as he turned away from the window.

"The first time I saw it, I was tripping," she said, "so I didn't think it was real. But I started dreaming about it and had to come back to see. To be sure."

Deacon stepped slowly away from the window, three slow steps and he was through the doorway and standing beside Sadie. "There," she said and switched the flashlight off. "All the way at the other end of the hall." For a long moment Deacon couldn't see anything at all, a darting, purple-orange afterimage from the flashlight and nothing much else while his pupils swelled, making room for light that wasn't there.

"Do you feel it yet, Deacon?" she asked and he started to say that he didn't feel a goddamn thing, but would she please turn the flashlight back on. And then he *did* feel something, cold air flowing thick and heavy around them, open icebox air to fog their breath and send a prickling rash of goose bumps down his arms. And it wasn't *just* cold, it was indifference, the freezing temperature of an apathy so absolute, so perfect; Deacon took a step backwards, one hand up to cover his mouth, but it was already too late and the gin and his supper came up and splattered loudly on the floor at their feet.

"Damn," she said, sounding surprised now, maybe just a little frightened. "Are you okay?" and he opened his eyes, wanted to slap her just for asking, but he only managed to nod his head as it filled with the cold and began to throb at the temples. "Do you want me to help you up?" and he hadn't even realized he was on the floor, on his knees and she was bending over him. His stomach rolled again and Deacon stared past Sadie, down the hall, that long stretch of nothing at all but closed doors and another tiny window way down at the other end.

"There," she said. "It's there."

Sadie was pulling him to his feet, but Deacon didn't take his eyes off the window, the distant rectangle less inky by stingy degrees than the hall. And he knew instinctively that what he was seeing was only the dimmest shadow of the thing itself, that fluid stain rushing wild across the walls, washing watercolor thin over the windowpane; a shadow that could be the wings of a great, black bird or long, jointed legs skittering through some deep and secret ocean. But it was *really* neither of those things, and nothing else he would ever understand, no convenient, comprehensible nightmare, and he shut his eyes again. Sadie was holding his right hand and squeezing so hard it hurt.

"Don't you *see* it?"

"Don't look at it," he croaked, his throat raw from vomiting, raw from the cold, and he imagined that the floor beneath him and Sadie had begun to soften, to tilt, and soon it would send them both sliding helplessly past the closed doors, towards the window, towards it.

"It doesn't want to be seen," he said, tasting blood and so he knew that he'd bitten his tongue or his lip. "It wasn't ever *meant* to be seen."

"But it's beautiful, Deacon," Sadie replied, and there was wonder in her voice and an awful sadness that hurt to hear.

Then suddenly there was the smell of burning leaves and something sweet and rotten, something dead left by the side of the highway, left to bake beneath the summer sun, and the last thing, before Deacon lost consciousness, slipped mercifully from himself into a place where even the cold couldn't follow, the very last thing—a sound like crying that wasn't crying and a wind that wasn't blowing through the long hall.

After Deacon has finished talking—the police and Soda's mutilated body, all the things he saw when he touched the bed, the nightmare—he stares down into his empty coffee cup and waits for Sadie to say something. The light brown stain there at the bottom of his mug like muddy water and right now he's so thirsty he could drink a whole goddamn river of whiskey. Sadie lights another cigarette and the pungent white-gray smoke leaks from her parted lips like an escaping soul.

"You didn't tell the police what you saw? Not any of it?" she asks and Deacon shakes his head and sets the cup back down on the coffee table.

"No, not yet," he replies.

"Why not?"

"Because they probably aren't going to listen to me. Because Chance doesn't want me mixed up in this. Because *I* don't want me mixed up in this. Take your pick."

"But this woman knows your *name*, Deke," Sadie says, reaching for an ashtray and Deacon shakes his head again.

"That was only a dream."

"Are you sure of that?" she asks him and taps ash into a huge, opalescent abalone shell. "I keep thinking of what Nietzsche said—"

"Nietzsche? I'm sorry, Sadie. You just lost me."

"You know, from *Thus Spake Zarathustra*? If you look too long into the abyss, the abyss might begin to look back into you?"

"Yeah," Deacon says and rubs slowly at the sandpaper stubble on his chin. "Right. Nietzsche."

"No, I'm serious. What you do, when you see these things, you don't know how it works. If you're picking up impressions left by other people, then maybe you're leaving impressions behind at the same time. And if Soda's killer was also sensitive, it could work both ways."

Deacon rubs his chin and stares at the stuffed raccoon on top of the TV. He's just noticed that it has a gold tooth.

"Hasn't that ever occurred to you?"

"No, Sadie. I can honestly say that has never occurred to me. But I'm sure I'll sleep much better now that you've pointed it out."

"Deacon, you should tell the police what you saw," Sadie says, and he thinks maybe she sounds afraid now. "And you should tell them about the dream, too."

"Did you know your raccoon has a gold tooth?" he asks her.

"He came that way. I found him at a yard sale."

"That's fucked up," Deacon says and leans back on the sofa.

"Why are you trying to change the subject?"

"I'm not trying to change the subject. I just never saw a stuffed raccoon with a goddamned gold tooth before."

"Please promise me that you'll go to the police," Sadie says.

"Do you think he got it before or after he died?" Deacon asks and points at the raccoon.

"Christ, Deacon, I don't know. He just came that way. Will you please shut the hell up about the raccoon and listen to me?"

"I should be heading home," he says, glancing at his wrist as if he wore a watch. "I should at least give Chance a call and let her know I'm not dead or drunk or something."

"Why would the cops have come to you in the first place, if they aren't going to take what you tell them seriously?"

Deacon turns towards her and silently watches Sadie for a moment while she squints back at him through a restless veil of clove-scented smoke.

"People don't always want to hear the answers to the questions they ask you," he says. "This Detective Downs guy, he's just going through the motions because someone higher up gave him an order. I guarantee you he was relieved when I told him I didn't see anything, and he's probably of the opinion that if he never has to look at my sorry face again, it'll be too soon."

Sadie frowns and stubs her cigarette out in the abalone shell, then immediately lights another one. "Then maybe his boss, whoever gave him the order, maybe he'll listen," she says.

"Maybe so," Deacon tells her, even though he doesn't really believe it. "And maybe Chance won't divorce me for getting involved in this shit."

"It's not like you volunteered."

"But I could have said no, Sadie. I could have told Downs to go fuck himself, that I had no idea what he was talking about."

"Yes, but you *didn't* and now this is something that you have to do. But you already know that, don't you? You knew that before you even came here tonight."

"Did I?"

"I think so. I think you just needed someone to tell you it was the right thing to do."

"Well, then," he says, sighs, and pats the yellow sofa cushion between them. "Thanks for the coffee, Miss Jasper. And thanks for listening."

"You're very welcome, Mr. Silvey. I wish you would come more often, that's all. Maybe if you brought Chance sometime, maybe then she'd see I'm not some Jezebel, luring you back to a life of vice and loose women."

Deacon smiles and "We'll have to see about that," he says. "After the baby's born, possibly. Right now, though, I don't think she's much for socializing with anyone."

"I have some fossil shark teeth and trilobites my uncle sent me from Morocco. I could show them to her. We could bond."

This time Deacon doesn't answer her, sits staring at his hands, the thick, callused ends of his fingers, his yellowed nails, thinking about the blonde woman from his vision, the woman from his dream. *You have a lovely wife, Deacon Silvey,* growled in that animal's voice, and he tells himself again that part was only a nightmare. Only his aching head and his anxiety, his worries over Chance and the baby getting caught up in the crazy shit he'd seen in Soda's apartment, his subconscious playing a game of mix and match.

"Do you have a pencil and a piece of paper?" he asks Sadie.

"Yeah, sure," she says, not asking what he wants it for. "Just a sec. I'll get it for you," and she goes away and comes back with a few sheets of blank typing paper and a nubby black pencil. The eraser's missing and Deacon can see her tooth marks gouged into the wood.

"Maybe you'll find something like this in one of your books," he says, and draws the circle from the wall above Soda's bed, the hard black line beneath it. "Like I said, there was some kind of writing all around the edges, but I can't remember it. If I can get photos from Downs, I'll bring copies of them by to you later."

"Sure," she says and Deacon hands her the drawing. "If I find out anything at all, I'll let you know. And you're going to call them in the morning, right? The police?"

"Unless Chance kills me tonight for wandering off like this." And he thanks her again for the coffee, the coffee and the company and the raccoon with one gold tooth, and she walks him to the door.

"Maybe you ought to call a taxi, Deke," she says, standing in the doorway and Deacon's already on his way down the stairs. "This really isn't the best neighborhood after dark."

"Before dark, either," he replies. "But no, I'll be fine. I'm a big boy," and then he's gone, and Sadie stands staring at the drawing, the circle and the slash, until she hears the front door of the apartment building slam shut.

Chance is eating salty, microwaved popcorn and watching television, an old black-and-white western, Jimmy Stewart in *Winchester '73*, when there's a knock at the apartment door. And her first thought is that it must be Deacon, that he forgot his keys when he left. She sets the half-empty bowl of popcorn down on the arm of the love seat and gets slowly, clumsily, to her feet.

"You're just going to have to hang on a minute, Deke," she mutters. Once she's standing, Chance pauses to get her breath, ignoring the pain in her back and feet, and stares down the dark hall leading to the door. The only light in the apartment is coming from the TV screen, flickering salt-and-pepper light that doesn't even reach into the hallway and so she switches on the floor lamp beside the love seat. But the far end of the hall is still very dark.

The knocking starts again, more insistent than before.

"I'm coming!" she shouts at the door and the knocking stops.

Halfway down the hall there's a switch for the overhead light in the foyer and she flips it on.

And the knocking starts again.

"Jesus Christ, Deacon," she says, because it has to be Deacon, all the locks and security codes downstairs to keep everyone else out, so it's either Deacon or a neighbor and all the neighbors keep to themselves. "I'm coming as fast as I can."

Chance reaches the door, turns the dead bolt and "Deacon?" she whispers loudly through the wood. "That *is* you, isn't it?" She wishes there were a peephole, but there isn't because the landlord says the building is secure enough already and they don't need a peephole. She's asked Deacon to install one himself, but it's on the long list of things he still hasn't gotten around to doing.

"Deacon?"

A tense moment of silence, just the abrupt sound of gunfire from the television, and Chance takes her hand off the doorknob and begins to back away.

"Mrs. Silvey?" a man's voice calls out from the other side of the door. "I'm here to see your husband."

"My husband isn't here," she replies, then thinks better of it and adds, "but he'll be home any minute now."

"I need to speak with him. It's very important. He's expecting me. Didn't he tell you he was expecting me?"

"No," Chance says. "He didn't tell me he was expecting anyone," but she reaches for the door again. The little voice in her head telling her that she's overreacting, and it's easy enough to imagine Deacon making an appointment to talk to someone and then forgetting all about it.

"Maybe you should come back later," she says. "He should be home soon."

"It's very important that I speak with Deacon, Mrs. Silvey."

"I understand that, but he isn't here. Maybe you should wait for him in the lobby."

On the other side of the door a woman laughs softly and then mumbles something Chance can't make out.

"There's no reason to be afraid of me, Mrs. Silvey, I assure you. I only want to talk to Deacon."

"I believe you," she says, trying to sound calm, trying to sound friendly, but she lets go of the doorknob for the second time. "I'm sorry. But he wouldn't want me to open the door to strangers when he isn't here. You should wait downstairs."

"I don't have a lot of time, Mrs. Silvey," the man says, and he's beginning to sound impatient. "I've come a long way to talk to your husband."

"I'm sorry."

"If you would just open the door, I can explain."

Chance glances over her right shoulder at the coat closet, the white folding doors pulled shut; some of her field gear is stored in there, a geologist's pick and a few chisels, and she takes a step towards the closet.

"Please, Mrs. Silvey. That's really not necessary," the man says and the woman laughs again. "You don't have to worry about defending yourself. No one's going to try to hurt you. I only want to talk to—"

"I'm calling the police now," Chance says, all the calm draining out of her voice as she opens the closet and searches for the pick on the shelf above the coats.

"Deacon's already talked with the police, hasn't he?" the man asks. "That's why I need to speak with him."

"I have a gun," she says, though she can't even find the pick and the most dangerous thing in the closet seems to be an umbrella. Her heart's racing now and her mouth's gone dry; from the television comes the sound of running horses.

"No, you don't, Mrs. Silvey. Please, don't be afraid. I didn't mean to frighten you. I'm sorry."

Chance's hand closes around the leather-bound handle of the pick and she pulls it free of a tangle of wool scarves and extension cords. One of the electrical cords tumbles off the shelf and lies like an orange rubber serpent at her feet.

"Leave *now* or I will call the police. I fucking swear!" she shouts at the door.

"Yes," the man says. "I suppose you will."

"You're goddamn right I will."

"You shouldn't get so excited, Mrs. Silvey. I'm sure it isn't good for you or the baby."

"I'm not going to tell you again, asshole," Chance says and

grips the pick tighter, raises it above her head, the point aimed at the door and whoever is standing on the other side.

"Okay. I'm leaving," the man replies. "But Deacon *will* want to talk to me. Tell him that I can help him. Tell him I know who killed his friend." And then he slips a small, folded piece of paper beneath the door. Chance stares at it, her heart pounding so loud now that she hardly hears what the man says next.

"Please have him call me at that number. It's a cell phone, so he can call me anytime. And I am very sorry that I frightened you, Mrs. Silvey. I don't mean you or your husband any harm."

"Just *go,*" Chance tells him and then listens to the sound of their footsteps growing fainter, the muted ding of the elevator all the way at the other end of the building. She doesn't reach for the piece of paper, but eases her body slowly, painfully, down to the hardwood floor, her back pressed against the wall and her strong legs to control her descent. And then she sits there, still clutching the pick, and waits for Deacon.

All the way home, all the bloody sights from Soda's apartment playing over and over again behind his eyes, the unquiet theater of Deacon Silvey's skull, and crossing the duct-taped bridge above the tracks he thinks that maybe his headache is coming back. The faint throb at his temples, like iron fingers tapping gently at his flesh, and he pauses and looks east towards the streetlights along Morris, picking out his and Chance's apartment from the rest. But no lights in their windows, so he figures that Chance is probably watching an old movie or else she's given up on him and gone to bed early. Farther east, past other bridges, other roads, the stove-pipe ruins of Sloss Furnace stand straight and tall as rusted watchmen, guarding the night from sunrise. A white and waxing moon hanging cold above the city, and Deacon moves on, takes the narrow alleyway at the end of the bridge down to Morris Avenue. By the time he's walked the remaining block to their building, the pain in his head has faded away again, false alarm, and he almost feels relieved.

At the top floor, the elevator doors slide open and he walks quickly past the apartments of the neighbors that they rarely ever see to their own door at the end of the hall. Deacon fishes his keys from a pants pocket, the rubber Bullwinkle key ring Chance gave him not long after they started dating.

"Deacon?" she calls out from the other side of the door. "Is that you?" Her voice is shaky, either very tired or very worried or both, and "Yeah, it's me," he says, opening the door, and she's sitting against the wall by the closet, holding on to one of her rock hammers.

"Christ, honey, what are you doing?" he asks and sees the folded sheet of paper half a second before he steps on it.

"There was someone at the door," she says and now there are tears leaking from her green eyes, rolling slowly down her cheeks. Deacon glances back at the door, still standing open, and the dull pain at his temples starts again.

"He kept asking for you," Chance says. "I told him you weren't here and I was going to call the police, but he wouldn't go away. I thought he was going to break in."

"I don't think you should be sitting in the floor like that," Deacon says and bends down to help her up. She doesn't let go of the rock hammer.

"Where the hell have you been, Deacon?"

"Just walking," he says and the tip of the pick jabs him in the ribs as he lifts Chance to her feet. "Trying to clear my head, that's all."

"I didn't think you were coming back," she says and holds on to him tight, holds him like she's afraid he'll vanish if she lets go, and she presses her face against his shirt; he can feel her tears leaking through the fabric, salt-warm drops of her to stain his skin, and "Of course I was coming back," he says and hugs her. "I just went for a walk."

"He said he knows that you talked to the police," Chance sobs and then she points at the piece of paper lying on the floor, tattooed now with the print of Deacon's boot. "And . . . and he said he wanted to tell you who the killer is. He said he knows."

"We need to get you to bed," Deacon says and Chance shakes her head no, lets go of him and wipes her nose on the back of her hand.

"I'm sorry. I was just so scared. I didn't know if he'd really gone, or if he was going to come back."

"He didn't tell you his name?" Deacon asks.

"No. He said you should call him," and Chance points at the piece of paper again. "He said there was a phone number."

"He slid that in under the door?"

"Yeah, he slid it under the door," Chance says, wipes her nose again, wipes her eyes, and hands Deacon the rock hammer. "I'm going to sit the fuck down now."

And as she heads down the hall, her left hand braced against the wall and her right resting protectively on her belly, Deacon picks the paper up and unfolds it. There's a ten-digit number and two words written below it, SCARBOROUGH PENTECOST. But he forgets the phone number and the words the moment he sees the thing drawn at the bottom of the page, the perfect circle in red ink and a wide black slash underneath.

CHAPTER SIX

As I Have Heard from Hell

From her high and secret place in the dunes, Narcissa listens to the roaring January gale and watches the tide coming in. The sea, thick and red as a butcher's heart, is surging into Ipswich Bay, mixing with the muddy, dark water spilling down from the Manuxet's lower falls. The twice-daily meeting of the waters, the deceitful river spilling all its secrets into the crimson bosom and crawling mind of Mother Hydra, everything it's learned in its meandering journey across and through the land, and Narcissa shivers and pulls her coat tighter. She squints through the snow at the black and hungry creatures moving about in the water of the bay.

"Are you planning on spending the rest of your life out here?" her grandfather's ghost asks. He's squatting somewhere behind her, digging for pirate treasure in the sand. And "I might," she replies, not taking her eyes off the rising tide.

"Complacency, child. Complacency's gonna be the bitter end of you yet."

"Where else would I go?"

For a moment, there's only the howling wind in her ears, and she thinks maybe he's gone away again, slipped quietly into one of the shallow holes he's dug and pulled the sand in after him. It wouldn't be so bad to be alone, she thinks. Genuinely alone and no noises inside her head but her own voice.

"You had a perfectly good house," the old man grumbles, so she knows he's still there somewhere. If she turns around to look, he'll only hide from her. "Old Iscariot saw to that. But you burnt it down, you ungrateful cur. You burnt it down, so it serves you right, having to live out here in the dunes like an animal."

"It was a haunted place," Narcissa says, still watching the dark things struggling to haul themselves free of the sea; all the shimmering chitin shells and scales and tentacles straining for evolution's first landward step, each wave to carry them within easy grasp of the rocks, only to drag them back into the bay. Mother Hydra's jealous womb, her endless tangled umbilici, her silt and barnacled placenta, and the old man laughs at Narcissa.

"You think these here dunes are any different? You think this whole damn world ain't rotten to its core?"

"To tell you the truth, Aldous, I try not to think about it," and far out beyond Ipswich Bay, beyond Castle Hill and nameless barrier islands, across the crests and troughs of the afterbirth and amniotic depths, Narcissa thinks she sees white sails strung against the storm-dimmed sky.

"That doesn't change anything at all," he replies, but it's getting harder to tell the difference between the old man's voice and the wind.

"Go back to sleep, Aldous."

"You don't know how things work," he sighs. "They won't let you stay out here forever. There are rules, even rules for a cur bitch like you."

"They'll never find me here."

"Don't you start in fooling yourself again, Narcissa. Every grain of sand is a staring eye and every gull a mouth to sing them songs. You know—"

"Go on back to sleep, old man. You're dead. You're nothing now but ashes."

Down among the rocks and mud, a great mass of raw pink muscle and slime has escaped the sea and lies still, gasping from a dozen puckered mouths, from the slits behind its bulbous eyes.

"You better wake up, child. They're coming."

Beneath the waters of the sea,
Are lobsters thick as thick can be—

"Hell, they're almost here now."

They love to dance with you and me,

My own and gentle Salmon.

Narcissa turns to face him, to drive him off again, but Aldous has gone and in the sandy hollow where her lean-to and the charcoal smudge of her driftwood campfire had been there's only an open door suspended on taut piano wire. She cranes her neck and stares up at the sky, trying to get a glimpse of whatever the wires are attached to, but they vanish into the low clouds somewhere overhead. When she takes a step towards the door, she can see the wooden stairs leading all the way down to the cellar of the house on Benefit Street.

Will you, won't you, will you, won't you, will you join the dance?

"I've been there, Grandfather. I've been there time after time and they turned me away."

Behind her, down on the shore, the gasping thing starts making a sound like kittens and water draining from a sink, and she knows better than to turn and look. Knows the sea is waiting for her to make that very mistake. Instead, she takes another step towards the open door, because it's beginning to rain and maybe all those other times won't matter. She catches a whiff of the musty cellar air and stops.

Would not, could not, would not, could not, could not join the dance.

"Apostate," the cellar hisses bitterly between dry, ebony lips. "You think you can run from us? You think there's more than one way this can possibly end?"

"Wake up, child," Aldous Snow whispers from the sand and snow beneath her feet and Narcissa opens her yellow eyes. The Colt gripped tight in her sweaty right hand and only an instant's disorientation before she remembers where she is, *when* she is, and Narcissa lies very still in her sleeping bag, listening to the big, empty house on Cullom Street. Listening for any sound that shouldn't be there, any anomalous creak or rustle, and *There*, she thinks. *There you are.*

The rat hears her, too, and stops halfway between the sleeping bag and the door leading out to the foyer. When she rolls over and points the gun at it, the rat shits on the floor and stares helplessly back at her with its terrified black eyes.

"Am I awake?" she asks the rat. "Or is this only another sort of dream? Am I ever truly awake, rat?"

Narcissa glances at the digital travel clock radio perched on the books near her pillow, 11:30 P.M. in the soft absinthe light of sunless worlds. So almost an hour since she closed the antique volume on Persian thaumaturgy and lay still, listening to the branches and twigs scraping loud against the house until she fell asleep. She flips the safety off the pistol and cocks the hammer.

"What did they promise you, rat? What did you *owe* them? Or maybe you thought you'd get lucky and find a thorn in my paw?"

The rat blinks at her, its eyes darting from her face to the barrel of the pistol and back again.

"Do all good mice go to Heaven?" she asks it and squeezes the trigger, shattering the night crowded thick inside the house and wiping the last sticky strands of the nightmare from her head.

Deacon is sitting alone on the sofa, chewing a thumbnail and staring at the creased and wrinkled sheet of paper with the phone number, the circle and the line, the two words printed in black ink—SCARBOROUGH PENTECOST—while Chance pretends to watch television. One of her old movies from the cardboard boxes of videotapes she keeps beneath the bed, her dead grandfather's videos, westerns and war movies, John Wayne and Henry Fonda, James Stewart and Gregory Peck. Sometimes they seem to make her feel better and so he's never told her how much he hates most of them. Black-and-white heroics, guns and cows and horses. He touches the center of the circle drawn on the sheet of paper and looks at Chance on the love seat.

"Are you going to call him?" she asks.

"Don't you think I should call the police instead and give this to them?" Deacon motions towards her with the sheet of paper and Chance turns back to the television screen.

"I don't know what you should do, Deacon. But I know you never should have gotten us involved in this. I know *that*."

"I wasn't trying to get you involved in anything."

"But that's what you did. Me and the baby. And you don't even know what's happening."

"Fuck," Deacon growls and crumples the paper into a tight little wad in his fist, imagining all his anger and confusion and fear, his thirst and the pain in his head, crushed into something so small, something he could hold in the palm of his hand. Something that would burn. Then he takes a deep breath and carefully smoothes the paper flat again.

"I couldn't have stopped him," Chance says, speaking to the cowboys on television. "Not if he'd really wanted in."

"Whoever it was, he just wanted to scare you."

"Well, he succeeded."

"This isn't about you, baby. I'm the one he's looking for."

"That's real goddamn comforting, Deacon."

"I'm sorry," he says, apologizing to Chance for the thirtieth or thirty-fifth time since he came home and found her sitting in the floor holding the rock hammer. "I didn't think—"

"*Bingo,*" she says and then turns around in the love seat and glares at him. "You didn't fucking *think*. You didn't stop to consider that your life isn't only your life anymore. Everything you do now affects me and it affects the baby."

"Yeah," Deacon whispers and reaches for Chance's cell phone lying on the coffee table.

"Can you even tell me why this was so important that you're willing to risk our lives?"

"This woman's out there killing people, Chance."

"And you're not a fucking cop. It's not *your* job to stop her."

Deacon sets the phone down again and glares back at her. "Then what *is* my job? What exactly is it I'm supposed to be doing day after goddamn day?"

"You *know* what I need from you. You know the *only* thing I need from you," but now the fire is deserting her and he can tell from the tremble in Chance's voice, the wet glint of her green eyes, that she's close to tears.

"I'm sober," Deacon says and runs his fingers through his hair, staring down at the paper again, the name, if it is a name, the phone number. "You wanted me to be sober and that's what I am. But this is different. If I do what you're asking *this* time and wash my hands of the whole business, what do we do the next time she kills someone?"

"What do you mean, what do *we* do? This hasn't got anything to do with us."

He watches her silently for a moment, looking for words that aren't there, explanations that have never been within his grasp and aren't there now.

"If you'd ever seen the things I've seen," he says finally, speaking slowly and softly, looking her directly in the eyes, her face washed in the gray shades of TV light and shadow. "If you'd ever seen the blood and the shit and the fucking rotting *meat* that one person can turn another person into, you wouldn't have to ask."

And then Deacon glances back to the note and the cell phone, impatiently waiting for her to tell him how full of it he is, and when she doesn't say anything at all he looks up at her again. Chance is staring at the television and there are tears rolling down her cheeks.

"I'm not some kind of goddamned martyr," she says. "I understand what's my responsibility and what's not."

"You didn't see what she—"

"You don't *know* what I see, Deacon. You don't even have the faintest idea," and she wipes her nose, her voice grown fierce again despite the tears. "Lately, I don't even know what I see."

"What are you talking about?"

"Nothing," she says. "It's crazy. And I'm not going to be crazy, too. One of us has to stay sane."

"What do you see, Chance?" and Deacon can hear the apprehension in his own voice, the guarded urgency, and maybe Chance hears it as well, because she turns her head and stares at him.

"I'm not crazy," she says again.

"Nobody's going to think you are."

"Only crazy people see things that aren't there."

"Chance, just tell me what you're talking about."

She looks quickly back at the TV, the tall, determined man with his six-shooter, as if maybe there's some way he can save her, too. And then Chance tells Deacon about the drive to Atlanta and the blood that was and wasn't on her forehead, the diorama and the gore dripping from the mouth of the *Megalopseudosuchus*. Deacon sits still and listens to everything she has to say, and when she's finished he picks up the cell phone and dials the number written on the piece of paper.

Deacon hasn't been inside a bar in almost a year, not since the binge that finally landed him in the hospital and "You've got a choice, Deke," Chance told him. "Either me or the liquor. Take your pick." He'd forgotten just how close he came to choosing the liquor, but now, sitting in a booth in the back of Cheese's Blues and

Oldies Club, sipping ginger ale, he remembers it very, very well. The sweet funk of spilled beer and decades of cigarette smoke, the eternal night behind painted windowpanes or drawn blinds, the gentle, pastel wash of neon. Deacon lights another Camel and stares past the old black men sitting at the bar, watching the door, waiting for a face he's never seen.

"I don't go to bars," he told the voice on the other end of the cell phone.

"Well, tonight you're going to have to make an exception," Scarborough Pentecost replied.

"Look, asshole, we're gonna do this my way or I hang up right this minute and call the cops."

"No you won't," Scarborough Pentecost said confidently.

"Why the fuck not?"

"Because I'm not your enemy. Maybe I'm not exactly your friend, either, but for the moment I'm the best you've got."

"I don't even know what you're talking about."

"Yes, you do. You've seen her, Mr. Silvey. Do you really think the police can protect you and your family from *that?*"

Deacon didn't answer, and for a moment there was only strained silence on the line while he tried not to remember the face from his nightmare, those blazing eyes, and wished he'd taken the piece of paper straight to Detective Downs.

"You still there?" Scarborough Pentecost asked.

"Yeah," Deacon said and looked across the room at Chance standing at the window, her back turned to him. "I'm here."

"So, do we do this or not?"

"Just tell me where," Deacon replied, so now he's sitting in a booth at Cheese's, listening to Screaming Jay Hawkins blaring from the jukebox and watching the front door. Every now and then, the fat, white-haired bartender or one of the customers gives him a suspicious look and he smiles his best *Don't mind me, I'm just a crazy white man having himself a glass of ginger ale and a few smokes* smile and they frown and turn back to the bar.

And then the door swings open and the pair that steps into the bar, the boy and girl like rejects from a Tarantino film, have to be the ones he's waiting for because they're white and the bartender glares at them the same way he's been glaring at Deacon. The boy is tall and thin as a pole, his leather biker jacket hanging loose on his bony shoulders. He's wearing tattered jeans and black biker boots, his long hair pulled back in a ponytail. The girl is pale and pretty and she must be at least five years too young to be hanging out in bars. She stands very close behind the boy, her arms crossed self-consciously and her eyes on the floor; all her clothes look secondhand. The bartender nods his head and points to Deacon's booth.

He finishes his drink while they walk towards him down the long, narrow aisle between the row of booths and the bar. Someone whistles at the girl and she looks embarrassed and buttons her purple cardigan.

"You two come here often?" Deacon asks as the girl slides into the booth across from him.

"You know, I saw this place in the phone book and couldn't resist," the boy says and slides in after her. "You think that guy behind the counter is Cheese?"

"Maybe you should ask him," Deacon replies and crunches on a melting ice cube.

"Maybe I will. Maybe that's just what I'll do." Then the boy in the baggy leather jacket holds out his left hand to Deacon. "I'm Scarborough Pentecost, by the way," he says.

Deacon stares at his slender hand, the long, tapered fingers, the symbol like a rune or Chinese character tattooed onto the center of his palm, but he doesn't shake it.

"No shit. Now, tell me why I'm here," Deacon says. "While you're at it, you can tell me why you broke into our building and scared the hell out of my pregnant wife."

Scarborough sighs, pulls his hand away, and glances sidewise at the girl; she shrugs and smiles sheepishly at Deacon.

"I wasn't trying to scare her," Scarborough says. "I am sorry about that."

"Is that a fact? And I'm just supposed to sit here and believe you because—?"

"Because, right now, Mr. Silvey, your options are somewhat limited."

Deacon takes a deep drag off his cigarette, exhales and squints at Scarborough Pentecost through the smoke.

"We don't have the *time* to argue, Deacon," the girl says, the words spilling out of her in a nervous, urgent gush. "If you really care about your wife, you need to listen to him."

Deacon stares at her for a moment and then stubs what's left of his cigarette out in the cut-glass ashtray on the table. Smoke rises slow and coils from the butt like a question mark or the ghost of a fakir's cobra.

"You've got twenty minutes," Deacon says, and he checks the glowing Schlitz clock on the wall behind the bar. In five minutes, it'll be midnight.

Scarborough nods, then reaches into his jacket and pulls out a large manila envelope. It's bent at the corners and has what looks like a coffee stain on one side; he places it on the table between them.

"All right," he says and smiles, wide and ugly smile that's almost a threat and Deacon lights another Camel. "So much for the bullshit prefatory chitchat. When you were working with Vincent Hammond in Atlanta, you solved a missing-persons case."

"I solved a lot of missing-persons cases."

"Not like this one," Scarborough says and taps at the envelope with an index finger. "Fifteen children, mostly infants, boys and girls, taken from their homes over a period of seven years. The last one was a four-year-old girl named—"

"Jessica Hartwell," Deacon says so he won't have to hear her name from someone else. His mouth so dry he wouldn't be surprised if sand started dribbling from his lips and he raises a hand to get the bartender's attention. "Yeah, I remember."

"The Hartwell girl was the one who tied them all together, but she was also the only one they ever found. You saved her life, Mr. Silvey."

"Well, whatever was left of it," Deacon mutters around the filter of his cigarette, his eyes on the envelope.

"She just started high school," the girl says and when Deacon glances up at her, her eyes dart nervously towards the ceiling. "She still has nightmares, sometimes, but she's alive. And she's happy."

"How the fuck do you know that?" but then the bartender's standing beside the booth, wiping his big hands on his apron and frowning down at them, no-bullshit frown to say whatever the three of them are up to, it better not start any trouble on his watch.

"What you want now?" he says.

"Do you have Jack Daniel's?" Deacon asks and the bartender shakes his head.

"You want bourbon, all we got's Wild Turkey."

"Wild Turkey will do just fine, straight."

The bartender points at Scarborough. "What about you two. Those things you're sitting on ain't park benches, you know."

"I'll have a Coke," the girl says.

"No you won't, 'cause we ain't got no Coke," the bartender replies. "We got Pepsi."

"I like Pepsi, too," she says and smiles her shy, sheepish smile again. "Pepsi will be fine."

"That's good, 'cause that's what we got."

Scarborough orders a beer and the bartender goes away again still wiping his hands. "I thought you'd given up the hooch, Mr. Silvey," he says and Deacon ignores him and picks up the manila envelope. It isn't sealed and he pulls out a sheaf of newspaper clippings and black-and-white photographs, police reports and several pages photocopied from a handwritten diary. There's a photo of a small and dilapidated old house on top of the stack, the wide front porch draped with crime-scene tape.

"Where'd you get these?" he asks.

"We're not police, if that's what you're wondering," Scarborough says. "And we don't work for the police."

"Great, but that still doesn't answer my question."

"It doesn't matter *where* we got them, Mr. Silvey."

Deacon lays the photo of the house facedown on the table and under it is a close-up of the front door. The wood looks dry and rotten, the paint peeling in ragged strips and patches like dead skin sloughing off the belly of a snake; there's a sign nailed to the door—BEWARE OF DOG.

He swallows, no spit but he swallows anyway, and "What does the Hartwell case have to do with Soda's murder?" he asks and lays the photo of the door facedown on top of the photo of the house. The next picture is almost identical, except the BEWARE OF DOG sign has been removed and there's a symbol carved deep into the wood it was covering.

"The people we work for, well, let's just say they had a vested interest in those children in Atlanta," and then Scarborough nods at the papers in Deacon's hands. "Same thing with the murder of your friend Soda."

"Who is she?" Deacon asks without bothering to look up, and

the next photograph is from inside the old house, the intricate arch at the door leading down to the cellar, woven from human bones and dried creeper and kudzu vines. Three skulls nailed above the arch and each one wearing a crown of rusted barbed wire, the words LAND OF DREAMS printed in neat black letters on the door underneath.

"You were the first person to go into the house, weren't you?" Scarborough asks, pointing at the photograph.

Deacon licks his parched lips and eyes the bar desperately, the thirst grown so big and the memory of the horrors from that day at the house almost enough to swallow him whole, enough to leave him as bare as the bones in the police photos. But now the bartender is busy talking to a skinny man in a Panama hat and shows no sign of getting their drinks.

"You're the one who *found* Jessica Hartwell."

"Hammond was right behind me," Deacon says and lays the picture of the arch and the doorway down on the table with the others he's already seen. Now he's looking at one of the photocopied pages from the journal of a dead woman, her sloppy cursive filling up the whole page from top to bottom.

"But you saved her life, Deacon," the girl sitting next to Scarborough Pentecost says again. "Mary English would have killed the child if you hadn't stopped her when you did."

"I opened the cage," Deacon replies, hardly speaking above a whisper now. "But Hammond, he came in right behind me."

"Yes," Scarborough says. "But *you* opened the cage. Policeman or no policeman, you're the one who saved Jessica Hartwell's life that day."

Deacon drops the remaining contents of the envelope on the table and takes a drag from his cigarette, but the smoke only makes him thirstier and he crushes it out in the ashtray. Scarborough's still talking, his voice as smooth and dark as molasses.

"Hammond gave you a drawing they'd found in the girl's bedroom, and when you held it you saw a vision of the house where she was being kept, Mary English's house in the woods. You saw the door leading down to her cellar, her 'Land of Dreams.' Did you know she took that from William Blake?"

"No," Deacon says. "I never knew what it meant."

"It was all right there in her journal—'Dear Child, I also by pleasant streams, Have wander'd all Night in the Land of Dreams; But tho calm and warm the waters wide, I could not get to the other side.' You held the drawing, Mr. Silvey, and saw that doorway to the Land of Dreams, and you led Detective Hammond to it."

"What are you getting at? I don't see what any of this has to do with Soda's murder."

Scarborough leans a little ways across the table and Deacon catches a whiff of something sweet and rotten on his breath. "Have you ever paused to consider the relativity of heroism?" he asks. "How one man's David is inevitably another man's Goliath?"

"I didn't come here to listen to riddles."

"It's not a riddle, Deacon," the girl says. "It's not even a secret anymore."

"She's right, Mr. Silvey. These days it's almost a truism. A goddamned fact of life."

And then the fat, white-haired bartender is standing over them again with a tray in his hands, two glasses and a bottle of Bud, and he sets the shot of bourbon down in front of Deacon. "That'll be six-fifty," the bartender says gruffly and Scarborough hands him a ten and tells him to keep the change. Deacon doesn't argue, too busy staring into the perfect pool of amber liquor to tell the creep on the other side of the booth that he can buy his own damned drinks. For a second or two, there's nothing else in the world but that one precious glass of whiskey, the universe collapsing down to a single wet point, a decision as simple as swallowing.

"You still with us, Mr. Silvey?" Scarborough asks, snaps his fingers, and when Deacon looks up the bartender has gone and the girl is sipping at her Pepsi.

"I'm right here," Deacon replies. "And if you don't stop calling me 'Mr. Silvey,' I'm going to punch you in the face, *Mr.* Pentecost."

"Told you," the girl says.

Scarborough picks up the photograph of the arch of bones and the cellar door, examines it for a moment, then turns it around so Deacon can see it again.

"Okay, *Deacon.* As I was saying—"

"I hope you were about to get to the fucking point, because you've only got about five minutes left," and then Deacon lifts the shot glass and a few drops of the whiskey slosh out onto his fingertips. He quickly sets the glass down again, his hand shaking so badly he almost drops it.

"That summer day you walked through this door, you might have become a hero, but you *also* became a villain. Now, are you following me or are you too busy trying to decide whether or not to lick the Wild Turkey off your fingers?"

"Scarborough, can we please just get this over with," the girl says. "I don't really want to spend the rest of the night in this dump."

"What do you want from me?" Deacon asks and Scarborough lays the photograph down again.

"That cellar was Mary English's own Land of Dreams and you, Deacon, you were her nightmare."

"She was a murderer. She killed fourteen children before we found her."

"The police never proved that. There were no bodies found, no graves."

Deacon reaches for his cigarettes, only one left in the pack and he fishes it out. "She had photographs of every one of the missing kids," he says. "She had clippings of their hair and fingernails."

"That proves she had contact with them, but it certainly doesn't prove she killed a single one of them, does it?"

"Look, motherfucker," Deacon growls. "I've had just about enough of this bullshit," and all the men sitting at the bar glance up from their drinks and conversation, their cigars and salted peanuts, and turn towards the booth. The bartender reaches for something beneath the cash register.

"Maybe you'd better lower your voice," the girl whispers and then she smiles and waves to the men at the bar. "I think we're beginning to wear out our welcome."

Deacon looks at the unlit cigarette and then glares at Scarborough. "The bitch was a murderer," he says again, lowering his voice. "What the fuck is it to you two, anyway?"

"Just *tell* him," the girl says and stirs the ice in her glass with a green swizzle stick.

"Little birdie, one of these days real soon you're gonna have to learn to keep your mouth shut."

"Yeah, well, maybe one of these days you can try to teach me."

Deacon pushes the glass of whiskey away, more of it sloshing over the rim onto the table, spotting some of the papers from the manila envelope. "Time's up," he says.

"No. Please wait," and the girl reaches quickly across the table, taking his hand in hers and squeezing gently.

"These people that we work for, Mr. Silvey," Scarborough says, "well, let's just say that Mary English worked for them, too. And the woman that killed your friend, the woman you've seen in your visions, she's become something of a problem to them."

"He's telling you the truth," the girl says, but Deacon shakes his head and pries her fingers from around his wrist.

"Right now, I can't begin to imagine what sort of sick game the two of you are playing—"

"Yes, Deacon," the girl interrupts, "you're right. It is a game. But not the sort you think. It's a terrible game."

"—or how you know what you know, but I'll tell you this, both of you. If either one of you ever comes anywhere near my wife again, if you so much as *look* at her from across the fucking street, I *will* kill both of you. That's a fucking promise."

Scarborough rubs his forehead and laughs a gravelly, dry scrap of a laugh. "Sit back down," he tells Deacon. "We're not finished."

"Fuck you, you psychotic son of a bitch," and then the bartender's talking, his voice booming like thunder, and when Deacon turns around the first thing he sees is the long, slick barrel of a shotgun aimed at his chest, its twin muzzles gaping like cannons. The fat man eases the hammers back and they click loud over the noise from the jukebox.

"I think it's about time you folks took your party somewheres else," he says, "if you get my drift."

"Yes sir," Deacon says. "I was just leaving. But I'd be grateful if you'd keep an eye on these two here until I'm gone."

"You got exactly two minutes," and now the big man points the gun at Scarborough Pentecost instead.

"Thanks," Deacon says and walks quickly to the door and out into the chilly October night.

Not the last case Vincent Hammond brought Deacon, not the one that finally broke the camel's back and so what if Hammond had gotten him a shit job at an all-night coin-op and slipped him twenties and fifties now and then. Not the last, but definitely the worst, and if he'd had the sense God gave a rock, if he'd had the courage or self-confidence to tell the detective to fuck off, if he'd ever been sober for five minutes at a stretch, it would have been his last.

"What do you see, Deke?" Hammond asked.

Deacon looked up from the girl's drawing, the crayon lines and angles, waxy blacks and greens and blues, and "A fat cop," he said. "Too lazy to do his own damn work."

"You're a goddamned comedian, bubba, that's what you are. A goddamn Groucho fuckin' Marx."

"I do have my moments," Deacon said and looked back down at the drawing in his hands. What might have been a face at a window, or something else entirely, those smudges that could have been eyes opening wider and wider, spilling a scalding kaleidoscope of broken sounds and images into him. The wild woman at the window, the witch who cries and whimpers and stares until you have to let her in and then she drags you off to meet the goblins, off to the wild, dark places underground to become a Child of the Cuckoo.

O, what Land is the Land of Dreams?
What are its Mountains and what are its Streams?

The heady smell of dirt and pine straw, blood and rotting meat, shit and spiders, and two hours later, still clutching the drawing, he led them to the old shanty house in the woods somewhere west of the city. Down a long dirt road, narrow logging road crammed with five police cars and an ambulance, their sirens to drown the locust wail from the trees, but not the voice whispering furiously to Deacon from Jessica Hartwell's crayon geometry. That voice growing louder and louder, swelling until he thought it would crack his skull in two and splatter his brains across the dashboard, *Does the Eagle know what is in the pit? Or wilt thou go ask the Mole?*

O, what Land is the Land of Dreams?

"You wait right here, you hear me?" Hammond said as the car rolled to a stop in a cloud of orange dust, but Deacon was already out, already running across the weedy yard towards the front door of the house. Hammond shouted at him to stop, ordered him to come back to the car, but the sun grown much too bright, the June heat and the voice squeezing itself between the cracks in his soul, and Deacon kept running. Three cinder-block steps up to the sagging front porch and the door wasn't even locked. As he turned the brass knob and stepped into cool shadows the voice became a hurricane behind his eyes, raging, singing, swirling around the still and silent heart of his pain.

Some are Born to sweet delight, Some are Born to sweet delight, Some are Born to Endless Night.

Through cramped and shabby rooms, down a hallway whose walls seemed to pulse and throb like living, membranous things, and at the end of it the arch of bone and vines was waiting for him, guarding the cellar door.

"Deacon! Where the fuck are you?" Vincent Hammond roared from somewhere nearby and still very far away, somewhere inconsequential, and the three skulls leered down at Deacon from their hollow, eyeless sockets. "Here!" he shouted back. "I'm over here," but the air around him turning thick and sour as clotted milk to muffle his words, to slip down his throat and slither up his nostrils. And when Deacon reached for the cellar door, the knob felt soft and warm.

"Land of Dreams," he whispered, "Land of Dreams," reading the words painted on the door aloud; the voice in his head flinched and shuddered and the air around him was only air again.

She saw the couches of the dead, and where the fibrous roots of every heart on earth infixes deep its restless twists . . .

The doorknob, cold and hard as any doorknob, turned oil-smooth in his hand and Deacon stared down the crooked wooden stairs at the darkness below. The musty stink of dust and mildew and tiny white mushrooms flowed from the open doorway and he reached for the light cord, pulled it and a single bulb flickered and burned dimly from its socket on the cellar wall. He could hardly hear Hammond and the others anymore, their voices and footsteps faded like a passing train, and Deacon stepped through the arch.

A land of sorrow and of tears . . .

"Jessica?" he called out and nobody answered, no one and nothing but the lunatic ranting in his brain. The stairs creaked beneath his feet and Deacon wondered if they would take his weight, if maybe it weren't only a trap after all and in a moment he would be lying broken and bleeding in the dark, broken and maybe dead. The whole damned thing too easy, too *urgent*, his mad dash from the car, the unlocked doors, and he retreated a step backwards into the hallway.

Past the weak glare of the bulb, an insectile *snick-snick-snick*, metal against metal, steel drawn repeatedly across steel or a whetstone, and "Jessica!" he yelled, louder than before. Around him, the house seemed to mutter to itself, smug, satisfied, triumphant, and the hurricane voice in his head paused for an instant, the meanest instant of silence, and then O, *what Land is the Land of Dreams?* it asked him again.

Deacon descended the cellar stairs as quickly as he dared. He kept his right hand pressed against the wall, fingertips to brush mold and cobwebs, to tell him when the pine boards changed to bare earth, and the stairs led him down and down and down, much deeper than he would have imagined the cellar to have been dug. The soft earth changing, finally, to rough-hewn stone, bedrock, and the light at the top of the stairs had grown as faint and distant as a star. There was no sign of Hammond or anyone else back there, and he began to wonder if they'd ever been there at all, if his entire life had not been spent on these stairs.

Art thou a Worm? image of weakness, art thou but a Worm?

There was surprise when he found the bottom, surprise but not relief, and more surprise when he realized that it wasn't dark anymore. The woman holding the kerosene lantern stared back at him with dewy eyes the color of moss. She wasn't old, but the lines in her face and the streaks of gray in her tangled black hair there to say that she'd seen and heard enough in her time that she might as well be a hundred. Her tattered yellow dress draped slackly over skin and bones, her bare feet, and she gripped a straight razor in her other hand.

"Is this a Worm?" she asked, and the voice in his head was only her voice now, had never been anything more or less. "I see thee lay helpless and naked, weeping, and none to answer."

"Where is she?" Deacon demanded and the woman smiled softly for him and held the razor up so it glinted in the lantern light.

"And none to answer," she replied. "None to cherish thee with mother's smiles."

"I'm not alone. There are police coming."

"Yes," she said and looked at the razor, her smile melting away to something like regret. "There are."

"Give me the girl and I promise no one will hurt you."

"You can't make promises for other men," she whispered.

Deacon glanced quickly from the razor in her hand to the gloom behind her and back again. "Is she here?"

"You have no idea, Deacon Silvey. You can't begin to imagine," and she pointed at him with the straight razor. "I'm only a conductor here, and this is only a transit station. That God would love a Worm, I knew—"

"Her name is Jessica," Deacon said and looked again into the shadows crouched behind the woman. There was something back there, something that seemed to hang suspended from the floor of the house a thousand feet overhead.

"But they won't let her keep that. No, Deacon, but they will let her choose a new name one day, when she's older and—"

"You need to show me where she is," Deacon said and the woman took a couple of steps back from him then and smiled again, this time a haughty, secretive smirk, and she shook her head.

"She's a Child of the Cuckoo now. Her name has already been written in the book and you can't ever have her back."

"They're coming to *take* her back."

At that the woman hissed and swiped at the air with her razor, cut a long slash in nothing only a few inches from Deacon's chest. Her thin lips curled back to show rotten teeth and black spaces where teeth should be.

"You better run, boy," she snarled, "while you still got two good legs under you. You better run straight back up into the light and tell the rest of them folks they better start running, too. That child ain't theirs no more, not—"

And then Deacon punched the woman in the face, hit her hard and fast and she dropped the razor, stumbled backwards and almost fell. He snatched the razor from the floor and folded it closed.

"Where is she?" he asked again, but then he could see for himself, the cage and the chain leading up into the darkness, rusted iron bars and the girl lying on her side at the bottom, curled fetal in a filthy bed of hay, her back to him so he couldn't see if she was alive or dead.

"You don't know what you've done," the woman said, tears in her eyes and running down her cheeks, blood oozing steadily from her nose, getting into her mouth, and she spat on the ground at Deacon's feet. "What wailing wight calls the watchman of the night? You don't know what you've done, Deacon Silvey."

The cage was locked, but he found the key ring hanging not far away on a railroad spike driven into the rocky wall, a loop of wire with a dozen keys, and while he searched for the one that would open the cage he talked to the motionless form of the child.

"Jessica, can you hear me? I've come to take you home."

The woman sat down on the floor, no fight left in her, no effort to escape, and she pulled her knees up underneath her chin and wept and watched Deacon with her mossy, angry eyes.

"You don't know what you've done," she said. "But you will, yes sir, one day, one day they'll *show* you what—"

"Just shut the hell up," he barked at her and came to the very last key on the ring, an antique brass thing with a small crimson gemstone set into the filigreed bow and letters he didn't recognize carved into the shaft. He slid it into the padlock and the tumblers rolled and clicked and maybe the red stone on the key sparked and shimmered for a moment, a tiny wink of ruddy light, and maybe that was only his imagination. But the hasp popped open and the child in the cage made a frightened sound, and far overhead he heard Vincent Hammond shouting his name.

An hour past midnight and the girl who calls herself Starling Jane finds Deacon alone in a small park at the end of a dead-end street. She stands in the trees for a while, silently watching him where he sits at a picnic table beneath the tar-paper roof of a weathered gazebo. Not far away is a limestone blockhouse set into the mountainside, the gated entrance to a tunnel, and it makes Starling Jane nervous. She thinks about going back to their motel room and telling Scarborough that she couldn't find Deacon Silvey, that she found him but he wouldn't listen to her, whichever lie is most convenient. The old tunnel seems to watch her warily from its two small windows, square and simple holes on either side of the entrance.

"You just mind your own business," she whispers at the tunnel. "I haven't got any interest in the likes of you tonight."

"Who's there?" Deacon asks, standing up quickly, startled, and she steps out of the shadows beneath the trees so he can see her.

"Me," she says. "Only me."

Starling Jane can't see the expression on his face, too much dark gathered there inside the gazebo, but she can feel his surprise dissolving quickly into anger.

"Oh," he says and sits back down. "Where's your little friend? Did he have words with that big fucker's shotgun?"

"No," she replies. "He's fine."

"I'm sorry to hear it."

"Scarborough thought I should talk to you alone. He thought—"

"Well he thought wrong, so fuck off," and he lights a cigarette, his face framed momentarily in the glow from a match.

"I wish I could do that, fuck off," she says. "I don't like this place."

Deacon doesn't reply, just sits there, staring towards the tunnel and smoking his cigarette. She takes a few steps nearer the gazebo and her feet make hardly any sound on the concrete path.

"What is that place?" she asks and points towards the tunnel.

"Go away," Deacon grumbles and the tip of his cigarette flares orange red.

"It's some kind of tunnel, isn't it?"

"Yeah, it's some kind of tunnel."

"People should be more careful where they dig holes."

"I'll remember that. Now leave me alone."

Starling Jane takes another step towards Deacon. "I'm sorry we upset you before," she says. "I know Scarborough can be a real asshole sometimes."

"Oh, you've figured that out, have you?"

Two more steps and she's standing under the gazebo. She lays the manila envelope on the picnic table in front of him and Deacon pretends not to have noticed, still watching the blockhouse, the ink-black eyes and mouth of the tunnel.

"I have to make you understand what's at stake here," she says. "Can I sit down?"

"Can I fucking stop you?"

"Your life's in danger, Deacon. And the lives of your wife and unborn child. That's why she's here, the woman you've seen in your visions."

Deacon turns his head and stares at her, his hard face slack, expressionless, his eyes hidden in the night. For a moment, she's almost more afraid of him than of the tunnel.

"And you two are my guardian angels, is that it?"

"No," Starling Jane says and sits down across from him. "No, we're not. But we can help you."

"*If* I help you first," Deacon says and she nods her head. He laughs and slowly grinds his cigarette out on the tabletop, flicks the butt away. "What if I say no? Why would I want to get myself mixed up in this shit?"

"That's what Scarborough was trying to tell you. You're mixed up in it already. You have been since the day you led those cops out to Mary English's house. That's why she's here, Deacon, the woman you saw, the woman who killed your friend, to find you and your wife."

"To settle the score, right?" and he laughs again, a weary and hollow laugh like a very old man, someone who's tired of living, but too afraid to lie down and die. "To teach me not to go poking my nose where it don't belong. No good deed goes unpunished."

"It's complicated, Deacon."

"So, what's the score? Is this some sort of Mafioso shit, these *people* you work for? Some sort of gang?"

"I can't tell you who they are. Who they are doesn't matter, not as far as you're concerned."

"No, of course it doesn't."

A sudden breeze blows through the trees and the dry leaves still clinging to the branches rattle and scratch loud against each other. Starling Jane shivers and hugs herself, glances nervously over her shoulder at the blockhouse.

"What do you want me to do?" he asks and she turns to face him again.

"Two days from now, on Sunday, call the detective who took you to see the body. Tell him you need to talk to him again."

"And what do I *need* to tell him?"

"That you've seen the killer, here, in your mind," and she puts her left thumb against her temple.

"Look, if I start telling him what I've seen, the last thing he's going to do is believe me."

"You *don't* tell him what you saw. You describe a man, a white man in his mid-forties. A man with a swastika tattooed on his back. There are a few more details in the envelope."

Deacon picks up the envelope and turns it over in his hands. "You want me to fucking lie to the cops," he says.

"You've lied to them already. You told them you didn't see anything when you did."

"Yeah, well. You've just got all the answers, don't you?"

"There's an address in the envelope. You tell them to go to that address and they'll find the evidence to support almost everything you say."

Deacon puts the envelope down again and scratches at his chin. "I don't get it. You say she's come after me and Chance, and that you're trying to help us, but now you're protecting her."

"We're not trying to protect her. We're here to kill her, Deacon. But you have to understand, the cops can't stop her and if they get close, she'll run."

"If she runs, she's not my goddamn problem anymore."

Another gust and restless, windblown leaves whisper among themselves, murmuring Starling's name in their wordless autumn language, and she says a silent prayer that Narcissa Snow hasn't learned to listen to the trees yet.

"She's not going anywhere until she finishes what she came here to do, Deacon. She believes that her life depends on it. If the cops catch on, she'll run, but not until after you're dead and your wife is dead."

"And that's all I have to do, this one little lie to the cops and I'm free and clear?"

"No," she says. "There will be other things, later on, but that's the first of it."

Deacon reaches into his coat pocket and pulls out a crumpled piece of paper, slides it across the picnic table to Starling Jane. She looks at it a moment, then looks back to him.

"That symbol," he says. "She drew it on the wall above Soda's bed, in his blood. What does it mean?"

"I don't know," she lies, because she's said everything she was sent to say, because there are too many things she can never tell him, things connected to other things, and she hands the sheet of paper back to Deacon. "We knew it would get your attention, that's all."

"What I said back at the bar, I meant it, you know. If either of you fuckers comes anywhere near Chance, I'll kill you. I wasn't kidding. She's the only thing I have left in the world."

"Then why aren't you with her, Deacon? Why are you sitting here in the dark by yourself? She needs you."

"And you promise you'll leave her out of this?"

"I can only promise I'll do my best," she says, and then there's a scrambling noise back towards the tunnel and Starling's heart flutters and misses a beat. The adrenaline burning hot in her veins, hotter than crank or cocaine, and she draws the pistol from the shoulder holster inside her sweater and points it at the tunnel.

"Relax, okay?" Deacon says. "It's just a raccoon. They're all over the place up here. They live under the kudzu and come out at night to eat from the garbage cans."

But Jane doesn't relax, all the trees still whispering among themselves, the night too full of phantoms or the threat of phantoms, and the gate to the tunnel like a gaping, hungry jaw full of wrought-iron teeth.

"It's only the old water works tunnel," Deacon says. "It runs all the way under the mountain to Homewood. Me and Chance and a friend of hers got stoned one night and broke into it, years ago, but Chance chickened out. We didn't get very far."

"Raccoons," Starling Jane says, taking a deep breath and lowering the pistol.

"Yeah, raccoons. Or maybe somebody's cat. Chill out."

Starling checks the safety and returns the pistol to its holster. "It's good that Chance was afraid. People should be more careful where they dig holes."

"You said that already."

"I have to go now, Deacon," she says, standing, stepping out from underneath the gazebo. "But everything you need to know is there in the envelope. And you have the number if you should need to reach us."

"I don't even know your name."

"Jane," she tells him. "Just call me Jane. Everyone else does."

"Don't fuck me over, Jane," he says. "You tell Mr. Pentecost I meant what I said at the bar."

"He knows that. I'll see you later, Deacon Silvey. You just do what we've asked and this will all be over soon."

And then she turns and walks quickly back down the winding path to the road, wanting to be far away from that haunted tunnel and the tall, gossiping trees.

CHAPTER SEVEN

Forests of the Night

The sun comes up slow and cold, heartless blue-white light to worm its way through the trees crowded close about the old house on Cullom Street and find Narcissa still squatting naked on the floor in front of the remains of the dead rat. A deep gouge in the wood from the bullet and she's picked the rat apart with her nails, has spread its innards and bones, its fur and teeth, like a deck of tarot cards. A meaning to every drop of blood, unspoken significance in each speck of flesh or tiny vertebra, and she has squatted there for hours teasing understanding from the gore. And finally, their intentions revealed to her in the torn membrane of a kidney, the acute angle of a femur to a rib, their intentions *and* their names, and, what's more, that they have gone to the seer. Narcissa grinds her teeth and stares at the morning light, then licks a bit of rat off her thumb and looks back down at the mess on the floor.

Did you think they'd just give up? one of the voices whispers, taunting her, someone coiled beneath her sleeping bag. *You can keep killing them from now until Doomsday and it won't make any difference.*

"What do you know?" Narcissa asks it. "You're just a scrap of something I couldn't digest."

We see things over here, the voice says and now it sounds more frightened than scornful. *Hell is full of windows. Some of them are your eyes, Narcissa.*

"Shut up," she says and pokes at the kidney again. "I knew they were coming. This doesn't change a thing."

You didn't *know they would go to find the seer,* Aldous mumbles smugly from his place in the closet. *And you didn't know that he'd listen to them. I bet you didn't know that.*

"It won't matter."

They've warned him about you, Narcissa. And that one, he just might be smart enough to listen.

"One day, old man, one day I'm going to cut you out of my head like a cancer. One day I'm going to seal your soul in a bottle and toss it into the sea."

And Narcissa glances from the dismembered rat to all her careful, irrelevant plans thumbtacked to the bedroom wall. Her photocopied map of the city and the diamond that she drew there, the one small red circle where she killed the boy three nights ago, the other points to complete the configuration.

You've made too much a game of it, Aldous sneers. *You always have to make a game of everything, sadistic little games when all you have to do is slit a throat or two and walk away.*

"The fucking game," and then she stops herself, licks anxiously at her lips, and continues. "The *plot,* that was for me. I wanted them to see. I wanted them to appreciate what I can do."

But they don't care, child, her grandfather says. *They don't give a shit and a holler about all your silly schemes.*

"Shut up," Narcissa snarls and realizes how empty her stomach is, reaches inside the circle of salt and powdered sage and eats the rat's heart and lungs.

You're not safe in this house, the voice beneath the sleeping bag says. *They'll come here soon. I wouldn't be surprised if they're already on their way.*

"They won't stop me," she says. "They're only changelings."

And what are you, granddaughter? Just what the hell are you?

"What am I?" she replies, a question to answer his question, and Narcissa turns her head to face the rising sun. "I am everything you could never be, old man. I'm exactly who and what you made me."

What will you do? a very small voice inside her asks, a nervous, twitching voice and Narcissa realizes it's the dead rat and that makes her smile.

"Everything I came here to do," she says and slowly rubs her flat, muscular belly, her hard and haunted flesh. "But it is a shame I'll have to rush things now."

Narcissa turns back to the morning sunlight, warm and reassuring against her face and shoulders, her breasts, warm against the place she cut her face with the razor blade two nights before. The shallow slice along her chin and she knows that it'll heal like all the others have before it, will leave behind no sign of a scar, no dent or blemish in her resilient, damning mask. The sunlight smells like squirrels and moldering, fallen leaves and Narcissa flares her nostrils, breathing in the day, trying to remember why she ever went to the trouble to rent this house. Time she thought she'd have, maybe, a place to be alone with her work and no paper-thin motel walls to worry about.

"One more, though, just to get Mr. Silvey's attention."

But he already knows, the voice beneath the sleeping bag reminds her. *They told him last night.*

Narcissa shuts her eyes, wishing the sun didn't feel so good, wishing she were stronger and could slip forever into the gentle darkness beneath Miss Josephine's house in Providence, the endless tunnels and cellars and wells linking a hundred graveyards.

You're insane, Aldous mutters. *No one else should have to die because you're insane,* but Narcissa ignores him, listening instead to her heartbeat, steady as waves on the ocean, and the twittering ghost of the rat lost and drowning in her stomach.

Sadie Jasper curses and squints at the morning stinging her sleepy eyes, hardly ever up this early, 8:35 by the pink plastic Kit-Kat clock hanging on the kitchen wall. She pours her third cup of coffee, hot and black and bitter, and sits down on her stool beside the window, the kitchen much too small for a table so she has to make do with the stool and a patch of counter space. In the winter, she has to sit farther from the window, because of the heat and steam from the half-sized radiator squeezed in beneath the sill. Her bowl of Lucky Charms is starting to turn soggy, but she isn't really hungry, anyway. She sips at the coffee and stares out the window at the street and the cars and a woman walking her ugly little terrier dog.

She was up most of the night with Deacon's sketch, the circle and the line, searching through her books for anything like it and coming up empty-handed. It might be Egyptian, she thought at first, maybe two hieroglyphs used together, but that was only a hunch and her hunches are usually wrong. About three thirty, ready to give up and go to bed, she found herself staring groggy-eyed at the frontispiece of Blake's *Europe: A Prophecy,* "The Ancient of Days," Urizen the measurer crouched inside the yellow sphere of the sun and reaching down towards an unseen world with his vast compass. And she wondered if it could be that simple, Deacon's symbol meant to be the sun, sunrise or sunset, and the black line underneath nothing more than the horizon.

"Yuck," she says and pushes the cereal bowl across the counter until it bumps into the microwave, a Christmas gift from her parents because she hates using the cranky old gas stove. Sadie reaches for her cigarettes and lights one, exhales tobacco and cloves. A draft immediately pulls the smoke out the open window. She glances at the clock again and the hands don't seem to have moved at all. The cat's bulbous eyes rock lazily from side to side, its eyes and its rhinestone-studded pendulum tail and *Hell,* she thinks, *I should have slept at least another fucking hour.*

And that brings her back to the question she's been asking herself since Deacon left the night before: Who's she doing this for? And why the hurry? Sadie sips the scalding chicory coffee and watches the Kit-Kat clock, her head nodding in time to its tail. There was a month or two when she thought she might be falling in love with Deacon Silvey, though she doubts he ever had any idea, the days and nights they spent talking books and drinking, but him in love with Chance all along—the school-smart girl from another world so far from Sadie's that it might as well have been another goddamned planet, the *normal* girl who didn't hang out with the freaks and slackers and ne'er-do-wells, didn't waste all her time in bars and punker clubs.

After the wedding—just a minister at the Jefferson County courthouse, so no big deal, none of Deacon's friends invited—a week or more of people asking her if she'd heard the news yet. "Did you hear Deacon married that girl he was seeing?" "Did you hear she's rich?" "Did you hear she's boring as Hell on a Sunday afternoon?"

And then one night at The Plaza, Sadie getting drunk on White Russians, and Sheryl had asked her if she was okay, if she needed to talk to someone. Sadie shrugged and finished her drink, stared a moment at her reflection in the big mirror behind the counter, her too-blue eyes framed in a smudgy raccoon mask of eyeliner.

"I don't know what you're talking about," she said and used a paper napkin to dab milk off her waxy black lipstick.

"Are you sure? Because I know how you felt about him—"

"I don't *need* Deacon Silvey around to remind me how to be a loser, Sheryl. Believe me, I know *all* about it."

"Okay," Sheryl said, *okay* but her voice full of uncertainty. "I just wanted you to know I'm here, if you *do* need to talk."

"Yeah, well, whatever," and Sadie ordered another White Russian. Sheryl said something motherly about how it was better to try and talk some of it out than get shit-faced, that talk was a lot cheaper than booze and didn't give you a hangover, but she brought Sadie's drink anyway.

Sadie watches the pink Kit-Kat clock and "That shit's ancient fucking history, ladybug," she says, setting her coffee mug down on the counter. It doesn't matter who she's doing it for, she reminds herself, only that she's doing something that might make a difference somewhere down the line, that one day someone might say, *Oh yeah, it was Sadie Jasper finally figured that out. Didn't you know? She helped catch the killer,* and maybe she'll even be there to see the disbelief and confusion on the faces of all the people who've never thought she'd ever amount to anything.

The clock's minute hand grudgingly moves ahead one tick, one tock, sixty seconds closer to nine; Sadie finishes her coffee and cigarette, then sets her cereal bowl in the sink, something she can deal with later, and goes to get dressed.

The Akeley Collection something the library's never gotten around to cataloging, a couple dozen books in two cardboard boxes, lots one and two from the Estate of Mr. Charles L. Patrick Akeley, donated in November 1963. Sadie fills out a request form and gives it to the balding gray-haired librarian.

"I swear," he says. "I don't think a single, solitary soul has ever once asked to look at those old things but you. One of these days, I'm going to have to find the time and money to take better care of them."

"You really should do that," Sadie replies. "There are some very rare books in those boxes."

"Well, like I said, one of these days," and the librarian smiles, showing off his perfect dentures, and reads the slip of paper in his hand. "You only need Lot Two today?"

"I think so."

The librarian nods his head slowly and stares at her, his thick glasses magnifying his eyes just enough that he reminds Sadie of Mr. Magoo.

"I hope you won't think I'm being too nosy or anything," he says, "but do people ever stare at you? On account of the way you dress, I mean?"

Sadie frowns and glances down at her long black dress, the spiderweb design woven into the velveteen, her black-and-white candy-striped hose and tall Doc Marten boots.

"I'm sorry," the librarian says. "I never should have asked you a personal question like that."

"No, it's okay. But yeah, people stare at me. Sometimes they do more than just stare," and Sadie lowers her voice an octave and affects a thick, redneck drawl. "'Yo, Morticia? You s'pposed to be some kind of vampire or somethin'? You wanna drink my blood?'"

"You don't, do you?" the librarian asks her.

"What? You mean drink blood? Oh no, not since I was a kid."

The librarian nods again and seems to consider that a moment, scowls at the slip of paper she's handed him, and then he looks back up at her.

"If you don't mind my asking, why *do* you dress like that?"

And Sadie just wants to get to work, the librarian's attention wearing thin, so she leans close to him and whispers the first thing that comes to mind.

"There are people, you see—mostly members of certain secret alchemical orders—who believe the world ended a long, long time ago and all the stuff we think we see and hear and all the people walking around, *everything's* only a ghost of that world which still hasn't figured out it's dead. So, it seems to me like someone ought to dress for the funeral."

The librarian's eyes grow the slightest bit larger behind his spectacles and he manages a dubious, slightly embarrassed smile.

"Well, all right then," he says and goes away, disappears into the claustrophobic maze of shelves behind his desk and leaves Sadie alone in the stuffy, overlit archives room in the basement of the library. The dropped ceiling so low that she can almost touch it and there are long wooden tables with a few green-shaded banker's lamps despite the rows of fluorescents overhead. The white walls are decorated with antique maps of Alabama and the other south-eastern states, priceless hand-tinted maps from the Civil War and colonial days. The room is crowded with file cabinets and a microfiche reader taking up one whole corner, a drooping, anemic-looking potted plant in another.

Sadie sits down at one of the tables to wait for the books, takes Deacon's drawing out of her notebook and stares at it, trying hard to imagine the design as he must have seen it the first time, not graphite on a rumpled sheet of typing paper, but traced in drying blood on a wall above Soda's bed, the dark line beneath the circle drawn in charcoal. The same thing, but something entirely different, something awful. Deacon said there was writing all around the circumference and she wishes she knew what it was, wishes she had the photographs the forensics people must have taken.

"Here you go," the librarian says and sets the cardboard box down in front of Sadie. "Lot Two of the Akeley Collection."

"Thank you," and Sadie opens her notebook to a blank page.

"No ink, remember. Just pencils."

"I remember," Sadie says. "Thanks."

The librarian lingers, wringing his hands and gazing down at her with his wide Mr. Magoo eyes.

"I hope you're not offended," he says. "I honestly wasn't trying to be offensive."

"I'm not offended," she says, which is mostly true, since she's only annoyed.

"You're absolutely sure?"

"Yes, I'm absolutely sure," she says. "Don't worry about it."

"Well, you let me know if you need anything else. Oh, and I'm afraid the Xerox machine's broken down again," he says and goes back to his desk.

Several years now since Sadie discovered the meager remains of Charles Akeley's library, these two boxes willed to the archives upon his death, but she knows there must once have been a hundred times this many books, the bulk of them sold off by his heirs. Akeley the wealthy grandson of a Birmingham steel baron who never married and spent most of his time traveling in Europe and Asia, chasing ghosts and collecting odd books on the occult. He even wrote one of his own, late in life, and published it himself— *The Mound Builders and the Stars: An Archaeo-Astrological In-*

vestigation—though Sadie's never actually seen a copy of the volume for herself. In the 1950s, he briefly served on the library's board of trustees, but abruptly resigned in disgrace following rumors of homosexuality and strange goings-on in his great-grandfather's mansion over the mountain. Finally, he committed suicide in 1963, only a few hours after the Kennedy assassination. From time to time, Sadie's entertained the idea of writing his biography, but has never gotten any further than a few pages of typed notes.

She takes a couple of books from the box marked LOT 2 in red Magic Marker, copies of Magnien's *Les Mystères d'Eleusis* and Benoist's *Histoire des Albigeois et des Vaudois,* sets them both aside because she hasn't had French since high school and they're not what she's looking for, besides. There are volumes on the Grail and alchemy, witchcraft and Masonry and the Knights Templar, a battered copy of Erich Neuman's *The Great Mother* and *The Idea of the Holy* by Rudolf Otto. The pleasant, nostalgic mustiness of the old paper, but she's more than halfway to the bottom of the box and Sadie's beginning to think this might be the wrong lot after all, is already dreading another encounter with the librarian when she finds what she's looking for hidden beneath a first edition of Charles Fort's *Lo!* Nothing stamped on the fraying cloth cover, but Sadie knows this one by sight, has read most of it at one time or another. She places it carefully on the table and opens the book to the title page, *Werewolvery in Europe and Rituals of Corporeal Transformation* by Arminius Vambery, London 1897.

"*There* you are," she whispers to the book, and gently turns its brittle yellow-brown pages, past medieval maps and woodcuts, a man with a wolf's head gnawing a bone. Searching for a passage she remembers or only thinks that she remembers and Sadie pauses to read Vambery's narrative of the Beast of Gévaudan, *la Béte Anthropophage du Gévaudan*; contemporary accounts quoted from the *Paris Gazette* and *Saint James' Chronicle* of something huge and wolflike that roamed the French countryside from 1764 to 1767, something murderous that was said to stand on its hind legs to gaze into the windows of peasants. Stories of slain women and moonlight sightings, strange tracks and the frustrations of the Chevalier de Flamarens, King Louis XV's Grand Louvetier. Vambery finishes with Gévaudan and goes on to describe other attacks in other places, other years, a creature that stalked Cumbria in 1810 and another in Orel Oblast, Russia, in July 1893. When Sadie glances at the clock, an hour has passed and she still hasn't found the passage. She looks at the sheet of typing paper and Deacon's drawing, and turns another page.

"Indeed," Vambery writes, "many of these accounts may be divided from fatal attacks upon persons by mere carnivorous animals, in the singular and grisly commonality that so few of the bodies are ever entirely devoured. Instead, the beasts frequently remove only the meanest portion from the corpse, often a vital organ such as the heart or liver, or have only drained the victim of his blood. No doubt, these selective, indeed almost surgical, habits must be related to rituals which remain unknown to us."

"How's it going?" the librarian asks and Sadie jumps, drops her pencil and it rolls away under the table.

"I'm so sorry. I didn't mean to startle you."

"No," she says, "that's okay," ducking beneath the table to retrieve her pencil, but it's nowhere to be seen. "I didn't know you were standing behind me, that's all."

"I thought you might need something else."

"No, I'm fine. I found the book I was looking for," and she gives up on the pencil, sits up again and the librarian is reading Vambery over her shoulder.

"Not for someone with a weak stomach, is it?" he asks and smiles his uncertain smile.

"No," Sadie replies, "I don't guess it is," wishing he'd go back to his desk, wondering if she has another pencil or if she'll have to borrow one from him.

"I was born in New Orleans," he says. "My grandmother used to tell us stories about the *Loup Garou.* She used to say there'd once been a house in the Quarter where they all met when the moon was full."

Sadie finds another pencil in her purse, but it isn't very sharp and doesn't have much of an eraser left.

"The house caught fire when she was just a little girl, on a night with a full moon, and her mother told her that it was God's judgment on the werewolves for having killed a parish priest. She said the firemen heard animals howling inside the burning house, but all the bodies they ever found were human."

Sadie turns around so she's facing the librarian, scoots her chair across the linoleum floor. "That's a really creepy story," she says. "You should write it down sometime."

"Oh, well, my grandmother, she knew a lot of creepy stories. Are you sure you have everything you need?"

"Yeah, I'm sure," Sadie says. "But thanks, though," and then the librarian returns to his desk and leaves her alone again with Lot Two. She turns back to Arminius Vambery and Deacon's drawing, his rising or setting sun, sun or moon, if she's right. Sadie finishes reading the account of the attacks in Orel Oblast, turns the page, and at last there's the one she's been looking for. She reaches for her notebook and prints ATTACKS BEGINNING 8 JANUARY 1874 on the top line of a blank piece of paper.

A string of unexplained killings in Ireland, mostly attacks on sheep and other livestock, and Vambery quotes at length from an article titled "An unwelcome visitor" from the *Cavan Weekly News,* April 17, 1874. "A wolf or something like it" the reporter says, slaughtering sheep near Limerick, as many as thirty in a single night, and several people bitten by the animal were admitted to the Ennis Insane Asylum, "labouring under strange symptoms of insanity." Another article from *Land and Water* dated March 28, describing footprints not unlike a dog's, but long and narrow, with marks made by strong claws. The throats of the sheep had been neatly cut and most of the animals drained of their blood, but the bodies left uneaten.

More newspaper accounts, the *Clare Journal* and London *Daily Mail,* a monotonous inventory of dogs shot and sheep mutilated, and then Vambery returns to the subject of the Ennis Asylum. One of the women from Limerick, Margaret Tierney, mauled by an animal she could only describe as a "great black beastie" and "Following the incident, the inmate has been gripped with some peculiar specie of obsessive mania," Vambery writes. "When given ink and pen to write her step-sister in Dublin, Margaret Tierney instead decorated the walls of her cell with the same symbol or design again and again. The symbol was described by the physician in attendance as a carefully executed ring or circular shape, underlined in each and every instance. It may be of interest to the reader and any future investigators that there still exists a tradition among the people of Co. Limerick of 'raths' or 'hollow hills' leading down into the subterranean realm of the Gaelic *Daoine Sidhe*. It is said the entrances to these 'hollow hills' are sometimes marked by ancient standing stones bearing graven emblems not entirely dissimilar from that drawn repeatedly by mad Margaret Tierney."

The story of the "Black Beast of Limerick" went on for several more pages and Sadie made a few notes with the dull pencil, dates and names, Margaret Tierney's insanity, the removed organs and surgical precision of the wounds. On April 27, an infant went missing from its cradle and tracks found in the soft earth beneath an open window matched those discovered at the scene of many of the beast's attacks. The mother was the last "victim" admitted to the Ennis Asylum during the incident, where she continued to insist that what had slipped out the bedroom window with her child wasn't a wolf at all. After the disappearance of the baby, the attacks ceased as abruptly as they'd begun. "In early June," Vambery continues, "a farmer in neighbouring Croom is said to have shot and killed a mongrel, which many believed to be the fiend. However, there are no records to tell us if the dog's spoor compared favorably with the queer tracks seen two months previous in Limerick."

And then he goes on to recount other horrors and Sadie closes the volume and sets it aside with the others. She copies Deacon's drawing into her notebook, and writes "Not sun, but moon" and underlines "moon" three times. When she looks at the clock on the wall she's surprised to see that it's almost twelve, so two whole hours now since the librarian brought her the cardboard box labeled LOT 2, and my how time flies when you're giving yourself the willies, she thinks. Sadie returns all the books to the box and then carries it back to the librarian's desk.

"Oh, you didn't have to do that," he says. "You should have asked. I'd have gotten it for you. That's what they pay me for."

"That's okay, I'm a big girl," and she thanks him again for his help and goes back to the table for her notebook, her purse and the stubby pencil.

"There's a pay phone upstairs, right?" she asks and the librarian points at the ceiling. "First floor," he tells her. "Right there across from the big portrait of Washington," and then he disappears into the stacks with the box of Charles Akeley's books.

*   *   *

The coffee and sandwich shop only a block from the library, hurried lunch-hour crowd of businessmen and their secretaries, the murmur of indecipherable conversations and when Sadie's finished talking, she hands her notebook across the table for Deacon to see. As if there could be something there to back up the wild things she's said, as if words on paper might be more convincing, but it doesn't matter, because he doesn't even bother to look at it.

"Werewolves and fairies," he says again in the same doubtful tone and pushes the notebook back across the table to Sadie. She closes it and shrugs, looks down at the cover instead of looking at him.

"You said see what I could find. That's what I found."

"I'm looking for a murderer, Sadie, not a monster."

Deacon pours milk into his coffee from the little cow-shaped pitcher that the waitress brought, stirs at it with his spoon until it's faded the color of roasted almonds.

"What you told me you saw," Sadie says, "it sounded pretty goddamned monstrous to me."

"Yeah, well, you know how that works. I know I've explained it all to you before. What I see isn't always gospel, Sadie. Sometimes I only see people the way they see themselves."

"So what about the design, then?" Sadie asks and reaches for a pink packet of Sweet'N Low for her own coffee. "You don't really think that's just a coincidence?"

"No, but I do think it's possible this woman's been reading some of the same books you have."

Sadie shakes the packet of saccharin three times and tears a corner of the paper, dumps the white powder into her cup and most of it floats on the surface of the coffee like a tiny island.

"'The moon came down and scraped itself raw against the horizon,'" Sadie says, quoting lines from Deacon's dream back to him. "'When I was a girl, the moon bled for me.' That's what you told me she said to you."

"Something like that."

"Lycanthropy is often associated with menstruation, and menstruation is often associated with the moon. She kills people and then draws the moon in their blood."

"Hell, Detective Downs should have come straight to you in the first damn place," Deacon says and blows on his steaming coffee.

"But you do see that it makes sense, don't you? That's what she meant about the moon coming—"

"Sadie, I think maybe it's best if you forget all about this mess, let the cops deal with it. The truth is, I never should have come to your place last night."

Sadie glances quickly back down at her coffee, just in time to see the mound of Sweet'N Low collapse and sink into her cup like doomed Atlantis swallowed by the ocean. She picks up her spoon and stirs at the hot black liquid for a moment, counterclockwise swirl, a tiny whirlpool to drag down her thoughts, and when she releases the spoon, the momentum carries it three or four more times around the inner rim of the cup.

"Mrs. Silvey wasn't too thrilled when she answered the phone and it was me, was she?"

"That's not what I mean," Deacon says. "This doesn't have anything to do with Chance."

"Sure. Whatever you say, Deke. But I think I have less trouble believing in those sheep-killing fairies."

Deacon sighs and takes a drink of his coffee, stares out the window at the street.

"Hey, look, don't worry about it," Sadie says and reaches into her purse, digs around until she finds three crumpled one-dollar bills, and lays them on the table.

"You're not listening to me," he says impatiently. "This thing's a lot more complicated than I thought and I shouldn't have ever gotten you involved. It's dangerous—"

"Great. So next time you feel the need to fucking unburden yourself, try telling your spook stories to Chance. Tell her about your bad dreams."

"For shit's sake, I don't need this right now, Sadie."

"Well, you know what? Neither do I," and she gathers her things, the notebook, her cigarettes and purse, and slides out of the booth. "I gotta run, anyway. Sheryl got me a few hours at The Plaza this afternoon and I need the money."

"I'll call you later."

"No you won't, Deacon. But that's okay, all right? It was fun pretending we were friends again," and she walks quickly past the woman at the cash register and back out into the breezy October afternoon.

*   *   *

Seven long hours at The Plaza tending bar for minimum wage and tips, two o'clock until nine to supplement the checks her parents send once or twice a month, seven hours before Bunky shows up and she can finally go home. Bunky Tolbert on time for once in his whole lazy life, and Sadie leaves the smoke-filled, clattery bar and steps out into the night. A chill in the air and her breath fogs, but there's no point wishing she had a car, because she wouldn't be able to afford the insurance, or even gas, for that matter; she walks along Highland Avenue, her quick, determined steps, arms folded and her hands tucked into her armpits to keep her fingers warm. Her streetlight to streetlight march, one halogen pool to the next, and Sadie tries not to think about Deacon Silvey or her empty apartment. She keeps her eyes on the sidewalk, step on a crack and maybe her mother has it coming.

The wind makes lonely, snake-rattling sounds in the trees and she doesn't look at the windows of the apartments and condos she passes, other people's comfort not meant for her. When she reaches the scruffy little hollow of Caldwell Park, Sadie stands there shivering, staring across the patch of grass already going brown from an early frost, a few scattered water oaks and pines, a swing set and picnic tables. A shortcut home she's taken a hundred times after dark, but tonight there's something in the air or under her skin and she pauses and looks back the way she's come. There are only the cars parked along the sidewalk and a few fallen leaves scuttling like giant insects along the road, and she steps off the concrete and descends sandstone and redbrick stairs leading down into the park. At the bottom, she stops again and looks back up towards the sidewalk.

"What the fuck's gotten into you?" she asks herself, wondering if it was the things Deacon told her the night before, or the stories she read that morning in Arminius Vambery's old book. Either or both or something else altogether, and she listens to the random interplay of the sighing wind and dry branches, the human sounds of the traffic along Highland and a radio playing rap music somewhere.

"Go home, Sadie," she says, prompting, just something to get her moving again, and she imagines how good a hot bath will feel, Mr. Bubble and her vanilla- and lilac-scented candles, how much better bed will feel afterwards. She turns back to the park and takes a few more steps towards the other side, no streetlights down here and so she walks faster than before. *If Deacon were here,* she thinks and then pushes the thought away, angry at him and more angry that she's getting freaked out over nothing, scared of the dark and jumping at her own shadow like a five-year-old.

"If Deacon *were* here," she says out loud, talking to herself and the shadows gathered beneath the trees, "I could kick him in the nuts." She laughs, but it isn't really very funny and doesn't make her feel any better, so she starts walking again. Sadie's halfway across the park when she hears a noise from the trees on her right, a heavy footstep in pine straw or the creak of rusty chains from the swings, some perfectly ordinary park sound, so there's no reason whatsoever for the way her heart has started racing or the tinfoil and ephedrine thrum of adrenaline in her veins. But a stray line remembered from Vambery's book, "When twigs crack, don't whistle," warning from mothers to their children during the terror in Gévaudan, and "Fuck off!" she shouts at the dark places the noise might have come from. "I have pepper spray!"

There's no way to pretend the laughter that floats back to her is anything else, a woman's soft, almost musical laugh, and Sadie reaches into her purse, hunting the tiny can of cayenne-pepper spray she keeps on her key chain.

"I'm not joking with you, asshole," she says, even though she can't find her keys hidden somewhere in all the other purse crap.

The woman laughs again, as Sadie's hand closes at last around the cold and spiky bundle of keys. She drops her purse getting them out and spills everything in a pile onto the grass at her feet.

"Oh my," the woman says, her voice like ice cream and rose thorns. "What big, big eyes you have, Sadie."

Sadie aims the pepper spray at the darkness, at the useless streetlights shining dimly from the far side of the trees, but her hands are starting to shake.

"What will it be, Little Red Cap? Which road will you choose?"

Sadie doesn't turn her back on the voice, but she does take another step nearer the edge of the park, another step towards home.

"What the hell are you talking about?"

"This fork in the road, child," the woman replies. "Which path will you choose? That of the needles, or the road of pins?"

"I'm not afraid of you," Sadie lies and there's a rustle high in the trees, the flutter of frantic, startled wings, skitter of small, sharp claws. And she squints into the night for a glimpse of the face behind the voice, but there's only black and a hundred thousand shifting shades of gray.

"I'm not afraid of you, bitch. Come out where I can see you."

"Oh, child," the woman says, and now she sounds almost kind, almost sorry for whatever's coming next. "Run. Run away fast."

And that sudden shift in tone enough to make Sadie drop the badass act once and for all, any pretense that she isn't scared all the way shitless and back again, and she *does* run. Never mind her spilled purse, never mind anything but the safety of lights and cars and people. She runs, and with her ears or only in her mind she can hear the thing following her fast across the grass and patches of dry, sandy earth, the thing that doesn't need a face because it has that voice and the whole damn night for a mask.

Sadie reaches the sidewalk and keeps running, out into the street and the deafening blare of a car horn, the squeal of brakes and tires hot against asphalt, the headlights like the dazzling eyes of God. The car misses her, but close enough that she can feel it rushing past, the gentle shove of air displaced, and then she trips on the curb and lands sprawling among the gnarled roots of an old poplar tree. She rolls over onto her back, the pepper spray still gripped tight in her right hand, and *Please, just let it be over fast, let it be quick,* but there's only the empty park back there, only the mute darkness holding its ground beyond the garish streetlights and the road.

All the way home from the park, past more apartment buildings, walking twice as fast through the long shadow cast by a freeway overpass, finally past The Nick and its rowdy parking-lot crowd, and every second Sadie listening for anything out of place, any incongruence, the most infinitesimal creak or shuffle or whisper that ought not be there. One knee and both her elbows bleeding badly from the fall, skin scraped raw and aching, and when someone calls her name from the crowd outside The Nick she smiles and waves, but keeps walking. All she has to do is get inside and call Deacon, and he'll come because he *has* to come, because somehow this is all his fault.

"Yo, Sadie!" someone shouts. "Is something wrong? You look like shit," but she doesn't stop and try to explain, nothing she could say that would make sense, anyway, nothing that wouldn't sound hysterical.

Through the front entrance of the building and up the stairs to the second-floor landing, her keys all that she has left now but all she needs, too, and it takes her a moment to find the one that fits her door. The pepper spray and the key to her parents' house in Mobile, the key to a blue Volkswagen bug she had years and years ago, four or five keys to nothing at all, just bits of shaped and polished metal she carries around because they make her feel less disconnected from the world. Her hands still shaking badly enough to make even such a simple undertaking a chore, but when she finds the right one, the brass key slides smoothly into the lock and it clicks softly and the knob turns easily in her hand.

"Hello, Little Red Cap," the woman from the park says and Sadie looks up to see her standing all the way at the other end of the hall. She smiles a wide white smile and reaches into her slick leather blazer the color of old motor oil. "I've been waiting here so long I thought maybe you weren't coming."

"I'll scream," Sadie says and opens the apartment door.

"And who do you think's going to hear you, child? Who do you think's going to care?"

Sadie steps quickly over the threshold into the dark apartment and slams the door behind her, turns the dead bolt and slides the safety chain into place. Only a little light from the street getting in through the curtains, but the telephone isn't far away, sitting in its cradle on a stack of books beside the television and she grabs the receiver and dials 911.

"They can't help you," the woman says, her voice coming from right outside the door now, bleeding through the wood. "By the time the police get here, it'll all be over."

"Leave me *alone!*" Sadie screams, and then the operator comes on the line and starts asking questions, easy questions, but Sadie can't remember any of the answers, and "They can't help you, Little Red Cap," the woman says again. "I wouldn't lie to you. I have no reason to lie to you."

"There's someone at my door," Sadie tells the operator, words rushing out of her in a frantic, breathless flood. She knows that she's crying now, because she can feel the wet, warm paths of the tears down her cheeks. "Please, there's someone trying to fucking kill me," and the operator tells her to stay calm, slow down and speak clearly, asks for her address in a perfectly reasonable, dispassionate tone, and then the doorknob begins to turn.

"This isn't my style, Sadie. Let me in or I'll have to let myself in."

"Please," Sadie says. "Hurry," and the door explodes with a crack loud as thunder, the old hinges giving way before the dead bolt, the doorframe pulling loose from the wall in a shower of splinters and plaster, and Sadie drops the phone and runs. She makes it as far as the beaded curtain dividing the kitchen from the living room before strong fingers tangle themselves in her cherry hair and pull her back. Sadie grabs at strings of amber beads and they go down with her.

"What are you running from, Little Red Cap? Didn't you *want* to find me? Didn't you go looking for me in a book today?"

The woman crouching over her, one hand locked tight around the back of Sadie's neck, sharp nails digging into her skin and forcing her face towards the hardwood floor, the yellow-orange scatter of plastic beads, and "The police are coming," Sadie sobs. "They're already on their way."

The woman laughs and slams Sadie's forehead against the floor. There's an instant of faultless nothingness before the pain and a fairy swarm of lights about her face, but she doesn't black out.

"And then what, Little Red Cap? Will they chop off my head? Will they cut open my belly to let you out?"

Sadie closes her eyes and opens them again, blinking back the pain, but the fairy lights are still there, and a chocolate-dark smear of her blood against the wood.

"Why do you keep calling me that?" she asks, more blood spilling from her lips and Sadie realizes that she's bitten her tongue, so maybe that's where the blood on the floor came from. The woman's mouth is pressed close to her face now, her hot breath like steam off summer roadkill, and her teeth nip playfully at the rim of Sadie's left ear.

"Come on, Sadie. Don't spoil the moment. You know exactly how this story goes, don't you? You know *all* the stories."

"I don't know what you're talking about."

"At last I find you, you old sinner," the woman says. "I've been looking for such a *very* long time."

"You're fucking crazy," Sadie says, spits out a mouthful of blood, and the woman smacks her head against the floor again.

"*No,*" she growls. "It's not half that simple, Little Red Cap. It isn't that simple at all."

The ballooning pain in Sadie's head and the sweet rot clinging to the mad woman's breath, the one as unreal as the other, and now even the fairies have deserted her and there's no light left in the world but a few reluctant shafts filtered through the apartment windows.

"The police are coming," Sadie says again, but her voice sounds weak, slurred, very far away, and she doesn't even convince herself.

"Then we'll have to hurry, won't we," the woman replies and she drags Sadie across the kitchen floor, drags her all the way to the little radiator beneath the windowsill. Sadie lies still at her feet, listening for sirens that aren't coming, staring up at the tall, blonde woman. Her eyes flash gold and scarlet, wild animal eyes, but Sadie knows that isn't real, either. The woman reaches into her leather blazer and takes out a shiny pair of handcuffs.

"Do you think Deacon will ever appreciate what you did?" she asks. "Do you think he'll even understand? Perhaps I'll tell him for you before I cut his throat."

"Deacon," Sadie whispers, her tongue too sore now to talk any louder. "He saw you in his dreams. He saw you—"

"He saw what I let him see. That's all, Little Red Cap."

"He saw *you*, bitch," and then the woman snaps one of the cuffs shut around Sadie's left wrist, the other around the radiator pipe. The steel cuff isn't cold, and such a small surprise brings Sadie back to herself a little. She blinks and now the woman is holding a long, sharp knife, stiletto glint, and Sadie wonders where the hell that came from.

"Magic," she mumbles and the woman kneels beside her.

"Maybe," she says. "My father was a cheap magician, but *his* father, his father was a wizard. Isn't that what you've been looking for all along, just a shred of magic in the world?"

"Hey!" a man shouts from the other room, from the apartment door. "What the hell's going on in there! I want you to know I already called the goddamned police!"

"A friend of yours? You know who that is, Little Red Cap?" the woman asks. Sadie shakes her head no, but it's old Mr. Farris from down the hall, Mr. Farris who yells at her in the hallway about her stereo and the sound of her typewriter in the middle of the night.

"Well, you stay put, child. I'll be right back, I promise," and the woman stands up. "Just a minute, please," she shouts back at Mr. Farris and leaves Sadie alone in the kitchen. A few seconds later and the old man starts yelling about the police again.

Sadie gets to her knees, dizzy and sick to her stomach, but she braces herself against the counter; she can just reach the stove, and she twists the control knobs for the four burners and the big one for the oven. Immediately, there's the hiss of escaping gas, the smell that's always reminded her of boiling turnip greens, and Sadie opens the silverware drawer and pulls out a handful of forks and spoons.

"I ain't afraid to use this," Mr. Farris says, and she figures he means the duct-taped aluminum baseball bat he takes with him on his afternoon walks, but it could be a gun for all she knows. Sadie has a feeling it could be a fucking howitzer and it wouldn't make any difference to the blonde woman.

"I fought in Korea and I ain't afraid to use this."

"Thank you," Sadie whispers to whoever or whatever might be listening and opens the cabinet door beside the stove. There's an aerosol can of Lysol disinfectant and she takes it out, so dizzy she has to stop and lean against the counter, wasting precious seconds, until the kitchen decides to quit spinning. The room on a carnival Tilt-A-Whirl, her skull trying to spin the other way round, and "I mean it, lady!" Mr. Farris shouts.

Sadie opens the microwave oven and dumps all the silverware and the can of Lysol inside, shuts the door and presses the button marked QUICK ON. The green LED display sets itself to *0* and she pauses, looks from the window to the kitchen doorway, and *Maybe if I scream,* she thinks. *Maybe he does have a gun and if I scream now—*

But then a shocked and gurgling sound like someone strangling, and so she knows that the blonde woman has used her knife, has cut the old man's throat, and "I'm sorry, Mr. Farris," she whispers and presses *9* on the microwave's touch pad. The oven hums and whirs suddenly to life and Sadie pulls herself to the window, up over the radiator and onto the narrow sill. Already sparks are flying about inside the microwave and she doesn't stop to think about how far it is down to the ground, or her wrist snapped and torn by her own weight and the steel cuff. No more time left for thought, not if she wants to live and Sadie Jasper has never known how badly she wants to live until this moment.

And then the blonde woman is back, standing there in the doorway, sniffing the poisonous air like a dog, revelation bright in her furious, golden eyes, and Sadie tumbles backwards out the window as the kitchen is swallowed in a blinding cascade of roiling blue flame.

CHAPTER EIGHT

Proverbs of Hell

Sunday, 9:30 A.M., and Chance is sitting alone at the little table in the nursery, sipping Red Zinger tea from a cracked coffee cup that she keeps meaning to throw out. But it was her grandfather's, his plain white cup with the glaze worn away to rough ceramic at the handle and most of the way around the rim, and so it always winds up back in the cabinet. Too little of him left, now that the house is gone, and Chance sets the cup down on a saucer and listens to the rainy sounds of Deacon taking a shower. Most of Saturday morning spent working on the nursery, Chance watching more than actually doing anything, watching while Deacon finished with the wallpaper border she'd ordered from a catalog—a dinosaur alphabet, crude stone letters and cute cartoon dinosaurs. A for *Ankylosaurus,* B for *Brontosaurus,* and he called her a geek when she complained that the proper name for *Brontosaurus* was *Apatosaurus* and everyone ought to know that by now.

Pretending their world was safe and sane and normal, and then the phone rang and his hands were full, so she went to the bedroom and answered it. The girl named Sadie, one of his old drinking buddies, *Hello, can I please talk to Deacon,* and Chance almost hung up on her. As though pretending were enough to keep the bad things at bay, when she's always known better.

"I asked her to do me a favor, that's all," Deacon said when they were finished talking. "I'll be back in half an hour." He wiped his hands on his jeans and reached for his jacket hanging on the bedpost.

"What if I said no?" Chance asked and he shook his head and looked at the floor.

"I'd have to go anyway."

"This is about the guy at the door, isn't it? The shit with the cops?"

"Thirty minutes, I swear," he said and Chance didn't say anything else, but she sat on the bed watching the alarm clock on the dresser until he came back. Forty-five minutes later, not thirty, but she couldn't see any point in complaining about the difference. He apologized, not for being late, for going, for Sadie's call, for everything, and went back to the nursery to finish the border.

C is for *Coelophysis*.

Chance sips her hot crimson tea and stares through the wooden bars of the cradle, her eyes tracing the soft ridges and valleys in a white flannel blanket. In the bathroom, Deacon turns off the water and she can hear his heavy, wet footsteps on the tile floor. The brief hiss of his spray-on deodorant, and then the sound of a door opening, and Chance turns to see him standing naked in the hallway, still rubbing at his hair with a towel. Wisps of steam rise from his lean shoulders, his body still so skinny that she can count the ribs, skinny but hard, strong despite the abuse it's endured over the years.

"You're dripping all over the floor," she says.

"Did you call Alice?"

"No, I didn't," she replies. "Now wipe that up. I'll slip and break my neck."

"Are you *going* to call her? I have to leave soon."

"I called Dr. Capuzzo's office and rescheduled for tomorrow."

Deacon stops drying his hair and stands there dripping and frowning at her.

"Why the hell'd you do that?"

"Because," she says, "I'm going with you today."

He rubs his rough, unshaven cheeks and sighs, stoops to wipe up the water.

"Honey, I don't think that's such a good idea. A police station isn't exactly the ideal place for pregnant women."

Chance takes another drink of her tea and shrugs. "Be that as it may, I'm still going with you. And we're not going to have an argument about it."

Deacon sits down, the wet towel draped across one knee, his bare ass on the varnished wood, and he's looking back at her with that familiar, weary expression that she knows means he isn't up to whatever it would take to make her change her mind.

"This is stupid," he says. "You know that, right?"

"I want to know what's happening. I *need* to know what's happening."

"I already told you—"

"*No*, Deke," she says, truly sorry that she sounds angry, but not sorry enough that she doesn't finish what she's started. "You've only told me what you thought I'd believe, or what you thought wouldn't piss me off. You haven't told me what you think is *really* going on."

"That's because I don't know what's really going on."

"But you know a lot more than you're telling me."

"Yeah," Deacon says, "I do," and then he rubs his cheeks again. "Shit, I forgot to shave."

"I wasn't brought up to believe in ESP. Hell, sometimes it seems like I wasn't even raised to believe in card tricks."

Deacon raises an eyebrow and coughs out the stale crust of a laugh. "Or God. Or the Easter Bunny. Or Santa Claus—"

"I did too believe in Santa Claus," Chance says indignantly. "I believed in him until I was six."

"No shit? Man, I bet that was a weed up Joe's ass."

Chance doesn't reply, because this isn't going to degenerate into a fight about her grandparents, that old bone already chewed down to the marrow ages and ages ago. She goes to take another sip of her Red Zinger, but the cup is empty, just a stain and a few bits of tea leaves stranded at the sticky bottom.

"I'm scared, Deacon," she says, finally. "I'm more scared than I've ever been in my life."

"And now you're starting to think that not knowing is worse than knowing, even if you don't believe?"

"Something like that," she says and dabs at the tea leaves with an index finger.

"But it doesn't always work that way, Chance. You need to understand that. Sometimes ignorance really is bliss."

"No, I absolutely can't accept that. I can believe in a whole hell full of ghosts and goblins, *or* a heaven full of angels, before I can believe I'm better off being ignorant about *anything*."

Deacon gets up off the floor, the wet towel slung around his neck, and he glances towards the bedroom door.

"I don't suppose I have to tell you about trying to put genies back into bottles, do I?" he asks and she shakes her head.

"That's why you went to see this Sadie girl, isn't it? Because you can't talk to me, but she'll always listen, no matter how crazy it sounds."

"She took me to see a ghost once," Deacon says. "Something like that sort of breaks the ice about shit like this."

"I have to know," she tells him and Deacon silently stares at her a moment, the indecision plain to see in his green eyes, and a small voice somewhere inside Chance insisting that maybe she doesn't want to know these secrets, after all, doesn't want Deacon to start telling her all the things he's told Sadie Jasper and the police, the things the man named Scarborough Pentecost has told him. But the fresh memories of blood that wasn't there as a counterpoint, blood dripping from her forehead into a rest-stop sink, the blood from the fiberglass maw of the *Megalopseudosuchus,* and she thinks nothing can ever be as terrible as the fear that she's losing her mind.

"Well, hang on a second," Deacon says and disappears into the bedroom. She can hear him rummaging about in the closet and when he returns, he's wearing a pair of blue-and-green plaid boxer shorts and carrying a manila envelope. "I have to get dressed. If you're serious, look at what's in here, and then we'll talk on the way to the station. But, Chance, if you're *not* serious, I can get through this mess without dragging you any deeper into it. And when it's over, we can go right back to the way things were before."

"No, we can't," she says, turning the envelope over in her hands. There's a coffee stain on one side. "Something's changed, Deacon, something *inside* me has changed, and I don't think it's ever going to be the same again. Are you going to shave?"

"I don't think it matters."

"No, I don't guess it does."

"I *will* protect you and the baby, Chance. Ain't nothing or nobody getting close to you again, not as long as I'm alive and breathing. Maybe you do need to know what this is all about, but I need you to believe that I can take care of you."

"I'm trying," she says. "I promise, I am," and opens the envelope, dumps the photographs and photocopied pages out onto the table beside her empty teacup.

"You don't have to do this."

"Yes, I do," she says, and in a moment Deacon gives up and goes back to the bedroom to finish getting dressed and Chance picks up a black-and-white photo of a ramshackle old house in the woods somewhere. And behind her, a sudden, shattering sound like breaking glass; she turns quickly and the window looking out onto the street and the buildings along First Avenue is washed in thick streaks of blood or something that may as well be blood. She takes a deep breath and starts to call for Deacon, a witness to tell her this isn't all in her mind, but then it's already gone, and there's only a nursery window again. Autumn sunshine bright through clear, clean glass, the sky wide and blue above the city, and the baby kicks so hard she gasps.

"Hush," she says, rubbing her belly. "That really hurt."

When Chance glances back at the window, there's a rock dove perched on the sill, watching her with its beady, dark eyes. She watches it too, for the minute or so before it flies away, and then Chance goes back to examining the contents of the envelope.

"It's good to meet you, Mrs. Silvey," the detective says and reaches across the clutter on his desk to shake her hand. "But this is a surprise," he adds. "I was under the impression Deacon would be coming down alone today," and then Chance catches the confused, what's-going-on-here expression on his face when he looks at Deacon.

"It's *Dr.* Silvey," Chance says and squeezes the detective's hand as hard as she can.

"Right," Detective Downs replies, smiling an uncomfortable smile to show off his wide nicotine-stained teeth. "*Dr.* Silvey, it's nice to meet you." She releases his hand and he stares at it a moment, as if maybe he's counting his fingers to make sure they're all still there. "Too bad it's not under more pleasant circumstances."

The detective's stuffy office smells like stale cigarettes and staler coffee, the walls painted the lifeless color of oatmeal and too many pieces of furniture crammed into much too small a space, his desk and three chairs, a bookshelf and metal filing cabinet, a coatrack stuffed into one corner. The heat's blowing from a small vent overhead and Chance has already started to sweat.

"So, what are you a doctor of, Dr. Silvey?" the detective asks and then Deacon lays a sheet of paper on the desk in front of him, the address from the manila envelope the girl gave him.

"Yeah, what's this?"

"That's the best I can do," Deacon says. "You need to go to that address this afternoon. I think you'll find something there that will help you locate the killer."

"You *think?* Have you been holding out on us, Deacon?"

"It doesn't always happen right away. I told you that before."

The detective picks up the piece of paper and leans back in his chair, chews thoughtfully at his thin lower lip while he reads the address printed there aloud. He glances skeptically at Deacon.

"Is that all? An address?"

"Sometimes it's a whole lot less," Deacon replies.

"But you didn't actually *see* the killer? That's what I'm asking you, Deacon."

"I didn't see very much."

"But you saw something more than this address?"

Chance shifts uncomfortably in the chair, wishing she'd used the rest room before being herded into the detective's office, wishing someone would turn off the goddamned heat.

"Do you really believe he saw anything at all?" she asks and the detective shrugs and rocks forward in his chair.

"There wasn't much," Deacon says again. "A white man in his forties. He has a tattoo on his back, a swastika."

"You're telling me this guy's some sort of Nazi?"

Deacon takes a very deep breath, like a swimmer before a dive into cold, deep water. "No," he says. "Not necessarily. The swastika goes back a lot farther than the Nazis. I don't know what it's supposed to mean to him. It could have another meaning."

"Is that all?"

"He wears a Masonic ring, and I think his eyes are blue. Blue or gray."

"And we're gonna find him if we go to this address?" Detective Downs asks and taps the sheet of paper.

"That's not what I said. I'm not sure what you'll find there, but it's something important."

"You never answered my question, Detective," Chance says.

"Do *you* believe he really sees anything, Dr. Silvey?"

"I'm still trying to figure that out," she replies and the detective smiles at her.

"Well then, I guess that puts us both in pretty much the same leaky boat. We'll see what's waiting for us at this address here and then maybe I can answer your question and you can answer mine."

"I'm sorry there's not more," Deacon says and wipes a bead of sweat off the tip of his nose.

"I'll tell you what, man, I should have my fucking head examined for letting myself get involved with this crazy hoodoo horseshit in the first goddamn place."

"You called Deacon," Chance reminds the detective. "Not the other way around."

"That I did, Dr. Silvey, but I promise you it sure as hell wasn't my idea."

"So whose idea was it?" she asks and Deacon takes her hand and squeezes it gently.

"Is there anything else, Detective Downs?" he asks.

Chance turns and glares at him, suddenly too hot and pissed off about too many things at once to focus, to turn her anger into words, but she pulls her hand free, enough sweat that it slips easily from Deacon's grip.

"Actually, there is. I suppose I really should have mentioned this first. You know a young lady named Sadie Jasper, lives over on the ass end of Twenty-second, down by the projects?"

"Yeah," Deacon replies and Chance catches the guarded hint of apprehension in his voice. "I do. Why?"

"There was a fire last night. I'm surprised you didn't hear about it on the news this morning. Maybe you don't watch—"

"But Sadie's okay," Deacon says, as if he already knows, as if he has some say in the matter, and the detective nods his head.

"She's alive. A little worse for the wear, but the docs say she'll be fine. She's a lucky girl, though. Half the damn building burned to the ground before the fire department got things under control."

"Jesus," Deacon whispers. "I saw her yesterday afternoon."

"Was anyone else hurt?" Chance asks and now she reaches for Deacon's hand, but he pulls away.

"There was one fatality, but we don't think it was the fire did him in. The coroner says someone cut the old man's throat before the fire ever got to him."

Chance looks at Deacon a moment and then back to Detective Downs. "Cut his throat," she says.

"Yeah. And broke a few bones in the bargain. But, and here's the thing, Deke, it looks like Miss Jasper was the one started the fire in the first place. No one's pressing charges yet, but I think it's only a matter of time."

"That's fucking crazy," Deacon says. "Why the hell would Sadie have done something like that?"

"Well, she claims someone was trying to kill her and she did it to protect herself. Claims a blonde woman broke in and hand-cuffed her to a radiator in her kitchen."

"Come on, baby," Deacon says, standing up, helping Chance to her feet, and then he turns back to the detective. "Where is she, which hospital?"

"They've got her stashed over at St. Vincent's, but listen, man, I've still got some questions here I need answers for. Sadie Jasper says you told her about the case, that we'd brought you in on it. I thought we had an understanding—"

"I don't remember making any promises," Deacon says, reaching for the door leading back out into the hallway. "Maybe you've been thinking just a little bit too hard."

"Deacon, she says this woman's *looking for you.*"

Chance is already halfway out the door and she stops and stares first at Deacon and the detective. "*What?*" she asks, not at all sure she wants to hear the answer, but the asking almost automatic, like the new layers added to her dread. "What do you mean, she's look-ing for Deacon?"

"Hey, I'm just telling you guys what Sadie Jasper told us. She says the woman was going to try to kill Deacon. She also seems to think this woman's the one who killed Charles Ellis."

"Who?"

"Soda," Deacon says.

Chance takes a step back into the office, back towards the de-tective behind his desk, and Deacon lays a hand on her shoulder.

"You're the one who got him mixed up in this," she says.

"And I assure you we're prepared to do whatever is necessary to protect the both of you, but—"

"I'll call you later," Deacon says. "I've got to see about Sadie now. After I've talked to her, *then* I'll talk to you."

"Fine, Deke, but listen, we both know the clock's ticking on this one, right? You understand that?"

"Right now, Detective, I don't understand much of anything at all. But I'll call you, soon as I can."

"You do that," the detective says coolly, big man speaking with the glacial composure of authority. "I'll be waiting."

And then Deacon puts an arm around Chance and leads her out of the tiny, overheated office, and in just a little while they're back outside, Deacon digging the keys to the Impala out of his pants pocket, the keys on his Bullwinkle J. Moose key chain, and Chance remembers how badly she needs to piss.

"It only hurts when I breathe," Sadie says, a grimace where a smile was meant to be, and Chance gets up and goes to the window looking out and down on the city.

"I'm so sorry," Deacon says again and Sadie closes her eyes.

"Why?" she says. "You aren't the psychotic bitch that tried to kill me. There's nothing for you to be sorry for."

The air smells like disinfectant and the big, gaudy bouquet of flowers on the table across the room, yellow and purple daisies, baby's breath and ferns, flowers from Sadie's parents in Mobile. The much smaller bouquet of white roses Deacon and Chance bought downstairs in the hospital gift shop is still lying in Sadie's lap, wrapped in tissue paper and cellophane. Sunlight streams in warm through the parted curtains, eclipsing the cold and lifeless fluorescents set into the ceiling.

"Anyway, Mom and Pop will be up here tonight. I think that's the worst part," Sadie says and opens her drug-clouded eyes again, glances at Chance standing at the window.

"Deacon, why don't you get her to sit down. Her feet must be killing her."

"I'm fine," Chance says. "I don't need to sit down."

"We can come back later, if you don't feel like talking right now," Deacon says and Sadie's watery white-blue eyes drift his way.

"No. There are things you need to know."

"It can wait, Sadie."

"No, Deke, I don't think so."

Deacon leans back in the hard, plastic chair, molded plastic almost the same color as the ugly pea-green walls. Better to look at the floor beneath her bed than at Sadie in her white plaster cast and bandages, the strawberry-red and violet-black bruises on her face, so he stares at the tile instead.

"I was right," she tells him. "She thinks she's a werewolf."

Chance sighs a loud, long exasperated sigh, and "I'm going for a walk," she says, "I'll be back later." Deacon nods his head, but doesn't do anything to stop her, knows better than that by now and the very last thing Sadie needs is to have to listen to the two of them bickering.

"Thanks for the roses," Sadie tells Chance as she walks past the foot of the hospital bed and "You're welcome. I hope you feel better soon," Chance replies, and Deacon can tell she's at least trying to sound like she means it.

"I won't be much longer," Deacon says.

"Take however much time you need. I just—" but she doesn't finish the sentence, leaves the room as quickly as she can, and neither Deacon nor Sadie says anything else until she's gone. He sits listening to the sound of her footsteps growing fainter and farther away, the squeaky soles of her tennis shoes against the shiny, sterile floors.

"Someone's not a happy camper," Sadie whispers and Deacon shrugs.

"Don't take it personally," he says. "This whole thing's got Chance bent out of shape. I can't really say I blame her."

"She knows what's going on? You *told* her?"

"A little," Deacon says, but *Not enough,* he thinks, even less than he's told Sadie.

Sadie presses a red button and an unseen motor whirs and raises the bed a few more inches, so she's almost sitting upright now, and Deacon tells her to be careful, take it easy.

"Would you believe this is the first time I've been in a hospital since I was born?" Sadie asks him. "I've never broken a bone in my whole life. Guess I'm making up for it in spades, hunh?"

"You don't have to be so damned nonchalant about it, Sadie. You could have been killed."

"That's what everyone keeps telling me."

"That's because it's the fucking truth. You know the fire took out half the building?"

"I fell out the kitchen window, didn't I?" Sadie asks him and shuts her eyes again. "It's so weird how I keep forgetting things."

"It'll pass. You just need to rest."

"She handcuffed me to the radiator, Deke. If that old prick Farris hadn't come along, she really *would* have killed me. He's dead, isn't he?"

Deacon shifts uneasily in his chair, unsure what to say next, and "They found a body," he says. "A man. His throat had been cut. They didn't tell you?"

"No," she says and opens her eyes. "They haven't told me much of anything at all. The police came in and asked me a lot of questions. I suppose I probably shouldn't have answered them. Anyway, my father's bringing his lawyer with him."

"So you did start the fire?"

"What the hell else was I supposed to do? I'm sad to say my ninja powers ain't exactly what they used to be."

Deacon laughs, something good, something unstained, to drain a little of the tension from the antiseptic air. Sadie laughs, too, then moans and settles back into her pillow.

"But you want to know the god's honest truth?" she asks, her words slurring together slightly. "I thought I *was* dead, Deacon. I thought, there's no fucking way I'm getting out of this alive, not a chance, not a snowball's chance in hell, but maybe I can take this bitch out with me. Maybe I can at least keep her from hurting anyone else. But I didn't, did I?"

"It doesn't look that way. Then again, you're not dead."

"No," she says. "No, I'm not."

"How's that bum wing feeling?" he asks, points at Sadie's right arm, and Sadie frowns at the cast that extends from her shoulder all the way down to her wrist, where it ends in a mass of bandages and drainage tubes.

"You don't want to know. They're afraid I'm gonna lose the use of that hand, at least for a while. I guess I'm going to have to learn to hunt and peck with my left hand."

"That bad?" Deacon asks, though he can see for himself, and who really needs to know all the gory details.

"It's a wonder I didn't tear my goddamned hand off. Dislocated my shoulder, fractured my collarbone, broke three ribs, broke my wrist and three of the bones in my hand."

"Metacarpals," Deacon says, because he can't think of anything else to say.

"Yeah, right, metacarpals. But that's not the worst of it. You ever heard of 'degloving'?"

"No."

"Yeah, well, me neither. But that's why they had to operate last night. My hand slipped out of the cuff, and the firemen say that's probably what saved my life, but I peeled loose a big flap of meat on the back of my hand. They're talking about skin grafts," and her voice cracks and she shuts her eyes again.

"But you're alive," Deacon says.

"Yeah, but she's still out there somewhere. Christ, Deke, I thought I was tough. I mean, I thought I'd *seen* some shit, you know? But now, *fuck.*"

"It's over, Sadie. I want you to stop thinking about her and worry about getting well."

"She's not just insane, Deacon. I wasn't even sure I believed in evil before last night, not *real* evil, but now . . ."

And Deacon takes a tissue from the box beside the bed and wipes Sadie's face, the tears leaking from the corners of her eyes and winding their way down her cheeks.

"I'm sorry. I don't want to cry. I hate crying in front of people."

"I think you've earned it," Deacon says and dabs at a wet spot on her chin. Then Sadie grabs his arm with her good left hand, holds on tight, and her eyes are open wide now.

"Listen to me, Deke. It doesn't matter if this woman's really some kind of werewolf or not. It only matters what she *thinks* she is, okay?"

"Yeah, sure," he replies, trying hard not to sound as anxious as her spooky blue eyes and the urgency in her voice are beginning to make him feel.

"Did you ever see that movie, *The Company of Wolves?*"

"Sure," Deacon says and he wipes more tears from her face. "I saw it."

"Remember what the old woman told her granddaughter? She said that the worst wolves are hairy on the *inside.* And just before I fell, right before the explosion, I saw inside *her*, Deacon, through her eyes. Her eyes are yellow—"

"Sadie, you need to calm down now, okay? You're just going to make yourself sicker."

"She kept calling me Little Red Cap," and now Sadie's almost hysterical, and there's no point trying to wipe away all the tears, the clear liquid running from her nose. "Do you know what that means? You told me parts of Soda's body were missing, didn't you, and there were bite marks?"

And Deacon reaches for the call button above the bed, pushes it, and Sadie's still hanging on to his hand, hanging on like she's too afraid to ever let him go again. The last thing keeping her from slipping off the edge of the world, and "Sadie," he says, "I've called the nurse," and he smells oranges and rotting fish.

"Little Red Cap," Sadie sobs desperately, squeezing his hand now so hard that it's starting to hurt. "It *is* a moon, Deacon, a red moon like an eye—"

"I've called the nurse," he says again, and a flash then, blinding light that isn't light pouring out around him, light that's somehow the opposite of light, swallowing him in searing, brilliant jaws. And now he's the one holding on, as the flash scalds away the world and he's watching Sadie on the windowsill, and the blonde woman where the curtain of plastic beads used to be.

She smiles for him, for Sadie, and *That's where the light's coming from,* he thinks, the light that isn't light, black hole ejecta, and the woman takes a step towards him.

"O, what land is the Land of Dreams?" she asks, smiling. "Father, O Father! What do we here, in this land of unbelief and fear?"

On the countertop, the microwave throws orange-white sparks and buzzes like there's a furious swarm of red wasps locked up inside its guts.

"The Land of Dreams is better far," the woman says, and sniffs the gas-fouled air. "You have my key, Deacon Silvey," she growls, "but I'll take it from you soon," and then the wasps explode from the microwave and set the air on fire with their poison barbs.

"Mr. Silvey!" the nurse says, shaking him so hard the world opens up wide and sucks him back into the hospital room. The black light gone and now there's only the irreconcilable mix of sun and fluorescence, and the nurse shakes him again.

"Deacon?" Sadie whispers, afraid, still crying, her blue eyes the antithesis of the blonde woman's sickly golden stare. "Can you hear me?"

"I'm here," he says and the nurse is helping him into the pea-green chair.

"Do you need me to call a doctor?" she asks, and "No," he tells her, his last bit of strength to muster enough insistence that she'll believe him. "I'll be fine. Just give me a minute or two to catch my breath and I'll be fine."

"Are you an epileptic?" the nurse asks.

"No, I just got a little dizzy, that's all," and Deacon shuts his eyes and waits for the pain to begin.

He finds Chance sitting in the lobby downstairs; rows of Naugahyde chairs the color of Thanksgiving cranberry sauce, furniture that hasn't been fashionable since the early 1970s, low tables scattered with piles of old magazines—*Reader's Digest* and *Prevention*, *Woman's Day* and *Southern Living*—and Chance is pretending to read from a *National Geographic* with a frog on the cover. His head already so bad that throwing up is beginning to seem like a good idea, and frantic purple fireflies have started to flit before his eyes. Past the information desk and the low murmur of people around him seems distant and unreal, the loved ones of the dying and the sick, plate glass and potted plants, too much sunlight for the fireflies' liking, and Deacon moves along in his migraine bubble, apart from them all.

"Are you done," she asks him, not bothering to look up from her magazine.

Deacon sits down beside her, slumps into the cranberry chair, rests his head against the back. "I'd give my left nut for a shot of Jack," he says.

"That's not funny," and she tosses the *National Geographic* back onto the table with the rest.

"That's why you don't see me laughing."

"Your head?" she asks and he frowns and shuts his eyes for an answer.

"She could have been killed," Deacon says. "I almost *got* her killed."

"She'll be fine."

"Will she? That arm will probably never be right again. Just because she went to the goddamn library for me. And then I had the gall to fucking laugh at her when she tried—"

"Why does your head hurt, Deke? What happened after I left?"

"It's nothing," he says, but puts one hand over his closed eyes to keep out the light slipping through his lids, stabbing rusty needles at his pupils.

"So what'd she try to tell you yesterday that made you laugh at her?"

"Nothing, Chance. Nothing at all."

"Why don't you just tell me to fuck off and get it over with?"

Deacon opens his right eye and squints at her, shading his face with his hand. The last thing he needs or wants right now, a fight with her, but the headache is growing a will of its own and it isn't half so reluctant.

"Don't you think for a moment it hasn't crossed my mind," he says and the quick and subtle changes on her face to tell him that he's hit home, bull's-eye, bingo, and already Deacon's wishing he could take it back.

"The way you were looking at her up there, the way you fussed over her—I'm not blind, Deacon."

"Jesus, Chance, someone tried to *kill* her last night."

"Did you ever sleep with her?"

Deacon covers his eyes and "I am *not* going to have this conversation," he says.

"Were you in love with her?"

"I'm going to pretend that's just the hormones talking."

She grabs his hand and pulls it away from his face, letting in the sunlight again, the rusty, stabbing needles, and her eyes are bright and wet. Her anger like a mask, so thick, so solid, impenetrable contempt and he thinks for a moment she's going to hit him.

"Don't you do that, Deacon. Don't you fucking do that to me."

"Do *what*?"

"You know exactly what I'm talking about. Don't you dare start condescending to me like that."

He pries her fingers loose from his wrist and sits up, looking her in the eyes now, her furious green eyes like living emeralds, and glances at the two receptionists watching them warily from the information desk.

"Tell you what, babe," he whispers, speaking low now so maybe no one else will hear, so maybe the women will decide to mind their own damned business and not call security. "We'll make a trade. I'll tell you the truth about Sadie Jasper if you tell me how many times you and that sour old dyke Alice Sprinkle got it on. Sound fair enough to you?"

She watches him a minute, not a word, just her hot green eyes and the tremble at the downturned corners of her mouth, Chance's voiceless rage building up and up until the air around them seems to crackle and hum and finally Deacon looks away.

"I'm sorry," he says. "I didn't mean that."

"There are two policemen outside," she replies calmly, calm to mock her anger and the pain in Deacon's skull. "Detective Downs wants you along when he goes to that address you gave him."

"What the hell for?"

"Ask him. I'm going home."

"You know I didn't mean that, Chance. My head hurts and—"

"Forget it," she says and gets clumsily to her feet before he can turn and help her up. "Whenever this is done, I'll be waiting for you," and she leaves him then, and the receptionists go back to their computer screens and clipboards.

Past downtown and into the maze of back streets and warehouse ruins on the decaying north edge of the city, Deacon riding up front with Downs in an unmarked car. There are two black-and-whites close behind them, no sirens or flashing lights, but it's still a long way from inconspicuous and Deacon wonders if that makes any difference. The sky has turned from blue to gray, the ash and charcoal cloud wall of an advancing cold front sliding like a velvet curtain across the world. *There'll be rain before dark,* he thinks around the jagged shards of his headache, staring up past the buildings at the clouds while the detective asks questions Deacon doesn't want to answer.

"Since I was a kid," he replies. "When I was eight, I found my mother's car keys."

"No shit? If you don't mind my saying so, that's not a very auspicious beginning for someone with your rep."

"We all gotta walk before we can run," Deacon says, reciting his lines like someone in the movies. Better that way, canned dialogue to match whatever lies and misdirection Scarborough Pentecost has laid out for the cops.

"What'd your folks think about their kid being, you know, psychic?"

"As little as possible."

They turn up a narrow, unpaved alley and a thick cloud of red-brown dust almost obscures his view of the two cars behind them.

"You really don't like talking about it, do you?" Downs asks, and Deacon rolls up his window because the dust is getting in.

"Nothing slips by you, does it?" he says.

"Look, man, I'm just trying to make a little polite conversation. Ain't no cause for you to go gettin' nasty on me."

The car bumps through potholes and over an old set of trolley tracks, half-buried by gravel and dirt and weeds. Deacon covers his eyes, wishing the clouds were heavier, wishing the sky were as black as pitch and then maybe the pain would back off an inch or so.

"I think there's an extra pair of sunglasses in the glove compartment there," Downs says, but when Deacon looks he can't find them. Nothing but piles of receipts, a box of .38 Smith & Wesson cartridges, and a rolled-up copy of *Hustler*.

"Deke, what's waiting for us at the end of this alley?" the detective asks him and Deacon shrugs his shoulders and closes the unhelpful glove compartment.

"If I knew that, I'd have told you. It might not be anything at all. I've been wrong before."

"Well, right or wrong, we're here," and Deacon looks up as the car comes to a stop beside a concrete loading platform crowded with rusting green barrels and the battered remains of a drill press. "X marks the spot," Downs says and points at the huge red swastika spray painted on the wall of the building.

"Do these things really stop bullets?" Deacon asks and pokes doubtfully at the heavy Kevlar vest that Downs made him put on over his shirt before they left the precinct.

"That depends whether or not some asshole decides to shoot you in the head."

"Thanks for the peace of mind."

"You just stay real close behind me, Mr. Silvey, and odds are you'll be right as rain," and then Downs checks his service revolver and opens the car door, letting in the dust. Deacon coughs and opens his own door, wondering if there's a word for the taste in his mouth, the metallic-flavored residue of pain and adrenaline, dread and uncertainty, and *Chance might know*, he thinks, and steps out into the day.

There's a fleeting moment of light before the abandoned warehouse swallows them all.

There's no electricity in the building, just the bright flashlights of the policemen, restless white beams to bob and sway and divide the darkness; Deacon does as he's told and stays between the detective and a tall street cop named Ledbetter. It's cold inside, musty, mildew-soured air, air that hasn't seen the sun in years, and he's trying not to shiver.

"This place is fucking huge," one of the cops whispers, not Ledbetter, someone else. "What the fuck are we looking for, anyway?"

"What's that over there?" Downs asks and the cop aims his light at a wooden door hanging loose on its hinges. Another swastika, and this time there's something else scrawled beneath it— the familiar red circle and straight black line. The detective touches the swastika and then looks at his fingertips, as if checking to see that the paint is dry.

"I'd say *this* is what we're looking for, wouldn't you, Deke?"

Deacon doesn't answer, steps to one side as Downs tries the knob. It isn't locked, but the sagging door drags loudly on the cement floor when he pushes it open.

"Oh hell," the detective mutters. "Holy fucking Moses," talking more than half to himself now, the voice of a man who's seen his share of bad shit and maybe this is the worst yet. Maybe this is the worst by far, and he takes a deep breath and crosses the threshold into the room behind the door.

"Simpson, you get on the radio and get an ambulance out here. You tell forensics to get their fat asses over here fucking yesterday."

Ledbetter steps into the room after Downs, and Deacon follows them, more afraid of being left behind than of what's inside, disoriented and his heart beating much too fast; this room even darker than the hallway and he blinks and follows the flashlight beams as they play back and forth across something pale hanging from the ceiling. The sudden, cloying stink of shit and blood and Deacon covers his nose and mouth.

"Is he dead?" Officer Ledbetter asks.

"That supposed to be some kind of goddamn joke? The son of a bitch doesn't have a head, so yeah, he better be fucking dead," and now Deacon can see the ragged stump of the corpse's neck, the wet glint of bone and gristle. The man's naked body is suspended from the high ceiling by its ankles and there's a steel washtub sitting on the floor directly underneath. Deacon sees that it's at least half full, a dull skin forming on the surface as the blood cools and begins to clot.

"Motherfucker's still bleeding out," Downs says. "He hasn't been dead long," and Deacon turns his head and gags, squeezes his eyes shut tight and leans against the doorframe.

"Hey, man," Downs shouts at him, "if you're gonna puke, do it out there in the hall."

"No, I'm okay," Deacon says, even though he's far from okay, and rests his dizzy, aching head against the wall.

"Don't nobody touch jack shit," the detective growls. "You hear me?"

"So where the fuck's the *rest* of him?" one of the cops asks and "Over there," Downs says, "and over there, and over there," and Deacon doesn't turn around, easy enough to imagine, he doesn't have to see it for himself.

"And you're telling me you didn't have any idea this was here," Downs says, and "No," Deacon replies and then he gags again. "I didn't know this was here."

"Just look at the fuckin' walls," Ledbetter says and Deacon raises his head slowly, so much agony from such a simple act, and glances to his right. The unsteady flashlight beam to reveal the graffiti frenzy scarring the brick and plaster: leering, demonic faces and blazing eyes, wolf jaws and SS insignia, at least a dozen more swastikas. A Confederate battle flag, and there are long shelves lining the wall, crude things built from cinder blocks and warped and sagging two-by-fours, jammed to overflowing with books and pamphlets. Deacon looks down at the floor and tries to concentrate on not vomiting.

"I have to get out of here," he says and takes a step towards the hall, stumbles and grabs the doorknob for support.

"Deke, I need to know if you're getting anything," Downs says. "I mean anything at all," and then a jolt like an electric shock from the brass knob, something cold that burns, and Deacon cries out and tries to pull his hand back. The blackness flinches, then surges hungrily around him, pulsing like a rotten heart, and he sinks to his knees on the cement floor. The policemen are talking again, talking *still*, calling out his name, but that's already some other time ago, sometime that hasn't happened yet and might never happen now so he doesn't try to respond.

The Land of Dreams is better far . . .

The boundless, heaving blackness—India ink and razor-sharp obsidian flakes, poisonous roiling smoke and seawater a mile or more down, all those things and not one even half this perfect black—tugs at the softest parts of Deacon's brain, and then it melts suddenly away and he's watching Scarborough Pentecost hoisting the dead man's body. The nylon rope tied tight around his ankles and somewhere overhead a rusted pulley squeaks noisily.

"Upsy-daisy," Scarborough says and tugs on the rope again.

"Do you think they'll come?" the girl asks, the girl sitting cross-legged on the floor, cradling the head in her lap. Blood up to her elbows, her clothes washed red-black and a crimson smear across her mouth and chin.

"They'll come," Scarborough says. "Don't you worry. They'll come."

"I didn't expect him to fight so much," she says and gently strokes the dead man's hair with her sticky fingers. "Why's a bum gonna fight so hard to stay alive? I mean, he ate out of garbage cans."

"Everyone fights, little bird," Scarborough says and strains at the rope. "Nobody ever goes down to the nightlands without a struggle."

"I won't fight," she says and reaches for the trash bag lying on the floor nearby. "There are worse things than dead."

"You say that now, but just you wait. Just you wait till it's your turn, then we'll see how much you fight."

"Madam Terpsichore told me it won't be so bad."

"With all due respect, Madam Terpsichore hasn't ever died, now has she?"

"I could ask Miss Josephine," she says and lifts the head by its matted hair. "She would know, wouldn't she?"

"Will you please just put the head in the goddamn bag," he tells her and now the body hangs ten or fifteen feet above the floor of the room, above the washtub, swaying slightly like a pendulum carved of flesh and bone. "We haven't got all day."

"Put the head in the bag," she sulks. "Put the head in the bag," mocking him or merely repeating what he's said, and the plastic bag makes an empty, rustling sound. She ties it shut and looks up, directly at Deacon. Her lips part and her eyes grow wide.

"He sees me," she whispers.

"He's fucking dead, Jane," Scarborough says. "Trust me. He doesn't see anyone anymore."

"No, not him. *Him,*" and she points a red index finger and Deacon tears his hand off the doorknob, wonders how much of himself he's left behind as the blackness swallows him again. The kind and sightless abyss to wrap him in its ebony amoeba folds and rock him senseless, acid night to dissolve his soul if he only knew how to hold on long enough. But he doesn't, or it won't let him, and when he opens his eyes there's only the headache, worse than before, and Detective Downs is squatting there beside him.

"You still with us, man?"

"Yeah," Deacon replies, his throat so dry it burns and he sits down on the floor.

"That's good. Thought for a second there maybe we'd lost you," Downs says. "Think you can walk back to the car? We ought to get you out of here before the circus starts."

"Yeah," Deacon says again, though he isn't at all sure if he's telling the truth. The cop puts an arm around his shoulder and helps him to his feet. Deacon's head swims and he slumps against the door, careful not to touch the treacherous brass knob.

"One of you guys give me a hand over here," the detective says. "We gotta get Mr. Silvey back outside."

"I'm okay," Deacon tells him. "Just give me a minute."

Downs nods and spits on the floor. "I don't know what you got goin' on in that head of yours, mister, but I'll tell you, this shit's the damnedest thing I've ever seen. You did good, Deke."

"Did I?" he asks. "Is that what you think I did here?" and then the doorway leading back to the hall, the hall leading back out to daylight, bleeds a hundred satin tendrils that slip unseen past the detective and wrap themselves about Deacon, drawing him back down to the floor and merciful, numb oblivion.

CHAPTER NINE

In Caverns of the Grave

"You're sure about this?" Sheryl asks again and this time Deacon doesn't even bother to answer her, his glare worth at least a thousand words, his eyes to say everything that needs to be said, and she sets the mug of Budweiser and the shot of Jack down on the bar in front of him.

"Fine," she says. "You're a grown man, Deacon Silvey." And then she takes a step back from the bar, crosses her arms, and watches him.

"What? You've never seen a drunk fall off the wagon before?"

"I'm not saying a word. This is between you, your pregnant wife, and the bottom of a bottle."

Deacon stares at the two glasses and then stares at Sheryl, then stares at the beer and the bourbon a little more.

"What's that crap on the jukebox?" he asks and wipes sweat off his forehead.

"Someone else's quarter," she replies.

"Well, it sucks ass. You know I hate that hip-hop shit."

"So find somewhere else to get smashed," and then someone shouts at her from the other end of the bar, and Sheryl leaves him alone with the two drinks. He touches the rim of the shot glass, a single drop of whiskey on his index finger and then places his finger to the tip of his tongue. The sweet, hot taste of Heaven, the fire to burn away his headache, and Deacon shuts his eyes and tries not to listen past the monotonous *whump-whump-whump* from the jukebox to the soft rise and fall of voices and laughter, the careless clink of glasses, the reek of cigarettes and alcohol, all the sounds and smells of The Plaza at 6:25 P.M. on any Sunday evening. Seedy bar symphony to calm his jangling nerves and soothe the edges off the migraine, if it wasn't for the goddamn rap music. He thinks about getting up and unplugging the jukebox, but Sheryl would probably kick his ass out on the sidewalk if he did. And this is where he told Scarborough Pentecost to meet him—The Plaza at 6:30 or I tell the cops every goddamn thing I know.

Deacon opens his eyes and the two glasses are still there, waiting patiently on the scuffed and dented bar, gold and amber, and he picks up the shot of Jack and sets the edge of the glass against his lower lip, taking a breath, drawing the aroma deep inside himself. "Coward," he whispers, trying hard to think of Chance instead of the decapitated body dangling from the warehouse rafters, instead of the things he saw when he gripped the doorknob. Enough to send fucking Superman scuttling back to the booze, even a whole mouthful of kryptonite better than the memories and the pain and knowing what it all might mean, not being certain what any of it means.

"Fucking pussy," he mutters, no longer sure if he's trying to bully himself into or out of taking the drink.

"You're talking to yourself, Deke," Sheryl says as she walks past and keeps on going.

"Never a good sign," Scarborough says and sits down on the empty stool next to him; the raggedy, thrift-store girl named Jane is standing behind him. "Fella starts carrying on the circular discussions and next thing you know, it's Thorazine and electroshock therapy."

"You're early," Deacon says.

"I'm a busy man."

Deacon draws another deep breath, imagines the whiskey molecules absorbed directly through his nasal passages, his lungs, one big toe in the pool just to see how cold the water is before he takes the dive.

"Yeah," he says. "I just had a good look at some of your handiwork. Do you get paid for that or do you do it just for kicks?"

"Six of one, half dozen of the other," Scarborough Pentecost replies and shouts at Sheryl to bring him a beer. Deacon, the shot glass still held up to his trembling lips, turns around and the girl smiles a sheepish, guilty smile at him.

"You really don't have to do that," she says.

"Why? Don't you think he's earned a drink or two?" Scarborough asks her. "You'll have to forgive her, Mr. Silvey. Someone let her read *The Lives of the Saints* once upon a time and she hasn't been the same since."

Deacon sets the glass back down on the bar.

"Who was he, anyway?"

"Who?"

"The man we killed and left for the police to find," Jane says before Deacon can answer. "That's who he means."

"Hey, now, why don't you just climb up on a table and tell the whole goddamn room about it?" Scarborough snaps and she frowns and glances back towards the door.

"Maybe that's not such a bad idea," Deacon says. "Maybe that's exactly what *I* ought to do."

"Maybe you should just have that drink there, and then have a few more after it, and *then,* Mr. Silvey, think long and hard about Chance and the baby."

Deacon laughs and rubs at his aching head, the grinding, infinite expansion of pain in his skull, turning circles trapped inside turning circles and no limit to the largest or the smallest wheel.

"Mention Chance one more time, you dickless freak, I'm going to break your goddamn neck."

And then Scarborough Pentecost leans very close to Deacon, smiles his wide and toothsome grin, wicked-mean smirk like some cartoon Big Bad Wolf, and "Personally, though, it's no skin off my nose, one way or another," he says.

"Both of you stop it," Jane hisses under her breath and then Sheryl brings a bottle of Pabst for Pentecost.

"Are these two supposed to be friends of yours?" she asks Deacon, glaring suspiciously at the tall man and the ragged girl.

"Not especially," Deacon mumbles and picks up the glass of bourbon again. "Maybe you should bring the bottle."

"Maybe I shouldn't," and she looks back up at Scarborough and then slips away with a wet gray bar rag in one hand and an inky shot of Jägermeister in the other.

"I know you *think* you know the score," Scarborough says. "You think a killer's a killer, a monster's a monster—"

"You set me up, asshole. You made me a fucking accessory to murder."

"We only helped you show the cops what we needed them to see."

"It was necessary, Deacon," the girl says, tracing something on the bar with the ring finger of her right hand, watery geometry of condensation and surface tension. "It had to be perfect. We couldn't take any chances."

On the jukebox, the rap song finally ends and is immediately replaced by Nick Cave crooning about God and Tupelo.

"We need you," Scarborough Pentecost says, his smile fading like a sunset. "And you still need us. She's still out there."

"Everything I need, Mr. Whoever-the-hell-you-*really*-are, well, I got it right here in my hand," and Deacon tips the shot of Jack towards the tall man, make-believe toast to end the charade, all the charades that hold his life together, and then Scarborough plucks the glass from his fingers before it even gets halfway to his mouth.

"You think you know the score, Deacon," the girl says, gazing intently at the invisible things she's drawn on the bar. "Where the darkness ends and the light begins, all the sins that turn angels into demons. But you don't. Not yet."

Scarborough drains the shot glass and sets it down in front of Deacon, wipes his lips with the back of his hand, and the tip of his tongue darts out to catch a stray drop of liquor lingering at the corner of his mouth.

"Best listen to her, buddy," he says and jabs a thumb at the girl. "She's nutty as squirrel shit, but every now and then she starts making sense."

Deacon nods his head and then wraps his left hand around the empty glass, making a fist, imagines it shattering and the splinters burying themselves deep inside his palm. A long time since he's been in a fight, but not so long that he's forgotten anything that matters, anything important, and he swings so hard and fast that Scarborough Pentecost doesn't have time to dodge the blow. Deacon's knuckles connecting with the tall man's nose, the faint snap of bone a second before the shot glass breaks and blood spurts from his hand and Scarborough's nose in the same red instant.

Scarborough grabs for the edge of the bar, misses and tumbles backwards off his stool.

"Did you hear that, *buddy?*" Deacon asks and when he opens his hand, the few pieces of glass that aren't embedded in his skin fall to the floor; fresh pain to clear his mind a little bit, welcome counterpoint to the headache's incessant throb. "How about it, Jane? Am I starting to make sense?"

The raggedy girl glances at Scarborough lying on the floor, cursing and clutching his bleeding nose, and she frowns and looks up at Deacon. "You're just wasting time," she says.

"You don't say?" and when Scarborough tries to get to his feet, Deacon kicks him in the crotch. "Seems to me, I got time enough. Hell, I got just about all the time in the whole goddamn world. Ain't that right, buddy?"

"We have to find Narcissa *tonight,*" the girl says.

"Who or what is Narcissa and why, exactly, do I give a shit?" he asks and realizes that almost everyone in The Plaza has stopped whatever they were doing and is now staring at him and the man writhing on the floor. Sheryl's reaching for the phone near the register.

"Stop her, Deacon," the girl says. "Stop her or I'll have to."

Deacon looks down at Scarborough, curled into a moaning, fetal lump at his feet.

"I can't let her call the police," Jane whispers and there's an edge in her voice more threatening times five than anything Scarborough's done or said to him, a *promise,* and Deacon stands up and yells across the room at Sheryl.

"Yo, Sher, there ain't gonna be no need for that. Cross my heart and hope to fuckin' die. My *friends* and I were just leaving," and she glares furiously back at him, her fingers resting indecisive on the telephone's touch pad.

"I absolutely do not need this crap tonight, Deke," she says and he apologizes and drops a twenty on the bar.

"That's cool. We're already out of here," and he squats down beside Scarborough. "You been listening to all this, buddy? That nice lady over there wants us out of her bar, *tout de suite.*" And then Deacon seizes him by his ponytail and begins dragging him towards the door. Jane follows, keeping an eye on Sheryl. Scarborough flails and snarls and grabs at the strong hand tangled in his hair until Deacon kicks him in the ribs and he stops.

"Thanks, Sheryl," Deacon says as he opens the plate-glass door painted over in messy crimson strokes to keep out the sun.

"Fuck you," she replies. "I ought to make your sorry ass come back and mop the blood off the floor."

"Someday, baby, I'll make it all up to you, and then some," and he hauls Scarborough Pentecost out into the gravel parking lot, into the streetlight shafts coming down through the trees and kudzu crowded around the little bar. Jane eases the door shut behind them and sits down in the gravel next to Scarborough.

"You sure she won't call the police?"

"Yeah, I'm sure," Deacon says. "Sheryl fucking hates the cops. She used to be married to one of the motherfuckers."

Scarborough groans and rolls over onto his back, stares up at the night sky through the branches, his face streaked with blood and snot and spit. Every time he exhales, fresh droplets of gore spray from his broken nose.

"You shouldn't have done that," Jane says to Deacon. "We're going to need him later on."

"Who said I was finished?" and Deacon plants a boot squarely in the center of Scarborough's chest, pinning him to the ground.

"You can't go up against Narcissa alone."

"There's that name again," Deacon says and puts a little more weight on Scarborough's chest. "When do we get to the part where I stop asking questions and you tell me what the hell you're talking about?"

"Not here, not out in the open like this. She might have spies," and the girl looks warily up at the trees. "There are always spies."

Deacon follows her gaze, but all he can see are dead leaves and a few strangling kudzu vines, the sky gone dark so soon, a moment of confusion until he remembers the time change—spring forward, fall back—Sunday, so it's an hour later than it was this time the day before. He shakes his head and looks back down at Scarborough, who's smiling his wolfy smile again and pointing a large handgun at Deacon's head.

"Now move your goddamn foot," he growls and Deacon does as he's told, but keeps his eyes on the barrel of the gun. He takes a step away from the man lying in the gravel and Scarborough tightens his grip on the trigger.

"Jane, you better hope no one else sees him waving that thing around out here, not if you're really so worried about the police showing up."

"He's right, you know," she says to Scarborough. "You're not helping things any."

"You just shut up a minute, little birdie, and let me deal with Mr. Joe Badass here. You broke my goddamn nose, you son of—"

"Put away the gun, Scarborough," Jane says very calmly, the way someone tells a child it's time to turn off the television and go to bed, and Deacon takes another step backwards.

"Don't think that we can't do this *without* you," Scarborough snarls. "Don't think for a minute there's any reason in the world for me not to pull this trigger and blow your goddamn head off."

"The thought never crossed my mind," Deacon says very softly.

"Just put it *away,* Scarborough," and Jane's voice is still calm, but firmer this time. "You're not going to shoot him and we both know it."

"Maybe what you know and what I know are two entirely different things," he replies and starts to sit up, moans and slumps back into the gravel.

"Maybe *you* need to try a little harder to remember what we're doing here," the girl says sternly and then she snatches the gun, moving so fast that Deacon almost misses it altogether—one second Scarborough's holding the pistol and the next it's in her hands.

"I didn't come all the way from Providence to watch you get into a pissing match," she says and Scarborough curses them both and shuts his eyes, covers his bleeding nose with his left hand.

Deacon looks longingly at the front door of the bar, the burnt-out neon sign that's always been hung upside down so that it reads ɐzɐ1Ԁ ǝɥ⊥, the panes of red glass and the GO AWAY—WE'RE OPEN placard, hoping that maybe Sheryl called the cops anyway. But there's no reason to think his luck should start changing now, no point in spoiling a perfect losing streak, so he kicks Scarborough in the ribs again.

"That's for pointing a gun at me," he says and then, to the girl, "What do you say I just take my toys and go home?"

"You called us, Deacon."

"Yeah, I know, but I think I'm over that now."

Jane sighs and wipes a trickle of blood off Scarborough's chin, then wipes her hand on her jeans.

"She'll kill you before the night's over. And then she'll kill Chance. You've seen her. You know what she can do."

"Narcissa," Deacon says and Starling Jane nods her head.

"She came here to kill you both and take your child. It's the child that really matters to her."

"Like Mary English."

"We really shouldn't talk out here in the open, Deacon. She—"

"—has spies. Yeah, I know. I heard you the first time around."

"There is so much at stake here," the girl says and wipes more blood from Scarborough's face. "You cannot begin to imagine."

"What if I took Chance and went somewhere else?"

"Then she'll follow you, dickhead," Scarborough mumbles. "She'll follow you all the way to Hell and back, if that's what it takes. You can't run from this shit, any more than we can."

"Can you walk?" Jane asks and Scarborough grunts, either a yes or a no, but Deacon isn't sure which.

"We have to go someplace where it's safe to talk," she says. "There's not much time. Help me get him up, Deacon."

Deacon looks down at his mangled left hand, a few shards of the shot glass still buried in his bleeding palm, no telling how many stitches he's going to need, and he realizes that it's beginning to hurt more than his head. *Well, at least that's something*, he thinks, and offers Scarborough his good hand.

"I don't need your help," Scarborough tells him and "Yes, you do," Jane says. So Deacon takes him by the sleeve of his leather jacket and hauls him roughly to his feet.

"Do you two have a car or broomsticks or what?"

"That isn't funny," Jane replies. "We have a car, right over there," and she points at the line of vehicles parked in the shadows and streetlight puddles along the road. Something sleek and white slips out from under the front bumper of an old Volkswagen Microbus and seems to glide over the asphalt, vanishing quickly beneath the wheels of a battered pickup truck, and Deacon tells himself it's only a cat, or maybe a possum, nothing that shouldn't be out on an October night, then looks back to Jane and Scarborough.

"I have to call Chance first," he says.

Scarborough spits at the ground and licks his lips. "Five minutes and then we're out of here, Mr. Silvey," he says, "with you or *without* you."

"Five minutes," Deacon replies and heads for the door.

"Are you dying, Narcissa?" her grandfather whispers in her ear and she opens her eyes, flinches at the pain, and lies staring up at the ceiling of the bedroom in the old house on Cullom Street. It's finally dark outside, so it's dark inside, too, and it takes her a moment to remember why she hurts.

"No," she says. "I was only sleeping. I was dreaming about the night I burned the house."

"She got away," the old man taunts. "The pretty girl got away from you. No one's *ever* gotten away from you before, Narcissa."

"I was standing out in the dunes, in the snow, watching the flames." And she starts to roll over onto her right side, but it hurts too much, so she lies still and watches the yellowy windowpane reflections on the white drywall overhead.

"You look like a big ol' lobster someone left boiling in the pot too long," her grandfather snickers. "And the pretty little girl got away from you, didn't she?"

Narcissa shuts her eyes again, only wanting to go back to sleep, to slip away, back down to the numb place by the sea where the snow whipped through her hair and the fire was much too far away to ever reach her. She imagines the icy, howling wind off Ipswich Bay, so loud she can't hear the breakers or the blazing demon picking the house apart. So loud there's nothing else that matters, the memory alone almost enough to deaden her blistered face and hands, that frigid wind she thought would sweep the world away.

The first night that Aldous' ghost came to her, charred and skulking across the snow-dappled sand, leaving no footprints but leading the way for the loping, yellow-eyed things that had come out of their holes to watch the house burn. Leading them to her.

"You might have changed their minds," her grandfather murmurs behind her eyes, "but you weren't much of a fuck, they said."

Is that what happened? she wonders. *Is that what* really *happened, or was it something else entirely?* Did she only sit in the sand, shivering and smelling the sea, while the flames licked at the cloudy underbelly of the sky? Time and the pain have muddied her recollection, the pain and Aldous' whining, simpering voice, and she can't be sure. Perhaps the ghouls didn't come for her until sometime later, the long nights she lived alone in the dunes with only the noisy gulls and Aldous' ghost for company.

"The girl doesn't matter to me, old man," Narcissa says. "She never mattered. The girl was only a very small thing, a garnish—"

"Liar," her grandfather purls. "She *saw* you, Narcissa. She knows your face. They'll never, ever have you now."

Will you, won't you, will you, won't you, will you join the dance?

"They won't have any choice, Aldous. Not when they see what I've done for them, not when they see my gift."

"They'll piss on you *and* your idiotic gift. They'll pick their teeth with its bones."

Would not, could not, would not, could not, could not join the dance.

"If they *wanted* that child, Narcissa, they'd damn well come and take it for themselves."

Narcissa can hear the old man pacing restlessly back and forth across the floor now, his bare and bony feet loud on the varnished wood, but she doesn't open her eyes. Lies completely still in her fevery cocoon, the faint, maple-candy stink of Neosporin ointment, her hands swaddled in layers of gauze, a big Band-Aid where her left eyebrow used to be. He *wants* her to look, wants her to see what she's made of him, so she keeps her eyes shut and only watches the distant, burning house, the flames mirrored in the black waters of the bay.

"I bet you didn't think twice about spreading your legs, when they finally came sniffing around, did you, child?"

You were there, she thinks. *Weren't you?* and maybe she's dreaming again, because the girl named Sadie Jasper slips over the windowsill, the handcuffs pulling tight, almost tearing the radiator pipe loose. And the tiny kitchen fills up with blue-white fire. If she hadn't smelled the gas, if she hadn't guessed and stepped back from the doorway, and she tries not to notice the way all the vampires in Miss Josephine's parlor are staring at her.

"You should forget us," Madam Terpsichore says, "while there's still time to live the life you have."

"I don't want the life I have," Narcissa tells her. "There's no place for me out there. There will never be any place for me but here, with you."

"No, she isn't dying," one of the other voices whispers, a runaway she met on the road to Baltimore months and months ago. "She'll heal. More's the pity."

"You don't *know* that, you little fag," Aldous growls. "You don't know she won't die."

"Hell won't have her," the dead boy says, "and Heaven's full."

"You don't know that either, so why don't you just shut the fuck up. How could Heaven ever be full?"

The fire spreading so quickly there was no time for the pain, less time to wonder if the girl would escape, and Narcissa jumped from a bedroom window as the apartment filled up with smoke and the hungry roar of the inferno pouring itself free of the kitchen. In the dunes, the gale carried the billowing smoke away towards Cape Anne and the wide, indifferent Atlantic. She didn't have to smell it at all, just the clean snow and salt smells, the winter's night to keep her safe from the heat and soot and ash. She watched the gabled roof sag and collapse as the house shuddered and fell in upon itself, and an eight-year-old girl imagined entire cities at the mercy of such a perfect, merciless beast.

"Ask me, she smells like any chunk of human meat," the ghoul named Barnaby said to Madam Terpsichore and sneered at Narcissa. "Soft and pink, but maybe when she's dead, maybe when she's aged a bit, there might yet be something of interest come of it."

And then Madam Terpsichore reminded Barnaby that no one had asked him anything and he went back to work, dividing skin and silk-white fascia from red muscle. Upstairs, the vampires must have begun the evening's waltz, the way the floorboards have begun to creak and dust sifts down into the darkness, into the snowy night, sifting down from the ceiling of the old house on Cullom Street to settle on Narcissa's burned skin. Motes like scalding embers as she turns a page of her mother's journal, the smell of the paper to ease her soul, and "The universe," she wrote, "is only strings and knots. Most of the knots were tied ages ago, but we tie a few ourselves, and then spend the rest of our lives trying to untie them again."

"Did you see that, Grandfather?" Narcissa asked and Aldous shook his head, squinting out to sea.

"It hurts," one of her dead voices mumbles in her ear.

"Not so bad," she replies too quickly, too eager to prove the ghost a liar. "I've been through worse."

The wind off the sea flutters the pages of the journal and Narcissa reads by the light of the burning house:

Loose threads are all the power and all the loss that has ever been and ever will be. They are ours to tie, or to leave be. When I lie in bed at night, my eyes only just half-shut and the moonlight coming in through the window, I can almost see the strings. There are at least a hundred in this one room alone, crisscrossing spaces we'd rather believe are empty. They spring from my flesh like silver hairs.

"Well, it looks like it hurts," the voice says and Narcissa tries to remember which one this is, which death, which sin, but her head is too full and the names rush past like snowflakes.

"You learn your place in the scheme of things," Madam Terpsichore says, "or someone has to teach it to you. I recommend the former." And then the ghoul glances up at the basement rafters, the rhythmic stomp and shuffle of shoes in time to antique music from Miss Josephine's Victrola. Narcissa hears, or only imagines that she hears, the swish of crinolines and petticoats from upstairs. Madam Terpsichore looks back down at the corpse on the dissection table and her long fingers move swift and sure, claws so sharp she has no need of scalpels.

"We all dance," she says. "But only a damned fool dances to someone else's fiddler."

"Isn't she dead yet?" Aldous asks and one of the other voices laughs at him.

Everything my mother knew, left for me in a hole in a wall. All her careful knots and loose threads . . .

The face gazing back at her from the mirror above the bathroom sink, skin scorched lobster pink just like the old man said, her eyes starting to swell shut, and she dabs more of the ointment on her cheeks. Never mind the pain, the pain is just her due, it's the inconvenience that matters. Running out of time because everything that flies and scampers and crawls through the night has been set against her, because Deacon Silvey is starting to suspect, even if he never believes. Because she should have killed the girl named Sadie

in the park and left her body hanging from a tree. Should have
strewn her in messy, gaudy shreds across the dry grass and there
never would have been a fire. A fat blister at the corner of Narcissa's mouth bursts and that much more of her leaks out; dead
skin and new, raw flesh exposed to the air, and she reaches for another Band-Aid.

"You're not going to be very damn inconspicuous anymore,"
her grandfather says from his seat on the toilet behind her.

"When was I ever?"

"Oh, you ain't never been half so different as you'd like to
think," he replies. "It's almost eat you up alive, too, living inside
that ordinary hide of yours. Now, you should have seen your
grandmother—"

"I will, one day."

"How do you expect to live without a house? Where do you
think you're gonna sleep?" and the mirror is only the night sky
above the burning house. A shrieking cyclone of sparks and smoke
swirling up to meet the moon, the low red moon hung on meat-
hook spurs against a velvet sky. Her mother's eye, that moon, and
Madam Terpsichore's cruel, dismissing glare, and Narcissa turns
her back on it. Better if there's only the sea, the pure, pale beam of
a lighthouse somewhere to the north, winking on and off, off and
on, sweeping out across the waves. Better if Aldous had caught her
unawares, had cut her throat and carried the body down to the
hungry things waiting in the tunnels beneath the house.

"No more time for dreams, child," he says. "You started this
business. Tonight you gotta finish it, one way or another."

Narcissa sits down in the sand and the snow and tries hard to
ignore him, watching the lighthouse, the bobbing masthead beacon
of a fishing boat a long way off. Nothing *she* began, this business,
as he said, so that's a goddamned lie. The life she was dragged into
from her mother's womb, squalling and helpless to turn back, the
life that has followed her soul across a century of madness and
monstrosity; no more than a consequence, inevitable as death, the
thing she has become, no more or less than she ever might have
been.

"Don't you try to fool yourself like that, Narcissa," and that's
either Aldous speaking, or Madam Terpsichore or one of the murdered voices woven deep into her bones. "There might be strings

and there might be knots, but it's nothing you couldn't have cut or untangled, if that's the way you wanted to go. Be a killer if you want, if that's all you got left inside, but don't pretend you never had a choice otherwise."

She opens her eyes again, because there's nothing left to say, nothing left to dream, and the pain sings her awake and spreads the night out before her like a butchery.

Chance hangs up the telephone and then stands at the kitchen counter, staring at it, the sleek black plastic shell and orderly buttons with all their numbers and letters printed in white. Her mouth is dry and she can still hear Deacon's voice inside her head.

"So where the hell is he?" Alice asks from the sofa behind her and Chance turns around and forces a crooked smile.

"A bar," she says and Alice curses and goes back to watching the television, even though the sound's turned all the way down.

"He isn't drinking. At least he says he isn't drinking."

"Of course he does."

"He didn't sound drunk. He just sounded scared," and that makes Alice look up again, fresh worry to take some of the edge off the anger in her eyes. "He's asking the police to send someone over," Chance says.

"Why don't you just pack a bag and we could—"

"No, Alice, he says I'm safer here. He says the police will send someone and not to be afraid."

Alice drums her thick fingertips on the back of the sofa and shakes her head. "Safe from what?" she asks. "Afraid of what?"

"Would you like some tea? I think I'm going to make myself a cup of tea."

"Will you please stop pretending that you don't hear me whenever I ask a question?"

Chance takes the teakettle off a back eye of the stove and begins filling it with water from the tap. "I'm not pretending I didn't hear you. I just don't know what I'm supposed to say."

"Well, you could start by telling me what it was that Deacon called to tell you not to be afraid of."

Chance sets the full kettle down in the sink and shuts off the water, and "It's not that simple," she says. "Most of it wouldn't even make sense."

"Try me."

Chance picks up the kettle, pours out some of the water because she's filled it much too full and then puts it back on the stove.

"I can see that you're scared. I know you want someone to talk to," Alice says. "Why did you call me over here if you didn't?"

"I needed some company, that's all. It's been a really strange day and I didn't want to be alone."

"While your husband is off doing god only knows what—"

"Alice, you're not my mother, okay? Stop acting like you are."

Alice Sprinkle glares at her a moment, then makes a disgusted, huffing noise and goes back to watching the silent television. Chance gets a Red Zinger tea bag down from the cabinet and holds it under her nose, breathing in the flowery sweet scents of hibiscus and rose hips, licorice and lemon grass. Smells to soothe her shot nerves, a fleeting hint of something normal, and she wants to tell Alice everything she knows or thinks she knows, everything she suspects. But she can't begin to imagine the words she would need and it would only turn into an argument she couldn't win. *This is how Deacon feels when he needs to talk to me,* she thinks and quickly pushes the thought away, goes to the dishwasher for her grandfather's old white coffee mug.

"Is he selling drugs?" Alice asks.

"No, he's not selling drugs."

"Yeah, I suppose that would be a little too much like work."

Chance realizes that she forgot to turn on the stovetop and sets the burner on high. In a few seconds, the drops of water on the bottom of the kettle have begun to sizzle and steam, and she drops the tea bag into the white cup.

"Is it one of those silly hipster girls he used to—"

"Alice, can you cut it out for five minutes? You're not doing anything to make me feel better."

"You *have* told him that you're pregnant, right?" and this time Chance decides it's better to ignore her, not taking the bait, and she stares instead at the calendar thumbtacked to the kitchen wall. A Christmas gift from Deacon, something he found at the bookstore or ordered online, a color photograph of a different trilobite for every month of the year. October's bug is a spiny odontopleuroid named *Dicranurus monstrosus* from the Devonian of Africa, bizarre little beast even for a trilobite, its recurved occipital spines coiled like tiny ram's horns. Chance glances past the blocky string of days towards the end of the month, Halloween, then flips the page over to November and there's Sunday the fourth circled in red Magic Marker, her due date.

"This is why I don't have cable," Alice says. "Sixty-seven channels of nothing worth watching."

"There's usually a movie," Chance replies, counting off the days in her head, less than two weeks left between her and that red circle. "Try AMC or TCM."

"What the fuck does Birmingham need with *two* golf channels? Hell, what does it need with one?"

"You see that?" Chance whispers to her belly, whispering so Alice won't hear her. "Time's getting short, butter bean."

"I had to play golf in high school. God, what a stupid game."

"Try the National Geographic Channel," Chance suggests, sick of hearing Alice bitch about golf. "There's usually something worth watching on it."

Alice presses buttons on the remote and "It's something Egyptian," she says. "The Sphinx, I think."

"Egypt's not so bad."

"Why don't you come in here and sit down?" Alice asks her. "You've got to be exhausted."

"I'm waiting for the water to boil. If I sit down now, I'll just have to get up again in a few minutes."

"No, you won't. I'll get it for you."

"I'd rather do it for myself."

"Fine. Have it your way," and Alice turns up the volume on the television. The narrator is busy describing the effects of acidic pollution on the 4,500-year-old structure, crumbling limestone and hopeful proposals for restoration.

"I've always wanted to go to Egypt," Alice says.

"Isn't Alabama hot enough for you, you have to want to go all the way to Africa?"

On the stove, the teakettle has begun to make small crackling and popping sounds as the metal heats up and expands, and Chance watches the red-orange glow of the burner instead of the television screen. Wishing that Deacon were home, that she hadn't started the stupid, pointless argument with him at the hospital, wishing she could think of anything but the way he sounded on the phone. *Don't be afraid,* he said. *It'll be over soon, all of this crazy shit, and, Chance, you have nothing at all to be afraid of, I swear. Nothing in the world,* but the murmur and hum of the bar in the background to underscore and undermine his every word, the clattering, muttering voice of all her doubts. No longer even certain what to call that fear, or where it begins and ends, and the trip to Atlanta seems like a century ago. That ordinary day of perfectly ordinary worries and wonders, all her anxiety and misgivings occupied by her pregnancy, the welfare of her fossils, the wording on an exhibit banner.

But it wasn't really *an ordinary day, was it?* she thinks and walks over to the kitchen window. The streets are dark and deserted and there's no sign of police cars anywhere. Any fall night in this city, except Alice Sprinkle is on her sofa and Deacon's gone and she's here waiting for policemen to come and keep her safe from a killer.

"I think I have to go to the bathroom," she says out loud and Alice looks up from the television.

"Are you okay? Is something wrong?"

"No, I'm fine. Watch the kettle for me."

"Yeah," Alice says, "if you're really sure there's nothing wrong."

"No, I just have to take a piss," and Chance doesn't wait around for Alice to start asking for all the gory details, heads down the long hallway to the bathroom. Behind her, someone on television is speculating on the fate of the Sphinx's missing nose. The bathroom door is standing partway open and she can see her reflection in the wide mirror above the counter and the sink, her bloated silhouette, and it'd probably be depressing and disorienting if she were a little less afraid.

I swear I'll be home as soon as I can, Deacon said.

Miles to go before I sleep, Chance thinks, some part of her brain running on autopilot, dredging up useless, unconscious flecks of memory; she stops at the bathroom door and reaches inside to flip the light switch. Her fingers touch something damp and sticky and she jerks them back, but there's nothing on her hand, no stain, no unclean smudge, and she stands there staring at her fingertips for a moment.

"Just be cool, baby," she whispers, trying to make the words sound exactly the way that Deacon would make them sound. "You're all wound up and starting to freak yourself out." But she doesn't sound much like Deacon, and Chance wipes her hand on her overalls and reaches into the bathroom again. This time there's only the plastic switch and switch plate.

"Silly goose," she says, and that's her grandfather's voice inside her head, Joe Matthews scolding her for being afraid of thunder or the sound of pecan branches scraping against the window of her attic bedroom. She flips the switch and clean white light floods the bathroom, washes the forest-green walls, the colorful Mucha prints hanging on her left.

"Silly goose," she says again, because it felt good the first time, and she smiles at herself in the big mirror. Chance steps into the bathroom and eases the door shut behind her, closing out the noise from the television. She starts unbuttoning the bib of her overalls, but stops after only one button.

And miles to go before I sleep . . .

In the mirror, the door and the bathroom walls behind her have completely vanished and in their place there's a wide gray sky spread like a million mockingbird wings pinned above a narrow beach and a stormy sea. She can even smell the salt breeze and the faint, unpleasant odor of dead fish. Her heart like something small and frantic, caged in flesh and wanting out, and Chance takes a deep breath and turns around very slowly. But there's only the door, the dark green walls, everything exactly as it ought to be.

"You're all wound up, freaking yourself out," she says again, but she can't even remember what the words are supposed to mean. She glances back at the mirror and the impossible seascape is there again, if it ever went anywhere else.

"Not real," she whispers and takes a step towards the sink. "Not real at all."

A gull soars high above the whitecap sea and she can hear it, its caw and the low roar of the surf against the shore.

"Alice," she says, but the sound of the ocean has grown suddenly so much louder, drowning her out. She shuts her eyes, but when she opens them, nothing in the mirror has changed.

"Don't turn around again," a woman says, her voice as wild as the whirling hurricane clouds inching their way across the sky, as wild and as dangerous, and Chance doesn't take her eyes off the mirror. She can see the woman standing in the distance, beyond the point where the white bathroom tile ends and sand and sea oats begin, much too far away for Chance to be able to hear her above the wind and the raucous, screeching gulls, but she can hear her anyway. The woman is tall and wears a blue coat, a long navy-blue pea coat, and her eyes sparkle gold in the gloom. She's holding a knife and she looks over her shoulder at the waves.

"Mother Hydra," she says. "Don't mind her. I don't think she's ever going to wake up again."

And as the first contraction hits, the first hot pain to drive the breath from Chance's lungs, the woman in the navy pea coat raises her arms to the terrible, hungry sky. The second contraction and Chance's knees buckle so she has to grip the edge of the sink for support. Lightning flashes across the gray sky and blood begins to drip from the woman's outstretched hands.

"Not *real*, not real at all," Chance says and the woman balls her hands into tight, bleeding fists as the seascape comes apart in shredded kaleidoscope tatters, everything swept away in an instant by salt-damp wind and mercury-silver brilliance. And then there's only the bathroom wall behind her, and the closed door, and the kettle screaming from the kitchen like a dying gull.

When Scarborough and the girl named Jane have finally finished talking, have done with their long and impossible story of monsters and changelings, secret societies and half-breeds, when she's finished stitching up the gash from the broken glass, Deacon sets down the lukewarm can of Coke he's been sipping. He stares at his bandaged left hand, maroon blotches showing through the gauze.

"This is bullshit," he says. "And I'm going home."

"It's the truth," Starling Jane replies flatly, sitting on the floor in one corner of the shabby little motel room, her knees tucked up beneath her chin.

"It's total fucking *bullshit,* and even if it *was* the truth, that's all the more reason I should be at home. I should be home with Chance."

"Why? Because you still think you can protect her?" Scarborough asks. He's just come out of the bathroom again, keeps having to get up from his seat on one of the beds to get fresh toilet paper because his nose won't stop bleeding. There are crimson-stained wads of tissue scattered like strange flowers about the room.

"Because I think I'm supposed to be there to try."

"That's what she's counting on, Deacon," Jane says. "As much as Narcissa has a plan, killing you before she kills your wife is part of it."

Scarborough laughs softly to himself and sits back down on the bed closest to the door. Deacon watches him from the other bed, taking what small satisfactions he can from the raw tapestry of cuts and bruises on the man's face, his ruined nose, the left eye already starting to turn a bright reddish purple and it'll be a real shiner by morning.

"Your friend Sadie hurt her," Scarborough says. "Maybe even slowed her down just a little if we're real damn lucky."

"Yeah, well, I'm the luckiest motherfucker on the planet," Deacon mutters and Scarborough laughs again.

"A whole lot luckier than you have any goddamn right to be," he says.

"I should have punched you in the mouth, instead."

"You should stop running from the things you know better than to disbelieve. You should start trusting what you *see*, Mr. Silvey, not what you think you know."

"If you'll help us, we might be able to stop her," Jane says from her spot on the floor. "With your sight."

"Listen, *screw* my sight, okay? I mean, if I hadn't led the cops to Mary English, this crazy bitch would never have come looking for me and Chance."

"You can't undo the past, Deacon," Jane tells him. "You can only see it for what it is, what it truly is, and then try to set the present in order again. You've always known that."

"Fuck me," Deacon whispers and runs his fingers through his hair, looking at neither the girl nor Scarborough Pentecost now, staring straight ahead at the cheap wallpaper, faded yellow green with tacky flecks of gold and a bamboo pattern, bamboo stalks and leaves. Someplace for the tigers to hide, their eyes burning bright as the golden eyes of madwomen.

"We need you to believe us," Jane says and she stands up then, brushing absently at the seat of her jeans. "And there's really no more time for us to convince you."

"Fine. If you two need to go find this woman, that's your business. But I have to go home now. Thanks for keeping me sober."

And then Scarborough takes out his pistol again, slips it from the black leather shoulder holster and points it at Deacon's chest.

"You won't shoot me," Deacon says, trying hard to sound like he believes it. "I'm no good to you dead."

"No, but it doesn't sound like you're going to be any good to me alive, either. And I gotta tell you, Mr. Silvey, it'd sure as hell be satisfying to pull this trigger." A trickle of blood leaks from Scarborough's right nostril and he licks it away. "And, to tell the gods' honest truth, I couldn't give a sick what happens to your wife *or* your kid. That's not why I'm here. That's not why they sent me down here to this backwards shithole of a city."

Deacon swallows, his mouth gone dry despite the sticky soda aftertaste from the Coke and, "Tell me this, Scarborough," he asks, "can you even take a piss without that thing in your hand?"

"There's no more time for talk," Jane says, scowls a disapproving, furtive scowl at Scarborough, and then she steps between them, between Deacon and the barrel of the gun. "We've told you as much of the truth as we're allowed, a lot more than we should have told you. So now I'll have to *show* you, because you haven't left me any choice and there's only one way this night can end."

"You better get out of my way, little girl," Scarborough growls. "I've had enough of this prick. I can take care of this—"

"You just shut up for a goddamn minute," she snaps back, and he does, disappointment smeared across his face like a mean dog coming unexpectedly to the end of its chain, but he doesn't put the gun away.

"Show me what?" Deacon asks her.

"Secret things," she replies and gently presses her middle fingers to his temples. "Terrible, beautiful things. Whatever it takes to make you believe."

"Not everything I see is true. You know that."

"Yes, Deacon, I do," and then Starling Jane bends down and kisses him on the lips, her breath like tendrils of cinnamon and newly turned earth slipping down his throat, up his nose, spilling into the convolutions of his brain. Before he can blink them away, she presses her thumbs lightly against his open eyes, and the last dregs of the migraine dissolve like sugar sinking into warm water.

"You stay close," she says. "It wouldn't do to get lost, not where we're going."

And the world slips, or cracks, or was never really there to begin with, unless it's only him that's come apart, shattered by her touch. Falling into her, the deepest, softest folds of her, and if there are even colors here, he's never seen them before and wouldn't know what to call them; if there is light here, it's the alien light hidden beyond the edges of the spectrum open to simple human eyes.

"All your life, since you were a child," she says, her voice dripping down from the uneasy place where the sky should be, "you've lived at the muddy boundaries of so many different worlds—the past, the present, life and death, waking truth and dreaming truth. The borders are thin for you, but there are still borders, and they've almost driven you insane. In time, Deacon, they will."

He tries to shut his eyes, but her thumbs are still in the way, her grip like iron wrapped round his skull. There's more familiar light now, flickering yellow-white candle points, luminescent insects burning themselves alive, and the sudden smell of mold and cellar dust, like the basement of Chance's old house. Something moves, bristling fur and eyes like gold coins washed in blood, and "What are you doing, Jane?" a cold and guttural voice asks from the swarm of candlelight.

"I couldn't find any other way," she replies.

"For your sake, child, indeed, for *all* our sakes, I hope you are wiser than you seem."

"Will it matter, Master Tantalus, if the mongrel has her way?" and the darkness, which he knows was never really true darkness at all, releases Deacon Silvey to the candles and the milder glow of phosphorescent fungi clinging to the walls of the vast ossuary. Jackstraw pillars of thighbones and toothless skulls that seem to rise up forever, broad arches of dry brown ribs and vertebrae, and all of it only a frame for the creatures squatting in the shadows. The wirehaired things watching him with glittering eyes, crouched there on their spindly legs, and he sinks to his knees in the filth and bits of bone covering the floor of the necropolis.

"The Land of Dreams," Jane whispers in his ear, and now he sees that she's standing there beside him. "Mary English's Land of Dreams. And Narcissa Snow's Land of Dreams."

The smell and taste of rotting flesh and age-brittled bones so thick in the air that he gags, and Jane kneels down beside him and wipes the tears from his eyes.

"But she can never come here, Deacon. Narcissa is neither *ghul* nor changeling, neither a lurker in the wastes nor a child of the cuckoo. But that's all she desires, and she means to have it."

"I don't believe any of this," Deacon mumbles and the stooped things in the gloom laugh and bark and click their ebony claws against the earth at their feet.

Jane cleans away the spittle leaking from Deacon's trembling lips, brushes the sweat-soaked hair back from his eyes.

"It *is* real, Deacon, and somewhere inside, you know that it's real. That part of you that found Mary English, that part of you that can see what others leave behind. *That* part of you will always know this place is real."

"You could die for this, Starling Jane," one of the creatures snarls and squats in the dirt in front of Deacon. "You have broken the covenant."

"But he had to see. He had to see for himself," she says and when the thing curls back its black canine lips and bares its teeth, she shows it her throat and Deacon vomits at its feet.

"Then it has seen enough. Take it back and finish this," and the creature turns and lopes away into the shadows, trailing the smell of carrion and candle wax.

"Have you seen enough, Deacon?" she asks him. "Have you seen enough to understand what's at stake?"

"She isn't one of you," he whispers hoarsely. "But she wants to be. She thinks . . . she thinks if she brings our child to this place, you'll have to let her in."

"Can you stand?"

"I don't know. What difference does it make?"

"There are things here you shouldn't be bowing to," she says, so he struggles to his feet and the creatures laugh at him again.

"Madam Terpsichore will hear of this," one of them whispers. "You would be sweet on the slab, child."

"Tell her what you wish. Maybe she'd prefer to do her own dirty work from now on."

"Please, get me out of here," Deacon stammers, his body beginning to shake uncontrollably as he wets himself. He grabs her hand and clings to it, the only still point in the storm raging between their minds. "I can't stand up much longer."

"Hold on very tight," she says, as if there were any chance he'd ever let go, and she folds herself around him again, sews him up inside herself, against that welcoming, starving void and only this thin girl to keep it from pulling him apart, eating him alive. A moment, or an hour, or ages beyond reckoning, but when Jane takes her thumbs from his eyes, there's only her face and the light from the lamp between the motel beds.

CHAPTER TEN

The Pool of Tears

The ride in Scarborough's long black Cadillac Coupe deVille, not more than ten minutes between the parking lot of The Schooner Motel and the address on Southside, the house at the dead end of Cullom Street where the girl named Starling Jane said they would find Narcissa Snow. Deacon stares out the passenger-side window of the old car at the streets and buildings flashing past outside, familiar sights made strange and foreboding by this night and its circumstances. Scarborough behind the wheel, watching the road and speaking only when Deacon says something to break the not-quite silence, the sound of the wheels on the asphalt, a ping somewhere in the Caddy's guts, the distant sound of thunder from the sky.

"She didn't have to go," Deacon says, repeating himself but it's better than nothing. "I talked to Downs before we left the bar. The cops are watching the building."

"When are you gonna wake up and smell the beans?" Scarborough replies and slows down for a red light, looks both ways, and then runs it. "If the police could stop this bitch, I never would have had to fucking leave Boston."

"Is that where you're from? Boston?"

"Yeah. Well, most of the time," Scarborough mumbles and then glances at himself in the rearview mirror. He gingerly touches the end of his nose with one fingertip and winces. "Where the hell did you learn to fight, anyway?"

"Out behind bars, mostly," Deacon replies. "It used to be sort of a hobby."

The first scatter of raindrops speckles the windshield and Scarborough stares up at the clouds slung low above the trees and rooftops. "Just what I fucking need," he grumbles and turns on the wipers. Deacon watches as the rubber blades smear the water back and forth across the glass, hitching pendulum swing that doesn't really make it any easier to see.

"Those things she showed me—"

"—are strictly between you and her," Scarborough says before Deacon can complete the sentence. "Whatever it was, I don't even want to know."

"Then I *wasn't* supposed to see any of it, was I?"

"Jane does things her way, I do things mine," and Scarborough turns up Twentieth without signaling, leaving behind the small pentangle of bars and restaurants at Five Points, the people and the lights, and heads up the side of Red Mountain. "If she fools around and gets herself killed, that's just one less thing I have to worry about."

"Turn right onto Sixteenth," Deacon says. "It'll get us there."

"I know where I'm going, Mr. Silvey. I don't need you to give me directions."

A thunderclap, lightning, and the rain grows suddenly harder, countless tiny drumbeats against the top of the car, and Scarborough curses and switches the wipers to a faster setting.

"So I guess you're the original coldhearted motherfucker," Deacon says, pressing his good right hand against the window to leave a print in the condensation there. "You watch your own ass and the devil take the hindmost."

"I haven't met anyone yet that I'd be willing to die for, if that's what you mean."

Deacon draws a circle around his handprint, five points inside a circle like a charm to keep back the storm and whatever else is coming at them through the night.

"What about these . . . these things you work for? The Great Old Ones, whatever the fuck you call them?"

"I said that I haven't met any*one* I'm willing to die for, not that I hadn't found any*thing*."

"There's a difference?"

"They gave me a life, Mr. Silvey," Scarborough says and stares straight ahead at the rain and the wet street and the metronome sweep of the wiper blades.

"Or took one away from you."

Scarborough glances away from the road just long enough for Deacon to see the look in his eyes, the slow-burn fury to tell him it's time to shut up or at least change the subject.

"Am I allowed to ask questions?"

"Haven't you seen enough already? I thought you were the *reluctant* clairvoyant. I thought you didn't want anything to do with this freaky shit."

"That was back when I still thought maybe I had a choice in the matter, before your little pal jabbed her thumbs in my eyes and gave me the nickel tour of Hell."

"And now you want the two-bit tour?"

"No, but I'd appreciate you telling me who Narcissa Snow is," Deacon says. "I mean, if she isn't one of you, or one of your Morlock buddies, then where'd she come from?"

Scarborough shakes his head and cuts the steering wheel right, guiding the sleek black Cadillac off Twentieth and onto Sixteenth, this narrow avenue to carry them closer to the top of the mountain.

"Narcissa Snow's just an unfortunate oversight," he replies. "A mess that someone should have cleaned up twenty-six years ago."

"So I guess that sort'a makes you like a janitor," Deacon says and turns back to the window.

"Yeah, Mr. Silvey, I suppose it does. But a house is only as strong as the people who keep it in order."

Deacon chuckles to himself and stares out at the lights of the soggy, rain-shrouded city laid out below; it only takes him a moment to locate Morris and the roof of his apartment building, the safe place where Chance is waiting for him.

"That's a good one," he says. "If you ever get tired of pointing guns at people for a living, maybe you could get a job writing fortune cookies."

Scarborough runs a stop sign, bounces through an overflowing pothole, and the rear of the car fishtails slightly. Behind them, someone blows their horn.

"You know, if you get pulled over for driving like a lunatic, it could put a real crimp in your plans for the evening."

"How about you let me worry about that, Mr. Silvey. You just worry about whether or not we get to her before she gets her shit together and makes a beeline for your wife."

"And what am I supposed to do when we find her?" Deacon asks, and then wipes his handprint off the Cadillac's window. High above Birmingham, lightning flashes and stabs searing, electric fingers at the world. A split second of noon, and then the rainy night washes back over everything.

"Try not to get yourself killed," Scarborough says, and turns another corner.

Chance is sitting on the sofa in a carefully arranged nest of cushions, her feet propped up on the coffee table and another cushion under them. The television is still on, the National Geographic Channel and the Sphinx, because Alice hasn't thought to turn it off. Chance rests her dizzy head against the back of the sofa and stares up at the ceiling, the heavy wooden beams and crisscrossing pipes of the old factory.

"Were they contractions or not?" Alice asks and Chance shuts her eyes. Better in the darkness, the near-dark behind her eyelids, better to pretend the things she saw in the mirror were never there at all.

"They stopped," she says. "I don't think it was anything at all. They wouldn't have come so close together."

"Chance, just tell me if you want me to call Dr. Capuzzo and I'll do it."

"No, I'm fine now. I think I'll be okay."

She can hear Alice get up from her chair and begin to pace about the room again, her window to window to window circuit, and she starts grumbling about the police cars. Fifteen minutes ago, a cop named Conroy Adams came to the door and told them there'd be three cars watching the building until Detective Downs said the coast was clear. She'd laughed when Alice told her that, that the man had actually said "when the coast is clear."

"It couldn't have been Braxton-Hicks," Alice says. "Not if they hurt."

"I'm not even sure they hurt."

"You *said* they hurt."

Chance opens her eyes and all the beams and pipes are still up there, the sprinkler system and smoke alarm like a tiny white flying saucer hovering fifteen feet overhead.

"Will you please turn off the television?" she asks. "It's making me nervous. I think I'd like to listen to some music," hoping it might calm her nerves, that something easy and familiar might make here and now more real than the gulls and gray-blue sky, the woman with the knife and golden eyes.

"I wouldn't know what to play," Alice says. "You know all those cars are parked on the same side of the building? Shouldn't they have someone around back?"

"I'm not a cop, Alice. I don't know where their cars ought to be."

"Well, they shouldn't be all bunched up together like that."

Chance shuts her eyes, asks Alice again to please turn off the TV, to put on a CD, instead, and Alice Sprinkle mumbles a handful of disparaging words about compact discs.

"I don't even know what you want to hear," she says.

"*Exit West* by Daria Parker. It's right there on top of the stereo. If you can't find it—"

"I found it," Alice says. "*Exit West*. Isn't this that girl from Birmingham?"

"Yeah," Chance says, "that's her," and she swallows against her nausea, wishing she had the unfinished cup of Red Zinger tea now to settle her queasy stomach. "She used to be in a punk band, but now she does mostly folky stuff."

"God, I fuckin' hate punk," Alice says. "It was almost worse than disco. Don't you have something else?"

"It's *not* punk. I said that she *used* to be in a punk band. Do you like Sarah McLachlan?"

"I liked *Fumbling Towards Ecstasy*."

"Then you'll like this, too. Anyway, she's also a big old dyke, so you'll probably fucking love her."

Alice's heavy, brusque footsteps, crossing from the kitchen window to the television set, switching off the narrator halfway through something about Nubian slavery during the reign of Khafre. For a few long seconds, there's only the noise of the rain beating hard and steady against the roof of the building, a sound that's never made Chance nervous before, but it does now. Alice starts cursing at the stereo buttons, Chance keeps her eyes closed, looking for deeper shades of black hiding inside herself, trying to ignore the rain, and finally she hears the tray on the CD player slide slowly open.

"You don't even *own* a turntable, do you?" Alice asks and the tray slides shut again.

"Just press play," Chance tells her and in a moment the room fills with piano chords and the watery sounds of a twelve-string guitar, the gentle, rolling susurration of synthesizer keys and drum machines. The first track, "Carbon White," and Chance opens her eyes and blinks at the ceiling; no sanctuary left inside herself anywhere, only onionskin layers of doubt and fear, and she wishes Deacon would come home.

"You gave me a scare in there, kiddo," Alice says, sitting down again.

"I think maybe it was just the stress."

"Are you going to tell me why there are three police cars all bunched up together outside your building?" Alice asks and Chance suppresses a groan, only wanting to pay attention to the music.

"Just let me listen to this song," she says. "I feel better now, really."

"I didn't *ask* how you felt, Chance. I asked why there's a goddamn stake-out downstairs."

But Chance is trying not to think about the police, too busy concentrating on the music, the words, the singer's voice like sandpaper against velvet, and "Deacon saw her a few times when she was still in Birmingham," she says. "Before she got famous. I never went to shows. I think she lives out in San Francisco now."

"Lucky her," Alice whispers. "I need a cigarette."

"You could go out to the stairwell. Deacon smokes there when it's raining."

"I don't think I should leave you alone."

Chance turns her head towards Alice, her cheek pressed against the soft fringe at the edge of a cushion. She smiles, trying to put Alice at ease before she gives them both a heart attack, but that only makes her frown more dramatically.

"I'm fine, really. I promise. I'm just going to sit right here and listen to the music. You won't even be more than a hundred feet away from me."

"I might not be able to hear you—"

"That doesn't matter, Alice, because I'm okay now and there's not going to be anything for you to hear."

Alice cracks her knuckles and glances anxiously at the blank TV screen, stares at it as though there might be some answer hidden somewhere inside the dark glass. But only the wide room reflected back, a subtly convex doppelgänger to mock her unease and she sighs and cracks her knuckles again.

"I won't be more than five minutes," she says. "I swear."

"Take your time. I'm not going anywhere."

Alice gets up, her strong, broad shoulders to eclipse the warm light of the nearest lamp, and she stands beside the coffee table, looking worriedly down at Chance.

"You know how much I care about you," she says, her voice grown softer by scant degrees, but a fine distinction Chance can hear right away. "You know how much you mean to me."

"I think I know," Chance replies.

"If anything ever happened—"

"No, Alice. Don't say that. Nothing's going to happen. I've got Deacon and I've got you and I've got three whole carloads of police sitting outside. I'm probably the safest pregnant lady in Alabama right now."

"I told your grandfather I'd always watch after you," Alice says and then lightning and a thunderclap so loud there's no point in anyone saying anything else until it's done and the big windows have stopped rattling.

"And you always have," Chance tells her, leaning forward a little and upsetting some of the cushions so they tumble off into the floor. "Every single time I've ever needed you, you've always been there for me. Now, please, go smoke a cigarette and stop worrying for a little while."

Alice stoops and retrieves the fallen cushions, tucks them back into place around Chance. And then she leans over and kisses Chance lightly on the lips.

The singer's voice leaking from the stereo speakers, too pretty to be husky, too hard to be sweet, *I've lost myself inside your light, and burning doesn't seem to scare me anymore, here everything is carbon white, and ash.*

"Alice," Chance says uncertainly, and immediately Alice's cheeks flush bright pink and she backs away, almost tripping over the coffee table.

"I'm so sorry," Alice mumbles and wipes at her forehead.

"Don't apologize," Chance says and touches her lips. "I understand."

"You think so? Then you've got a leg up on me, kiddo."

"I'm okay, Alice. Go on. I'm just going to sit here and listen to my music for a little while."

And Alice does go, then, walks quickly down the hall to the front door, leaving Chance alone on the big sofa in her nest of cushions. Chance licks at her lips, the faint, musty taste of Alice Sprinkle lingering there, and *Come home, Deke,* she thinks. *Come home now,* because she doesn't feel anything like okay. The things she saw in the bathroom mirror, the yellow-eyed woman and her carving knife, the angry, gull-haunted sky, and she closes her eyes and tries to think of nothing but Daria Parker's song.

The fire behind your eyes is burning me alive, no reason left to fight, the light inside you shining, shining carbon white.

"There are many evil places in the world, sick places, *terrae pathologica,*" Madam Terpsichore said, when Jane was only seven and a half, still a whelp but starting to forget her vague, intangible memories of the world before. "And if you should die in a sick place, child, the evil things there will trap your soul and, if it is a very clever sort of evil, you might spend all the rest of eternity looking for a way out."

Huddled in the leaky shelter of the loading dock of an abandoned warehouse or factory, shivering and trying hard not to let the cold and wet distract her from watching the narrow cobblestone street, but Starling Jane can't keep the *ghul*'s words out of her head. Can't stop thinking of the dread she felt that first day she and Scarborough came to this city, that day on the overpass above the old iron foundry, or the night she went to Deacon Silvey and saw the blackness crouched jealously just inside the gated tunnel leading deep into the heart of a mountain. Those things and all the dead and crippled that Narcissa Snow has left scattered in her wake like broken toys.

"Even we shun those blighted places," Madam Terpsichore said and licked her thick black lips, her long tongue slipping about the edges of her muzzle for any stray bits of supper caught in her fur. "Even the darkest folk among us aren't that bold."

"Why are the places sick?" Jane asked and the hounds laughed and then went back to gnawing their bones.

"There were things here ages before us, child, terrible things that will still be here when we're gone. The sick places are where they sleep, and wait."

"Wait for what?"

"Don't ask so many questions," Madam Terpsichore said. "It's not healthy," and then she turned her back on Starling Jane and wandered away into one of the tunnels leading down towards Swan Point Cemetery and the muddy Seekonk River.

"Silly old cunt," Jane whispers, but it doesn't make her feel any better, and so she reaches inside the raincoat that Scarborough bought her at an army surplus store back in Atlanta. The reassuring butt of her gun tucked into its holster, the knife tucked into her boot. There's a brilliant, scalding flash of lightning, then, and she ducks her head, flinching instinctively; the thunder chasing its dazzling heels is so loud that she covers her ears and waits for it to pass.

"Fuck it all," she whispers, almost able to hear herself over the rumbling sky. Starling Jane pulls her raincoat tighter and watches the old-fashioned lampposts along the street, gaslights with electric hearts. Nothing but the night and the storm, the water gurgling noisily from aluminum rainspouts and filling up the gutters, swirling away down storm drains.

There are lights burning bright in a few of the windows, nineteenth-century warehouses and livery stables gentrified into pricey yuppie cocoons, but at least that's something this awful, alien place has in common with Providence. History dusted off and smothered under layers of paint and varnish, renovated for the unseeing people of sunshine and blue skies. Across the street, a pretty young man with red hair and glasses stands at one of the windows for a moment and then goes away again.

If things had been different, she thinks, *if the world had turned another way and the Cuckoo hadn't chosen me, I might live in a place like that. If things had been different, I might live another night.*

"Regret is your worst enemy," Madam Terpsichore said once, when she found Starling Jane huddled in a corner with a magazine she'd found abandoned on a park bench, crying over the glossy photographs of perfect, smiling people. "You are strong and can survive anything, so long as you keep regret at your back. *This* is the way your life has gone. It will not now go another way."

Starling Jane shivers and checks her wristwatch. They should be getting to the house soon, and in another half hour it will all be over and done with.

The sudden creak of straining metal overhead and she looks up, the rain dripping into her eyes, half blinding her before she can blink it away. But not before she sees that there's something crouched there on the bottom landing of the fire escape only a dozen feet above her, something with iridescent golden eyes peering down between the rusted strips of steel beneath its feet.

"Do you even know *why* you're hunting me, little girl?" the thing on the fire escape asks. "Has anyone even bothered to tell you?" Its voice is sweet and smooth as honey on lead crystal, worming its way into her head so she can't think straight, blurring her thoughts like the rain's already blurred her vision.

"For the things you've done," Jane says very quietly and slowly reaches for her pistol.

"*No,*" the thing on the fire escape growls back at her. "Because you've been *ordered* to hunt me. That's why you're here. Don't pretend you're doing something noble. Don't pretend you're anything but a lapdog."

Starling Jane draws the gun and aims it carefully at the darkness framed between those flashing, amber eyes. Sighting down the pistol's snubby barrel and she knows perfectly well that she'll only get one shot, if she's really fucking lucky she'll only get one shot off before Narcissa Snow slips over the edge of the fire escape and tears her apart.

Narcissa laughs at her, and it's a sound so cold, so absolutely empty, all the wasted places of the earth sewn up in that laugh, that Jane almost drops the gun and runs.

"You're not going to use that," Narcissa says confidently.

"Why the hell not?" Jane whispers.

"The three police cars out front, that's why the hell not. Don't you think they'll hear the shot? What if you missed? How can you keep all your precious fucking secrets if you miss and they find your body and have to come looking for me themselves? What if they catch me, instead? All the things that I could tell them, all the things that I could *show* them."

"Asylums are full of lunatics," Jane says, flipping off the safety and tightening her grip on the trigger. "Every one of them knows the secrets of the universe."

"But I have the *proof,* baby doll. That's the difference."

She wants you to keep talking, keep listening, she wants to confuse you, pull the trigger and she's dead, pull the trigger and it's all over.

"No one would ever believe anything you said," Jane replies, not even persuading herself.

"Then shut up and *shoot* me. Even a ribsy little bitch like you should be able to hit me from this distance."

But Jane lowers the gun, instead, releasing the trigger, praying to all the dark gods of the hounds that there's time to draw the dagger tucked into her boot before Narcissa gets to her.

"Smart girl," Narcissa purrs and the rusty fire escape pops and creaks, swaying just a little as she shifts her weight, as she moves like a living, liquid shadow flowing down to engulf and drown Starling Jane.

Alice finishes her cigarette and stubs the Winston out against the railing, flicks the butt away into the spiraling depths of the stairwell. There are others littering the steps, dirty little secrets no one has bothered to sweep up, so the building keeps them to itself, here where hardly anyone will ever see. Dozens of Camel butts and she figures those might be Deacon's, though they could just as easily belong to someone else on the third floor. She looks at the half-empty pack of cigarettes lying next to her, there where she's sitting on the topmost stair, and thinks about lighting another one. Her nerves already shot before that messed-up little scene with Chance, the silly fucking kiss, and she swears to herself she'd give up a year of her life just to take back that one moment. The whole thing fucked up more ways than she cares to count, never mind that Chance is pregnant, that she's *married* and pregnant, plenty bad enough that Alice could be her goddamned mother, that she made so many promises to Joe and Esther Matthews.

"It wasn't anything at all," she says, even though she doesn't mean it, and takes out another Winston. It's a little bent from riding around in her shirt pocket all day, and she straightens it with her fingers.

"It didn't *mean* anything," she says.

Alice flips open the lid on her silver Zippo, thumb on the strike wheel, and then she hears a sound coming from somewhere beneath her. Clattering noises from a lower floor or the parking garage all the way at the bottom of the stairs, and she takes the cigarette from her lips and listens. But there's only the incessant drumming of the rain against the roof, the low and muted howl of wind around the corners of the building. She looks over her left shoulder at the door to the stairwell propped open with a piece of cardboard, one flap torn off a cardboard box and wedged in level with the doorknob so the lock can't catch.

What the hell are you so nervous about? she thinks, returning the Winston to the crumpled pack. Then remembers the three police cars sitting out front, the telephone call from Deacon and the frightened, furtive expression on Chance's face. All that forgotten for a few minutes, her mind too busy worrying over the unfortunate kiss, too busy wondering if she's managed to screw up her friendship with Chance. One foolish, impulsive action that might be strong enough to invalidate all those years, the disproportionate cause and effect she's seen so many times before. The too-familiar weight of guilt, and Alice shuts her eyes for a second and listens to the rain and thunder. Nothing to be frightened of there, nothing that she doesn't understand, and she wishes Chance had called someone else to keep her company, then feels ashamed for wishing it.

On the first or second floor, somebody opens one of the other doors into the stairwell and there's a sudden downdraft, musty, warm air sucked in from the third-floor hallway behind Alice, before both doors, the one below and the one at her back, slam shut in unison. Startled, she jumps and drops her lighter. It clatters end over end down the steep cement steps and lies glittering in the dim light of the landing.

"Mother*fucker,*" Alice hisses, getting quickly to her feet and she tugs at the door handle, but it's locked tight; the useless piece of cardboard has slipped all the way down to the floor and she kicks it hard enough to hurt her foot. No way Chance will ever hear her, not with the stereo blaring and so much distance, so many walls and doors, between them, so she'll have to go all the way downstairs and out through the garage, then use one of the call boxes to get Chance to buzz her back into the building.

She bangs on the door a few times, just in case someone's in the hall, someone who might hear and let her back in. When no one does, she leans out over the railing and bellows down the stairwell.

"Why the *fuck* did you open the damned door, you dickhead?!"

Only the storm raging above her for an answer, the rain to remind her that she'll probably end up soaked before this is over, standing in the downpour, waiting for Chance to get to the phone.

She glares at the locked door one last time, the traitorous hunk of cardboard, then takes the fourteen steps down to the landing and picks up her Zippo.

"Hell," she mutters, "the way things are going, I'll probably drown out there. Or get myself struck by lightning."

Alice tries each door on the way down, but they're all locked, just like they're supposed to be. Past the first floor and on down to the ground level, a burned-out row of bulbs there that no one has bothered to replace and so the dark has claimed the foot of the stairs for its own. But at least that door opens when she turns the handle, a fluttery second or two of panic when she thought it might not after all, but then the darkness is washed away by the pale, fluorescent light from the parking garage. For decades, the building next door was a spice warehouse, and so the air down here stinks of curry and black pepper and paprika, the smell strong enough it always makes Alice's eyes start to itch and water. She eases the door shut behind her and the click of the latch seems very loud in the vast silence of the garage.

Shiny rows of cars divided neatly by yellow lines and square concrete pillars, great teetering piles of junk stacked back against the walls, everything the tenants have no place or use for, but can't quite bring themselves to throw away, either, so all of it stored down here, almost out of sight and mind. Alice walks past Chance and Deacon's space, 307 stenciled in canary-yellow numerals on the dirty gray cement and Chance's Impala parked in front of their own share of the garage junk—big boxes of paperback books, wooden crates of fossils and tools, a bicycle with one wheel, a broken halogen floor lamp.

Outside, the thunder rumbles furiously, muffled now by these thick walls of brick and steel and mortar. Alice tries the lobby door first, the quickest route to a call box, but of course it's locked, too.

"Goddamn paranoid yuppies," she grumbles and starts to kick the door, then remembers hurting her foot upstairs and thinks better of it. There's another thunderclap, much louder than the last, and the lights flicker.

"Oh no, you don't," she says, staring up at the ceiling only a few feet above her head. The unsightly tangle of exposed pipes and wiring and "No," she says again. "The universe has pissed on me enough for one night and the power is *not* about to go out and leave me stranded down here in the dark. The lights are *not* fucking going to go out," but she forgets all about the lobby and walks quickly to the big electric door on the other side of the garage. Down the short car ramp to the control box mounted on the wall, just two black buttons, UP and DOWN, and she presses UP. Somewhere nearby a motor whirs sluggishly to life, accompanied by the clang and rattle of chains, and slowly the door begins to rise.

"Yeah," Alice whispers. "That's a girl." She takes a step backwards as the wind whips in, blowing in a spray of icy, cold rain to soak her ankles right through the cuffs of her jeans. Then the lights flicker again and the door makes a hitching, grinding sort of sound and stops. Alice curses and jabs the UP button repeatedly until it finally clanks reluctantly back to life.

And the dripping, shaggy thing standing on the other side of the garage door blinks her golden eyes at Alice Sprinkle and smiles. She's standing over a body, a hunting knife clutched tight in her right hand, and the convenient rain to wash away the blood.

"Hey, old woman," the thing says. "Did you know the sky's falling?" and then more thunder, and the lights flicker one last time and wink out for good.

Through the storm, to the shaded place where Cullom Street ends, and the house is waiting for them there like everything else that's inevitable. No lights from its curtainless windows, only the darkness past the last streetlamp, a hole torn in the night and left like a dry, forgotten well beneath the branches of the old pecan trees.

"Shit," Deacon hisses, watching the house through the rain-slicked windshield of the Cadillac. "That fucking figures."

"What?" Scarborough asks him, not taking his eyes off the house.

"The spider-girl house," Deacon replies and laughs a dry, sick little laugh. "It would have to be the fucking spider-girl house."

"What are you talking about?"

"Come on, Scarborough. You're a spooky guy. You're supposed to be up on this sort of shit."

Scarborough frowns and shakes his head, but doesn't reply, wipes condensation off the glass with the palm of his hand.

"It's the local haunted house. Kids get stoned and dare each other to sneak into this place. It's been going on for years."

Scarborough kills the engine and switches off the headlights, and then there's only the dark and the thunder, the dripping trees and the uneasy sounds the wind makes coming down the side of the mountain.

"You think this place is haunted?" he asks and Deacon catches the faintest hint of trepidation in his voice, not quite dread but close enough for horseshoes.

"No, I *don't* think this place is haunted. It's just, you know, a fucking urban legend, something all the teenagers pass around to freak each other out. A girl who used to live here is supposed to have hung herself in one of the bedrooms. And she kept spiders for pets. Now her tormented ghost is damned to walk the night, dripping poisonous spiders from her hair, blah, blah, blah. So, ergo, it's the spider-girl house."

"But you don't think any of it's true?" Scarborough asks and then he leans closer to the windshield, squinting through the night at the house.

"I don't fucking believe I'm hearing this, okay? You go out and whack some guy, gut him like a pig and leave him swinging from his ankles for the cops to find, and now you're scared of ghost stories?"

Scarborough Pentecost shakes his head again and reaches into his leather jacket, pulls out the biggest handgun Deacon's ever seen and checks to make sure that it's loaded.

"Bad things happen, Mr. Silvey," he says. "Very bad things leave behind stains on the world."

"Yeah, right, and I read Shirley Jackson, too. You know, while we're sitting here having this profound moment, Narcissa's probably slipping out the back door."

"No, she's not," Scarborough says. "Narcissa Snow doesn't run. That's part of the problem," and now he's fumbling about beneath the seat with his right hand. He bumps his chin hard on the steering wheel and curses.

"Did you lose something, chief?" Deacon asks and then a flash of lightning so bright that it may as well be a summer day, white to sear its way through his pupils and scorch the back of his skull. For half an instant, he can see every single tree, every soggy, fallen leaf piled against the low shrubs, all the vertical and horizontal lines of the house stark as an architect's blueprints. And something else, something the light can't touch moving swiftly across the yard, slipping from the shelter of one shadow to another.

"Do you know how to use one of these?" Scarborough asks, and Deacon turns to see what he's talking about, but it's hard to see anything through the swarm of purple-white fireflies the lightning has left in his head.

"Which is it?" he asks. "A crucifix or holy water?" and he blinks at Scarborough.

"A gun, Mr. Silvey. It's a gun," and then he puts something heavy and cold in Deacon's hand. "Do you know how to shoot?"

"Yeah," Deacon says, blinking down at the gun, turning it over and over in his hands and trying to decide whether or not he should tell Scarborough Pentecost he's never even held so much as a BB gun before. "You point it at the bad guys and pull the trigger."

Scarborough sighs and licks his lips, stares silently out at the dark and patient house.

"Okay, listen," he says a moment later, "when the time comes, all you'll have to do is take off the safety, hold the gun in your good hand, finger *off* the trigger," and he demonstrates with his own pistol. "Then you pull back the slide like this, and just let it go. That'll chamber the first round. And don't forget that you have to *keep* pulling the trigger if you want it to keep firing. It's semiautomatic, not magic. I left the safety on. It's that little switch on the—"

"Yeah, sure, I got it," Deacon grumbles. "So how many bullets do I have in this damned thing, anyhow?"

"Don't you worry about that. All you need to know about the bullets is that they make a big hole going in and a *very* big hole coming back out. One way or the other, this will be over fast, so I can guarantee you aren't going to need a second clip."

"That's about the most reassuring shit I've heard all night."

"She knows we're coming," Scarborough says. "I'm sure she's watching us right now, from one of those windows, so there's no point even pretending that we're going to surprise her."

"And if she's not here? If she's already on her way to—"

"I told you—"

"I *know* what you told me, asshole," Deacon says and he cocks the pistol exactly the way that Scarborough showed him. "You just better be right, that's all I'm saying," and he wonders briefly if he's fast enough, if maybe he could put a couple of shots in Scarborough Pentecost's face and drive away from this place, straight back home to Chance, where he's supposed to be.

"You just better be right," he says again.

"Just keep your head down, Mr. Silvey, and watch where you point that thing. I've already got enough irony in my life without killing this bitch and then getting my head blown off by you. Are you ready for this?"

"I'm waiting for you," Deacon replies.

"All right. On five then," Scarborough says, and Deacon listens to him counting and tries not to think about the blonde woman from his visions, or about Chance, or the oil-skinned thing he might have seen rushing across the yard on long and jointed legs.

The stereo has just begun the fifth track of *Exit West* when the music stops suddenly and Chance opens her eyes on the darkened apartment. Only the palest watercolor-gray light shining in through the big loft windows, so she knows the streetlights have all gone out as well, that it's probably a blown transformer somewhere. There are candles and matches in one of the kitchen cabinets, but she decides to wait it out, the darkness not unpleasant and, besides, the power will probably be on again in five or ten minutes. And Alice is probably already on her way back from the stairwell, convinced she's scared half to death.

"Doesn't make much difference to you one way or the other, does it?" she asks her belly. "I didn't think so."

A dazzling flash of lightning and another thunderclap, a drawn out, throaty rumble that seems to roll back and forth across the sky.

"You're not afraid of nothing, are you, butter bean?"

She turns her head towards the windows, wondering what the cops parked outside are doing, if they'll all have to leave now to deal with traffic lights that aren't working and things like that. But maybe they've been told to stay put, no matter what, and the thought of being protected, the thought that she might *need* to be protected, is too disturbing and so she dismisses it. Chance is still watching the window, the rain battering itself against the glass, when she hears a small, shuffling noise somewhere on her right and turns her head.

"Alice?" she calls out. "Is that you? I didn't hear the door." But no one answers her and she's left staring into the deeper night filling up the hallway, the dim window glow barely making any difference at all. And then a curling wisp of oyster-white to ruin the gloom, a formless movement that seems to drift just above the floor, there and already gone again, and Chance gets to her feet as fast as she can.

"Alice?" she asks again, but she knows this isn't Alice, knows instinctively this isn't anyone or anything she wants to see.

I might not be able to hear you, Alice said.

"It's nothing," Chance whispers, whispering like she's in a library, like she's afraid someone might hear. "It's just the dark and I've never been afraid of the dark in my life."

The child steps out of the blackness, then, *not* out of the hallway, but out of the blackness itself, trailing tattered bits and shreds of the clinging night about its face and shoulders. A soft, intangible brilliance leaks from its wide brown eyes, and a warm shimmer off its naked body, like something that knows it can't be seen unless it learns to make its own light. The child holds out a hand to Chance.

"She's coming," it says in a smooth and completely sexless voice. Chance takes a step backwards and bumps into the sofa.

"Who are you? How did you get in here?"

"No, stop asking questions and listen. You can't waste any more time, Mother. She's coming. She's coming now."

"Mother," Chance says, still whispering, but now the tremble in her voice much more than fear, and then the kick inside so hard she gasps and sits back down. She forces herself to look away from the child and stares instead at the safe and simple shadows between her feet.

"Would you mind coming with me, Piglet?" the child asks. "In case they turn out to be Hostile Animals?"

"I read you that story," Chance whispers and when she looks up again the child is standing very close by, watching her intently with its glinting, brown eyes. *Deacon's eyes,* she thinks. *Deacon's eyes stained brown. Watching me with Deacon's eyes,* finally beginning to understand, even if she can't believe.

"You'll fight," the child says and smiles a sad smile for her. "You'll do everything you can, but it won't be enough."

"Alice will be back soon," Chance replies and realizes there are tears running down her face. "She'll be back any minute. Will you wait for her? Will you please let her see you, too?"

"No, Mother. Alice isn't ever coming back. But she tried. She fought for us."

"Can I touch you?" Chance asks and the baby kicks again.

"But you're touching me now," the child replies, and something like confusion washes across its face. "You've always touched me."

"Then I'm dreaming. I was listening to the stereo and fell asleep and this is only a dream. Alice will be back soon, and she'll wake me up. I'll tell her that I dreamed about you and you were so beautiful."

"She's coming," the child says urgently. "She's almost here."

Chance reaches out for the child, imagines her fingertips brushing gently across its smooth white skin, but it pulls away from her and shakes its head.

"There's no more time left. Are you deaf? Can't you hear her coming? Can't you hear her teeth?"

"No," Chance replies, "I can't," and then there's another blinding flash of lightning and the thunder comes right behind it—a mindless, booming creature made from clouds and discord, chasing down the fleeing light, nipping at its crackling heels, tumbling at last into the empty place it's left behind. Chance blinks once, blinking back her tears and the electric afterimage, but now the child is gone and she's alone in the living room with the unconsoling sound of the wind and the rain.

Soaked to the skin and shivering from the short dash across the yard, and Deacon is crouched on one side of the front door of the spider-girl house, feeling idiotic and terrified at the same time, feeling surprised that he's still alive. Scarborough's crouched on the other side, one ear pressed against the wall, his eyes shut, and Deacon thinks again about just shooting him and going home.

"I can't hear her," Scarborough whispers and frowns. "I can't *feel* her anywhere."

"I told you," Deacon whispers back.

"No, she's here. She has to be here somewhere. It's just a trick."

Lightning and the wind blows the rain about like a chilly, invisible veil, driving it up under the cover of the wide porch.

"This is bullshit," Deacon hisses and Scarborough opens his eyes and glares at him.

"You just do like I do and maybe you'll live to see the other side of this thing."

"I'm fucking freezing to death. And my wife is alone in—"

"Your wife isn't alone, Mr. Silvey. Not yet. Now stop worrying about her and keep your mind on the here and now."

"Fuck you," Deacon grumbles as Scarborough stands up quickly and tries the cut-glass knob; it isn't locked and he turns it, moving so slowly, with such confidence and a hint of a smile on his face, that Deacon can almost believe he knows what he's doing. Whatever he's getting them both into, and the door swings smoothly, silently open onto total darkness. Another surprise, because in Deacon's head the hinges should have creaked very loudly, haunted-house cliché to complete the scene, and he glances down at the pistol in his hands as Scarborough slips inside.

"This is crazy," he whispers and wonders why they're whispering and sneaking about if Narcissa Snow already knows they're here. *Just keep moving,* he thinks and, before he can talk himself out of it, follows Scarborough into the house.

"Stay close," Scarborough says from someplace near, though Deacon can't see him, the darkness beyond the porch that complete, and he turns his head to see why there's no light at all coming in from the open door.

"Don't let it spook you," Scarborough says. "It's only a fascination she's put on this spot. Just light and shadows. The door's still right there behind you."

Deacon takes a couple of steps backwards and he's standing on the porch again, the dim light of the stormy night and the shaded porch about him, and a solid wall of blackness held tight inside the doorframe. He puts his right hand into the black and then pulls it quickly out again when it vanishes up to the wrist.

"We don't have time to play Mr. Wizard," Scarborough whispers from the inky nothing and Deacon takes a deep breath and steps through the door again. The blackness closes back around him like frigid, thick water.

"She's using the house," Scarborough says. "Using its bad

memories against us. All you have to remember is these things are only illusions. She can hurt you. They can't. They can only cause you to hurt yourself."

"How are we supposed to find her if we can't even fucking see *each other?*"

" 'Chance favors the prepared mind,' Mr. Silvey," Scarborough replies. "Louis Pasteur said that." And then the blackness isn't quite so black anymore, its perfection marred by a faint bluish glow somewhere in front of Deacon. "That's sort of appropriate, don't you think?" but Deacon doesn't reply, not even sure what he's being asked, and, besides, he's much too busy watching the bluish glow ebb and swell, pushing back the edges of the gloom until he can see Scarborough again, his pale face and the small, pulsing sphere of light floating just a few inches above his left palm. Vivid powder-blue light that streams towards the ceiling and seems to make the black cringe and flinch, pulling itself back like something scalded, and Deacon laughs in spite of himself. Things too awful and wonderful to be real, but here they are, anyway.

"Can I touch it?" he whispers. "Can I hold it?"

"That would be a very bad idea," Scarborough says, and then holds the light up so Deacon can see something scrawled on the wall in what looks like drying paint, but he's pretty sure is actually drying blood.

"Silly quim," Scarborough smirks and shakes his head, holds the light in his hand closer to the writing on the wall. "I've had about enough of your drama."

The letters two or three feet tall, smeared neatly across the plaster, and Deacon recognizes the writing from the wall of Soda's apartment, the exact same alphabet that surrounded the circle drawn above the bed. Nothing he can read, but then it's really nothing he *wants* to read.

"Is that the spell?" he asks.

"Not a spell," Scarborough replies. "Just a fascination—"

"Yeah, whatever. Is *that* it?"

"No, it's not. It's just a sick little love note for you and me, something to waste our time."

Deacon thinks briefly about asking Scarborough to read it out to him, to translate the strange, flowing letters. "What's that language supposed to be?" he asks instead.

"It doesn't have a proper name. It's a tongue of the dead, that's all. She's showing off."

Deacon nods his head slowly, as if he even begins to understand what Scarborough's talking about, and his eyes follow the scabby and meandering trails of blood down towards the baseboard and the floor. There's a pile of dead birds and chipmunks there, illuminated by the blue light, and he looks quickly away.

"So, what's next?" Deacon asks, trying not to think about those small bodies heaped together on the floor, matted fur and feathers, dry and gaping wounds.

"We keep looking for Narcissa. She isn't trying to hide. She just wants to disorient us. She's looking for an edge."

"Well, she's about got me ready to shit myself," Deacon says. "I don't mind telling you that."

"Keep your fear to yourself, Mr. Silvey. I don't need it cluttering up my head, and neither do you." Scarborough turns away from the wall and now Deacon can make out a closed door on their right, and a doorway on their left. Then he catches a faint, greasy smell, like a pork roast simmering in an oven, something out of place in among the musty old house odors, and Deacon notices the blistered spot on Scarborough's hand, just beneath the blue ball of light.

"Doesn't that hurt?" he asks and points.

"Like a motherfucker in heat," Scarborough replies. "But that's the way it goes. Now, stop asking stupid questions and pick a door, Mr. Silvey. Left or right?"

"What? How the hell should I know?"

"'Cause you're the dude with the million-dollar eyes, that's why. You're the man with a hot line to the past stuck in his head. You don't think I just brought you along for shits and giggles, do you? Now pick one."

"This is bullshit," Deacon says again.

"Almost everything is," Scarborough chuckles. "Everything under Heaven, anyway. Do we go left or do we go right?"

"Jesus," Deacon mumbles to himself and tucks the pistol into the crook of his left arm, his hand too stiff and bandaged to hold it, then presses his right hand flat against the closed door. But it only feels like any door should, smooth wood grain underneath the white paint, neither particularly warm nor particularly cold—just a door.

"We don't have all night," Scarborough says.

"I don't even know what I'm looking for here."

"Traps, Mr. Silvey. The kind most people never see until it's too late to avoid them."

Deacon takes his hand away from the door and stares down at his palm and fingers for a moment, which makes him think of Scarborough's scorching flesh again.

"Look man," he says. "All I can tell you is that's a fucking door. I'm not getting anything at all."

"Then what about that way there?" and Scarborough motions towards the open doorway on the right with the muzzle of his gun. "Put your hand on the wall there and tell me if you get anything."

"You're starting to sound a lot like the cops, you know that?"

"Just do it," and so he does, does as he's told because he only wants this to be over, only wants to get out of this terrible house and back to Chance. He presses his reluctant fingertips to the door-jamb, shuts his eyes, and waits, for the pain and the vision, or for nothing at all. Outside the thunderstorm seems to be building rapidly towards some crescendo, some frenzied epiphany of lightning and rain, pricking at his senses, getting in the way. Five seconds, ten, fifteen, and Deacon opens his eyes to Scarborough's pulsing blue light and the mangy edges of Narcissa Snow's darkness.

"Nothing," he says, not caring if Scarborough hears the relief in his voice. "Nothing there at all."

"You're absolutely sure about that?"

"I've never been *sure* of anything in my whole goddamned life, so don't you expect me to start now," and he takes the pistol in his good hand again and is surprised to find some faint solace in the weight and solidity of it.

Scarborough glances uncertainly from one side of the tiny foyer to the other, left to right and back again, and mutters something hard and angry through his gritted teeth that Deacon can't make out.

"Hell, maybe we should flip a coin," he says and Scarborough glares at him.

"I can't hold on to this thing forever, Mr. Silvey," and he nods at the ball of light hovering above his hand. The blistered spot on his palm has grown much larger, seared almost black at the center. "I'm not much of a magician. I'll have to release this soon or it may be beyond my control." Deacon can see that there are beads of sweat standing out on his forehead now, or it's only the rainwater leaking from his wet hair and trickling down his brow, crystal droplets to catch the blue light and flash it back more brightly.

"Tell me the truth, Scarborough," Deacon says, looking back to the high and bloody letters scrawled on the wall, the mound of empty, dead things lying underneath. "This isn't exactly what you expected, is it?"

"Not exactly," Scarborough replies and his hand trembles beneath the light.

"And we're in some very deep doo-doo, aren't we?"

For an answer, Scarborough raises his pistol and points it at the open doorway on the left; Deacon wonders if he's going to pull the trigger, as though the darkness clotted there was something he could drive away with bullets and gunpowder.

"You just stay real close," he says and steps through the doorway, the blue light parting Narcissa Snow's blackness like a living curtain of latex and India ink. Deacon hesitates only a second or two, the brief space squeezed in between heartbeats that it takes for the murk to begin to reclaim the foyer, for the cold to sink its teeth into him, and then he follows Scarborough and the fading blue glow. He steps quickly across the threshold, trading one room for the next, falling farther in, but Scarborough's impossible beacon gutters and grows dimmer instead of growing brighter.

"I can't see you," Deacon calls out, shouting and to hell with the whispering if she knows they're there anyway.

"Over here," Scarborough calls back, and his voice seems stifled and very far away. And then something soft and damp brushes across Deacon's cheek and he winces, but doesn't cry out. The incongruous, salty sweet smells of the ocean and rotting meat washing suddenly over him like a poison breathed out by the darkness, and the woman's voice behind him so close that he can feel her hot breath against the back of his neck.

"It's cold in Heaven," she says. "Cold and dark and the stars are farther away than God."

Deacon spins around and blindly aims the gun at the nowhere place her voice might have come from. His finger on the trigger, but he can't find the safety, can't remember if it's on or off.

"She's here!" he shouts to Scarborough.

230 Caitlín R. Kiernan

"I *know* she's here," Scarborough calls back from at least a mile away.

"No, she's *here*," and the sticky, wet thing brushes against Deacon's face again, leaving behind the smell of decay and the sea, salt and putrescence, and he realizes the thunder isn't thunder anymore; waves pounding against a rocky shore, picking apart the world one ancient quartz grain at a time.

"Did you think you could come for me the way you came for poor Mary English? Did you really think it would be that easy?"

Deacon squeezes the trigger, and the gun clicks uselessly.

"Scarborough, where the fuck are you, man?" and now there's no answer at all, or there's so much distance between them it simply doesn't matter anymore.

"The changelings can't help you, Deacon Silvey," the woman says, the mad woman from his dreams and visions, the woman with eyes of molten gold. "They never could."

Deacon takes a step backwards, one step away from the taunting voice, and fumbles for the safety.

"Did they tell you that I was insane?" she asks and the darkness around him flutters like hundreds of small and leathery wings. "Did they tell you I was only a half-breed, mongrel whore?"

"They didn't have to tell me jack shit. You tried to kill Sadie," and then Deacon finds the safety and flips it off with his thumb. He squeezes the trigger three times and the gun roars, deafening demon voice to shatter the nothing packed in all around, to cut great, ragged slits and let the light come pouring through, and the unexpected recoil knocks the pistol out of his hand.

"When I was still a little girl, the moon bled for me," the woman says. "One of these days, she's going to bleed again."

Deacon looks down, blinks at the daylight stinging his light-starved eyes, and the pistol's lying in the brown- and white-sugar mix of sand and snow at his feet, and the crash of the breakers and the shrieking wind through the dunes are even louder than the gunshots were. Reverberating sound like deep-sea pressure, how many decibels per square inch before his skull finally collapses and the cacophony grinds his sorry soul to jelly?

"You really have no notion how delightful it will be," Narcissa Snow begins to sing in a tittering voice stolen from a crazy child, a voice that rises somehow clearly above the seashore's wail. "When they take us up and throw us, with the lobsters, out to sea!"

And Deacon finally sees her then, standing at the crest of a dune and looking down on him. The wind whips her blonde hair about her white face, blonde coils to hide and then reveal her blazing eyes, her naked body shimmering, skin like pearls, beneath the maritime sun. Slowly, he stoops down and reaches for the gun, never taking his eyes off her. Narcissa's voice sails to him on wheeling gull wings, woven tightly into the gale.

"'What matters it how far we go?' his scaly friend replied. 'There is another shore, you know, upon the other side.'"

His hand closes around the butt of the pistol and he lifts it slowly from the sand.

"Yes. That's right, isn't it?" she asks and smiles, showing him her glistening, dagger teeth. "You've read the stories, haven't you? All the pretty fairy stories. You have to try to be the hero, don't you, Deacon? Slay the ogre, save the princess—"

"You're not an ogre," he yells back at her and the greedy wind snatches his voice from his lips and scatters it carelessly across the dunes. "You're *nothing,* nothing but some twisted little girl who wanted to grow up to be a monster and didn't get her wish!"

"Am I not monstrous?" she shouts at him, the smile fading, and she looks up at the low and steel-bellied sky. "What I am, the things I've done?" and Narcissa lowers her head and her feral eyes flash scalding embers at Deacon. "The things I'll do before I'm done?"

Deacon squints into the stinging wind, struggling to keep his hand steady as he aims the barrel of the gun at a spot just above her left breast. Narcissa takes a step towards him.

"They've been lying to you, *using* you, you sad, stupid man. The Children of the Cuckoo," she sneers. "A couple of lapdog curs, that's all they are, those two. That's all they'll ever be."

Deacon pulls the trigger, but the shot goes wide; Narcissa doesn't even flinch. She takes another step forward, her bare feet in a drift of snow, her long legs and those eyes to burn his resolve to cinders.

"They need you, Deacon. They need your sight to find what I've taken from them."

"Shut up," he says and tries to steady the gun by propping it against his bandaged left wrist. She's no more than ten feet away from him now, and Narcissa takes another step, closing the space for him that much more.

"Who's watching Chance?" she asks. "Who's minding the baby?"

Deacon pulls the trigger and the slug tears a hole in the soft depression beneath her windpipe; blood sprays out across the sand and she stops, staggers, and puts a hand over the wound, the smile returning to her lips.

"Your child will be such a prize," she says hoarsely. "She has her father's eyes."

He fires again and this time the shot catches Narcissa squarely between her breasts and knocks her to the sand. She sits there, smiling triumphantly up at him, a trickle of blood escaping from her open mouth, blood leaking thick and dark between the fingers still pressed futilely to her throat. But the hole in her chest isn't bleeding at all.

"See me now, Mother Hydra," she croaks. "Lady of the Abyss, Kraken Daughter," and then she stops talking and shuts her eyes. Deacon takes a cautious step towards her and the sea salt and rot smell grows suddenly stronger than before, the stench so thick it seems to cling to the insides of his nostrils. He gags helplessly and Narcissa reaches out, taking his hand and the pistol and pressing it against her forehead. She opens her eyes again, but the fire is gone from them, leaving behind only sickly yellow irises and shrinking, black-hole pupils.

"Finish it, Deacon," she says. "Kill the monster," and a fresh gout of blood spills from her lips and flows like syrup down her chin. "Will you, won't you, will you, won't you, will you join the dance?"

Deacon pulls the trigger for the seventh time, lucky seven, and overhead the sky rumbles so loud he can't even hear the shot. The sky pulling itself apart, ripping itself open at the seams with lightning hooks and needles, and Narcissa slumps back into the sand as her body comes apart in a feathery burst of raven wings. A dozen big black birds where her body lay an instant before and they rush past Deacon and are gone.

And he's standing in the old house at the end of Cullom Street, storm-dim light through the windows so he can see Scarborough's body lying lifeless at his feet. The body and the circle drawn on the floor in blood and shit and charcoal, the bleached bits of bone laid out inside that stinking wheel. He lets the gun slip from his fingers and it clatters loudly against the floor, and the sound echoes through the empty house.

By the time Deacon gets back to Morris Avenue, the storm has passed, has dragged itself away north and east across the smarting, shell-shocked sky, leaving the city to glitter wet beneath the street lamps. Driving like a maniac, running stop signs and red lights and it's a miracle he doesn't get pulled over or have a wreck; finally the wheels of Scarborough Pentecost's long black Cadillac bouncing hard over the cobblestones, bouncing so hard that Deacon bites his tongue and his mouth fills with the taste of salt water and old pennies. He's still a block away when he sees the strobing lights, an epileptic's nightmare of swirling, flashing blues and whites and reds. *Too late,* he thinks. *Too late and she's dead,* and then there's a pissed-off-looking cop standing in the road with a whistle frantically waving him towards the curb.

Deacon cuts the wheel sharply to the right and stomps on the brake, but the Cadillac's tires couldn't care less what he wants and keep moving over the cobbles, too fast, too wet for traction, and the big car slams over the concrete curb and crashes into one of the cast-iron lampposts. It comes loose from the sidewalk and lands on the hood of the car in a sizzling spray of yellow-orange sparks, denting chrome and puncturing steel, shattering the windshield. Deacon wipes at his forehead, trying to figure out why he's bleeding, why there's blood on the steering wheel and his head hurts. When he looks up, the cop has started shouting at him, shouting words that Deacon can't quite make out and he pulls the handle to open the Cadillac's door.

"You just stay right the hell where you are," the cop yells, reaching for something at his waist, his gun, handcuffs or pepper spray, and Deacon doesn't think it really makes much difference which. "Are you fucking high or something?"

"No," Deacon says and starts to get out of the car, but that just makes the cop yell at him again.

"We've had enough crazy shit down here tonight without some drunk plowing into a lamppost."

"I'm not drunk," Deacon tells him.

"Well, how about you just stay put and let me figure that out for the both of us, okay?"

Deacon shakes his head and looks back up at the blizzard of swirling colored lights, all the cop cars and two ambulances crowded in at the back of their building, a fire truck parked right in the middle of Twenty-third Street, and "My wife," he says. "My wife is in there."

"Mister, ain't nobody left in there," the cop replies and glances warily at the ruined streetlamp half-buried in the hood of the black Cadillac, still spitting up a few lazy sparks. "You better just sit still until I can get someone from EMS over here to take a look at you."

"Look, man, I fucking *live* there," Deacon growls, losing patience as his head begins to clear, and he stabs an index finger in the general direction of the building. "My wife is pregnant. She was in 307. I've got to find her."

"Oh crap," the cop says and then starts speaking fast into his walkie-talkie, but there are already other people running across the wet cobblestones towards the Cadillac, their shoes loud in the night—four or five more cops and a fat paramedic, a tall fireman in green rubber boots and Detective Downs bringing up the rear.

Downs whispers something to the cop with the whistle and bends down beside the open car door. "Where the sam hell have you been?" he asks. Deacon doesn't answer him or take his eyes off the building, off the windows of his and Chance's apartment.

"Listen to me, Deke, I'm gonna need you to stay real fucking calm, you hear—?"

"Where is she? Where's Chance?"

"That's what we're trying to figure out. We just got the power back on a few minutes—"

"What the fuck do you mean?" and then Deacon's up and out of the Cadillac, shoving his way through the bodies packed in around the car, already halfway across Morris before the fireman and one of the cops can stop him.

"She's not *in* there," Downs says. "Now don't make me have to put the cuffs on you. You gotta believe me, there's nothing in there you want to see right now."

"Oh god," Deacon whispers. "You were supposed to be here.

You were supposed to protect her," and he starts to take another step, but Downs is there to block him.

"Where were you tonight, Deke? What is it you're not telling me about all this shit? You knew she needed protection, but you weren't here to do it."

Deacon looks away from the apartment windows and stares directly into the detective's bloodshot eyes; whatever Downs sees there is enough to make him take a cautious step or two backwards.

"Arrest me or turn me the fuck loose," Deacon says, his voice gone flat and mock calm, spending almost everything he has left just to keep from punching the detective in the face.

"You are bound and determined to make this as hard as possible for both of us, aren't you?"

"Arrest me or get out of my way."

"Deacon, your wife is *missing* and we've got this other woman's corpse splattered all over your parking garage like a piece of modern fucking art, all right? We got *another* girl they found out in the street there and she's gonna be real damn lucky if she makes it through the night. Right now, arresting you is just about the only thing that does make sense, but I don't want to do it."

"I know who did this," Deacon says. "I know exactly who did this and I know why, and you and all your little bad boys in blue here aren't ever going to catch her," and for a few seconds Downs stares silently back at him, then nods his head.

"Right now," he says, his voice strained thin and brittle, "forensics is in your apartment. When they're done, I'll take you up. But, Deacon, in the meantime, you're gonna sit your ass in the backseat of that cruiser over there and you're gonna keep your mouth shut, do you hear me?"

"You don't know what's—"

"I *asked* you if you fuckin' heard me."

"Yeah, sure thing," Deacon mutters, but he can see the relief pooling like thick, glycerin tears in Downs' eyes. "Whatever you say, Detective."

"I swear to you, we're doing everything we can."

"You're wasting your time," Deacon says and he glances at the apartment windows again, at the safe incandescent glow through the glass.

"We'll find her," Downs says. "You just gotta keep believing that. You just gotta let us do our job."

"The girl you found out back, can I talk to her?"

"She isn't even conscious, Deke. Do you know who she is?"

"Maybe," he says, "and maybe no one does," and then he lets one of the other policemen lead him away to a black-and-white parked in the street, catty-corner to the building. The cop asks if he'd like some hot coffee and when Deacon says no, shuts the door, locking him in. Deacon leans back in the seat and stares up at the clearing sky through the rear windshield—the last purple-gray wisps of the storm clouds sailing by high above the rooftops, a handful of stars and the cold moon, almost full now. In a little while, he closes his eyes, waiting for Downs to come back for him, for whatever Narcissa Snow's left upstairs, and Deacon Silvey prays for the first time since he was a child.

PART II

The Hounds of Cain

In what distant deeps or skies
Burnt the fire of thine eyes?
On what wings dare he aspire?
What the hand dare seize the fire?

And what shoulder, & what art,
Could twist the sinews of thy heart?
And when thy heart began to beat,
What dread hand? & what dread feet?

—WILLIAM BLAKE (ca. 1792)

CHAPTER ELEVEN

Lullaby

In the soft half-light behind her eyelids, Chance listens to the airplane-propeller hum of the tires on the road, the comforting, consoling thrum that has carried her from one weightless hour to the next. Morning sunshine warm on her face through the windows, bathing her like honey; no time here, and the fear is far away, unimportant, so long as she doesn't think about it. So long as she keeps the whys and hows at arm's length, where they belong.

"When I was seven," the child says to her from the backseat. "Do you remember when I was seven and I broke my arm?"

"Yes," Chance replies, even though she doesn't.

"You told me to be careful, climbing trees."

"Did I?"

"Of course you did, Mother," the child replies.

"You should rest now," she says. "You'll need your strength."

"Is it very far, the place we're going?"

"I don't know. I can't remember if I know or not," and the thing behind the steering wheel, the werewolf, the monster with the sun trapped inside its smoldering skull, tells her to shut up.

"Faster!" the child squeals excitedly. "Don't try to talk!"

"I'm sick of listening to you babble," the werewolf growls.

"Faster! Faster! I wonder if all the things out there move along with us?"

"I don't know," Chance says. "I can't see them."

"Well, you could, if you'd open your eyes," but that's the last thing she wants to do, better here in the warm honey-light with the constant, soothing thrum of the tires, better if she doesn't have to see the face of the beast, the waxy mask it wears so other people don't see the things it's shown Chance.

"Let me sleep a while," she says to the child, trying to sound firm, but also trying not to scold and the werewolf growls again.

"Maybe I'm giving you too much," it says. "Or maybe I'm not giving you enough. Maybe if I give you just a little more next time you'll shut the fuck up for a while."

"I'm fine," Chance tells it. "I'll stop talking."

She hears the click of the radio knob, static, white noise to get in the way of the wheel sounds, and then a man's singing a gospel song. *That's not so bad,* she thinks, curious to hear how the radio voice slips so easily in between the rays of light, through her skin, between the tires and the asphalt.

". . . I once was lost, but now I'm found . . ." and then the crackle and pop of more static and Chance almost asks the werewolf to put it back, that she wants to hear all the song, but then decides it's better if she keeps quiet for a while.

But now I'm found, and *No,* Chance thinks. *I'm not found at all, am I? I'm still very, very lost.*

"You can be the White Queen's Pawn," the child says unhelpfully. "And you're in the Second Square to begin with. When you get to the Eighth Square you'll be Queen—"

"You should be quiet for a little bit," Chance says. "We'll talk more later. Later on, I'll tell you a story."

"There's that same old tree again," the child says and laughs, a high, wind-chime laugh that Chance is glad the werewolf can't hear. "I think we've been under this tree the whole time, Mother."

"Go to sleep," she says. "I need to go to sleep."

"You need to shut the hell up for five minutes," the monster growls and snaps its jaws. Now there's rock music blaring from the radio, nothing Chance recognizes or wants to recognize, and she tries to hear the tire hum through the writhing maze of electric guitars and drums.

"You can sleep when you're dead, girl," the child says, just like Deacon, and it surprises her so much that Chance opens her eyes partway and squints painfully at the brilliant day, the sun and the hills rolling past outside the car.

"I need to pee," she says, trying not to mumble or slur the words. "I'm thirsty and I need to pee."

"There's no place to stop here," the werewolf tells her. "You'll just have to wait. You shouldn't drink so damn much."

"I'm pregnant," Chance replies impatiently. "Pregnant women drink a lot of water and then they pee a lot. Didn't anyone ever tell you that?"

"You drew a trilobite on my cast," the child chimes in from the backseat. "And a red *Tyrannosaurus.*"

"No one ever told me they talk so goddamn much," the werewolf growls and turns up the radio. "I ought to cut out your goddamn tongue. It's not like you're going to need it."

"It's not me talking. It's the needles," Chance says, though she meant to say "It's the shit *in* the needles," but part of it got lost in all the racket coming from the radio. "I really do have to pee," she whispers and the child with Deacon's strange eyes laughs, but she doesn't turn around to see why. She stares out the window, much too much trouble to close her eyelids again, now that they're open, watching the steep, wooded hills, autumn-colored hardwoods and grass that's still mostly green, wondering where they are, how far they've driven, how many nights and days since the werewolf came slinking out of the storm to take her away.

"Where are we?" she asks and "We're under the tree," the child answers. "I fell and we're waiting for Daddy."

"No, I mean where are we *at,* not where are we *when.*"

"What difference does it make?" the werewolf growls.

"Maybe it's someplace I've never been before. Maybe I'd just like to know."

The car passes between gray-white limestone walls, a small slice of the world taken away long ago to let the road come through. "See, I think those rocks are Mississippian," Chance tells the werewolf. "But they might be Ordovician. If I knew where we were, I could tell you which."

"Why the hell do you think I care?"

"I care," Chance says. "The Ordovician's not so interesting, but the Mississippian—"

"We're in Virginia. We've been in fucking Virginia forever. Now will you zip it?"

"Virginia," Chance says, repeating the word because it takes her a second to remember exactly what it means. "Then they probably are Mississippian after all."

"I've got a scalpel and clamps in my bag in the trunk—"

"But I might bleed to death," Chance whispers, sly whisper that makes the child in the backseat laugh out loud again. "We can't have that, can we?"

"I'm a real whiz with a needle and thread," the werewolf barks back. "Trust me, you wouldn't bleed to death."

"Anyway," Chance says. "I'm going to pee on your seat and the floorboard and then I guess you'll have to steal *another* car."

"She does that later, after the fire," the child says.

"Oh," Chance replies and the car passes through another road cut, higher walls than the last one, and for a moment the sun is eclipsed by the exposed rocks. A moment of chill air and Chance shivers and starts talking again so she doesn't have to think about cold, dark places.

"Are we in the Valley and Ridge Province?" she asks, but doesn't wait for the werewolf to answer before she continues. "If we are, then it probably is only Ordovician. Shallow water carbonate deposition predominated, up until the Taconic Orogeny began, anyway. There's the Conococheague Formation. Isn't that a wonderful name? And the whole Beekmantown Group—"

"What's an orogeny?" the child asks.

"When mountains get made," Chance replies, and then they're out in the sun again and she'd already forgotten how good it felt on her face.

"I see," the child says thoughtfully. "Are there dinosaurs in those rocks?"

"No. There won't be dinosaurs for a long time yet, not for hundreds of millions of years. But there were lots of trilobites and brachiopods, and bryozoans. Remember me telling you about bryo—?"

"Jesus fucking *Christ!*" the werewolf snarls and it cuts the steering wheel like it's decided it's a better idea to try driving straight through the pastures and trees. The car bounces off the blacktop and onto the narrow shoulder, slinging gravel, plowing up red mud and tall brown stalks of ragweed and yellow goldenrod. It rolls to a stop beside a listing wooden billboard that reads REPENT SINERS FOR THE END IS NEAR; sun-faded crimson paint on peeling white, letters taller than Chance.

"That's not how you spell 'sinners,' " Chance says, pointing at the sign. "I don't think that's even a real word."

"Just get out of the damn car," the werewolf growls at her and snaps its ivory teeth at the sizzling, Naugahyde air. "Get out and take your fucking piss and then shut the fuck up."

"But someone might drive by and see me."

"Then go behind the sign," and Chance looks up at the billboard again, stares at it a second or two, trying to remember if she's right about the proper spelling of "sinners," and then she nods her head.

"Okay. Sure. That'll do. But I need toilet paper."

The werewolf curses and grabs a wad of paper napkins from the dash, leftovers from someplace they stopped for hamburgers last night, and she shoves them into Chance's hand.

"Don't try to run, Mother," the child says from the backseat. "You won't get far. She's fast."

"Don't worry," Chance replies, smiling and looking over her shoulder, but she can't see the child so maybe it's hiding in the floorboard. She'd hide, if she could fit. "I'm just gonna pee. I'll be right back," and then, to the monster in the driver's seat, "Don't try to leave me here. I don't even know where we are."

"Just get out of the fucking car," it snarls back at her and Chance unlatches her seat belt and opens the door. She leaves it standing open, so it'll be more trouble than it's worth for the werewolf to drive off and leave her stranded. Dizzy when she stands up and she almost falls, has to lean against the car until her head stops spinning. "Just the morphine," she says, because it scared her until she re-membered the needles, the white powder, and she turns her back on the car and starts pushing her way through the tall weeds. Small brown grasshoppers leap out of her way, hundreds of grasshoppers, it seems, and a bumblebee buzzes loudly past her head.

"Deacon's coming," she whispers to the insects, quiet so the werewolf won't hear her. "He's coming with the starlings to take me back home. So all I have to do is stay alive until he finds me."

The sign looms above her, declaring doom and damnation and hope like a hostage, and Chance tries to focus on where she's put-ting her feet, watching out for poison oak and copperheads. *Now, wouldn't that be ironic?* she thinks and wonders if the werewolf has anything in its bag of tricks to treat snakebite. Another dizzy spell and so she leans against one of the signposts this time until it passes and "Deacon's coming," she says again.

The hills above the sign are very steep, the forest like a fortress wall on the other side, and maybe if she ran she *could* get away, if she could only make it up the hill; the sky so wide and blue above her and there must be a hundred thousand places to hide in there. To make herself very small and burrow deep down into the fallen leaves and detritus, pull the soil up over her head and wait for Deacon to come and take her home. Down with the worms and grubs and the werewolf would never, ever think to look that far down.

"Yes, she would," Chance says with the child's androgynous voice. "That's the very first place she would look. Monsters are always looking down."

Chance steps behind the sign and unbuttons the denim straps of her overalls, lets them fall down around her ankles. Just her oversized T-shirt and violet panties to deal with now and she pushes the panties down and squats with her back pressed firmly against the signpost, so she doesn't lose her balance and go rolling head over heels out into the road.

"Try not to pee on yourself this time," she says, knowing she probably will anyway. Too awkward, too clumsy, and the weeds are poking at her and starting to make her itch. The sudden sound of the warm urine rushing from her aching, distended bladder reminds Chance that she's thirsty, has been thirsty forever it seems, and she wishes she had a Coke or a cold bottle of water. And then she sees the dead thing, half-hidden in the tall grass only a few feet away from her, sees it and smells it in the same instant, and covers her mouth and nose.

It's hard to tell what it used to be, before, to start with; a big possum or a raccoon, once upon a time, a small dog maybe, or a fox, but now there are only a few matted tufts of gray-black fur clinging stubbornly to the bones and rot, a noisy, iridescent cloud of greenbottle flies hovering in the air above the corpse. Sharp white teeth still set in its slender jaws, and Chance thinks if only *she* had teeth like that, maybe she could have fought off the werewolf and wouldn't be pissing behind an end-of-the-world sign in the mountains of Virginia right now. And her child would be safe, and Deacon would be safe, if she had teeth like that.

"They didn't save him," the child says unhappily, speaking with her tongue, her lips, and Chance starts crying and the last few trickles of piss splash against her overalls and left shoe. She leans back against the signpost and stares up at the sky, wishing she believed in anything at all, anything watching down on her.

"Motherfucker," she sobs, trying to think clearly through the fear and the haze the morphine has spun behind her eyes, trying to remember how long since Birmingham. "Where are you, Deke? Where the hell are you?"

"He's coming," the child reassures her. "You just have to be strong. You have to be strong for both of us now."

"Stop it!" Chance shouts up at the vast Appalachian sky. "You're not real, so stop making me fucking promises!" and then she's crying too hard to say anything else.

The wind whistles and blows through the trees, rattling the dry leaves, pulling more of them free of the twigs, and the flies buzz undisturbed around the dead thing. In a couple more minutes, Chance wipes herself dry, pulls her clothes back on, and makes her way slowly, carefully, back down to where the werewolf and the child are waiting in the car.

Narcissa drives until the pain from her burned face and hands is finally more than she can stand, until the exhaustion begins to blur and double her vision. Escaping the hilly purgatory of Virginia back roads sometime towards dusk, and she slips as quickly as she dares along US 11, through a sliver of West Virginia and then across the dark Potomac as the western horizon swallows the sun. An even stingier sliver of Maryland afterwards, but she makes it into Pennsylvania, the wilderness just past Greencastle, before she nods off the first time and almost runs off the road.

"You won't be satisfied until you've killed us all," Chance mumbles and Narcissa slaps herself hard, never mind the burns, and starts looking for any place safe enough to pull over and rest a few hours, maybe even get some sleep if she's lucky.

Past the junction with State 16, a few miles more, and she finds the deserted, burned-out shell of a motel, a tall metal sign that she can't read in the darkness of the mountains. She pulls off the road, across a wide gravel parking lot, and Chance turns and looks into the backseat again.

"I think we're here," she says and smiles sadly.

"You've gone crazy as a fucking loon, you know that?" Narcissa tells her. "Who the hell do you think you're talking to back there?"

"No one," Chance says too quickly, like she's been rehearsing the response in her head all day and yesterday too. "No one at all."

"Well, you and Mr. No-one-at-all back there are driving me apeshit and I'm telling you I'm too tired to listen to it anymore."

The car rolls past sooty brick and concrete ruin, charcoal and melted glass, and the limestone gravel crunches loudly beneath the tires of the rusty old Ford Thunderbird the color of dirty snow that she stole back in Tennessee.

"Stop giving me the shots and I'll stop talking," Chance says. "The shots make me talk."

"In your dreams, crazy lady."

"They'll hurt the baby," Chance says, a little more forcefully and Narcissa glances in the mirror at the empty backseat.

"No, they won't. Well, nothing permanent. Don't worry about the baby, I did my homework. I always do."

"I don't believe you."

"I don't give a shit."

Narcissa drives around to the back of the building, well out of sight of the highway, and parks the Ford beneath and between two huge oak trees. Twisted limbs like the massive, knotted arms of the forest, forked branches like its claws, straining to rake the wasted motel and everything else into its leafy gullet.

"I don't know why you don't just get it over with," Chance whispers. "I don't know why you don't kill us and be done with it."

Narcissa shifts into park and cuts the engine. "You got me all wrong," she says. "No one and nothing is going to hurt your precious fucking baby. I don't really give a shit what happens to you. In the end, you're just an incubator as far as I'm concerned, but nobody's gonna hurt the kid."

"Then it doesn't even make sense," Chance says and Narcissa thinks about shutting off the headlights, reaches for the knob, but then something small moves at the edge of the woods and she stops and stares at the patch of briars caught in the beams.

"Well, there's no money. Not if that's what you think you're going to get out of this."

"I don't *need* anybody's fucking money," Narcissa sneers, still watching the patch of blackberry briars twined in between the roots of the two oaks.

"No," Chance says. "She's not going to hurt you. She just said she wasn't going to hurt you, didn't she?"

"You think you're talking to the kid, don't you?"

"I don't know," Chance whispers very quietly. "I don't know what's happening to me anymore."

"Must be a bitch, that big ol' rational brain of yours trying to take all this crap in, trying to trick it into something scientific."

"The drugs . . . ," Chance mumbles, trailing off, and closes her eyes.

"Yeah, that's right. Blame it on the morphine. Keep it up as long as you can. None of this is real."

"None of this is real."

"Maybe it's all just a bad dream," Narcissa says and reaches across the seat, brushing Chance's sweat-stringy bangs from her face. "Maybe you'll wake up soon and open your eyes, and before you've even finished breakfast you won't be able to remember my name."

"I *can't* wake up," Chance mutters. "I've been trying to wake up forever and ever."

"Then maybe you're trying too hard. Didn't you think of that?"

"Where are we going, Narcissa?"

"Down to the sea," she replies and leans closer to Chance. The smell of her, sweat and urine, the spittle dried to a crust on her lips and chin, her breath, and Narcissa flares her nostrils, taking it all inside. "A secret place I know."

Chance opens her eyes, flinches when she sees how very close Narcissa is, and immediately shuts them again. "You're in pain," she says. "You got those burns when you tried to kill Sadie Jasper, didn't you?"

"Yeah. It's a shame you don't have her determination, her resourcefulness. You might not be in this fix right now."

"A shame you didn't fucking die in that fire," Chance whispers and Narcissa laughs and licks at her left earlobe, just a little taste, and Chance screams. The sound is very loud, trapped there inside the closed car with them.

"Oh, come on now," Narcissa growls softly. "It can't really be as bad as all that," and she nips playfully at Chance's ear, catching it and holding it between her sharp teeth. Feeling Chance's whole body grow tense before she finally lets go, and then Narcissa doesn't say anything else for a few seconds, sits savoring the salty, living taste of this woman, salt and a bitter hint of the drug coursing through her veins. Enough that Narcissa forgets the pain for a moment, almost enough that she could forget herself and reach for the butterfly knife tucked beneath the seat.

"Your friend, Alice—that was her name, wasn't it, Alice? She didn't seem to mind—"

"I *know* you killed her," Chance says, spitting out the words like venom and nails and now there are tears streaking her cheeks. "You don't have to tell me what you did to her."

"No," Narcissa says, sitting up straight again, and she looks back at the briars tangled between the trees. "I guess I don't. I expect you've figured most of it out for yourself by now."

"I know you killed her."

"She shouldn't have tried to stop me," Narcissa says and the something at the edge of the woods moves again, its small, bright eyes flashing back the headlights. A lanky jackrabbit cowering in the thorns, and Narcissa takes a pair of silver handcuffs from a pocket of her leather jacket and cuffs Chance to the steering wheel.

"You getting hungry, crazy lady?" she asks and when Chance doesn't answer, Narcissa glances in the rearview mirror again. "Well, what about you, Mr. No-one-at-all-back-there? You ready for some solid food yet?"

"Fuck you."

"I'll be back soon," Narcissa says, not taking her eyes off the rabbit, helpless and cringing in the lights. "Scream if you want. Blow the horn if you want. But I don't think anyone's going to hear you way out here." And then she opens the door and slips out of the Ford and into the night, the darkness a balm against her blistered flesh, and leaves Chance alone for a while.

When there is little more left of the rabbit than skin and the bones she's broken open to get at the marrow, Narcissa sits shivering in the underbrush, trying to ignore the pain from her burns and watching the Thunderbird parked behind the motel. The headlights are still on and if she doesn't go back soon, the battery will run down and they'll be stranded.

"It breaks my heart to see you like this, child," her grandfather says. Aldous Snow is sitting behind her on a fallen sycamore log, smacking his gums and picking through the discarded remains of the jackrabbit. "Lost and adrift in the wide, wide world."

"I'm not lost," she murmurs. "I know exactly where I am. I know where I'm going."

"And that's the reason you'll *stay* lost," he says.

"Only two days till the full moon," she says. "Two days until Halloween. And there she is, right there in the car. They'll come for her, old man."

"They'll come all right," he grumbles and tosses aside a handful of ribs and fur. "They'll come to put an end to you, once for all."

The wind whispers cold through the tall trees and there's an owl hooting loudly somewhere close by, probably close enough she could see it if she only turned her head and looked. But she doesn't. Doesn't take her eyes off the Ford.

"It's a shame Death didn't see fit to make you any less bitter," she says. "It's a pity you're such a jealous ghost."

"Oh ho," Aldous exclaims. "You missed a speck of something here. I think it might be liver."

"Because they wouldn't come for you or mother, you would have killed me to keep them from coming up for me."

"Yes, it *is* liver."

"You can't eat, old man. You're a ghost. Put it down. Leave it for the ants and maggots."

Narcissa imagines that there's movement from the car, then, sudden movement behind the windshield, but it's probably only Chance shifting in her morphium-flavored dreams. Nothing for her to be afraid of, nothing left to stop her now. The late October breeze breathes unkindly against her face and sets off a new wave of chills and she shuts her eyes for a moment, waiting for them to pass.

"I'll eat whatever I damn well please," Aldous mutters behind her. "Arrogant little hussy. Selfish, arrogant bitch."

"Fine, old man," she says, gritting her teeth together to try and stop shivering. "Knock yourself out."

"You're hurting, aren't you?" he asks and then smacks his gums uselessly around the mean scrap of rabbit flesh. "Why don't you just use a little of that shit you're shooting into your Madonna down there? Fix you right up, I bet."

"I have to keep my head clear, Aldous. It's not over yet."

"Your head doesn't seem too clear to me, child. Sitting up here in the dark, talking to ghosts and hurting like you are."

"So fuck off," Narcissa says. "I didn't invite you."

"Didn't you? Are you sure?"

"Mother Hydra will stir with the moonlight," she says, ignoring his inconvenient questions. "Like you told me, old man. In her sleep, she'll open one great black eye for me and keep me safe from harm."

"I never told you that. You made that up, hiding in that room of yours, talking to yourself."

"Mother Hydra, Father Kraken. They guide my hands," Narcissa says and shivers again. "But you, you tried to poison my mind against her, make me fear her like you wanted me to fear the tunnels beneath the house. Like you wanted me to fear *everything* that mattered."

More movement from the car and this time Narcissa gets slowly to her feet, brushes her left hand against a creeper vine and almost cries out when a thorn tears its way through a blister to the new, raw skin growing underneath. She bites her tongue, hard enough to taste blood, and doesn't make a sound, but Aldous laughs at her. Chance has rolled her window all the way down and is resting her head on the doorframe, half in, half out. Probably just wanting a little fresh air, that's all, and Narcissa considers staying beneath the sheltering forest a while longer. Wishes that she weren't too anxious to close her eyes and drift off for ten or fifteen or twenty minutes. Wishes she *could* pop a few milligrams and sleep until she began to feel more like herself again.

" 'Below the thunders of the upper deep,' " she whispers to herself. " 'Far, far beneath the abyssal sea—' "

"How precious," Aldous sneers. "Our Lady of the Cephalopods, Patron Saint of Mollusks. It was only a fairy tale, Narcissa, and if it wasn't, you best hope it was. Ain't no one and nothing down there watching out for you. No one at all."

" 'Until the latter fire shall heat the deep,' " she continues, speaking fast, forgetting lines but it's the thought, the faith, that counts. " 'Then once by man and angels to be seen, in roaring—' "

"You're pathetic," Aldous says and goes back to digging noisily among the scraps of bone and skin. "That's only a sorry bit of fucking Tennyson. You make it sound like scripture."

"Sometimes, in dreams, even men see things. You read me Blake yourself."

"Blake was a damned schizophrenic," the hungry ghost replies. "They just hadn't invented the word back then."

"How often is a changeling of such worth offered up to them? Maybe once in a century? Once in five hundred years?"

"That doesn't change what you are, Narcissa," Aldous says and snaps a tibia between his insubstantial fingers. "More important, that doesn't change what you are *not.* There's not half-enough of the blood of the hounds in your veins to make a decent poodle, much less a *ghul,* and all the pretty gifts on earth can't change that. They don't bargain with humans, and that's all that you are. Never mind what you stole from them, never mind you blackmailed them."

"You'll see," she says, and then Chance begins to blow the horn over and over again.

"Your guest is growing restless," Aldous cackles. "Perhaps she needs fresh linens."

"No. She just has to piss again," Narcissa says. "And it's about time for another injection," and then she catches the pattern in the blats from the Thunderbird's horn. Three short, three long, three short, and Aldous must have caught it, as well, because he begins to giggle from his seat on the fallen sycamore.

"Better watch yourself, child," he snickers. "Maybe this one here's got her own sort of Mother Hydra."

Narcissa shakes her head, wipes some of the dried blood from her lips and chin, and when she's sure that Chance isn't going to stop blowing the horn, isn't tiring of her pointless SOS, she leaves the ghost of the old man alone in the woods and goes back to the car.

A few miles past Red Bridge, the crest of Kittatinny Mountain rising hazy in the west to catch the morning sun, and the werewolf pulls into a combination diner and Texaco station because the Ford's gas tank is getting close to empty and, besides, Chance thinks it must be tired of listening to her complain about being

hungry and needing to piss. The whole long night spent behind
the burned-out motel and the werewolf is growing impatient,
Chance can see that, doesn't understand why, but even through
the drugs it would be hard for her to miss the anxiety building behind those hard yellow eyes. When Narcissa came down out of
the forest, blood drying to tacky smears on her face and hands,
she gave Chance another injection that swept her along to dawn,
and then another before they rolled back out onto the highway.
After the second shot, the child in the backseat grew suddenly
quiet, sullen, and then went away altogether, and she has to keep
reminding herself it was only an hallucination to begin with, that
they didn't leave it behind somewhere, that the werewolf hasn't
murdered it.

"I'm going to fill the tank first," Narcissa says, glancing nervously towards the big diner windows decorated with gaudy, smiling Halloween pumpkins and skeletons. "I can't use the cuffs
because there are people watching, but you're going to sit your ass
right here and not move a muscle, you got me?"

"Yeah," Chance tells her. "Sure. But then we'll get something
to eat?"

"Whatever," the werewolf growls and slams the door.

Chance looks forlornly into the empty backseat, then across the
parking lot towards the diner, then at the backseat again.

"It doesn't really matter if you're real or not," she says, whispering, in case Narcissa is listening. "You can come back if you
want. I miss you, butter bean. I'm afraid."

But the child doesn't reappear and she turns and stares out the
Thunderbird's dusty window at the diner, the three other cars and
one pickup parked out front. The car is filling up with gas fumes
and the smell of asphalt warming in the bright morning sunshine,
so she cracks her window just enough to let in some fresh air, then
realizes that's where the bad smells are coming from in the first
place. A red-orange neon sign in the diner window spells out GOOD
HOMECOOKING, and even with the gasoline and blacktop fumes
working their way up her nostrils and making her nauseous, the
sign gets her mouth watering. Her stomach gurgles loudly and the
baby kicks.

"Yeah, I know you're hungry, too."

The pump makes a dull, whirring sound and she looks away

from the diner, watches Narcissa and the gray LCD numbers ticking off pennies and ounces, dollars and gallons.

"We're going to eat in a little while. She promised," Chance says and gently massages her belly through her overalls and the T-shirt underneath. "If I had your books, I'd read you a story and you'd forget you're hungry. I'd read you Pooh or Dr. Seuss, but they're all back in Birmingham. I could sing to you, instead. Would you like that?"

Sometime later, and for all Chance knows it's hours or only a few seconds, the werewolf opens the driver's-side door and glares in at her with its wide, jaundiced eyes and she stops singing "Hey Jude" to the baby and points at the diner.

"I need to eat," she says. "*Real* food."

The werewolf frowns and gets back into the car, sliding in behind the wheel, but never takes its eyes off her.

"I keep my promises," it says, and then Narcissa looks at herself in the rearview mirror. "Fuck," she growls.

"You don't look so bad," Chance says hopefully and her stomach gurgles again. "I think the burns are better than yesterday."

"It's not the burns I'm worried about, crazy lady, it's the eyes," and Chance sees that she's holding a white contact lens case in her left hand, but can't remember where it came from; something Narcissa might have gotten out of the trunk while the gas was pumping or maybe it came from somewhere else entirely. She opens the right side of the case and dips an index finger into the clear solution inside, removes a translucent lens and slips it into her right eye. She blinks two or three times and then turns towards Chance.

"See? Just like magic," the werewolf growls at her, and now one of its yellow eyes has gone a deep, discordant blue. "And if anyone asks about the burns, I'll tell them it's a skin condition, a sun allergy."

"Fine," Chance says. "Just put the other one in. That's really creepy-looking."

"If you think that's creepy, then you got a whole lot of bad shit ahead of you, Mrs. Silvey."

"I'm hungry," she says again, insistent, watching while Narcissa puts in the left contact and blinks until it slides into place.

"Now," the werewolf growls, its new blue eyes like something stolen and plugged inside its skull. "I'm only going to tell you this one more time, so I really do hope you're fucking listening."

"I'm listening," Chance replies and decides she'd rather look at the front of the diner than those phony blue eyes.

"I do the talking. *All* the talking. If you say anything, to anybody, one single fucking word, a whole lot of people that don't have anything to do with this are going to get killed. And it'll be your fault, understand?"

"I won't say anything to anyone," she murmurs. "I need to eat, that's all."

"I know you're not awfully sure right now exactly what's real and what's coming out of those syringes, but I need you to believe me when I say that I have absolutely no problem whatsoever killing anyone that tries to help you."

"Anyone who," Chance says.

"What?"

"Not 'anyone that,' but 'anyone *who*,' because—"

"You have got to be fucking kidding me," the werewolf barks in its coarse, sandpapery monster's laugh. "Here I thought you were some sort of geologist, not a goddamn English teacher."

"Well, there's no point in sounding ignorant," Chance replies, wondering if restaurants this far north serve grits.

"I speak nine languages," Narcissa says. "Three of them don't even have names anymore and I don't need a lecture on English from a rockhound on morphine. Now, *s'il vous plaît,* are you going to behave yourself in there or should I just keep going until we come to a drive-thru?"

"I'll behave," Chance says. "Do you think they have grits?"

"I don't even know what the hell a *grit* is. You just sit still and I'll come around and open your door."

"I can open it myself. I'm not an invalid."

"I said sit your fat ass still," the werewolf growls, and Chance wonders where it's from, that no one there eats grits. Someplace cold, she imagines.

Chance unbuckles her seat belt, wiggling free of the shoulder strap, and waits while Narcissa walks around the front of the Ford and opens her door. The werewolf reaches in and takes her hand and Chance pulls away instinctively, not wanting that filthy thing touching her, because if it's touching her it's touching her baby, too. Those scalded, blistered hands that were stained in rabbit's blood last night, the same hands that tried to kill Sadie Jasper and that murdered the kid that Deke called Soda. The same hands that killed Alice. Unclean hands that have done unspeakable things, and "I don't fucking need your help," Chance says sharply. Narcissa shrugs and takes a step back, giving Chance room to haul herself slowly out of the Ford.

"You just remember what I told you," the werewolf growls. "Not a word to anyone."

"I'm pregnant," Chance says, "not deaf."

"You're stoned and you're scared," the monster says. "That makes you two kinds of stupid."

A minute or two later and Chance is finally out of the car and standing on her feet, her legs weak and shaky from the dope and hunger, so many hours on the road, and she has to lean against the Thunderbird until her head stops spinning and she begins to feel a little stronger.

"People are starting to stare at us," Narcissa mutters, jagged flickers of anger showing at the edges of her words.

"So what?" Chance asks, trying to get her breath, wondering if she can walk as far as the diner's door. "Maybe the women in Pennsylvania don't get pregnant and shoot up."

"You're making a scene."

Chance shuts her eyes, looking for some still point deep inside, well beyond this morning and the morphine, beyond the small distractions of her hunger and thirst, her full bladder and aching body, beyond her fear and the werewolf's contempt; the dead calm of a hurricane's eye to give her the strength and resolve to do whatever has to be done next, to keep moving ahead until Deacon can find her.

He is coming, she thinks. *He is, soon. He's almost here.*

The safe, inviolable place beyond the counterclockwise spin of the towering indigo and charcoal edges of the cloud wall, and she's only a small boat, bobbing at the still heart of the tempest.

Wherever she's taking us, it's still a long way off. And Deacon's coming fast.

"Look, bitch," Narcissa says. "I'm not going to stand around until someone in there decides to play Good Samaritan."

"Fine. Then *you* help me," Chance spits back, impressed that she can sound so angry herself. The storm spins madly around her, eternal, insane, unearthly, but she's found the center even it can't reach.

"I don't think I can walk that far."

The werewolf growls and puts an arm around Chance, supporting her, buoying her up. For one long, disorienting moment, Chance feels weightless and imagines she could fly away, sail high above the hurricane, above these craggy mountains, and then she'd be able to find Deacon on her own.

But he's almost here, she reminds herself. *No point wearing myself out. He'll be along any time now.*

"Come on then," Narcissa says and Chance opens her eyes as the werewolf slams the Ford's door shut with her free hand. The day seems even brighter than before, a summer's day lost in late October, dazzling sun dogs flashing from the front of the diner and the roofs of the cars and truck, and Chance has to squint to see.

"It wouldn't hurt to smile," the werewolf growls.

"What the hell have I got to smile about?"

"You're still alive. How's that?"

"Not very encouraging," she replies, but manages a weak smile to keep the monster happy.

"That's better," Narcissa says, and then a big candy-apple red 4x4 bounces into the parking lot and pulls in beside the other truck.

"That just fucking figures," Narcissa grumbles and so Chance squints at the man who gets out of the 4x4, smiles at him and he smiles back. Sturdy man with his hair cut down to stubble, blond stubble and a baggy camouflage jacket and pants like deer hunters and army men wear.

"Don't you say a goddamn *word*," the monster whispers in her ear so the man can't hear what it's saying.

"You two ladies need some help this morning?" he asks, still smiling and *He doesn't even see what she is,* Chance thinks, disappointed, but not surprised. *He can't see that she's a werewolf.*

"We're fine," Narcissa tells him. "But I'd appreciate it if you could get the door for us."

"Yes ma'am," he says. "You got it," and when he opens the plate-glass door Chance hears a cowbell jingle. The delicious aroma of frying meat, bacon or sausage or ham, maybe all three, wafts out of the diner and makes Chance's stomach rumble again.

"How much longer you got till the happy day?" he asks her directly and grins a little wider.

"Oh, almost any time now," Narcissa answers quickly, before Chance can. Not that she's forgotten what the werewolf told her, not a single word, so she only nods for the man and keeps smiling.

"Well then, congratulations," the man says. "You hoping it's a boy or a girl?"

"A boy," Chance replies and Narcissa hurries her through the door into the warm and greasy diner air.

"Thank you," Narcissa says to the man in the camouflage jacket. "We sure do appreciate it."

"No problem, any time at all," and then to Chance, "Good luck, ma'am."

There's an empty booth, sickly avocado-green upholstery and the stuffing poking out in a couple of places, but not too far from the door and Chance points at it and asks the werewolf if they can please sit there.

"Why not," it growls very softly. "But I don't want to hear another goddamn word out of you. I *mean* it."

"You're not being very smart, you know," Chance tells her, trying hard not to slur, to pull her thoughts together, and she taps an index finger against her left temple as Narcissa helps her into the booth. The werewolf stands there, staring down at her a moment or two with those false, unreadable blue, blue eyes and then she takes the seat facing the diner door.

"Is that a fact?"

"Yeah."

"Are you going to tell me *why,* or are we playing twenty fucking questions now?"

Chance takes a laminated menu covered with gaudy color photographs of food from a metal stand behind the salt and pepper shakers and a bottle of ketchup.

"You're trying so hard not to attract attention," she says, squinting at the menu, "but you want to do *all* the talking. That guy asked me a simple, harmless question. The only way he would've thought there was something funky going on is if I *hadn't* answered him. Keep this up and, at the very least, you're gonna have these people thinking we're a couple of dykes," and then she's distracted by two large crows that have lighted near the front bumper of the old Ford and are pecking about at the tarmac.

"Just do what I told you," Narcissa says. "Tell me what you want and I'll order for you."

"Yeah, that won't look the least bit suspicious," Chance says, wanting to laugh but somehow managing not to, not taking her eyes off the glass and the crows. The pair has been joined by a third and she's pretty sure they're the biggest crows she's ever seen. "You gonna tell the waitress I'm mute or what?"

"Just fucking do what I said," the werewolf growls. "Decide what you want and stop staring out the goddamn window."

"Those are three very big crows, aren't they?" Chance asks and when Narcissa doesn't answer, she turns to see what's wrong, and the werewolf is watching the birds, too, and has one palm pressed flat against the glass. Her eyes are wide and her lips are moving very quickly, shaping words, but there's no sound coming from her mouth.

"They're just crows, Narcissa," Chance says. "I don't think there are ravens this far south."

And then a fat woman in a yellow Opryland sweatshirt and hot pink sweatpants is standing beside the booth, a stubby pencil and a pad clutched in her hands, waiting to take their order.

"I want scrambled eggs and toast, please," Chance says, "and sausage—link sausage—and some—"

"We only have sausage patties," the fat woman says, scribbling on her pad. Narcissa is still staring out the window and doesn't even seem to have noticed that Chance is talking to the waitress.

"Patties will be fine. And grits. Do you have grits?"

"No, we don't," the fat woman says.

Disappointed, Chance glances at the menu again.

"We got Quaker oatmeal," the waitress says, "and Cream of Wheat, but we ain't got grits."

"No, that's okay. But I want some orange juice. And a great big glass of milk."

"Whole or skim?"

"Whole, definitely," Chance says and when she returns the menu to its place behind the ketchup bottle, Narcissa's head snaps suddenly around, fixing her with the fake blue eyes.

"What did you just say to her?" the werewolf growls.

"Whole," Chance replies. "I asked for whole milk."

"Is that y'all's car sitting out there at the pumps?" the waitress asks and "Yes," Narcissa replies without bothering to look away from Chance.

"Well, I'm afraid you'll have to move it. You can't leave it sitting there while you eat. We might have other customers wanting to buy gas."

"Yeah. Fine," Narcissa says and she reaches across the table for Chance's hand. "We'll move it."

"Oh, no, there ain't no need for both of you to have to get up," the waitress says, and then, to Chance, "I mean, not in your condition."

"And my feet hurt," Chance says and looks back out the window at the three crows, not particularly surprised to see that they have been joined by a fourth. *Four for a birth,* she thinks and "I can wait here," she tells the werewolf.

"Sure, you just go ahead and give me your order, ma'am, and then you can pull the car up front here while the food's cooking."

"Are you coming?" the werewolf growls, a low rumble building down deep in its throat, like hearing thunder coming from somewhere far away.

"I'll be fine," Chance says, feeling sleepy again, wondering lazily if there will be more crows. "I'll just sit here and wait on you. My feet hurt."

"Maybe we should just leave."

"Don't be silly. I'll be fine, Narcissa."

The waitress scribbles something else on her pad and then clicks her tongue once, loudly, against the roof of her mouth. "That certainly is an unusual name," she says. "Narcissa. I don't think I've ever once met anyone named Narcissa before."

"It's Greek," Chance tells her, watching the four crows, and she pulls her hand away before the werewolf can touch her again. "Like Narcissus."

"Well, I can't say I ever met anyone named Narcissus before, either."

"It's a very old name," Chance says sleepily, "from a Greek myth. Narcissus was a beautiful young boy who fell in love with his own reflection in a pool of water."

The waitress clicks her tongue again, but not so loudly as before. "Is that so?" she asks. "Guess I should of paid more attention in school," and Chance nods her head. A fifth crow lands in front of the car and *Five for rich,* she thinks. The other birds flap their wings and make room for the newcomer.

"Well, anyway, you'll still have to move your car," the fat woman says.

"I'll be fine, Narcissa, I promise. I'm just going to sit right here and wait for my breakfast."

Narcissa turns back to the window, just in time to see two more crows light on the hood of the Ford.

"Seven for a witch," Chance says out loud and laughs before she can stop herself.

"Excuse me," Narcissa growls, sliding quickly out of the booth, pushing her way roughly past the fat waitress. "I'm going to move the goddamn car," and then to Chance, "I meant what I said. You just remember that."

"I know," Chance replies. "I'll watch from here."

"You do that," the werewolf snarls. The cowbell over the door jingles again and Chance is left alone with the waitress.

"She your sister or something?" the fat woman asks.

"No, I don't think she has a sister. I think she's an only child."

"I only ask 'cause she seems so protective and all. I'm sorry, about the car I mean, but Burt—he's the owner—he rides my ass about shit like that."

"No problem. We shouldn't have left it there. We just forgot to move it."

"Well, I hope she's seeing a doctor, your friend, about those burns she's got. You can't be too careful about a thing like that."

"Oh, we're fine," Chance replies, and then the black birds all take to the air at once, scattering noisily as Narcissa walks quickly across the parking lot towards them. Chance can hear their wings and taunting, cawing voices, even through the glass.

"Damn dirty crows," the waitress sneers. "They shit on everything and get in the trash, strew it all around, you know. Someone ought to just kill all the dirty old things and be done with it."

"Give her time," Chance whispers, and the fat woman goes away, muttering and clicking her tongue; Chance takes a deep breath, leans her face against the window and waits for Narcissa to come back.

The murder of crows shatters before her like a living sheet of black glass, each ebony shard an eager, shrieking spy hurrying back to its

master's ears. Feathers and bone and bird flesh to give up all her secrets, and Narcissa stands in the silent space they've left and
watches as they all shrink down to pinprick stains against the pale
mountain sky.

"What the hell are you doing now, child?" Aldous asks. "You
never should have stopped here." Narcissa looks around, but
doesn't see him anywhere. Maybe he's crouched behind one of the
cars or trucks, peering out at her with his dead man's eyes, but she
decides not to try to find him, that she won't give him the satisfaction.

"*You* saw them," she says. "The crows. Were you the one who
told them where to find me?"

"You left her in there *alone*, Narcissa."

"Yeah, I did. Now why don't you leave *me* alone."

"That fat cunt of a waitress, she knows your name now, and
your face. By the time you get back in there, she'll probably know
it all."

"Did you call the crows down on me, old man?"

"You better forget the damned crows. They were just birds. But
those people sitting in that restaurant, they're all watching you
right this moment, and do you know what *they* see?"

Narcissa turns and stares anxiously at the long plate-glass window, the neon GOOD HOMECOOKING sign, Chance's sleepy face gazing back at her.

"I'll tell you," Aldous whispers. "They see a madwoman standing in a parking lot, talking to herself, that's what they see," and
he's so close now that she can smell the faint scent, like dried sage
and mildew, that clings to the flimsy shadows of ghosts.

"At this very moment, I expect that fat cunt is picking up the
phone to call the police."

"No, she isn't," Narcissa says, and forces herself to turn towards the Ford again, so no one inside can see her lips move.
There's a big gray-white smear of crow shit on the windshield and
she thinks about getting something to wipe it off before it dries.

"She'll describe you and that pregnant woman. She'll tell them
about your burns. Someone will connect the dots—"

"Get in the car," another of her voices mutters urgently, one of
her killings and it doesn't much matter which one anymore, far too
many for her to count or keep track of, too many faces and every-

one's blood is the same ten thousand shades of red. "Get in the car and drive. If you go right now, right this minute, you might make it. They might not catch you."

"Oh, they'll catch her," Aldous snickers in her ear. "One way or the other, you can bet on it. They'll catch her and shoot her down like a rabid dog. They'll catch her and stick her in some jail somewhere to rot until it's time for her turn in the electric chair."

"Go to Hell," Narcissa whispers.

"Been there, child. Been there these past fifteen years, just waiting on you to join me."

"It won't be long now," another of the voices chimes in.

"They'll have a big ol' party in that yellow house on Benefit Street," Aldous says. "Soon as the news gets back, they'll throw a soirée fit to wake the dead."

Narcissa takes a hesitant step towards the Ford and then she sees the child sitting in the backseat, watching her with its deep brown eyes that are not quite male and not quite female.

"Everywhere you turn, girl," her grandfather laughs, "everywhere you'll ever go, there's something got its eyes on you."

"Get in the car and drive. Drive fast."

"No," Aldous says mockingly. "She ain't gonna run, not this one. Not when she's *so* damn close, not when she's got Mother Hydra watching her ass and such a fine, plump offering for the Hounds."

The child in the backseat is pointing a finger towards the diner now, and when Narcissa turns around to see, the fat waitress is standing in the open door, hands on her wide pink hips, shouting something Narcissa doesn't understand. Something she doesn't hear, because now so many of the voices are talking all at once, crammed in behind her throbbing eyes and squabbling for her attention. But Aldous Snow's papery voice rises clear above the din.

"I count seven heads," he says. "But you can't be sure how many might be hiding in the kitchen. Better get started, girl."

"Yeah," Narcissa whispers, as she draws the Browning 9 mm. from her jacket, pulls back the slide, and aims at the fat woman's head. "Now shut the fuck up, old man, and let me do this."

And for an instant, the time it takes to squeeze a trigger, Narcissa sees the world through the eyes of seven crows, looking down on the world from their privileged places in the sky, and through the glassy, titan eyes of something ancient and unthinkable, half-buried at the bottom of the sea. She sees herself through the widening eyes of the fat waitress in the doorway, and Chance, and the eyes of the unborn child still watching Narcissa from the backseat of the Thunderbird. And finally her grandfather's ghost, her *father's* ghost, grinning triumphant from the scabby hole he's dug in her soul. All these things, and more, rolling faster than starlight through her head, damning slide-show blur before the pistol roars and kicks and the waitress drops like a broken doll.

"Is that the way you want it, Aldous? Like that?"

"That's one," he says, and Narcissa nods her head and begins retracing her steps to the diner door.

CHAPTER TWELVE

Stations of the Cross

The same dream every time Deacon closes his eyes long enough to begin drifting down towards sleep, the same dream or close enough that it may as well be, all the horrors of Sunday night replayed again and again as if he's looking for some way to make it all come out differently. Some alternate, happy ending yet to be discovered and hidden deep within the minutiae, right there for the taking if only his stubborn subconscious self is allowed to pick through the broken pieces enough times. Guilt and regret and a loss that he's only just beginning to comprehend, not even two days between him and the loss of her, and there's only the bourbon in his belly and the migraine that doesn't get any better no matter how much he drinks.

"Where the hell were you, Deke?" Downs asks him again, but then Deacon remembers that it's only the dream, so this time he doesn't have to answer if he doesn't want to. He's standing in the hallway outside the apartment, looking at the bloody handprints on the open door, deep gouges in the wood like someone's been at it with a knife or an awl, or some other sharp, gouging tool.

"Or claws," one of the policemen says. "That's what it looks like to me, like a big ol' dog's been at the door. You got a dog, Mr. Silvey?"

And for the fifteenth or twentieth time he says no, no, he doesn't have a dog, he hasn't had a dog since he was a kid, and the cop shrugs his shoulders, for the fifteenth or twentieth time, and says well, it sure looks to him like something a dog would do. Deacon tries to ignore him and steps quickly across the threshold, before he can think better of it and change his mind, change his mind and wake up, because then he'll just have to start the whole dream all over and there's absolutely nothing behind him that he ever needs to see again. The meandering blood trail from the parking garage, beginning at the butchered mess that used to be Alice Sprinkle, winding up the fire stairs and down the third-floor hallway, all the dark and drying splotches and smears, the boot prints on the scruffy brown carpet leading to the door and into the apartment, and then leading back out again.

"You know, maybe he had a dog with him," the cop says and "Who?" Downs asks. "Maybe who had a fucking dog?"

"The perp," the cop replies. "It'd help explain the condition of the body down—"

"Are you a goddamn detective?" Downs asks him. "Is anyone paying you to be a goddamn detective? Did some asshole hand you a promotion when I wasn't looking?"

"Look, all I said was—"

"Carter, why don't you just shut the hell up until someone's stupid enough to *ask* for your goddamn opinion."

Deacon wants them both to shut up and go away, but knows they won't, not yet. He's been here and now enough times to know that they'll follow him inside, Downs watching him like a hungry, attentive vulture, the street cop sulking in the detective's shadow.

Scarborough Pentecost is standing near the bedroom door, his blood-stiff clothes and one of Chance's fossils, a dark, tightly coiled ammonite, in his right hand, the black hole like a third eye in the center of his forehead.

"Jesus, man, you look like shit," Scarborough says and then goes back to inspecting the fossil.

"You been anywhere near a mirror lately?" Deacon asks him and then turns his head, his eyes following the boot prints towards the front of the apartment, the raisin-colored streaks along the tall hallway walls. Halfway to the living room, there's a huge circle drawn on the wall in blood with a smeary line of charcoal underneath. The circle and the line, Sadie's red moon for a werewolf, red moon for vengeful Gaelic fairies.

"Well, hell, at least you haven't lost your sense of humor," Scarborough sighs and sets the fossil back down in its place on a small walnut curio shelf hung on the wall between the bedroom and the nursery.

"Isn't this shit bad enough already, without having to talk to you every fucking time?"

"Hey, it's not my dream," Scarborough replies. "I'm not the one who keeps sticking me here."

"It looks like she put up a fight," Downs says, and Deacon knows he can't see or hear the changeling's ghost skulking about at the end of the hall. "She didn't go easily. There's a knife in the kitchen we think she might have tried to use as a weapon."

"Where were your men?" Deacon asks, reciting the question like a stray line from a play, something learned through painful, tiresome repetition, and the detective coughs but doesn't answer him.

Scarborough laughs and shakes his head. "Aren't you getting tired of this yet, Mr. Silvey? It isn't ever going to get any prettier, you know."

"She isn't dead," Deacon says and that only makes Scarborough laugh again.

"Yeah, well, maybe not, but she may as well be. In fact, right about now, she's probably starting to wish she were."

"She isn't dead," Detective Downs says, straining to sound hopeful and Deacon takes a deep breath before he touches the blood smeared down the wall. The throbbing in his head swells expectantly.

"You keep picking at that thing," Scarborough whispers, "it ain't ever gonna heal."

Deacon sets the tips of his fingers against the drywall at the center of Narcissa's circle and the wall feels soft and warm, sticky, and he's done this enough times now to be pretty sure it has a pulse. He presses gently and there's a faint popping sound before his hand sinks in up to the knuckles.

"We're going to find her," the detective says. "But you gotta help us, Deke. You gotta start telling us the *truth*—"

"Maybe he don't know the truth," the cop named Carter says. "Maybe he don't even *want* to know the truth."

"Didn't I just fucking tell you to shut the hell up?" Downs snaps and Deacon's hand sinks deeper into the wall, wet and living flesh closing tightly about his wrist and holding him there, too late to turn back now, and he glances past the bickering cops at Scarborough before it begins.

"Better be careful," Scarborough says, looking around the corner at Deacon. "I've seen people lose fingers that way."

"Frankly, it's not my fingers I'm worried about," Deacon replies and now he's digging about inside the wall, plaster and raw muscle, greasy lumps of fatty tissue and fiberglass insulation, and he's starting to think maybe this will be one of the dreams where he can't find what he's looking for. One of the dreams where he doesn't even get on the roller coaster and it'll cost him another half-pint of booze just to stand in line again. "Come *on*," he snarls, grimacing, driving his arm in up to the elbow, forcing it past the reluctant lips of the slit.

"It might be a breech birth," the cop named Carter says, glancing over Deacon's shoulder. "My wife had a breech birth with our second girl."

"So now you're a goddamn obstetrician?" Downs grumbles.

"No, but we've had three girls and you learn a few things if you pay attention."

Deacon closes his eyes, shutting them all out, the cops and Scarborough Pentecost, as the entire universe pulses to the sick rhythm of his headache and then slowly contracts down to a single speck of pinprick brilliance. The whole cosmos to pass effortlessly through the eye of a needle, and Deacon knows he must be in the wall up to his shoulder now, can smell the rotting flesh, the mildewed softwood studs.

There it is, he thinks through the blur of pain and stars. *Right in there.*

And then his hand closes around bone, a rib or the smooth shaft of a femur, something Chance would know blind, would know by touch alone, but it really doesn't make any difference to him. The brass ring, that's all it is, and he holds on tight as the universe begins to swell, reexpanding about him. The wall makes an angry, squelching noise and tries to push him out again. No place he was ever meant to see, nothing he was ever meant to touch, the infinite, slippery dimensions crammed in between time and space, flesh of her flesh, blood of her blood. Something broken deep in his soul, that he knows these things at all, can slip back along these paths that have been rolled up forever and hidden away from prying eyes and curious brains.

The scraping sound, like claws against the apartment door,

stainless steel claws to dig deep gouges before Narcissa Snow is done having her fun and simply picks the locks. Deacon opens his eyes, but it's still too dark to see, still dark because the lights are out all over town.

"Little pig, little pig," Narcissa whispers through the door. "Let me come in."

"Fuck off, bitch!" Deacon shouts back, wondering why no one even tried to help, the neighbors on both sides, until he remembers that the guy in 306 was out of town and 308's still sitting empty.

"Little pig? Can't you hear me? Aren't you listening?"

"Leave her alone," he shouts and the scratching sounds stop, a moment or two of nothing but the thunderstorm raging overhead before he can hear her start to work on the locks.

"No? Well, that's okay," Narcissa says. "I can let myself in."

And when Deacon turns his head, there is a little light back that way, right there behind him, hazy gray light through the tall living room windows and Chance silhouetted at the end of the hallway. She's standing very still, staring through him towards the door, and there's a bread knife in her right hand. He can't see her face, her eyes, but he *knows* how afraid she is, can hear her heart racing and can smell the electric adrenaline charge coming off her. The air around her sizzles and cracks and she takes a step towards him.

"No," Deacon says. "You can't stop her, Chance. Nothing can stop her."

"I have a gun," Chance says, trying to sound brave but her voice too unsteady, unconvincing, and she grips the handle of the knife tighter. There's a loud click, then, as the dead bolt is unlocked, the rolling of well-oiled tumblers like the thunder from the sky, and she takes a step back towards the living room.

"Do you?" Narcissa asks. "Do you really?"

"Yes," Chance tells her. "I do."

"Then I'll have to watch myself. I shall have to be very careful, shan't I?"

"Go to the window *now*," Deacon says, talking fast because he knows he's running out of time, that Narcissa is almost done with the second lock. "Open a window and start screaming. Scream your goddamn head off. Someone will hear you. Someone will hear you and—"

"You're wasting your time, Deacon," Narcissa says, and when

he turns around again she's crouched there in the open doorway, watching him with her golden eyes, backlit by the soft crimson glow of the emergency lights in the outer hall. "You know she can't hear you. She can't do the tricks we can do."

"I'll find you," he says. "I'll find you if it takes the rest of my life."

"I'm sure you'll try, poor thing," she replies and drops down on all fours, her nude body slicked with blood and gore, the wiry mane running down her back matted and tangled with it. And then she isn't even Narcissa Snow anymore, something else terrible creeping towards him on long legs and claws that click against the floor. Its eyes are on fire now, the gold irises gone molten and burning away to show some stranger metal underneath.

"Oh god, no," Chance whispers and drops the knife.

"Too late to start praying, little pig," the monster growls. "Unless maybe you want to try praying to me."

"Give it up, Mr. Silvey," Scarborough sighs from some other world, the haunted place where Deacon's losing his tenuous hold on the wet bone buried inside the wall, the time when all this is already history. "Stop torturing yourself like this. You don't want to see any more, believe me."

"Please," Deacon whispers, pleading with the monster as it comes closer, moving low to the floor like a cat stalking a bird or a squirrel. "Don't do this again."

"You think you can change the past, Deacon?" it asks him. "You listened to those changeling lapdogs. You fucked it all up, let me get to her, let me *have* her, and now, now you think I'm going to give you a *second* chance?" And then the thing in the hallway laughs at its own joke and acid drips from its scalding jaws and hisses on the floor. A single paw to shatter him like crystal, to send the jagged shards skittering away as Deacon loses his grip and the wall spits him out. Spits him up and out of the dream, back into the sunshine streaming through the thin motel curtains, back to the stink of whiskey and vomit and sweat. He lies still a while, half-lost in the migraine and the fading shreds of dream, before he finally opens his eyes.

Tuesday afternoon and Deacon finally goes to see Sadie, because there's no one and nothing else left for him. Nothing but The

Plaza and Sheryl has already made it abundantly clear that she's not going to let him sit there on a stool and drink himself to death. So, he goes to the hospital, with its sterile waiting rooms and endless hallways, its suspicious, watchful nurses and disinfectant air. He put on a clean T-shirt and underwear first, but he can still smell himself, the sour reek of old sweat and alcohol trapped in the elevator with him. A bell dings too loudly, counting off the floors. Every floor a fresh nail driven into his aching head, his roiling stomach, and he's beginning to wish that he'd stayed in his room at the Travelodge motel on Twenty-first Street, the place where he's sleeping because he can't stand to be in the apartment with the police and the FBI agents. Not after the things he's seen, awake and dreaming, not with all the empty places where Chance isn't.

The elevator doors slide open and he walks quickly past the nurses' station in the lobby, a bouquet of yellow gift-shop daisies clutched in his hand and Deacon grits his teeth, smiling for their leery glances and clean blue and white scrubs. One of them, a woman with a stethoscope hanging around her neck, smiles back, but it's a wary, conditional sort of smile. Down a long hall to a private room at the very end and he stands outside her open door for a moment, listening to the voices coming from inside; Sadie's voice, drowsy and thin, and another, older woman's and Deacon guesses that it's her mother. He looks back the way he's just come, thinking again that maybe this wasn't such a good idea. Nothing Sadie can say to make any difference at all and nothing he can say to take back the harm he's done to her, so what's the fucking point?

"Are you here to see Sarah?" someone asks and Deacon turns back to the door. There's a tall, thin woman with salt-and-pepper hair and the same pale blue eyes as Sadie standing in the doorway, watching him intently, expectantly.

"Sarah?" he asks uncertainly, exchanging one question for another, and glances nervously down at the daisies. He wonders if maybe he went the wrong way at the nurses' station and the blue eyes are just a disquieting coincidence.

The woman frowns and an exasperated sigh whistles out past her teeth. "Sadie," she says. "You probably know her as Sadie."

"Yes ma'am," Deacon replies. "I do."

The woman stares at him for a moment, silent and still blocking the doorway, chewing nervously at one corner of her lip. Almost all the pink lipstick's worn away from that side of her mouth.

"You're Deacon Silvey, aren't you?" she asks finally and this time Deacon only nods his head.

"I thought so. I'm Sadie's mother, Anna."

"Well, I brought these for her," Deacon says and holds out the flowers. The green cellophane makes a loud, crinkling noise, but she doesn't take her eyes off him.

"I saw a picture of you on CNN this morning," she says.

"You're kidding."

"No, I'm not. You and your wife, actually. But I must say, you did look better in the picture than in person. What happened to your hand?"

"I cut it," Deacon says and belatedly hides his bandaged hand behind his back.

"Are you drunk?"

Deacon coughs into his good hand and shrugs his shoulders.

"It's a simple question, Mr. Silvey. Are you drunk?"

"I'm not sober," he says and offers her the flowers again.

"I didn't think so. You smell like a distillery. And not a very clean one, either."

"Yeah, well, look. Why don't you just give these to Sadie for me. Tell her I hope she's feeling better."

But she doesn't take the daisies, leans an inch or so closer to Deacon and he catches a hint of something on her breath, gin maybe. "From what I understand, you're the reason my daughter's lying in that bed in there," she says, speaking very quietly now. "You're the reason she might never be able to use her hand again. Don't you think you could at least have the decency to give them to her yourself?"

"Yes ma'am," he says and Anna Jasper steps to one side to let him pass.

"I'm going downstairs to the cafeteria to get some coffee," she whispers. "I'll be back in about twenty minutes and I'd honestly prefer if you weren't here."

"Fine," Deacon says. "Anything you say."

"And I am very sorry about your wife."

"I'm sure you are," he replies, and Anna Jasper nods her head, but doesn't say anything else, turns and walks away down the hall.

Deacon stands in the doorway watching her, listening to the sharp clack of her heels against the linoleum. When she reaches the end of the hallway, stopping there to speak with one of the nurses, he goes into the room and eases the door shut behind him. Sadie's bed is raised to a sitting position, but her head's resting on a pillow and her eyes are closed. There's an IV tube in her right arm leading up to a plastic bag hung on a shiny steel pole, filled with clear fluid.

"Yo," Deacon says softly. "Anyone at home?"

Sadie's eyes flutter open and seem to take a few seconds to focus, a few seconds to recognize his face.

"Oh, Deacon," she says, sounding surprised in a sleepy sort of way, and she smiles a weak smile for him. "I'm so sorry. I saw the news this morning and—"

"I brought you these," he says, before she can finish, and holds out the daisies. "You like yellow, right?"

"Yeah," she says. "I like yellow a lot."

"Good. That's what I thought," and he lays the bouquet in her lap instead of trying to hand it to her. "They had white ones, too, but I thought I remembered you liking yellow."

She picks up the daisies, her left arm moving stiffly and she winces before she sniffs them.

"They doing right by you in here?" he asks and she nods and smells the flowers again.

"You're drunk, Deke," she says and looks up at him, those eyes like her mother's, but so much younger, so much brighter.

"Yes, I am. But I'm afraid you're just gonna have to forgive me on that count."

"I saw the news," she says again. "You don't need me to forgive you for anything."

"I called my AA buddy first, told him what had happened— well, no, *some* of what happened—and he started going on about surrendering to my Higher Power and taking things one day at a time. I listened for a few minutes and then told him to go fuck himself and hung up."

Sadie smells the daises again and "It was her, wasn't it?" she asks.

"Yeah," Deacon says. "It was her."

"So, what have you told the police?"

"Sadie, how about let's not talk about the police, okay?"

"Then what *do* we talk about?"

Deacon doesn't answer her right away, rubs absently at the stubble on his face and stares at the daylight slipping in through the window on the other side of the room.

"Who says we have to talk about anything," he says finally. "I just wanted to see you again, that's all," and then Deacon sits in a chair near the foot of the bed. It's good to have the weight off his feet, good to be sitting down so that things don't spin so much and gravity isn't such a pressing concern.

"I thought talking might help."

"Just look where it's gotten us so far."

"I know there's a lot you haven't told me. How do you know if it would help or not if you won't even try?"

Deacon leans back in the chair, tilting it up on two legs and squints at Sadie with her yellow daisies and IV drip. "Don't you think you've already been hurt enough because I didn't know when to keep my goddamn mouth shut?"

"Now you're starting to sound like my mother."

Deacon lets the front legs of the chair rock back to earth, bump to the floor, and he turns towards the closed door, half expecting Anna Jasper to come walking in fifteen minutes early and right on cue.

"You're not gonna like what I'm about to say," he mumbles, reluctant to take his eyes off the door. "But you are gonna listen."

"Now you sound like my father," Sadie says and the cellophane crinkles so loudly that Deacon turns back to the bed to see if she's getting ready to throw the whole bouquet at him. But she's only pulled one of the flowers free of the rest and is rolling the thick green stem back and forth between her left thumb and index finger.

"Maybe it's time you started listening to them."

"And maybe you're drunker than you look."

"Chance is *gone,* Sadie," he says, says it out loud like the words have no power over him. "Gone. And it's a miracle you're not dead. This isn't a game. It isn't fucking tarot cards and Ouija boards and it isn't fucking *Scooby-Doo.* So, from here on, you can play Nancy Drew on someone else's dime if that's what it takes to get you through the day. But you might be the very last person left alive I give two shits about and whatever demons I have to deal with, I can do it without you."

Sadie hasn't stopped rolling the flower stem between her fingers, her head bowed slightly as she watches the spinning petals and chews her lip like her mother. He can tell she's close to tears and maybe that's exactly what he wants, what he needs, the real reason that he came here, to hurt her enough he's sure she'll stay the hell away from him forever.

"You came to me," she says, still watching the flower. "You wanted someone to talk to. You *asked* for my help."

"That's because I'm an asshole, Sadie. Sooner or later, you probably would have figured that part out on your own."

Sadie snaps the stem between her fingers and the broken daisy falls onto the hospital sheet covering her legs.

"You have no idea how bad I need a cigarette," she says and wipes her nose.

"I want you to tell me that you heard what I just told you. I want you to tell me you fucking understand what I'm saying to you."

"But I saw her, Deacon. How the hell am I ever supposed to forget that? How am I supposed to forget what it means?"

"You saw a crazy woman and that's all you saw."

"You don't believe that. I *know* you don't believe that."

He opens his mouth to reply, but then the words get lost somewhere between his brain and his tongue, and he sits staring at Sadie Jasper, listening to the clock on the wall ticking off the seconds and all the antiseptic hospital sounds seeping through the walls. There are tears running down both her cheeks now, wet streaks on her pale skin, and she closes her eyes and turns her head towards the window and the sun.

"But I hear you," she says. "I hear you loud and clear."

"That's all I wanted you to say."

"I'm always going to worry about you, Deke, and, I swear to God, I will always miss you. I don't think you're ever going to know how much I'll miss you."

He stands up and there's a moment of dizziness, the world playing carnival-ride tricks on him, and he leans against the bed until it passes. When things are reasonably still and level again, he goes to Sadie and kisses her lightly on top of the head, but she doesn't open her eyes or turn to face him.

"I gotta go now," he tells her. "Your mother will be back soon and I think it'll be better for all concerned if I'm not here."

"You're going to find Chance," Sadie says, almost whispering. "I know you don't believe it, but you will."

"Yeah, well, how about you just concentrate on getting better and getting out of this place before your mother drives you nuts."

"Don't give up on her, Deacon. Don't you dare." And then she's crying too hard to say anything else and he leaves her alone with the flowers and sunshine, and walks back down the long hall to the elevator.

Deacon has been sitting in the small room alone for almost fifteen minutes, small room with dark gray walls and a tiny window looking out on the street below, a table and four chairs, air that smells like nothing much at all but the smoke from his cigarettes. There's a security camera mounted on the ceiling in one corner and it stares at him with its glassy, cyclops eye, the red light to tell him that it's recording his every move. The FBI field office because he refused to go back to the apartment, told Downs they could stick his ass in jail if they wanted, but he's not ever going back there again. One of the agents showed him to this small room and left him alone, promised they'd be with him soon, assured him there was nothing to be nervous about, just routine questions with a case like this. Gaps they hope he can help them fill and anything he can do makes it that much more likely they'll find her alive. Deacon takes a drag off his cigarette and then taps it against the rim of the ashtray on the table. He looks at the red light on the camera and then at the tiny window, then watches the door, waiting for it to open, starting to wonder if it ever will.

He stubs out his Camel and immediately lights another. His headache isn't any better and, worse yet, he's beginning to feel the first solid edges of sobriety. He glances up at the clock, mounted not far from the security camera, is busy trying to remember just how long it's been since he finished off the pint bottle of George Dickle before leaving the motel to visit Sadie, when the door opens and spills Detective Downs and two FBI agents in matching blue suits into the room.

"Sorry that took so long, Mr. Silvey," one of the agents says, and the FBI men take seats at the table. Downs shuts the door, but doesn't sit, walks over to the window and turns his back to Deacon.

"No problem," Deacon replies. "I got time to burn."

"We do appreciate how cooperative you've been through all this," the other agent says. "We understand how hard it must be for you right now. But . . . we still have a few more questions we hope you can answer."

"And I'm afraid that a number of discrepancies in your story have turned up," the first agent adds.

"My *story*," Deacon says and takes another drag off his Camel, exhales and blinks at the agents through the smoke floating just above the table. "Do you two have names or should I just feel free to make something up?"

"They're here to help, Deacon," Downs says from his spot at the window, but doesn't turn around. "You need to keep that in mind."

"It's all right, Detective," the first agent says, and then, to Deacon, "Yes, Mr. Silvey, we have names. I'm Agent Broom and this is Agent Gorman. I'm with the Birmingham office and Agent Gorman's from our office up in Atlanta."

"Where's that guy I talked to yesterday? Peterson, wasn't that his name?"

"He's still at your home, Mr. Silvey, in case the kidnapper tries to make contact."

"I already told him, nobody's going to be making contact with anyone. She's got what she wants."

"And how can you be so sure of that, Mr. Silvey?" Agent Gorman asks. He's older than the Birmingham agent, his red hair going gray at the temples, and he has a long scar just above his left eye.

"Hasn't anyone told you?" Deacon asks. "I'm a fucking psychic."

"We're aware of your work with the police in Atlanta, and with Detective Downs here," Agent Broom says. His hair is the color of a tea stain and his small, dark eyes remind Deacon of the pet rat he had when he was in college. "I can't say that I personally buy into the whole extrasensory thing, but there's no denying you have an impressive record."

"Are you also aware I'm a drunk?" Deacon asks.

"Yes," Agent Gorman replies, exchanging impatient glances with the Birmingham agent. "We are. You'd been sober for what, the last year or so?"

"Give or take a month or two," Deacon replies. "Fortunately, I'm all better now."

"He gets migraines," Detective Downs says. "That's why he drinks."

"Jesus, man, are you like my fucking den mother now or what?" and Deacon glares past the two agents at Downs' back.

"I just don't see any point in you making this shit any harder on yourself than it has to be," Downs says. "That's all."

"Then maybe you can get me something to drink, 'cause a bottle of Jack or Dickle would sure make this a whole lot easier."

Agent Broom coughs and Gorman puts his elbows on the table and leans towards Deacon, squinting through the cigarette smoke with his beady rat eyes.

"What I'm still trying to figure out," he says, "is why you lied to Detective Downs here in the first place, why you told him you thought the killer was a man."

"Sometimes I'm wrong. I keep telling people that and nobody ever listens."

"It's a pretty big mistake, don't you think? First, you tell him he's looking for a white man in his forties with a swastika tattoo. Then you decide, no, it's really a woman with yellow eyes named—" and he stops and looks expectantly at Agent Broom.

"Narcissus Snow," Broom says.

"Narcissa," Deacon says.

"Pretty damn big mistake, wouldn't you say?"

"Think you could do better?" Deacon asks, then adds, "But I was right about the tattoos. She has two, one on each side of her ass. They aren't swastikas, but I still think I should at least get a half-credit for that."

"So, why didn't you tell us about the fight at the bar?" Gorman asks.

"What fight?" Deacon replies and looks at the ashtray so he won't have to look at Gorman.

"We talked to a friend of yours who tends bar there," Broom says. "She says there was some kind of trouble Sunday evening, you and some guy with a ponytail and a biker jacket. She said there was a girl with him."

"Is that a fact?"

"Deacon, you really don't want to start screwing around with the FBI," Downs says and Deacon shrugs his shoulders.

"Gentlemen, I've been in a whole hell of a lot of fights," he says. "I can't be expected to remember them all."

Gorman nods his head and leans a little closer. "The description the bartender gave us of the girl was a dead ringer for the chick we found out behind your apartment building."

"Then why the hell aren't you talking to her?"

"What was the fight about?" Gorman asks. "We know that's how you hurt your hand," and he points to Deacon's bandaged left hand.

"I broke a glass. That's how I hurt my hand."

"Well, at least that's half-true," Gorman says. "Why are you lying to us, Mr. Silvey? Who are you trying to protect? I'll tell you, if someone had just kidnapped my pregnant wife, I think I'd try to be a little bit more helpful."

Deacon takes a last drag off the Camel and adds it to all the other butts piled in the ashtray, but doesn't look up at Gorman. Too obvious that this man's baiting him, digging for a rise, and Deacon doesn't feel like giving him the satisfaction.

"Deacon, maybe it's time you started thinking about talking to a lawyer," Downs says.

"Do I look like I know any lawyers?"

"Perhaps it's time I introduced you to a couple."

"Listen, Mr. Silvey," Agent Gorman says and begins tapping a middle finger loudly against the wooden tabletop. "Every hour, every *minute*, that ticks by makes it that less likely we'll find your wife alive, or that we'll even find her *dead*—"

"I already told you—" Deacon begins, but Broom interrupts him.

"He's trying to stress that time is of the essence."

"Fuck that," Gorman says. "I'm trying to make this sad sack of shit here understand that if he doesn't shape up and stop bullshitting us, we're going to find his wife rotting in a ditch somewhere."

"No," Deacon replies calmly, watching Gorman's tapping finger now instead of the ashtray. The man's nails are thick and yellow. "I don't think that's what's going to happen. I don't think you're going to find her at all. I don't think you'll ever find a single trace of her."

"Who's the girl we got in the hospital?" Gorman asks and Deacon shakes his head.

"Are you saying you *didn't* talk to her at the bar Sunday night?"

"No, I'm just saying I don't know who she is, that's all. She told me her name was Jane. I think she might have said she was from Providence."

"Providence, Rhode Island?" asks Agent Broom.

"Yeah, Providence fucking Rhode Island."

"And who's your sparring buddy in the leather jacket?" Gorman asks and stops tapping on the table.

"I never caught his name," Deacon says. "We had a little disagreement over a glass of whiskey, that's all."

"So you kicked his ass?"

"What?" Deacon asks. "You think I might have overreacted?" and then he pushes his chair back from the table. It makes an unpleasant scrunking sound, sliding across the floor. Gorman sits up straight again and fidgets with his tie.

"You kicked his ass," he says, "then called Detective Downs to warn him that your wife's life was in danger, and then you got into a car with these two people. The same car, by the way—a black 1959 Cadillac with Massachusetts plates—that you showed up in at—"

"Am I under arrest, Agent?"

The two men exchange glances again and then "No," Broom says. "You're not under arrest, Mr. Silvey. I do want to make it clear that it wouldn't look very good if you left the city right now. But no, you're not under arrest."

"So I'm free to go then?"

"Deacon, I don't understand why you won't at least *try*," Downs says and finally turns around. "Who the fuck are these people that you're too afraid of them to even give us information that might save your wife and child?"

"I'm not afraid of them. I just don't know who they are and my head hurts too much to make up anything interesting."

"If we want to talk again," Agent Gorman says, looking over his shoulder at the clock, "we better not have any trouble locating you."

"Don't worry," Deacon says, "I'll cancel the vacation to Cancún," and he stands, picks up his pack of cigarettes and the book of matches from The Plaza. "But I'm leaving now, unless someone has a better idea."

"We didn't call you in just to bust your balls," Broom says. "You've got enough to worry about. I just wish we could make you believe that we are trying to help."

"Oh, I believe you are. I imagine that's exactly what you *think* you're doing. It's just that I know better and I'm tired of playing footsie. It's easier if I go ahead and give up now."

"Sounds kind of like the coward's way out to me," says Gorman and Deacon looks him in the eye and nods his head.

"Maybe that's exactly what it is," he says. "But that's really none of your goddamn business, now is it?"

"It's my business to find a woman who's been kidnapped and who's also unfortunate enough to be your wife."

Deacon takes a step towards the agent, one hand on the corner of the table like he means to shove it out of his way, and then Downs has him by the shoulders, strong hands holding him fast, and Gorman takes a quick step back.

"Maybe," Deacon says, his voice grown low and threatening, "you weren't paying attention. Maybe you missed the part where I really don't give a shit what happens to me anymore."

"Let's go for a walk," Downs says and is already leading Deacon towards the door. Gorman watches him go, while Agent Broom busies himself with a ballpoint pen and a little black spiral-bound notebook.

"You know better than that," Downs says, shutting the door after they've stepped out into the hallway. "At least I thought you did. Hammond said you were a pretty levelheaded guy, all things considered."

"I'm not in the mood for good cop–bad cop right now. And I need some water. I've got to take some Excedrin."

"I think there's a cooler at the end of the hall. But, Deke, you need to know these guys are looking for any excuse to arrest *anyone* right now, you or anybody else."

Deacon follows the detective down the wide hall, marble floors and walls, frosted glass doors with names and titles printed carefully in gold paint, and the white, white light pouring down from the ceiling is making his headache even worse. There isn't a cooler at the end of the hallway, but there is a men's rest room and Deacon tells Downs that'll do, just give him a minute, but the cop follows him inside.

"Did you ever think maybe I needed to take a piss?" he asks and fishes a couple of lint-covered tablets from his pants pocket.

"Sorry, but we need to talk someplace I know nobody's going to be listening. Well, someplace I'm pretty sure nobody's listening."

"All these G-men making you nervous?" Deacon asks and dry-swallows the two Excedrin, then bends over to drink from the tap.

"I don't mind telling you, right now, everything makes me nervous."

Deacon stares at himself in the mirror above the sink, wipes away the water dripping from his chin. The detective is checking the four stalls behind him to be sure they're alone, and Deacon runs some more water, splashes a handful across his face. The circles under his eyes have gone as dark as bruises.

"This isn't only about you and Chance," Downs says. "And I'm about to tell you some shit that I'm not supposed to, but I think you have a right to know, even if you're determined to act like a horse's ass."

"You ought to know I'm not so good with secrets," Deacon says, smoothing his hair back and wishing he could have stayed longer with Sadie, wishing he'd said all the things he meant to say.

"Then you're just going to have to make an exception."

"I'm not so good at making exceptions, either."

"Christ in a rusty wheelbarrow, Deacon, will you just shut the hell up and listen to me for a minute or two?"

"I know she's gone," Deacon replies, turning away from the mirror, away from the sickly, haggard face frowning back at him. "And I think *you* know that I'm probably right. So what do you have to say that I could possibly want to hear?"

"Maybe nothing," Downs says and leans against a closed stall door. "Not if you're so certain she's dead."

"She's dead or I can't get to her before she dies, and either way it's the same damned thing."

"The Feds have been after this psycho for months now. This isn't the first time they've gotten close to her. A few weeks ago, back in September, she killed one of their agents in Atlanta."

"No shit," Deacon says and takes out a cigarette, but Downs points at the THANK YOU FOR NOT SMOKING sign on the wall, the sign and a smoke detector, so Deacon curses and puts it back in the pack.

"No shit. They got eighteen murders, all down the East Coast, all with the same MO as that Charles Ellis kid and that guy you led us to in the warehouse. Eighteen, Deacon, and now our three plus a kidnapping, in the past six months alone. Fucking heads in garbage bags, disemboweled corpses, missing organs, bite marks that don't match human teeth, and that symbol—"

"It's the moon," Deacon says.

"What?"

"The symbol. It's the moon, rising or setting, I'm not sure which. Unless it's the sun."

"When'd you figure that out?"

"I didn't. Sadie Jasper did. That's why she's in the hospital right now. She also thinks that Narcissa Snow believes she's some kind of werewolf—"

"Why the hell didn't you tell us this already?"

"What difference would it have made? You want to go back in there and tell those two suits that they're looking for a woman who turns into a monster?"

"You said she *thinks* she's a werewolf. You didn't say—"

"I ain't said jack shit, because there isn't any point."

"They have a profile, from one of their people at Quantico."

"And it's totally worthless," Deacon says, reaching for a paper towel from the dispenser on the wall. "They're probably looking for a man, white, let's say someone between twenty-five and thirty-five, average appearance, below-average IQ—"

"But you've already told them the killer's a woman. You've given them her name."

"And how do you think that stacks up against their computers and some BSU think-tank nerd with a PhD? Do you know how rare female serial killers are?"

"I have an idea," Downs says. "But there are precedents. I think they're starting to believe they're looking for a woman, or at least a cross-dresser."

"Oh Jesus," Deacon laughs and wipes his face with the paper towel, then balls it up, tosses it at a toilet bowl and misses. "So they're after a transvestite with a pit bull?"

"Deacon, what if you're *wrong*? What if Chance isn't dead?"

"I've heard enough of this for one day, okay?"

"We have APBs out based on your description of this woman. You said she had yellow eyes. Now, how many people you think have yellow eyes? Sooner or later, someone's going to spot her."

"What I see isn't always true," Deacon groans and rubs at the back of his neck, the sore tendons there, only wanting the detective to shut up and let him go back to the motel. "How many times do I have to say that? Maybe she only wants to have yellow eyes. Maybe it's part of some fantasy. Maybe she wears yellow contact lenses whenever she kills people. Maybe she's a hepatitis carrier—"

"Or maybe she has yellow eyes," Downs says and Deacon shakes his head and looks at the floor, the white ceramic tile with flecks of gold.

"Yeah, and maybe she's a fucking werewolf," Deacon mumbles.

"Look, man, I don't care if I gotta go lookin' for the pope in a goddamn pink bunny suit, as long as we find her and get your wife back in one piece."

"So what exactly do you want me to say, Downs? You wanted me to touch the wall, so I touched the fucking wall. You wanted me to answer a few questions, so I answered your questions. Now what the hell do you want?"

"The same thing those two assholes from the FBI want. I want you to stop lying and tell me the truth."

"You're assuming I know the truth."

"I'm assuming you know a lot more than you're telling anyone. For starters, who's the girl in the hospital?"

"Sadie Jasper?" Deacon asks and kicks at a loose, cracked tile. "Well, her mother calls her Sarah."

"No, dickhead, the girl named Jane. The one Narcissa Snow attacked out behind your apartment not two hours after you were seen with her at that bar."

"Oh," Deacon says. He kicks the tile again and half of it pops out of place and goes sliding across the floor. The empty space it leaves is the color of ripe avocado skin. "That girl. Did you try asking her?"

"Yeah. And she's even less talkative than you."

"She's just someone that tried to help," Deacon says.

"Well, let me tell you something else about her. When she wouldn't give us a name and we couldn't find any sort of ID on her, we ran her fingerprints. And we got a match, for a baby girl named Eliza Helen Morrow who was abducted from her home in Connecticut back in 1986. Kinda weird, hunh?"

Deacon doesn't answer, keeps his eyes on the hole left by the missing tile, remembering her thumbs pressed against his open eyes. Remembering the secret, unthinkable things she showed him.

"Turns out, there's a whole slew of unsolved infant abductions from Connecticut for that year and the next. And a few from Rhode Island and Massachusetts, to boot. So, tell me something, Deacon. When do the coincidences stop being just coincidences?"

"That's something I've been asking myself my whole life," Deacon says and looks back up at the detective.

"I know it seems like it's easier to go ahead and give up now than hope she's still alive somewhere. I *know* that, Deacon."

The rest-room door opens and a very short man with a toupee and a yellow tie stands staring at them for a moment.

"Am I interrupting something?" he asks.

"Can I talk to her?" Deacon asks Downs. "To Jane, I mean."

"You can try," Downs replies.

"Without any cops around?"

Downs glances thoughtfully at the man in the toupee and, "I'll see what I can do," he says.

"I'm not making any promises," Deacon tells him.

"Hey guys, you know, I can go downstairs," the man says, but looks longingly towards the stalls.

"No," Downs says. "I think we're finished for now. Be my guest," and then he walks Deacon back down the hall to the elevator.

Another hospital, this one only a few city blocks south of the great gray Federal Building, over the railroad tracks and past a squalid wasteland of vacant lots and fast-food drive-thrus. Deacon stops at a package store on the way and buys two bottles of Jack Daniel's and a fifth of scotch, three packs of cigarettes, puts it all on one of his credit cards. Enough to last a day or two, maybe even enough to beat this headache, and he drinks half of one of the bottles of Jack in the parking deck of Cooper Greene Hospital before he can find the nerve he needs to get out of Chance's Impala and go inside. Downs promised that he wouldn't have any trouble seeing her, but there would be a guard, because she's being held in protective custody.

Another hospital and another elevator, and Deacon's beginning to think he's going to spend the rest of his life riding goddamn elevators. At least this one doesn't buzz or ding to count off the floors, though the gears and cables creak and groan as it hauls him up. There's an old black man in the elevator with him who smells of menthol and wintergreen; the man smiles at Deacon and keeps shifting his dentures around in his mouth.

"You here to see your wife?" the old man asks around his loose uppers.

"No sir," Deacon says uncomfortably, watching as the round white buttons with black numerals printed on them light up, one after the next. "I'm not. I'm here to see a friend."

"I'm here to see my wife," the old man replies. "She's got a bad heart. Doctors keep telling us she's gonna die any day, but she keeps not dying. Swears she ain't gonna die till Judgment Day."

"Oh," Deacon says, because he doesn't know what else to say and doesn't want to say anything at all.

"Yeah, she keeps on sending money to one of them TV preachers, but you ask me, I don't think she'll make it that long."

Then the button with a 5 printed on it lights up and the elevator doors open.

"My floor," Deacon says. "Hope your wife feels better soon."

"She always does," the old man replies. "You watch yourself, boy. You keep hitting the bottle like that and they'll stick you in one of these rooms, sooner or later. Mark my word."

"I'll do that," Deacon says, as the silver doors shudder and then slide slowly shut again, taking the old man away. Deacon turns around and there's a very small waiting area, just a few chairs and a table buried under old magazines, a potted plant that looks wilted even though it isn't real, artificial rhododendron leaves covered with a thick veneer of dust. He has the room number written on the back of the matchbook from The Plaza—Room 534—and he tries not to make eye contact with anyone at the nurses' station. There's a plastic jack-o'-lantern, orange and black and grinning like a skull, filled with candy, sitting on the counter.

"Can I help you?" one of the nurses asks him anyway and Deacon tells him he's looking for Room 534. The man in mint-green scrubs consults a clipboard, then a computer monitor, and "That's our Jane Doe," he says. "She's not allowed visitors. Police orders."

"I have permission," Deacon says uncertainly, wondering if the call's come through, if maybe Agent Gorman decided it wasn't such a good idea. "Detective Downs was supposed to call."

"Ah, wait a sec," the nurse says and pulls a yellow Post-it note off the computer monitor. "Here we go. Are you Deacon Slivey?"

"Silvey," Deacon corrects him. "Yeah, that's me."

"Just take the hall on the left, turn at the first right, and you'll have to check in with Officer Merrill."

"Thanks," Deacon says and then starts walking before the nurse decides that he's not Deacon Slivey after all. Down the hall and he turns at the first right, stopping outside the room with #534 on the door and a bald policeman sitting in a chair that's much too small for him, reading a copy of *Field & Stream.*

"Detective Downs sent me," he says, feeling like an idiot, and the cop stops reading and eyes him suspiciously.

"You don't say?" the cop asks, closing his magazine; there's a photograph of a wild tom turkey on the cover. "You that Deacon Slivey fellow?"

"Silvey," Deacon says. "Deacon Silvey."

"You got some kind of ID on you, Mr. Silvey?"

"Just my driver's license. Will that do?"

"Not if you don't show it to me, it won't," the cop says, so Deacon takes out his wallet and finds his license, hands it to the policeman who looks at it a moment and then looks at Deacon again.

"You drunk, Mr. Silvey? You smell like you've been drinking."

"Is that a problem?"

"No," the cop replies, handing back Deacon's license. "Agent Broom said you might be, that's all. Sorry as hell about your wife."

"Yeah," Deacon says and then the cop frisks him before opening the door.

"Okay, you're clean. You got thirty minutes with her, that's all. I'll be right out here if you need anything."

"I feel safer already."

"Hey, man, joke all you want. But that's a spooky little lady in there. Damn good at gin, too."

"You've been playing cards with her?"

The cop opens his magazine and goes back to reading. "It was her idea," he says. "Thirty minutes, don't forget."

"Don't worry," Deacon says and goes in, shutting the door behind him, half expecting the bald cop to open it again, but he doesn't. The girl named Jane is sitting in a wheelchair near the window, staring at him. Either she's wearing the same raggedy clothes as the last time he saw her, or different raggedy clothes that look exactly the same as the others.

"I was beginning to think you wouldn't come," she says. She's wearing dark wraparound sunglasses and there's a big white bandage on her forehead. "I thought maybe they weren't going to let you in."

The room is a little smaller than Sadie's and a lot dingier. There are no flowers or get-well cards and the curtains are drawn. The little television bolted to the wall is tuned to MSNBC, but the sound's muted and nothing comes from the anchorwoman's lips when they move.

"You knew I was coming?" he asks her; she nods her head and rolls the wheelchair a few feet closer to him.

"I knew you'd try, sooner or later. Where else would you go?"

"I wasn't planning on coming," Deacon says. "I didn't really see any point."

"What changed your mind?"

"Maybe I haven't changed my mind, Jane," he answers and sits down on the bed because his head hurts too much to stand any longer. "Maybe I'm just curious. So, what's the damage?" and he points at the bandage on her head.

"Just a mild concussion. I lost a tooth, too. Some scrapes and bruises, a few stitches. Your wife's friend probably saved my life by opening the garage door when she did."

"Lucky her," Deacon says. "They told you she's dead, right?"

"Yeah, they told me. But I saw it happen. There wasn't anything I could do to stop it. Scarborough's dead, too, isn't he?"

Deacon holds an index finger to his lips and nods towards the door, towards the cop and his *Field & Stream*.

"That's okay, Deacon. I knew he was. I felt it."

"What about Chance? Have you felt anything about her lately?"

Jane takes off her sunglasses and squints at Deacon. "The light hurts my eyes," she says.

"The concussion."

"Yeah. It'll pass. Are you asking me if Chance is dead?"

Deacon stares at her a moment, weighing the consequences of his reply, of any reply, wondering how much less pain there will be if he walks out of the hospital room right now and keeps walking. No answers, no hope, no disappointment, no distance left to fall because he's already found the bottom.

"We shouldn't have lied to you," she says. "I could tell you it was all Scarborough's idea, but there's no reason for you to believe me, is there?"

"Lied to me? When'd you lie to me?" Deacon asks before he thinks better of it.

"Scarborough never intended to protect your wife," she says. "I'm not sure he ever even intended to try to kill Narcissa."

"Then what the fuck were we doing in that house?"

"You might want to lower your voice," Jane says, barely speaking above a whisper now. "I've discovered that our friend in the hall has very keen ears."

"What the fuck were we doing in the house?" Deacon asks again, whispering, but he can hear the edge creeping into his voice, the anger that won't take very long to grow too big for whispers.

"Narcissa took things, important things, things that we had to try to get back from her. Scarborough hoped that she'd hidden them somewhere in the house—"

"What are you telling me? That you used Chance as *bait* so the house would be empty?"

"She's only one woman. There are many lives at stake here, Deacon."

"No way," Deacon says, looking down at his broad right hand now, the deep lines in his palm, the fine wrinkles and creases at the ends of his fingers, wondering if he can kill her before Officer Merrill figures out what's going on and stops him. "You did. You fucking used her as bait."

"I tried to stop her, Deacon. I stood between Narcissa and Chance as long as I could."

"And Scarborough took me along for the ride because he thought maybe I could help him find whatever the hell it was the two of you were after. You were using us all along."

"It was his idea, Deacon."

"But *you* went along with it."

"Yes, I did. I didn't see any other way. But it was also my idea to go to your apartment, to try and stop her. I was dead anyway, after all the things I showed you at the motel."

"What the hell's that supposed to mean, you were dead anyway?"

Jane glances towards the closed door, then sighs and slips her sunglasses back on.

"When we are taken," she says, speaking slowly, carefully, the way a teacher addresses his pupils, "when we're still just babies, we're bound to the Hounds by an irrevocable blood oath. And if we ever break that oath, as I did last night by showing you images of the Providence necropolis, then we forfeit our lives. I was already dead. I'm dead now. I'm just waiting for them to send someone to—"

"What about the cop out there? You're protected."

"He can't stop them, any more than the police can stop Narcissa, any more than Scarborough and I could have stopped her."

"So you're just sitting here waiting to die?"

Jane rolls the wheelchair forward an inch or two, then rolls it back again. "I can't very well run," she says. "Besides, I knew the price of my actions. I don't think it would be right of me to run, do you?"

Deacon closes his eyes and rubs hard at his temples, wishing that Downs had never followed him into the rest room, wishing he'd taken the bottles and gone straight back to the Travelodge.

"Is she still alive?" he asks without looking at the girl in the wheelchair.

"I think so," Jane says, no longer whispering, but not speaking very loudly, either. "We know a little about what Narcissa's trying to do. If we're right, she has to keep Chance alive until moonrise on the thirty-first. But she's not sane, Deacon. Something might have happened."

"Something," Deacon says, and when he opens his eyes Jane's standing at the foot of the bed, staring back at him through her sunglasses.

"We told you about Narcissa," she says. "About her grandfather, Iscariot, and her father, Aldous. About her intentions."

"Yeah," Deacon says. "You told me. She's ticked off because she wants to be a real monster and the other monsters won't let her join the club. She thinks giving them our kid will buy her way in."

"And there's a . . . a birthing ceremony," Jane says and her voice is growing hesitant, shaky. "But it can only be performed at moonrise on certain nights, only on four nights each year. The next is All Hallow's Eve. That's when Narcissa will call up the Hounds to receive your child."

"This is entirely fucking insane, you know that?"

"Deacon Silvey, I have already given up my life so you would believe me. You've seen them for yourself. You've *stood* in—"

"Yeah, but what I see—"

"—isn't always the truth?" she asks, finishing his declaration as a question, turning his defenses back on him. "Does it really matter whether or not you believe? Do you think it matters to Chance, or to Narcissa?"

"Will they come to her?"

"Yes, they'll come. She's learned enough that they'll have to come. There are rules."

"But not to take her back?" Deacon asks and Jane glances nervously towards the door.

"Oh, they'll take her back," she says and smiles, a furtive, vengeful smile. "But not the way that Narcissa thinks, not the way she *wants*. They have plans."

Deacon stops rubbing his head, not like it's making the pain any better, the pain that only gets bigger and bigger, that only wants to swallow him alive. He stares at the silent television screen, because it's better than the girl's smile. A fire somewhere and there's video that must have been filmed from a helicopter, aerial views of a column of black and billowing smoke and the red-orange flames writhing just underneath. An eager, pricking sensation at the back of Deacon's neck, and déjà vu so strong it sends chill bumps up and down his arms.

"Where's the remote?" he asks and Jane doesn't answer, but looks back over her shoulder at the television on the wall.

"I don't like television," she says. "The noise bothers me. I don't know how people stand it all the time."

"I need to hear this."

"It's a fire," she says observantly. "You can see it's a fire without the noise, can't you?"

The remote is lying on the table beside the bed and he aims it at the set, hits the mute button, and the anchorwoman's voice fills the room.

"—the scene near Red Bridge, Pennsylvania, this morning. The fire is still burning out of control and officials have yet to comment on what could have caused the blaze. But they are saying that as many as seven or eight people may have died in the fire."

"Oh," Jane says, turning her back on Deacon, removing her sunglasses and squinting up at the television. "I see."

"*What* do you see, Jane? What the fuck's going on? How did I know that—?"

"Because there are rules," she says again and takes a step nearer the TV. "And there are lines, lines in the void that tie us all together."

"It's impossible to say at this time what may have ignited the tanks," the anchorwoman says as the camera circles a safe distance from the roiling boundaries of the inferno. "Fire crews from nearby Chambersburg are still fighting to contain the flames."

"It was her, wasn't it?" Deacon asks. "Narcissa did that," and the girl nods her head very slowly, not taking her eyes off the screen.

"Like I told you, she's not sane. Something was bound to happen, sooner or later."

"Then she's only made it as far as Pennsylvania?" he asks. "She still has a long way to go, right?"

"Yes," Jane says. "If she's still alive."

"Where's she going, Jane?"

"I can't tell you that," the girl says and holds one hand up like she's about to touch the screen, but she doesn't. "I can't *tell* you, but I *can* take you there. There's still time. Get me out of here, Deacon, and I can take you there."

"What do you mean you can't tell me?"

"Get me out of here and I'll take you there," Jane says again.

"And just how the fuck am I supposed to do that? We got Officer Friendly sitting right outside your door and the police and the FBI are both breathing down my neck."

"You would never find it on your own, Deacon. Not in a hundred years. But I can show you. I know the way."

"Maybe you got more going on in there than a concussion," he says and touches his thumb to the side of his aching head. "Maybe it's affected your hearing, too."

She turns, then, and that hungry smile is back, that smile and her pupils dilated until her irises are only eclipse rinds of color to ring ebony pools.

"I can deal with the policeman," she says. "I've already been working on him, just in case," and she produces a dog-eared playing card, the ace of spades held between her thumb and middle finger, as if she's plucked it from the sterile hospital air.

"I don't think he's going to be impressed by card tricks," Deacon says.

"You let me worry about him. But I'll need you to create a disturbance of some sort. Something that will get everyone's attention," and she looks quickly back over her shoulder at the television and the burning gas station. "Find a fire alarm," she says. "Find a fire alarm and pull it."

"She's *dead*," Deacon says, getting up from the bed, fighting back the dizziness and nausea. "I *know* she's dead."

"You don't *know* anything," Jane says, her smile fading now, becoming an angry, impatient scowl. "Until you see her corpse, until you hold it in your arms, you don't know anything and I'm tired of listening to you whine."

"I'm leaving," he says and takes a step towards the door, but she holds out a hand to stop him.

"Find an alarm," she says. "You won't get another opportunity. Neither of us will."

"You just said you were dead, that they would send someone to kill you for showing me what you did."

"That doesn't mean I don't still have a duty. If we hurry, and help each other, maybe it's not too late to do the things we were supposed to do to begin with. In my dreams, I saw you, Deacon. I heard you tell Narcissa you would *find* her—"

"An alarm," he says doubtfully. "A fire alarm," and she nods her head. Deacon wipes sweat off his brow and looks down at his bandaged hand for a moment. "Have you ever been to jail?" he asks her.

"I've been lots worse places," she says, sitting down in her wheelchair again, as the door opens and Officer Merrill sticks his bald head into the room.

"Time's up, Mr. Slivey," he says and then taps his wristwatch to prove the point.

"Yeah, I guess it is," Deacon whispers and Jane nods her head.

"Thank you for coming," she tells him. "I'm sorry I couldn't be of more help. But don't worry, they'll find her."

Deacon glances at the TV again, the firemen with their swollen hoses, white arcs of water to keep a demon at bay. "I suppose we'll see," he says and, as he leaves Room 534, Jane asks the cop if he feels like another game of gin.

CHAPTER THIRTEEN

At the River's Edge

"It's three thirty-four," the child says, looking at the wristwatch that was Chance's grandfather's, the watch she'll never give her son or daughter for his or her tenth birthday. The child is sitting in the floorboard behind the front seat, wiping the sweat from Chance's forehead and cheeks with a scrap of cloth torn from the hem of its T-shirt. Chance turns her head so she can see its face, its perfect, pale skin, porcelain and morning light, that face, and the child smiles for her and wipes her forehead again.

"It's getting dark," she whispers, too hoarse now to speak any louder, her throat too dry, and the child shakes its head and looks up at the sky through the rear windshield.

"No, Mother," it says. "It's still only afternoon. There's still a lot of day left."

"Not a lot," Chance whispers. "Just a little, just a little more, that's all."

"Maybe it's enough, though," the child says reassuringly, still smiling, but Chance knows better. The long drive almost over, so everything's almost over, and just beginning, as well, but she'd rather not think about that part. Easier to accept that it's ending and whatever the werewolf has in mind, there won't be anything else for her afterwards. She looks at the back of the monster's head, its shaggy blonde hair tangled and moving like restless, writhing vines. Some colorless plant that can't grow aboveground, the opposite of photosynthesis for it to live, tendrils to drink up the blackness from the hidden places deep beneath the world.

"You don't give up," the child says, leaning close, its soft lips pressed to her ear. "That's not what happened."

Another contraction then, but no real pain, too much of the werewolf's morphine in her veins, clogging up her brain, for the pain to make it through. She gasps anyway, though, surprised at the force of the sensation, the pull of tightening muscles, and sits up a little.

"Be careful, Mother," the child says. "Don't wear yourself out. You'll need your strength."

Chance starts to ask why, then decides she really doesn't want to know, that she has a pretty good idea already, and, besides, she's sitting up enough now that she can see more than sky. Her back braced firmly against the door of the big steel-gray Lincoln they stole after the diner. After the fire, and Chance watches the unfamiliar countryside rushing by outside, the land turning flat and sandy, the last low, tree-crowned hillocks of glacial till quickly giving way to the salt marshes and a small river winding along between the rushes and reeds.

"Where the hell are we, Narcissa?" she asks, speaking as loudly as she can, forcing the words out as the contraction ends.

"Almost home," the werewolf growls back at her, watching her in the rearview mirror for a moment with its yellow eyes.

"Don't talk to her anymore," the child whispers. "That just makes her stronger."

"I have to know where it's taking you," Chance tells it and then she draws a deep, hitching breath, breathing deep while she can, before the next contraction begins. The stink of the marshes is getting in through Narcissa's open window, the musky, sweet salt and mud smell before the sea, more pungent than the smell of the ocean Chance held inside her for so many months, her own private sea until her water broke and that warm tide emptied out between her legs and across the backseat of the Lincoln.

"She likes the way your fear tastes," the child says. "Every time she hears it, she gets a little bit stronger."

"He isn't coming," Chance whispers and lies down again, too weak to sit up any longer, too stoned, and there's nothing out there she wants to see anyway. "He *would* have come, if he could. But there's no time left."

"Did you really think he would?" the werewolf asks. "You

think this is all some fairy tale and the brave woodsman saves Red Riding Hood at the last. Hell, lady, that's not even how that story's supposed to end. He got drunk. He got drunk and forgot all about you."

"Don't listen to her," the child says. "Please, please don't listen to her. She wants you to give up."

Chance turns her head towards the child again and there are tears running down its face. "He didn't get drunk," she says. "I know he didn't do that. And he didn't forget about us, either. But he isn't coming."

"If that's true, how can I be here?" the child asks and then looks at its wristwatch again. "If that's true, I wouldn't be here talking to you, would I?"

"It's all a dream," Chance says and gently touches the child's forehead, brushing the hair from its brown eyes. "You're here so I won't have to die alone. You're here with me now because I'm not going to get to see you later."

"No, Mother, that's not true. But if you start believing it's true, she can *make* it true."

Chance closes her eyes, silently counting off seconds, waiting for the next contraction. "What time is it?" she asks the child.

"Three thirty-seven," it replies.

"Your father is a good man," Chance says. "Whatever she tells you, whatever anyone else says, don't you believe them. He's a *strong* man. He would have found us if he could have."

"He's a drunk," the werewolf grunts. "A drunk and a coward."

"It's okay. I know she's lying," the child whispers in Chance's ear, and its breath smells faintly of cinnamon. "I know what's true and what's a lie."

"That's good," Chance says, "that's very good," as a contraction starts and she grips the fake leather upholstery. Her flesh like folding earth, she thinks, like continents grinding one against the other, changing the face of a planet, changing her.

"Can you sleep?" the child asks. "It would all be easier if you could sleep," and Chance manages to cough out a rough laugh.

"No," she says. "But I wouldn't want to. It would change the dream, wouldn't it? I want to be with you as long as I can."

She opens her eyes, fixing them on a thin, watercolor brush stroke of clouds set high in the blue New England sky, white clouds going yellow orange and indigo around the edges as the sun slips closer to the coming night, the coming darkness as unstoppable as the contractions. She watches the clouds and tries to remember to breathe, keep breathing for the baby, keep breathing because she still can because the monster driving the car hasn't taken that away from her yet. It will, the way it took the lives of all the people in the diner, but not until later, so she still has work to do, time to live through until the end.

"It'll be okay," the child says. "He *is* coming. He's coming fast with the starling girl to drive a stake through her black heart."

"I think that only works with vampires," Chance mumbles as the contraction finally releases her and she turns her head to face the child. But it's gone and now there's only the empty space behind the front seat where it was sitting, nothing but a couple of soft drink cans and a crumpled McDonald's bag lying there in the floorboard.

"Oh," she whispers. "No. Please come back. I can't do this by myself," but the only reply is the chilly wind whipping in through the open window, the angry rock music blaring from the car stereo, and the sound of the monster laughing softly to itself.

So many long red years since Narcissa Snow has passed through Ipswich, since she's driven this route north and east along Argilla Road, winding between the tall, swaying grasses of the Great Marsh and the dusky waters of the narrow Manuxet River, on this path of asphalt and potholes that eventually leads down to the bay and the sea. The road home, just exactly like she told the crazy woman lying in her backseat talking to children who aren't there, the ruins of the house her grandfather—not Aldous, but her real grandfather, Iscariot Snow—built in the dunes more than eighty years ago.

The home you burned, Aldous sneers from someplace inside her crowded head. *The home where you killed me.*

Narcissa ignores the ghost, too many years and too many miles, far too much murder done, to allow him to ruin this moment, this and all the moments soon to come. This is the evening she's worked for since the Benefit Street ghouls finally turned her away for the last time, and no memories of the distant, sour past will be permitted to spoil it, no matter how loudly they jabber and whine for her attention. Hardly an hour left until moonrise, but that should be time enough, time to find whatever the sea and wind have left of the house, the long, indestructible stone slabs upon which Iscariot Snow built it.

"Them stones were here before the Indians came," Aldous told her when she was a child. "Them stones might have been here since before there were people anywhere in the world. Sometimes, late at night, they sing."

And that much was true. More than one night she slipped out of the tall house and sat in the sand listening to the great blocks of black stone visible just beneath the bricks and mortar, their swooping, trilling song whenever the moon was bright and full and the stars shimmered overhead. A wordless, alien melody Narcissa could never quite remember the next day, no matter how hard she tried, and sometimes the stones gave her dreams of ancient days when the waters of the newborn Atlantic were as warm as summer and the skies were thick with dragons.

"You keep on listening close enough, child," Aldous said, "and one of these nights they'll serenade you all the way to Hell." But she listened anyway, almost every opportunity she got, not sure that Hell would be so very different from her life in the old house.

Guess you're home free, Aldous murmurs. *Guess even old Neptune on his throne of gold and starfish couldn't stop you now.*

"Why don't you shut up," Narcissa says, watching for the turn-off to the house, past the lower falls now and the sun glittering brightly off Ipswich Bay. "You lost the war, old man. You lost and now it's time for you to be a good phantom and just fade the fuck away."

In the backseat, Chance moans loudly and asks what time it is.

I suppose you're right. Ain't too much left for me to say, the old man sighs and she can feel his bony, ectoplasmic fingers slither across the convolutions of her brain. *You got the book, you got all the magic words, you got an offering fit for old Orc himself, all wrapped up safe and sound in its momma's innards.*

"They turned up their noses at me," Narcissa replies bitterly. "But now they'll see. They tried to kill me, just like you, old man. They're never going to underestimate me again."

Too damn bad Mnemosyne and that old whore Terpsichore couldn't have been around to see that pretty little piece of work you did back in Pennsylvania.

"Oh, they'll have heard," Narcissa says, remembering the way Chance sat perfectly still while she shot the people in the diner, one by one by one, the men and the women, the two children. Remembering the sound of her gun, the gas tanks going up as they drove away. "I'm sure the crows will have told them everything by now."

No doubt, Aldous snickers. *And one day soon, they're gonna write ballads about you, child. One day, your name's gonna be carved in the ebony door at the bottom of the Well of Despair.*

"Mock me all you want, Aldous, but you'll see. Very soon now, you'll see," and then she's come to the sandy, overgrown road leading down to the dunes and the place where the house once stood. Narcissa pulls over, bumping off the blacktop onto the low shoulder, and Chance cries out behind her.

"How you doing back there, crazy lady?" Narcissa asks and glances at Chance in the rearview mirror. "How much longer you think you've got?"

"Who were you talking to?"

"No one," Narcissa replies. "No one at all."

"You're making fun of me," Chance moans and shuts her eyes, gritting her teeth together.

"Well, I'd say you're about ready to pop," Narcissa tells her and then looks down the crooked, rutted trail leading away from Argilla Road. "You better hang on to something back there. I'm afraid this is going to be a rough ride."

You can't get a damn Lincoln Continental through there, Aldous says. *It's hardly even a decent deer trail anymore.*

"Well, I'm sure as hell not carrying her fat ass."

Make her walk, then. It's not that far. Walking her will speed the delivery. Narcissa starts to ask him how he knows that, but *I made your mother walk*, he says. *Didn't do her no harm.*

"She wasn't drugged," Narcissa replies. "And I bet she had a level floor to walk on."

"I'm not walking anywhere," Chance says, the words puffed out between her ragged breaths.

"Shut up, crazy lady. You'll do what I tell you to do."

"Why? Why should I? You're just going to kill me anyway."

She's got a point, you know, Aldous says and laughs, and the noise of his laughter wakes up the other voices in her head. *Maybe you're gonna be carrying her fat ass after all.*

Where are we? one of the dead children from the diner asks and another voice answers it. *The end of hope,* it says, and *All the way back at the start,* another mutters.

Narcissa leans over, reaching for the pistol tucked safely out of sight beneath her seat.

"You can finish it here," Chance says. "Whatever the fuck it is, you can finish it here."

There isn't any difference, another voice chimes in. *The start and the end, they're not even two sides of the same coin anymore.*

He's only a child, a mother's voice cuts in as Narcissa flips off the safety, turns around in the seat, and aims the pistol at Chance's head. *It's not fair for you to expect him to understand something like that.*

"You won't kill me," Chance says, her foggy eyes staring directly at Narcissa and the muzzle of the gun. "Not yet. You won't kill me, because you might kill the baby."

"Just when did you decide you have any idea what I will or won't do?" Narcissa asks her, wishing the voices would shut up again so she could think clearly, so close to pulling the trigger and unable to remember how much longer she needs to keep Chance alive.

"That would ruin everything for you, wouldn't it, if my baby dies?"

"Are you really that brave, crazy lady?" Narcissa whispers and raises the barrel of the 9 mm before she squeezes the trigger. The gun roars and the window above Chance explodes in a diamond-shard rain of safety glass. She screams, but Narcissa's head is already too full of the dead voices and the sound of the gun to hear her. The bitter, hot smell of gunpowder hanging in the shocked air and the sparkle of the glass scattered all over Chance and the back-seat like confetti, the spent shell lying on her chest, and Narcissa lowers the barrel again.

"It isn't a long walk," she says, her own voice barely audible over the ringing in her ears. "I'll help you."

Chance screams again, louder than before, and then covers her face with both her hands; there's a deep gouge near her left elbow, dark blood leaking steadily from the wound, and Narcissa wonders if there's any point in bandaging it.

Did you hear that? one of the dead children asks, frightened, and *What?* an old woman's voice calls back. *Did we hear what?*

The thunder. Did you hear the thunder coming?

Where's it coming from? the old woman inside Narcissa's head asks and another, younger voice giggles to itself and adds, *What's it gonna want when it gets here?*

"Tell them to shut up, Aldous," Narcissa growls. "Tell them all to shut up right this minute."

What makes you think I could do a thing like that? the old man replies. *What makes you think that I would even try?*

Listen, the old woman mumbles, *I will tell thee what is done in the caverns of the grave,* mumbling because she has no teeth, and now Narcissa remembers killing her in Baltimore or some other city that starts with a B.

What does she mean? one of the children asks.

Nothing, someone reassures it. *She isn't well. She's old and isn't well.*

"I fucking mean it, Aldous. Make them stop."

You're wasting time, child, sitting here talking to yourself when there's still so much left to do.

A noise outside the car, a sudden rustle from the tall grass growing at the edge of the road, and she looks away from Chance, looks up to see the old man standing in the fading daylight, watching her with the empty sockets where his eyes used to be. There are crows perched on both his shoulders, ebony birds with fiery red eyes and their beaks drip something thick and white. The ice pick is still embedded in Aldous' chest, right there where she planted it almost fifteen years ago.

"It wasn't my fault they wouldn't have you, old man," she says, uncertain if he's listening to her, but she says it anyway.

He smiles, or snarls, his lips folding back to bare tarnished silver teeth and rotting black gums. With one hand, he points a finger towards the sky.

Does not the worm erect a pillar in the moldering churchyard? the old woman's voice asks from some wet and writhing crevice of Narcissa's brain. *And a palace of eternity in the jaws of the hungry grave?*

"We have to go now," Narcissa says. "It won't be so hard. I'll help you walk."

Chance has moved her hands and is staring at Narcissa, more blood on her face, blood seeping from a dozen tiny cuts. Her eyes so wide and afraid, drowning in her tears, and she nods her head very slowly.

"First, you have to promise me you'll let me see it," Chance sobs and then shuts her eyes as another contraction hits. "Just promise me that, and I'll do whatever you want."

"Aren't you afraid that will only make it harder?"

"*Please,* Narcissa. Promise me."

"How do you know I won't lie to you, that I won't say yes now and then do something else later on?"

Chance opens her eyes and takes a deep, gasping breath. "You told me you keep your promises," she says. "And I don't have any choice. Just promise me you'll do it."

Narcissa takes her finger off the trigger and glances back at Aldous and the crows, but they've gone.

"Sure," she says. "I promise. Maybe I'll even let you hold it, if you'll stop giving me so much shit for—"

"Whatever you say. Whatever you want, I fucking swear."

Narcissa stares out across the marshes towards Castle Hill and the sea. Inside her head, the voices have all fallen silent and now there's only the sound of Chance sobbing and the distant, rowdy cry of a gull. She wishes she could see the beach from here, the cold waves throwing themselves against the shore, but tells herself it won't be much longer and opens the door of the Lincoln.

"That's not the right road," Starling Jane says. "It's another dead end." But Deacon turns anyway, only to find his progress blocked by a sprawling pile of trash and limestone gravel.

"*Shit,*" he hisses and shifts the car into reverse, his foot too heavy on the accelerator, spinning the tires, burning off more rubber.

"Keep that up and we'll have another blowout," she says.

"You said you knew the fucking way."

"I think you should go back to Ipswich. We should have turned south on High Street, not north."

Deacon squeals out of the dead end, backing onto the main road, and then hits the brakes so hard that Jane is thrown back against her seat, then forward again and she almost smacks her head against the dashboard. "What the fuck kind of sick joke is that supposed to be?" he asks her, pointing at a street sign.

"Labor in Vain Road," she says, reading it aloud. "Wé really should go back to Ipswich, Deacon, while there's still time. We should have turned—"

"Just admit you're lost, Jane. Please just fucking admit you have no idea where we are."

Jane looks away from the sign, stares silently at her empty hands.

"Yeah, well, fuck me," Deacon says, shifting into drive again. "What time is it?"

"You just asked—"

"Well, I'm just asking again. What time is it?"

"Three forty-three," she tells him, glancing reluctantly at her wristwatch.

"And moonrise is at four forty-five."

"We still have time. It's not that far from here, I swear. But we need to get back on the right road."

"She's going to die," Deacon whispers and slaps the steering wheel hard with the open palm of his good hand. "You fucking lied to me, Jane, and now Chance is going to fucking die because you fucking lied to me."

"No," she says very quietly, and then doesn't say anything else. He wants to hit her, wants to hit her more than he's ever wanted to hit anyone in his life. Instead, Deacon looks up through the bug-spattered windshield at the sky, the too-broad Massachusetts sky stretched out like a second-rate Maxfield Parrish painting, and starts driving again. Almost twenty-four hours now since they left Birmingham, slipping out of the city in the battered old piece-of-shit Camaro Jane pulled out of her ass with two calls from a pay phone, the car and two guns delivered to them like a pizza. No way they would have made it very far in the Impala, not once Downs and the FBI discovered they were gone. The phony fire alarm worked like a charm, and Deacon still has no idea what the girl did to the cop standing guard outside her hospital door, but he was way too busy counting and recounting her deck of playing cards to even notice when Deacon wheeled her out of the room and down the hall to the elevator. Too much panic and confusion for anyone to notice them, Jane in her sunglasses and wrapped in a torn and bloodstained raincoat that he'd found in her closet, Deacon keeping his head down and his eyes straight ahead.

"We'll be fine," she said. "Just act like you're doing exactly what you're supposed to be doing and nobody's going to look at us twice."

And nobody did, magic or luck or both, and he hasn't bothered to ask her which, no time for anything but the drive, the destination, an image of Chance burned into his mind like a dream of the Grail. His headache faded after the first day, about the same time they reached Virginia and the Camaro started overheating.

"We're not going to make it," Deacon says, not turning back towards Ipswich, following Labor in Vain Road east.

"Yes, we will," Jane whispers. "This has to connect with Argilla somewhere up ahead. There just aren't that many roads out here. Unless maybe it loops back around towards town. It might do that, you know?" and she looks back over her shoulder.

"Yeah, Jane, let's just keep thinking those happy fucking thoughts, why don't we? Why the hell are you whispering?"

"I'm not," she says, speaking so softly he could never consider it anything but a whisper. "But I think there's something following us."

Deacon glances at the rearview mirror and there's only the deserted blacktop behind them, a few trees and some scrubby underbrush, weeds and the litter scattered along the edges of the road. "I don't see anyone," he says.

"Just keep driving," Jane whispers. "Don't look at it. I think they know I'm coming."

"There's nothing fucking back there," he says, too scared and exhausted to humor her anymore, not after the way she's been freaking out on him every forty or fifty miles since they crossed into Connecticut, every time they passed a flock of blackbirds perched on a power line or a stray dog wandering along the highway.

"They probably wouldn't use anything you'd be able to see. Not this close to the warrens. By now, I expect they know you're with me."

The road begins to turn towards the southeast, winding past a small and shimmering lake on their left, a brief glimpse of a long-legged water bird with gray-black feathers standing in the reeds near the shore before the trees obscure the view. Jane looks over her shoulder again and then mutters something to herself, drawing some complex sign in the air with her hand, the sign of a cross with more than four points, and Deacon checks the rearview.

"I still don't see anything," he says.

"Don't look at it. Watch the road."

"Jane, there's nothing back there *to* look at. Except the fucking sunset."

"It's only three fifty-eight," she says quietly, calmly, staring straight ahead as the car rounds another bend and now the Camaro is traveling south.

"I didn't ask," Deacon says and starts to tell her this can't possibly be right, because now they're heading away from the sea, but Starling Jane opens the glove compartment and takes out her gun.

"I need you to promise me something," she says. "If you should make it through this and I don't—"

"Hold on. You think I owe you a favor?"

"No, but I'm asking you anyway, because there's nobody else left for me to ask. And I did bring you—"

"All you've done so far is get us lost," Deacon says and glances down at the speedometer, sees that he's only doing fifty and puts a little more pressure on the gas.

"We're not lost. We're getting close. You'll see."

"We're not even going in the right goddamn direction."

"The things Narcissa stole," Jane says, speaking so softly now that he can hardly hear her. "I think she'll still have it all with her. It's papers mostly, old books, journals, maps, that sort of thing. I think they'll be hidden somewhere in her car, the trunk probably."

"What the fuck do I care?"

"If I don't make it and you do, then I need you to take it all back to Providence for me. Don't even think about reading any of it. As long as you don't know exactly what it is, they won't hurt you."

"You're out of your mind," he says. "No way."

"Please listen to me, Deacon. There's a big yellow house on Benefit Street, just past the Athenaeum—"

"*No,*" he says again, more forcefully than before. "If we get through this shit and I don't kill you for what you and that asshole Pentecost have done to Chance, you'll be the luckiest little creep on the face of the earth. So don't start getting greedy."

"I'm sorry," she says, still staring straight ahead. "Fine. I won't ask again."

"Fucking Christ, you've got a pair of balls on you."

"Is it really necessary to use that word so much? You don't seem to be able to get through a whole sentence without it," and she checks her pistol to be sure that it's loaded, pops the clip out and shoves it in again.

"You're fucking kidding me, right?"

"No," Jane says, aiming the gun at the windshield, squinting through her wraparound sunglasses as she sets her sights on the remains of a very large brown grasshopper squashed flat against the glass. "I'm not. It makes you sound like a vulgar, ignorant man, and I know you're more than that. But you better slow down some. That's our turn."

Deacon starts to tell her to fuck off, considers putting her out right here and then whatever happens, he'll only have himself to blame, before he sees the road sign on his left and the stop sign on his right, and the sign reads ARGILLA ROAD.

"Left or right?" he asks, and switches off the Camaro's wheezy heater because he's started sweating.

"Left," Jane says. "The house was near the very end of the road. Probably not much more than a mile from here."

"That close?" Deacon asks and "Yeah, that close," she replies.

He takes the turn without stopping, hardly even bothering to slow down; the rear of the car fishtails and for a second or two, he thinks they'll wind up in the boggy, weed-choked ditch and have to run the rest of the way.

"Four o'clock on the dot," Jane says and Deacon looks anxiously at the dimming eastern sky, scanning it for any evidence of the full moon, praying that they're not wrong about moonrise, that they've still got forty-five minutes to go this final mile and find Chance. Jane turns completely around in her seat, gripping the loaded semiautomatic in her right hand. "It's still back there," she says. "But it's keeping its distance."

"So what happens next? Is that little pop gun of yours really going to do us any good against this bitch?"

"We have the shotgun, too. As long as we can stop Narcissa before she finishes the summoning, we have a chance."

"A chance," Deacon says and shakes his head, wishing that one of the empty whiskey bottles or beer cans in the backseat were full, wishing he had something besides fear and adrenaline to clear his muddled head. "That's really not very fucking funny."

"Sorry," Jane says, not sounding sorry, sounding distant and preoccupied, and she doesn't take her eyes off whatever she thinks is following the car. "I didn't say it on purpose."

"What are you doing? I thought you just said we shouldn't look at it."

"That's when I thought it was an assassin. Now I'm not sure what it is."

"So long as it stays out of my way," Deacon says, pressing the accelerator almost all the way to the floor, "I really don't give a rat's ass *what* it is."

"I think I saw it once before, years and years ago, but it was locked inside a little green bottle then."

Deacon hardly hears her, too busy watching the road and the speedometer, the Halloween sky bruising itself towards dusk, too busy trying to believe that they'll be in time and he and Chance will have the rest of their lives to heal from the things they've seen and done in the past week. The Camaro's engine roars and shudders like a weary, dying animal, swan song of pistons and crankshafts, belts and spinning fans, and the angry orange temperature light comes on again.

"Don't you even *think* about it, cocksucker," he growls and takes the wheel with his bandaged hand long enough to slam his right down hard against the dashboard. The orange light flickers indecisively and then winks out for good, but now there's white smoke or steam, probably a little of both, leaking out from beneath the hood.

"Deacon, we're not going to be much use to anyone if you kill us before we even get to the rath."

"What the sam hell is a *rath*?"

"You know the poem, 'and mome raths outgrabe.'"

"Is that what we're hunting? A jabberwock?"

"Have you ever used a shotgun?" Jane asks him.

"Not unless video games count," and she sighs and keeps watching whatever it is she thinks is tailing the dying Camaro.

"But you've used a pistol before?" she asks and "Yeah," Deacon replies, trying not to think about Scarborough Pentecost's body lying in the front room of the spider-girl house, or the gaping black hole between his eyes whenever he wanders into Deacon's dreams. "I've used a pistol. Once."

"Then I'll take the shotgun."

"You do that," and Deacon is starting to have trouble seeing through the steam coming off the engine, the smoke from burning oil; he considers turning on the windshield wipers, but decides that would probably only make things worse. Around them, the land is growing flatter, the thick stands of pine and hardwoods giving way to the marshes, a restless sea of yellow-brown grass marked here and there by gnarled and stunted trees. There's a small river to the east, snaking along between low and muddy banks. On their Rand McNally Massachusetts road atlas, it's only a pale blue squiggle labeled the Castle Neck River, but several times Starling Jane has referred to it as the Manuxet. There are a few old willows growing in sandy places near the water, their drooping, bare limbs dragging the ink-dark surface like woodsy tentacles. Deacon doesn't like the river, something he'd rather not even try to put his finger on, and he watches the road through the smoke and steam instead.

"It can't be much farther now," Jane says, turning back around, and Deacon glances at the speedometer. The needle's wavering uncertainly just above ninety miles an hour, and he eases some of his weight off the gas pedal. There's a sudden, violent rattling sound from the guts of the Chevy, metal grinding metal, and "It's a good damn thing," he mutters. "A few more feet and we'd have to get out and fucking push this piece of junk."

Jane sees the huge gray Lincoln first, parked at the side of the road underneath a crooked little oak. "There," she says. "That's it. That's her."

"How do you know? Is this—"

"Deacon, just stop the fucking car!" she shouts and he hits the brakes, screeching to a stop five or ten yards past the Lincoln.

"Do you have a god you pray to, Deacon Silvey?" Jane asks, handing him the pistol before he can pull the Camaro over to the shoulder.

"No," he says and she frowns and shrugs her bony shoulders, lost inside the raincoat. "No matter," she whispers. "It probably wouldn't make much difference anyway."

Chance is trying to think of the name of the bitter, ugly root that Narcissa made her chew after breakfast, trying to think of anything but the pain. She takes another step, the rutted, sandy road like walking in a nightmare, and realizes they've started going uphill again. Narcissa has one arm around her tight and is carrying a leather satchel in her other hand. "It's wearing off," Chance says. "The morphine," and stops as another contraction begins.

"It's not much farther," Narcissa says.

"I can't do this. I can't walk any more."

"Yes, you can," the werewolf replies, holding her up, holding her up and dragging her forward through the sand and thistles when Chance hurts too much to walk. "You can do all sorts of things, if you have no other choice."

She can't remember the name of the root, even though Narcissa told her twice, told her it would help get the contractions started, the root and the syringe full of oxytocin. Just like her, that she remembers the name of the drug and not the root. She wants to ask Narcissa what it was called, but she can't get her breath to speak. The air's gone cold enough now that it fogs when it rushes out between her teeth, forced out of her in dragon-smoky gasps whenever the pain comes, and she wishes she could think clearly enough to count the seconds, the minutes in between. Certain only that the distance between contractions is getting shorter and shorter. The air is cold, but the sweat's coming off her like she's hemorrhaging water, like she's just a little black rain cloud trying to wash the world away. She's started having chills and wonders if it's a fever, if she's burning up alive and maybe, if she's lucky, the flames will get Narcissa, too.

"Just over this hill," the werewolf growls, though Chance is beginning to doubt she really is a werewolf after all, beginning to think that's just another lie the morphine told her.

"I have to stop," Chance gasps as the pain releases her again. "Please, let me stop for a minute."

"No way, crazy lady. You sit down now and I'll never get you back on your feet."

"I can't climb this fucking hill."

"From the top you can almost see forever," Narcissa says, as if she hasn't heard a word Chance has said to her. "You can see the Annisquam lighthouse after dark, like the eye of a sea serpent rising up out of the bay. Sometimes you can see the top of Allen's Reef showing above the waves."

"I'm not a fucking tourist," Chance grunts, still trying to catch her breath, the sweat dripping from her matted bangs and stinging her eyes. "I don't really give a shit about the scenery."

"When I was a little girl," the werewolf says and then she's silent for a minute, pulling Chance along through the sand and brush. The wind whistles loudly through the dunes and there are seabirds squawking noisily in the sky. "When I was a girl," Narcissa says again, "Aldous would take me out near the reef sometimes in his rowboat. But he was always afraid to get in very close, afraid of the demons. That's what he always called them, the demons. Sometimes we saw whales spouting farther out. Sometimes we saw sharks."

A sudden gust blows the sand high and Chance shuts her eyes in time, but it gets in her mouth and nose, sticks to her sweaty face and hair.

"I want another shot," she says, but the werewolf shakes its head no and keeps dragging her towards the crest of the hill.

"I don't think so. I don't think more morphine would be a good idea at this point."

"What difference does it make?"

"Just shut up and keep moving," but then the next contraction hits her like a punch in the belly, knocks the breath from her and she can't keep moving. Chance tries to sit down in the sand, but Narcissa holds her up.

"You just better not forget our deal," the werewolf smirks, "not if you want to see the kid."

"I've seen it," Chance says, when she can speak again, even though she believes that even less than she believes Narcissa Snow could really be a werewolf. "Even if you don't keep your promise, I've seen my child."

"Sure," Narcissa says. "Whatever gets you through the day. Come on, crazy lady, we're at the top."

Chance blinks through the sweat and the grit clinging to her eyelashes, blinks through the pain, at the road winding steeply down the far side of the hill, this lone and stony hill lost out here among the dunes, and at first all she sees is the darkening sky and the white sand, stretching away to the edge of the ocean. The eastern horizon is turning a deep purple and the setting sun throws long, uneasy shadows across the dunes.

"Down there," the werewolf growls. "Down there near the shore."

"What?" Chance asks, teetering on the thin rim of another contraction, but then she sees it and sits down in the sand before Narcissa can stop her.

"I was born there," the werewolf tells her, so maybe it doesn't care that she sat down, maybe it isn't going to try to make her walk anymore. "It was a very big house. My grandfather built it."

"Well, there's no house there now," Chance mutters, taking a deep breath and wiping the sweat from her face. "There's nothing but a bunch of rocks."

"I thought rocks got you all hot and bothered, crazy lady. I thought rocks were practically your religion."

"Not rocks. The fossils I find in the rocks. There's *nothing* in these rocks. It's all igneous—"

"You hurt too much to fucking walk, but you can lecture me on geology," the werewolf barks. "Now, isn't that something?"

"They're only rocks," Chance says again and then the pain's back and this time she screams because it's easier than not screaming. Every second longer than the one before and the werewolf grabs her by the shoulders before she can lie down.

"Not just rocks," it snaps, its ivory teeth clicking loudly together, yellow-white blades that slice the evening to ribbons. "But you wouldn't know that, would you, because it's nothing anyone's ever had the nerve to put into one of your *science* books, is it? The Hounds built that altar to Mother Hydra and Father Kraken ten thousand years before the last ice age. Before Orc and all his children followed the night roads down into the earth, before men had even learned to build fires to keep away the monsters."

The contraction ends and Chance gulps the salty, cold air, shivering now, drinking the air like it's the sweetest water she's ever tasted. "That's the stupidest thing you've said yet," she says, trying not to let her teeth chatter, not wanting the werewolf to hear her discomfort. And then she forces herself to laugh, even though her throat hurts and she feels more like vomiting. But it's a clean sound, nonetheless, and she imagines the wheeling gulls laughing with her, opening their sharp, hooked beaks and letting Narcissa Snow know exactly what they think of her delusions. "The last ice age would have ground those boulders to dust, if they'd been here then. The glaciers were a mile thick. Do you have any idea how much a mile of ice weighs, Narcissa?" And she laughs again before the pain returns or the werewolf can think of an answer. "Is that what you dragged me all the way from Birmingham to see?"

"You'll never see past the lies that were put here to blind you," Narcissa says, and now she almost sounds like she feels sorry for Chance. "You'll never see the truth of things, the beauty and horror hidden just beneath the surface."

Chance stares down at the long, flat boulders, half buried in the sand, laid out in a rough, uneven sort of rectangle running parallel to the sea. There's some passing resemblance to photographs she's seen of megaliths in England and Ireland and other places, but not enough that it can't be coincidence, the work of tides and the weather, the random work of time, not designing hands. In places, she can make out the charred remains of brick walls built directly on top of the granite, and part of a crumbling chimney is still standing at the nearer end of the ruins. Here and there, blackened timbers rise from the sand like the scorched bones of a giant.

"You're beginning to sound like some of my students," Chance says. "You're not going to start talking about Noah and the fucking ark, are you?" and then the next contraction comes, but this time she digs her hands into the sand and doesn't scream.

"Maybe you'll get a glimpse, before you die," but Narcissa's voice is muted by the pain, Chance's body trying to rip itself into some new form and function, as her cervix strains to dilate the final few centimeters. She shuts her eyes tight, forcing her fingers deeper and deeper into the soft, dry sand. The Atlantic wind in her ears, the cries of the birds, and she can almost lose the werewolf entirely. She tries to think of Deacon, wishing him here, wishing she could see his face one more time, wishing Narcissa would give her another shot of morphine.

You think it's over, Mother, the child says. *You think it's over, but it's not. He's coming.* And Chance opens her eyes, but there's only Narcissa and the ruined house sitting at the bottom of the hill, only the pain and the things she's hurting too much not to want to be true.

The starlings are showing him the way.

"—on your feet. It's time. The moon will be along soon."

Chance exhales, breath like her life shuddering out of her, if only it could be that easy, and then, because it isn't, she draws more of the chilly ocean air deep inside her.

"I can't walk any more, Narcissa," she says. "I fucking swear to god. If you want me to go any farther, you're going to have to pick me up and carry me."

The werewolf squats down beside her, peering at her with its odd yellow eyes, peering through her, just a hint of fire around the rims of the irises now, and it licks its lips.

"Then the deal's off, crazy lady," it says. "I was keeping my end of the bargain."

"Just please shut up and get this over with," Chance tells her, and Narcissa Snow, who isn't really a werewolf, frowns and nods her head. The wind fingers through her hair, whipping it about her hard, pale face.

"Hold this," she says, handing Chance the leather satchel, "and don't drop it, I don't care how much pain you're in."

And then Narcissa lifts her off the sand, one arm around her shoulders and the other beneath the crooks of her knees, lifting Chance as though she were a hollow, weightless thing.

He'll never, ever stop looking for us, the child whispers, so maybe Narcissa won't overhear, and then the woman with eyes the color of sunflowers carries her down the hill.

CHAPTER FOURTEEN

Mother Hydra

"Go on ahead," Starling Jane says. "I'll catch up," and she pops the trunk of the Lincoln with something that almost looks like a bent paper clip. Inside, there's a jumble of cardboard boxes and suitcases, and she lifts the first box out and sets it on the road; as far as Deacon can tell, it's filled with medical supplies.

"We'll come back for this shit," he says as she takes another box out of the trunk, "*after* we find Chance."

"I said go on. Just follow the road. It'll take you there. I have to be sure it's all here."

"Bullshit," and he raises the pistol and aims it at her head.

Jane stops unloading the trunk and stares at him, a hint of a smile at the corners of her mouth, and then she glances at her watch. "You better hurry or you'll be too late."

"That wasn't the deal. First we find Chance, then you can worry about—"

"Isn't there enough blood on your hands, Deacon Silvey?" she asks, still smiling. "Wasn't Scarborough enough?"

"That was an accident."

"You think the police are going to believe that when they find his body? You think they'll believe it when they find mine? You're wasting time, and there's not much of it left to waste."

"You know I can't do this alone."

"I know we can't do it together," Jane says, glancing back at the trunk. "We can't stop Narcissa. No one can. Isn't that what you told Chance in your dream?"

"Fuck this shit," Deacon growls. "We'll find whatever you're looking for after we've found her. You're coming with me, Jane. Maybe we can't stop her, but we *are* going to try, *both* of us," and he cocks the pistol just like Scarborough Pentecost showed him.

"Deacon, are you going to stand here pointing that gun at me until the moon's up and your wife is dead?"

"Make up your mind. If we can't stop Narcissa, what the hell do I have to lose by shooting you?"

"Your last *chance*," Jane whispers purposefully, each word like a stone dropped into still water, and Deacon turns his head, turns to look down the overgrown dirt road winding away into a grove of cedars, because he thinks maybe he heard someone calling his name. Thinks maybe he heard Chance, but there's no one back there, just the murmuring trees and the dunes farther out. And then he hears Jane pumping the big shotgun, chambering a round, and he turns back to face her.

"You know, I'm getting pretty goddamned tired of the Jedi mind control shit," he says, looking directly into the twin barrels of the gun.

"Then turn around and start walking. Like I said, I'll catch up when I have what I came for. Four twenty, Deacon. You better get moving."

He swallows, his throat so dry it's hard to find so much as a drop of spit, and looks up from the shotgun, stares into the lenses of Jane's sunglasses instead.

"These people you work for, did they ever tell you your real name? Did they ever even bother to tell you where you were born?"

"That life was lost to me."

"You know the police took your prints, right?" and she nods and her finger tightens on the triggers. "Did you know they found a match?"

"Shut up," she snarls at him.

"Yeah. A missing kid from Connecticut—"

"I'm not going to tell you again. Turn around and start walking or I'm going to blow your head off."

"Then you might never know. You'll spend the rest of your life, whatever's left of it, wondering—"

"I don't want to have to shoot you, Deacon. I don't want your wife to have to die."

Then a sound from the opened trunk, wet and brittle noise like someone breaking eggs, at least a dozen eggs breaking all at once, thin white shells cracked to spill precious liquids, and Jane looks, startled, taking her eyes off Deacon. He slaps the muzzle of the shotgun hard with his bandaged hand and she drops it, a small, staccato gasp from her parted lips as it clatters to the pavement at her feet. And Deacon fires the pistol into the pitch blackness pouring out of the back of the Lincoln, the solid, intangible nothing rushing hungrily towards them.

"A trap," Jane says, sounding more surprised than scared, as the blackness flows thick around her, now you see her, now you don't, and there's not even time for Deacon to get off another shot before it's engulfed him, as well. The entire world wiped away, and he knows it's the same trick as the one Narcissa Snow used in the spider-girl house, the one that got Scarborough killed, the same perfect smoke screen made more terrible by its power over the fading daylight.

"Can you hear me?" he asks, half-afraid the blackness will slip down his throat and strangle him, will fill him until it's leaking from his pores, from his blind eyes, and "Yes," Jane says. "I'm still here. I haven't moved."

"Well don't. Stay right where you are. She did this when we went after her at the house. Scarborough made a blue light to—"

"I can't do that. I don't know photomancy. That was one of Scarborough's, but it isn't one of mine."

"That just so fucking figures," Deacon mumbles and slides his aching, bandaged hand into the pocket of his trousers. He can tell it's bleeding again, the wound torn open when he knocked the shotgun out of Jane's hands, but he finds what he's looking for, his cigarette lighter, and manages to get the lid open without dropping it.

"I can't breathe," Jane says. "I think it's going to suffocate us. I think that's what it does."

"No, it's just something she put here to slow us down. You're *not* fucking going to suffocate, so just stay calm," and he runs his thumb quickly across the strike wheel. The Zippo gives up a small shower of white sparks, an oily whiff of butane, and then a feeble yellow-blue flame that does nothing whatsoever to push back the darkness.

"I can't breathe," Jane says, her voice grown very thin and

strained, and Deacon tries holding the lighter up like a torch, but it doesn't work any better than before.

"Deacon, it's trying to get inside me," she whispers, and now she sounds very small and very, very frightened. "Oh god, I can *taste* it."

"It can't hurt you," Deacon says and he takes a step forward, moving towards her voice, towards the spot where she's supposed to be. "Don't you go losing your shit on me, little girl. That's exactly what she wants."

"It's not just a darkness. It's something she's called up. It's eating me alive—"

"*Stop* it, Jane! *Listen* to me. I want you to hold your hands out in front of you until you can feel me."

"It was a trap. It was a trap and I tripped it."

Deacon takes his finger off the strike wheel and the impotent flame vanishes immediately. He puts the lighter back into his pocket and takes another step towards Starling Jane.

"I don't want to die like this," she whispers and he thinks that she's started crying now. "I don't want her to get my soul. I want to know the name my parents gave me."

"Listen, I thought you were the hard-as-nails spooky bitch—"

"I can't find you," she says, but then her fingertips brush his right arm and she screams.

"C'mon, Jane. I thought you were the bad-ass monster slayer. Don't tell me you're afraid of the dark?"

But Deacon has started hearing things in the blackness, a sound like delicate, chitinous legs moving swiftly across the asphalt, a crisp and scuttling sound that seems to come from everywhere at once and nowhere at all. Jane clings tightly to his sleeve and "Do you hear that?" she asks. "Do you hear that, Deacon?"

"I don't hear anything and neither do you, you understand? She's just trying to frighten us. That's how Scarborough got killed."

"Something's coming. There's something in the dark with us."

"Listen to me, Jane. I need you to bend down and find the shotgun. It ought to be right there at your feet."

"I dropped it," she sobs. "You *made* me drop it," and the scuttling sounds are growing louder, a ceaseless, jointed susurration like busy insect legs, busy crab or lobster legs, moving swiftly through the blackness towards them.

"Just reach down and find it."

"I'm not letting go of you."

"Then I'll bend down with you," and he does, moving slow so she won't lose her grasp on his arm, and he can feel the scuttling things on him now, slipping fast across his feet and under the cuffs of his pants, probing claws and mouths pressed painfully against his skin.

"They're all over me—"

"They're not real, Jane," he says. "They're nothing. I fucking swear to god they're not real."

"I have it," she says a second or two later, only inches from hysteria now. "The shotgun, I found it."

"Good, now don't let go of it or me," he tells her. "Whatever you do, don't let go of me. I'm gonna try to get us out of here."

"They're all over me, Deacon!"

"It's only darkness," he says, struggling to sound calm, as much for himself as her. "It's only something to slow us down. Don't let go of me."

He takes a deep breath and lets himself fall backwards, away from the car, and for a moment they're tumbling together, arms and legs and guns, rolling across the asphalt, crushing a moving carpet of invisible, armored bodies beneath them. And then they're in the light again, twilight as bright as noon after the blackness from the Lincoln's trunk. They roll a little farther, off the road, across hard gravel, and into a shallow ditch filled with brambles and cold, stagnant water. Deacon sits up and looks at the car; there's nothing back there but the open trunk and the two cardboard boxes that Jane took out and set on the edge of Argilla Road.

"You can open your eyes now," he says. "I think it's over," and she does, her sunglasses lost in the escape, and she blinks and squints painfully at the light.

"Oh god," she whispers, wiping mud from her face. "It's beautiful, isn't it? It's the most beautiful thing in the world."

"Yeah," Deacon says. "It's absolutely fucking gorgeous. What time is it?"

A pause while Jane checks her wristwatch, holding it close to her face so she can see the hour and minute hands, and "Four forty-one," she replies reluctantly.

"How is that even possible? We couldn't have been inside that thing for more than a few minutes."

"Maybe my watch isn't right. Maybe it broke—"

"It's right," he says. "You know it's right and I know it's right." He gets to his feet, cold and dripping ditch water, pulling Jane up after him. "Are you coming with me or not?"

She glances at the gray Lincoln again and then down at the shotgun in her hands.

"You have to understand. The things she stole—"

"Simple question. In or out, yes or no. I don't need to hear a goddamn explanation," and before she can answer, he turns his back on the car, on her, and starts running down the dirt road towards the white dunes and the sea.

It's done, Chance thinks with no sense of relief at all. *At last, it's finally done.*

Lying there at the very center of the crude rectangle of black granite slabs, after Narcissa carried her down the steep hill and the moon began to rise above the horizon, a moon as red and swollen as an infection, malignant moon to stare hatefully down at them while Narcissa chanted and shouted and finally screamed at the sagging sky. While her hands moved ceaselessly over and inside Chance's naked body, drawing signs across her skin in fresh blood, in shit and saliva, and no moon was ever so full, ever half so wicked, as the bloated crimson thing leering down at them as the child slipped smoothly out from between her legs. Floating helpless in the freezing, saltwater pool hidden inside the stones, water not so deep that she would likely drown, deep enough her head kept going under, while Narcissa lifted the child by its feet, severing the umbilical cord, tying it, and a moment or a hundred thousand years later, the baby began to cry. Opened its tiny mouth and released the breathless wail like the bottomless loss spilling from Chance's heart, the voice of her desecration and emptiness, and neither that sound nor any other could ever fill the void.

And the red rain began to fall.

And the werewolf, the terrible, broken thing that's spent its life snared between the unseeing world of men and the unseen world of monsters, began pulling itself free, moth from its chrysalis shell, serpent from its egg, truth from the secret or the lie that's held it prisoner for so long. Chance fought not to lose sight of the child, so perfect, so fragile, beautiful beyond words or comprehension, clutched in the creature's claws, and how could she have ever fooled herself into thinking Narcissa Snow was only a woman, only something as frail and simple as herself?

It's over, she thinks, as her numb fingers lose their hold on the slippery walls of the pool, the moss-slicked masonry, and her head slips beneath the surface again. Salt water flooding her nose and mouth, salt water and the metallic, meaty taste of her own blood mingled with the blood from the ruptured sky. The water burns her throat and sinuses, but it's only more pain, only a very small pain, and she knows she'll never really hurt ever again.

I could stay here, Chance thinks. *I could stay down here forever, in the cold and the dark, until my bones are sand,* but then Narcissa has her by the throat, hauling her back into the air that's even colder than the water. Chance opens her eyes and Narcissa is cradling the crying baby in her other arm.

"I said I keep my promises," it growls, acid from its black lips, and she leans closer so Chance can see the child better.

"A girl," Chance tries to say, but she's shivering too hard to talk, crying even though she can't feel the tears.

"Yeah, you did a real good job, crazy lady. The moon is pleased with her. Mother Hydra is stirring in her sleep."

A girl, and it sounds much better if she doesn't try to say it out loud, if she only speaks the words inside. *My baby is a girl.*

The werewolf takes its hand from around her throat, growls contentedly and shakes itself, spraying thick droplets of the blood across the rocks and the water and Chance's face. Then it crouches at the pebbly edge of the pool and begins to lick the child clean.

Chance turns her face upwards, gazing into the foul, stinging rain, searching the clouds for some belated glimpse of the face of a god she's never believed in. There's a blue-white flash of lightning; it blinds her for a second and she lets herself slip beneath the surface again. Too weak to fight any longer, fighting when there's no point left to fighting, when losing is inevitable, when she's *already* lost, and at least it's not as cold beneath the water. Her contractions haven't ended, her body still struggling to expel the empty placenta, but the pain seems safely far away, held apart from her now, and the thought of drowning is not so bad. Only the dizzying, endless ache of regret to give her pause—that this monster has taken her child, that she'll never see Deacon's face again, that Alice is dead— and regret isn't nearly strong enough to keep her alive.

Go ahead, daughter. Turn loose now, the black water murmurs softly in its gentle seaweed and fish-scale voice, caressing her, wrapping her up in amniotic folds of numbness and oblivion; it soothes the cuts from Narcissa's sharp knives, the ragged wounds from her razor claws and teeth.

Come back to me. Back here to the start, where it all began, where everything always ends.

Chance opens her mouth, so the air in her lungs can get out, and the water whispers to her how easy death will be, letting it inside her, just letting it in to wash her away like a stain. She breathes out and the silver bubbles stream from her lips and nostrils. But then there are hands beneath her, buoying her up, forcing her back to the surface.

"I'm not going to let you die this time," the child says, and Chance opens her eyes, coughs and stares amazed into its pretty face. Not *its* face, *her* face, her hazel-brown eyes and mouse-brown hair, the face of her and Deacon's child already half-grown. "I figured it all out. You only have to hang on a little bit longer. Daddy's almost here."

The werewolf stops licking her baby and looks up at Chance, blinks at her with its searing golden eyes and runs its long pink tongue about the edges of its muzzle. "I thought you were dying," it sneers. "Would it be easier if I gave you a stone to weigh you down?"

"It doesn't have to end the same way," the child says. "I *know* that it doesn't have to end the same way every time."

"I would tie it around your throat," Narcissa snarls, "but there's no time left. They're coming," and she looks over her shoulder at the crumbling entrance to the tunnel near the pool, the flooded basement of a ruined house.

"Tonight the dream will be different," the child says, "and when I wake up, you'll be alive. When I wake up, everything will have *always* been different."

The werewolf takes a white towel from its leather satchel and carefully wraps the baby in it.

"I can hear his footsteps, Mother. The girl's coming with him and they'll be here any minute. This time, I won't let you go."

Chance looks back at the child's face, the tears streaming down its cheeks, the sorrow and desperation in its brown eyes, determination like a scar. And then she looks back at the baby, swaddled now in its clean white towel, lying on the ground where Narcissa has left it while she lifts a heavy, rounded stone free of the mud and sand.

"You," Chance whispers, her voice slurred and weak. She wants to touch her daughter, but can hardly even feel her arms anymore. "It's only . . . only a dream."

"You don't have to talk. I'm here. I'm holding you, Mother. Just be still and I'll hold you till he gets here."

"It's only ballast," the werewolf growls. "Be sure to show it to the ferryman when he comes," and then she wades back into the salty pool, splashing effortlessly through the insubstantial flesh of the child, though the girl doesn't seem to have noticed. Narcissa sets the big stone down on Chance's chest, lets go, and she sinks quickly to the bottom of the shallow pool.

Only a bad dream, she thinks, and now the child is underwater with her, a frantic shadow laboring in the darkness and the cold, trying to move the stone off her, trying to lift her again. *A nightmare and soon I'm going to wake up, any minute now, and I'll forget it all before I can even tell Deacon.*

And the child's splashing grows more distant, the thundering sky and its bloody moon only a rumor in this perfect, lightless place, and Chance lets go, and falls.

"Is she alive?" Jane asks. "Is she breathing?"

Deacon doesn't reply, holds Chance close to him while she gags and vomits brine and bile, her skin as pale and chilled as a corpse.

Twenty fucking minutes more, he thinks, rubbing her stiff and half-frozen hands between his own. *If I'd only been twenty minutes sooner. Fuck that, only fifteen goddamn—*

"Where's Narcissa?" Jane asks. She's standing at the edge of the pool, peering down into the glistening black water, as if there's anything left in there to see, anything left that matters. "Is she already in the tunnels?"

"Give me your coat," and she does, slips out of the big army-issue raincoat and hands it to Deacon. He wraps it around Chance and holds her tighter.

"Where's the child?" Jane asks. "Has Narcissa taken the child into the tunnels?" and Chance's eyelids flutter open, a tremble from her blue lips, and Deacon tells Jane to shut the hell up before he shoots her.

"I think she's in shock. I think she's fucking freezing to death."

"Do you want to save your child?" Jane asks, staring blankly into the pool again, watching the moon's rippling reflection.

"Oh, fuck me," Deacon whispers, trying hard not to see the things that Narcissa has done to Chance's body, trying not to hear Jane because he knows what's coming, the choice he's about to have to make, the gamble and either way he's damned. "We got lost, baby," he says. "We just kept getting fucking lost."

Sleight of hand and eye, misdirection, wrong turns and trunks stuffed with midnight, all of it playing over and over and over in his head now. What he could and couldn't have done differently, which wasted moments he might have possibly saved. And the cedars are the worst of all, because they were the very last, because they cost him that final handful of priceless, irredeemable minutes. Starling Jane caught up with him shortly after he became lost in the small grove of twisted, wind-stunted cedars only a dozen or so yards from the edge of Argilla Road. The trail leading down to the dunes and the shore had vanished abruptly under a vine-shrouded deadfall and Deacon had tried to go around it, had taken a few, hesitant steps into the trees and was immediately disoriented, disorientation that turned quickly into panic. His entire life spent in the cities and suburbs, navigating sensible, calculated forests of concrete and steel, asphalt and glass, and the prickling evergreen branches that clung to his jacket and hair, that scratched at his face, might as well have been demons placed there by Narcissa to block his way, to ensure that he would never reach Chance in time. Another fucking trick, another cheat, and Jane found him tangled in thorns and creeper vines, shouting curses at the trees.

"Be still," she said, cutting him loose with the small hunting knife she'd bought at a truck stop back in North Carolina. "You're only making it worse."

When he was free, she folded her knife closed and led him through the cedars and the underbrush, walking in what seemed like an endless series of circles, dead ends and switchbacks; a twilight maze without walls, that space so many times larger inside than out. And just when he decided that they were going to spend the rest of their lives wandering through those trees, they were standing beneath the sky again, standing on the other side, the dirt road only a few feet away on their left, and Deacon looked up and saw the low red moon risen clear of the horizon now.

"What time?" he asked her and she squinted at her watch, then shook her head. "You don't want to know that," she replied. "Just keep walking."

"There can't be very much time left," Jane says and Deacon shakes his head.

"There isn't any time left," he replies, wiping wet hair from Chance's eyes. "Baby, you gotta tell me what to do now. You tell me, because I can't make this decision on my own."

"I don't think she can talk," Jane says unhelpfully, without looking away from the pool. "Do you want me to go on without you?"

"Go," Chance says, her voice raw as the wounds carved into her thighs and chest. "Find her," and then she pukes up more salt water.

"There. You heard her."

"I can't just leave her here. She's fucking dying."

"She just told you to go. You asked her what to do and she told you what to do. And now you have to ask yourself if you have the strength, Deacon."

"Jane, she's my wife. She's dying."

"Simple question, Deacon. In or out, yes or no. I don't need to hear an explanation."

And he stares at her until she looks up from the pool and meets his gaze, her dark eyes as closed to him as the night pressing in around the ruins of the old house.

"You bitch," he hisses and Starling Jane only nods her head and unshoulders the big shotgun. "You want Narcissa dead so bad it's the only thing left you give a shit about."

"You're wrong. The Hounds will take care of Narcissa. She's called them here and now they'll deal with her. They don't need me to kill her anymore. But they'll take your child, as well."

"Please go," Chance whispers, her teeth beginning to chatter as her body steals a little of Deacon's warmth and she starts to shiver again. "Find her."

"It might not be too late," Jane says, and turns her back on the pool, turns to face Deacon. "If the Hounds haven't found Narcissa yet, then maybe we can do it."

"You said we couldn't fucking stop her."

"Yes, but maybe we won't have to. Maybe we only have to find her first."

"Please," Chance says again and shuts her eyes.

Deacon holds on to her tighter and strokes her hair, glances from Jane to the mouth of the tunnel leading into the black coiled beneath the fallen timbers and cracked foundation stones.

"Where does it go?" he asks.

"I can't tell you that," Jane says. "You don't need to know that. You just need to start moving."

He stares silently into the tunnel entrance for a moment, the darkness there, beyond the reach of the moonlight, as absolutely solid as anything Narcissa might have fashioned, and for all he knows she did. "I don't want to leave you," he says and Chance shivers, but she doesn't say anything.

"Now or never," Jane says.

"Go on ahead. I'll catch up," and she doesn't argue with him, three quick, short steps and the tunnel swallows her whole. He looks back down at Chance and kisses her forehead, pulls the old raincoat tighter around her before he takes off his own jacket and covers her with it, as well. "I'll be right back, I swear," and she doesn't open her eyes, doesn't speak, but nods her head for him. And Deacon lays her gently beside the pool, the pool where he found her weighted down with a stone on her chest, and follows Jane before he can change his mind.

The tunnel is hardly even as high as Deacon is tall, the walls and ceiling, the low roof, all braced with rotting timbers and the only light comes from his sputtering Zippo. He counts his footsteps from the entrance, leaving bread crumbs that will lead him back to the orange harvest moonlight and Chance. The walls are wet, dripping and fractured stone, and in places the uneven tunnel floor is flooded knee-deep with brackish pools concealing muddy, slick bottoms and he tries not to dwell on the things that might live in those pools. The soft, venomous things with stalked eyes and sharp pinchers, needle-toothed jaws and stinging tentacles, and

Deacon keeps moving, keeps counting. He's reached sixty-seven when the tunnel turns sharply away from the sea, turning south, sloping deeper into the earth, and Jane's standing there in the dark, waiting for him. He lets the lighter flicker out, too hot to hold anymore, and squats to cool the brass casing in the water at their feet.

"What's the story?" he asks, drying the lighter on the hem of his T-shirt.

"Not so loud," she whispers, and then, "I thought maybe we'd be able to hear the baby, if it's crying."

Deacon listens to the darkness crowded between the tunnel walls and there's hardly any sound at all, only the dripping ceiling and his own heart hammering inside his chest.

"I don't hear anything," he whispers.

"Do you still have the pistol?"

"Yeah, I still have the pistol."

"Well, you just make sure it's cocked and the safety's off," she whispers. "If we find them, we'll have to be ready."

"You fire that shotgun in here and you'll probably bring this whole place down on our heads," Deacon mumbles, glancing up at the tunnel ceiling hidden somewhere in the darkness overhead.

"It's more stable than it looks."

"Great. So what the hell are we waiting on," and there's a long moment of nothing but the measured *plop plop plop* from the dripping stone, and then Jane whispers, "You said you knew my name, Deacon. Were you lying?"

"My wife is dying out there," he replies. "My child is lost in here somewhere. I don't have time for this right now."

"I might not have time for it later. Were you lying?"

"No," Deacon says, and flips the strike wheel again, white-hot sparks and then the little flame to show their faces, etched starkly in the gloom. "I wasn't lying. Downs told me."

"I never . . . I didn't think anyone would ever know."

"We have to go," Deacon says. "We have to go now."

"Tell me," she whispers, leaning closer to him, her eyes gleaming faintly in the light from the Zippo. "Quick, and then we'll go."

And at first he thinks he might have actually forgotten the name the cop gave him, the infant vanished from its crib fifteen years ago. But there it is, waiting behind the fear and urgency. "Eliza," he says. "Your real name's Eliza Helen Morrow. You were born in 1986, I think."

"Eliza," Jane whispers, speaking so softly there's hardly more than the movement of her lips, and she smiles a sad and secret smile. "My name is Eliza Morrow and I might be fifteen years old."

"We have to go *now*," Deacon says and "Yeah," she replies. "Thank you, Deacon. Thank you for keeping that for me," and without another word she turns and heads deeper into the tunnel.

He follows her, carrying his puny light, walking fast to keep up with her. The air is growing warmer by degrees, but has begun to stink of mold and dank, rotting things. Deacon keeps counting, picking up at sixty-eight, nothing else to mark the time or distance; when he reaches one hundred and thirty-five, Jane stops and looks back at him.

"I think this opens into a cavern," she whispers. "I expect that's where she's waiting for them. Unless they've already come and gone."

"I still don't hear anything," Deacon says doubtfully.

"You wouldn't," she replies, but then he *does* hear something, a sudden *shhsssh* through the still and stinking air and then Jane drops the shotgun and clutches her chest with both hands. Four or five inches of rusty, bloodstained steel are jutting from her chest, the ugly, double-barbed point of some antique spear or harpoon, and she crumples silently to her knees in front of him. A dark gout of blood rushes from her open mouth, leaving maroon bubbles on her lips, and she grabs for Deacon. He sees the long shaft of the harpoon between her shoulder blades, sees that it really *is* a fucking harpoon and sees the rope tied to it; he reaches for her, their fingertips brushing as the rope goes taut and she's dragged away into the greedy blackness beyond the Zippo's reach. There and then gone so fast it can't possibly be real, as impossible as the rest of this shit, and he raises the pistol and aims into the dark.

"Run, Deacon," Jane calls out. "Run *fast*," a gurgling, wrecked phantom of her voice and then there's a loud cracking noise, wet snap of living bone, dry snap of metal, and he fires the pistol. The roar of the gun is deafening, like thunder belched up from the gut of the bottom of the world.

"Jane!" he shouts, his voice muffled by the painful ringing in his ears; no answer, but a few handfuls of sand and tiny bits of stone sift from a crack in the ceiling of the tunnel. A second or two later and there's an awful tearing sound before the girl named Starling Jane screams and is silent.

In the inky darkness up ahead, something begins to laugh.

And Deacon raises the gun, taking aim at the face of the pale shape lurching towards him through the tunnel, its skin streaked with blood and gore, its seething eyes to scald and shrivel the souls of angels.

"You think I still have what you're looking for, little man?" she asks. "You think you can take it away from me?"

Narcissa Snow, only a woman and nothing remotely human, and when she smiles, he pulls the trigger again.

Neither dreaming nor awake, living nor dead, Chance listens to the gunshots echoing from the mouth of the tunnel by the sea. She can't remember how long she's been lying there, wrapped tight in the strange girl's raincoat and Deacon's jacket, shivering and watching the stars moving overhead. All the constellations that her grandparents taught her to recognize—Ursa Major, Ursa Minor, Draco, Cassiopeia—and other stars she doesn't know, and the wind flutters the edges of the blue-white banner lying crumpled in a corner of the ruins, the one that reads AT THE OCEAN'S EDGE: FISH WITH FEET, when it ought to read AT THE RIVER'S EDGE, but Alice said it wasn't worth getting into an argument over. The sky so vast and brilliant, nothing like the sky above Birmingham, dull city sky half-hidden behind city lights, and she's beginning to think a few of those stars might take pity on her, might streak, screaming, across the velvet night and show her how to die.

But then the gunshots, and the girl's voice before that, words Chance couldn't make out, but the fear plain enough to hear.

"He needs you now," the child says. She's been sitting at the edge of the pool where she was born, dipping her fingers into the freezing water, playing tag with the tiny silver fish and phosphorescent trilobites, the waving arms of crinoids, and now she turns and looks sadly at Chance.

"Just let me lie here a few more minutes, please," Chance replies. "Just let me rest my eyes."

"There isn't time," the child says and then she smiles and dips her finger in the water again. "No, that's not right, is it? There's always time."

"I'm so sorry," Chance says, because she's just remembered how she got here, and that the werewolf took her newborn daughter into the tunnel. "But I couldn't stop her."

For a moment or two, the child watches Chance, still smiling, and then leaves the pool and comes to stand beside her. All around the remains of the basement, warm night breezes rustle the branches of towering tree ferns and cycads, and a gangly, young *Giganotosaurus* pauses to watch them, mother and daughter, with its flashing, nocturnal eyes, before vanishing into the foliage again.

"I made this place for you," the girl says. "I sewed it from pieces of your soul. When we're finished, you can stay here as long as you want. There's always time."

"You're very clever," Chance tells her, trying to sit up and the girl bends down to help.

"But we have to hurry now," she says. "He's hurt."

"Who? Deacon?"

"His gun ran out of bullets and he didn't have time to reach Starling's shotgun before Narcissa got to him."

Chance closes her eyes, hoping this is only a dream after all, her brain spitting up memories and wishful thoughts and white noise at death's door. The tropical Mesozoic air is sweet and it would be easy to sleep now, she thinks. Easy never to open her eyes again and this is so much better than drowning in a muddy, freezing pool with a stone on her chest.

"Wake up, Mother," the child insists and shakes her hard. "I'll help you, but *you* have to do this. It won't be finished until you do."

"It's finished now," Chance says, opening her eyes and the girl is frowning down at her. "What's your name?" Chance asks.

"I'm not allowed to tell you that. You'll find out later."

"You can't tell me, can you? Because you don't know. Because I never made up my mind about a girl's name, so you don't have one."

"Look, she'll kill him if you don't get up off your ass."

"Will she?" Chance asks and "Watch your step," the nameless girl replies, leading her along the wall of the dark tunnel. "It's slippery in here."

"What if he's dead already? What if we're already too late?"

"Then you'll know that you've done everything you could do," the girl replies. "You'll have done your best to help him."

"That's not enough."

"Then you should talk less and walk faster," but Chance can't walk any faster, can hardly walk at all, the child all but holding her up as it is. The stones have bruised and sliced her bare feet, and the water covering most of the tunnel floor is cold and smells like shit. She braces herself against the granite wall, pulls the raincoat tighter about her shoulders and wishes she were back outside in the sultry, jungle-scented night.

"There's light up ahead," the girl says and when Chance stares hard into the dark she can see it too, the sickly greenish glow, but it's hard to tell how far away it might be. And then she trips over Deacon's legs and almost falls. The child catches her and Chance kneels down beside him, her hands for eyes, and she's grateful for the blackness now, that she can't see his battered body slumped against the tunnel wall.

"Chance," he whispers. "How the fuck did you get in here?"

"You're not dead," she says and kisses him, tasting the blood drying to a sticky mess on his cheek. "I thought you were. I thought we were both dead."

"I couldn't stop her, baby. I emptied that goddamn gun into her and I still couldn't stop her."

"Shhhh," Chance whispers, crying again, but this time from relief and the tears are warm against her chilled skin. "That doesn't matter anymore. We're safe. We're *all* safe now, Deke. I just have to get you out of here."

"She didn't take the shotgun with her," Deacon says. "It's still here somewhere."

And *Look, Mother,* the child whispers. *Do you see? Do you see where she's taken me?* Chance stares past Deacon at the green glow filling the tunnel only forty or fifty yards farther along, light that seems to pulse faintly, light so terrible she wants to hide herself in Deacon's arms and never leave the dark again.

"I don't understand," she whispers. "I don't understand any of this."

"She would have killed me," Deacon says, "but someone down there started calling her name." He tries to stand up, grunts in pain and sits right back down again. "Just give me a few," he says. "I'll be okay. See if you can find that damn shotgun."

"It's right here," she tells him and picks it up from the tunnel floor. "But we're okay, Deacon. We're alive."

"She has the baby. She took it to them. Just let me get my breath."

The chartreuse light seems a little brighter now, or her eyes are adjusting, bright enough that she can make out Deacon's face, the wide and ragged cut above his eyes, the clean lines of the gun in her hands.

"I think I'm dying, Deacon," she says. "If I don't do this now I'm not going to have the strength to do it at all." He doesn't reply and she sees that he's shut his eyes. Chance leans close enough that she can feel his sour, alcoholic's breath on her face, can hear the regular rise and fall of his chest.

"You sleep," she says and kisses him again. "This won't take long, I promise."

"I wish it didn't have to end this way," the child says. "I wish the story could have a better ending. I wish it could end, 'And then they all left the tunnel, went home and never met another monster and lived happily ever after.'"

"That would be a fine story," Chance tells her. "That would be a very fine story."

And the child helps her to her feet again, holding her up when Chance thinks she can't walk another step, tells her not to look when they pass the headless body with the harpoon rising from its chest, but it's too late and she's already seen.

"She was trying to save us," the child says. "Daddy told me her real name was Eliza."

"Her real name," Chance whispers, too weak to speak any louder, and now the yellow-green light is so bright she can clearly see the tunnel walls, the face of her daughter, her own tattered flesh beneath the folds of the raincoat.

"I can't take you any farther," the child says. "You'll have to finish this alone, Mother," and there's a warm breeze, the ancient smell of the forest that isn't growing outside the tunnel, and the girl is gone. Chance leans against the stone wall, staring first at the shotgun in her hands, and then up at the place just ahead where the tunnel widens suddenly, the space filled up with the pulsing green light. And there are voices now, gravel-throated voices that hardly sound human, more like dogs or bears that have been taught to talk, some ingenious circus sideshow trick; she rests against the wall and listens and squints into the light.

"That's entirely beside the point. We did not *ask* you to bring us this suckling, Narcissa Snow. Had we wanted it, we would have gone for it ourselves."

"She thinks we need the likes of *her* to do our bidding."

"*If* she thinks, Terpsichore. If she even thinks at all."

And then Chance sees her, the werewolf standing naked and bleeding at the center of the chamber, and the baby bundled in a white towel at her feet.

"Its father wronged you all," Narcissa says, and Chance thinks that she sounds frightened. "He cost the warrens many infants when he led the police to the changeling Mary English."

"He caused us far, far less harm than you have, mongrel."

"You blackmail us, murder our charges, then whine that you've only taken vengeance on our enemies."

"She's insane, Lucius."

"She's an idiot."

Chance shuts her eyes tightly for a second, pressing her weight against the rough granite, waiting for a wave of dizziness and nausea to pass. *None of this is real,* she thinks. *It's only a dream.*

"There's nothing left to be said," one of the guttural animal voices barks. "We are finished with you, Narcissa Snow. It's a shame your father could not have handled you himself."

Chance opens her eyes again, opens up the shotgun's breech, this gun not so different from the one her grandfather taught her to shoot when she was a little girl, when they pretended to go hunting and usually just spent the days walking in the woods. There are two cartridges inside; she checks to be sure they're not spent.

A sound like laughter, if pigs could laugh, and Chance looks back into the cavern. Narcissa is holding a huge revolver, like a prop from an old western film, aiming it at the darkness lurking at the edges of the pulsing green glow.

"Look there, Terpsichore. Now she's going to *shoot* us," and the tunnel booms with barks and piggy laughter.

"I'm going to leave this child and I'm going to walk away," the werewolf says, her voice trembling now. "I swear, you'll never have to see me again."

"You swear?"

"But maybe we *want* you where we can see you, Narcissa Snow. Maybe we want you right where we can see you anytime we like."

Chance raises the gun, and maybe it looks like her grandfather's, but it seems to weigh a ton, something cast in lead instead of made of wood and steel. She blinks away sweat or blood, trying to clear her vision, and then fixes the werewolf in her sights.

"I fucking *belong* here," the monster growls, the stiff mane along its back bristling now and Narcissa pulls back the hammer on the revolver. "This is my birthright. I am the granddaughter of Iscariot Snow and this is my home."

"Be careful, Lucius. We want something left for the slab. It would be a shame to ruin her."

"I'll make it clean. I'll make it quicker than she deserves."

And then the shadows shift, twisting back upon themselves, folding, and something huge peers out of the gloom, watching Narcissa with blazing golden eyes. She fires the revolver once and the baby at her feet begins to cry; the werewolf curses and throws the gun at the beast rushing towards her across the smooth cavern floor, something tall and hunched, something to make her seem as harmless as the stolen infant. Narcissa Snow turns to run, to flee back towards the tunnel, back to the surface, but stops when she sees Chance and the shotgun.

"You," she says and smiles, smiles as if she's forgotten the creature bearing down on her, as if the gun in Chance's hands is only a toy. "Well, what are you waiting for?"

And Chance pulls the twin triggers and the gun howls, erasing Narcissa's face in a spray of blood and bone and flesh. The recoil knocks Chance off her feet, sends her sprawling in the mud, and the last thing she sees before the nothingness welling up inside her skull takes her, the very last thing, is the beast standing above her, and the confusion in its burning eyes.

Deacon Silvey hears the dry crackle of the fire, the hungry cries of the gulls, smells the ocean and the smoky fire before he opens his eyes. The distant, muted crash and sigh of the breakers, and he blinks and squints painfully into the late morning sunshine bathing the high, windswept dunes. He lies still a while, his head aching like he's been drunk six weeks straight, like he's just come down from the bender to end all benders, and watches the small fire burning itself out a few feet away. And then the baby in his arms, wrapped up safe inside the raincoat with him, begins to cry softly and he rolls over and lays it down in the sand at his side. And he sees Chance, her lifeless body stretched out on the other side of the fire, her eyelids half-open, as if she's watching her husband and child through the smoke.

Someone has put her in an old black dress, Puritan black and simple, and the cloth is stained and torn. He stares at her while the wind moans and whistles across the land between the marshes and the sea, while it all comes back to him, the time it takes to be sure that he's awake. And then he turns back to the baby, its fat, pink face and the deep blue eyes of newborns, eyes that haven't yet been scarred some plainer shade by all the things they will witness later on. He holds the child close, humming a song to comfort it because he isn't sure what else to do, and the wild, unending Atlantic gale seems to know the tune and carries it for him when Deacon finally begins crying too hard to sing anymore.

EPILOGUE

The Land of Dreams

Hardly an hour left until dawn and the long gray Lincoln cruises slowly along Angell Street, as unlikely a hearse as Deacon Silvey has ever imagined. The old trees and older homes of College Hill rise stately and mute on either side of the car, shielding him from the stars. Most of Providence is still mercifully asleep at this hour, but he wonders if he's waited too long, too close to sunrise and maybe he'll be turned away, maybe he won't find the house at all because maybe it doesn't exist. The radio is blaring to keep away the awful silence of the November morning, classic rock out of Boston, the Doors and the Byrds and Credence Clearwater Revival, but the baby doesn't seem to mind, seems capable of sleeping through just about anything.

It was almost dark by the time Deacon managed to get both the baby and Chance's body back to Narcissa Snow's car, retracing the path through the dunes to Argilla Road. And this time there was no deadfall waiting to send him wandering through the treacherous cedars, and no smothering blackness filled with scuttling legs when he put the boxes Jane had removed into the trunk again and slammed it shut. The keys were waiting for him in the ignition, strung onto a shiny brass key chain engraved with the initials C. A. S.; Jane hadn't even bothered to check for them before she'd started jimmying locks. He laid Chance out in the backseat, her arms crossed on her chest, and used one of the cardboard boxes, lined with his jacket and the towel, its contents dumped in on top of everything else in the Lincoln's trunk, as a makeshift crib. Deacon secured the box with the seat belt, and then drove away from the sea, through the whispering marshes and pines, through Ipswich to the highway.

Coming at last to the end of Angell Street and he glances at the brightly colored map folded open on the seat between him and the baby's cardboard box, "A Visitor's Map to Greater Downtown Providence," and sees that he's overshot the Athenaeum by several blocks. There are three teenagers standing on the corner of Angell and Benefit, drinking something from a paper bag and smoking cigarettes. They stop talking among themselves and stare at the Lincoln, only staring because it's something to see, but their eyes make Deacon nervous anyway.

Driving all night, skirting Boston because he didn't want to be that close to so many other people, people and their gaudy lights to keep the night at bay. When the car finally ran low on gas, he stopped at an Exxon station near Concord, bought a small carton of milk for the baby and a six-pack of Budweiser for himself. Then he used a pay phone to call Birmingham, dialing the number of their apartment on Morris because he figured that the FBI would still be there, waiting with their line-tapping machines and tape recorders, waiting for a break and he might as well give them one. He told a groggy Agent Peterson that he'd only talk to Downs, no one else, that he'd call back at 6 A.M. and Downs should be there if he wanted to talk, and then Deacon hung up. In the parking lot of the Exxon, he fed the baby a little of the milk, as much as it would take, and then headed south with no destination in mind, just driving because it seemed the only bearable course of action left to him. Sometimes he would glance at Chance's body in the rearview mirror, but mostly he kept his eyes on the road.

When he sees the big yellow house on Benefit Street, Deacon isn't surprised, even though he didn't genuinely expect it to be there. He wonders if it's the *right* yellow house, how many yellow houses there might be up and down this road, but pulls over to the curb and kills the engine. There are at least a half-dozen grinning jack-o'-lanterns on the porch, each one flickering orange light from its carved pumpkin skull, but all the windows are dark. Sitting in the car, staring up at the old house painted the color of caution, the color of sickness, Deacon begins to feel the way he felt the night he followed Sadie Jasper into the Harris Warehouse and Transfer

Building, the way he felt the day before when he first saw the narrow, winding waters of the Manuxet River.

"You're gonna have to wait here," he says to the baby, but it's sleeping now. He looks over his shoulder at Chance, and she doesn't look like she's sleeping at all. She just looks dead. He thinks that when he's done, he should find a blanket or a sheet to cover her with, before the sun comes up.

"I'll leave the radio on for you," he tells the baby, but turns the volume down a little. A Rolling Stones song ends and is replaced by Bob Dylan and the Band. "Don't you worry," he says. "I'll be back before you know it. I won't let you out of my sight," and he reaches for the slender leather satchel lying in the passenger-side floorboard. But then he waits until the Dylan song ends and the DJ starts talking before he gets out of the Lincoln.

He walks quickly across the cobblestone sidewalk and climbs the creaky, wooden stairs to the front porch, already wishing that he'd stayed in the car, wishing he'd just kept driving when he came to the exits for Providence. The porch boards creak even more loudly than the steps and Deacon stops and glances back at the parked car.

"You took your own sweet time getting here, Mr. Silvey," someone says and he turns around again and sees the girl he hadn't noticed before, either because he wasn't looking or she just wasn't there. She's sitting in a rocking chair, dressed in jeans and a gray cardigan, and her silver eyes flash back the jack-o'-lantern light. "We were about to give you up for lost."

"Were you?" he asks, unable to look away from her white face, her white lips, those eyes like polished ball bearings.

"The rest of the house is already sleeping," she says and leans towards him. "I told them all you weren't coming. I told them we'd have to send someone out to find you."

"So I guess you were wrong."

"I suppose I was. It's not the first time. Do you have something for me, Mr. Silvey?"

Deacon hands her the satchel and she nods her head, smiles but doesn't open it, sets it on the porch at her feet.

"I owed her," he says. "She helped me."

"Did she?" the silver-eyed girl asks. "That was very thoughtful of her, I suppose."

"It got her killed."

"Well, you know how that goes. No good deed and all that. Besides, it happens to the best of us, sooner or later."

"I just didn't want you people thinking she hadn't tried."

The girl nods again and then she turns her head, looking past him, past Benefit Street at the land sloping steeply down to the Providence River and Federal Hill, the western sky still dark as midnight but not for very much longer.

"I'd ask you in for tea and biscuits, Mr. Silvey, if there was time. Miss Josephine regrets she wasn't able to meet you herself. Perhaps if you'd come a little earlier in the evening."

"I have to be going anyway. I have to make a phone call."

The girl watches him a moment, still and pale as a waxwork, and then she rocks back in the chair and blinks her silver eyes.

"Does the child have a name yet?"

"No," Deacon says. "No, she doesn't."

"Well, see that she gets one soon. It's not safe for a child, being adrift in the wide, wide world without a name."

"Do you have one?" Deacon asks her. "A name, I mean?"

"Not one that you ever want to learn," and then she reaches for the satchel and stands up; behind her, the empty chair rocks itself back and forth a few more times. "Not one I leave lying around where just anyone can get at it."

"I should go now," Deacon says. "I have to make that phone call."

"You'll have an easier time with the police than you expect."

"Yeah, well, we'll see. I just didn't want you to think—"

"—she hadn't tried," the girl with shining eyes says. "Goodbye, Mr. Silvey. I'm sorry about your wife, but you have your daughter and you have your own life. That's something."

"Yes, I guess it must be."

"Never come here again. And never speak of this place to anyone, do you understand? If it ever did, this house no longer has a quarrel with you."

Deacon looks around him at the jack-o'-lanterns and shrugs his shoulders. "Who the hell would I tell?" he asks her, but doesn't wait for an answer, turns and walks quickly down the steps and back across the sidewalk to the Lincoln. Before he opens the door, he looks back at the wide front porch of the yellow house one last time, and the girl is putting out the candles inside the jack-o'-lanterns, one by one.

Caitlín R. Kiernan's first novel, *Silk*, received both the International Horror Guild and Barnes & Noble Maiden Voyage awards, and her second novel, *Threshold*, also received an International Horror Guild Award. Her critically acclaimed, award-winning short fiction has been collected in three volumes, *Tales of Pain and Wonder*, *From Weird and Distant Shores*, and *To Charles Fort, with Love*. Trained as a vertebrate paleontologist, she currently lives in Atlanta, Georgia.

Web sites:

www.lowredmoon.com
www.caitlin-r-kiernan.com